GLASGOW

Where the Bridge Lies is a work of fiction. Names, characters, settings and events are either the product of the author's imagination or used in a fictitious manner.

First published in Great Britain in 2019

By
Ringwood Publishing

www.ringwoodpublishing.com
mail@ringwoodpublishing.com

ISBN 978-1-901514-66-7

British Library Cataloguing-in Publication Data
A catalogue record for this book is available from the British Library

Typeset in Times New Roman 11

Printed and bound in the UK by
Lonsdale Direct Solutions

For Leo and Liam

"Even the most broken soul can be reunited
into Universal Harmony. The key is to
discover where the bridge lies."

Charles Fourier, *Le Nouveau Monde Amoureux*

One

Keir Connor edges across the rotten remains of a wooden pier. Beneath him the choppy Clyde surges and tugs at crumbling waterlogged piles. Most of the decking at the pier's margins has long since disappeared into the river. A small section, pocked by missing planks but still largely intact, survives in the lee of a stone jetty. There. The best viewpoint is there, he decides. He begins a careful traverse, taking time to assess the surface ahead before placing his foot and shifting his weight. Don't look down, he tells himself, but that doesn't stop his gaze flicking through gaps to where dark water crashes and gurgles.

He is glad to reach the surviving platform. It's in surprisingly good shape, its timbers weathered to hard grey rather than soft treacherous black. He surveys the wide river. A mile or so upstream the high curve of a suspension bridge makes toys of crossing traffic. The dreary rain that threw a blanket over the morning and drizzled on into afternoon has stopped. Low clouds are lifting. The sky is lightening. Downstream, raking shafts of sunlight sparkle the river and spotlight its banks, picking out a village here, a wooded hillside there.

Ahead, a ramshackle dredger moored in mid-river clunks and squeals as it drags bucket after bucket of silt from the navigation channel. Maybe that accounts for the troubling smell. An oiliness, a waft of eggy sulphur as if something long buried has been released, a hint of rotting sweetness that echoes within him. Don't go there, he warns himself.

He takes out a ring binder and opens at an aerial photograph marked "Henderson's Shipyard Kilbendrick 1960", one of the many items photocopied for him by that helpful young woman in the Blitz archive at Clydebank Library. He holds the aerial photograph at arm's length and begins to match it to

1

what now remains on the riverbank. Twenty years of closure have done the little shipyard no favours. Once plangent buildings are slowly losing themselves amidst an abandoned riot of weeds, rusting machinery, windblown rubbish and tidal flotsam. The breeze off the river creaks and clangs at loosened sheets of corrugated iron and whispers through the bared steel ribs of the skeleton that was once the platers' shed. A weed-resistant line of dead ground marks the bed of ballast that used to be the crane runway. All that remains of the slipways and building berths is a rubble-strewn slope that meets the river in a tattered edge.

And beyond the slipways, a line of ruined workshops.

Including the engine shop.

Where his father had worked…

As the clouds lift the wind rises, tugs at the folder in his hands. Pages turn in a ripple. Newspaper clippings. Black and white photographs. Shattered buildings burn. Suitcase-carrying survivors trudge debris-strewn streets. A collapsed tenement crushes a tramcar.

Herring gulls balance on the breeze. Their shrieks seem to be aimed his way. Scolding. Accusing. He has a sense of being swirled along, as if he is being pushed by something stronger than the wind. Something inside.

Be careful, he warns himself. Don't be drawn in. Heed the warning signs.

He needs to find a safe haven. Go back to Dr Rolfe's consulting room. To that last session.

Dr Rolfe spelt it out in his careful way: '… and your father's death is still very recent. You're vulnerable. Why put yourself under more stress? Are you sure you should leave Australia now? For months? Without support?'

Keir pushed the psychiatrist's concern back at him: 'But I planned the trip to Scotland long before my father died.'

'Yes. And I don't think you should rush into an assignment

now.'

'This isn't an assignment, Doc. It's a sabbatical, a family project.' He tried to sound persuasive, but wasn't sure he'd succeeded.

'Maybe. But it's also a story of war. There's bombing. There's death.'

Keir struggled to keep his tone reasonable. 'That's old history. C'mon. The Second World War finished thirty-five years ago. If my father hadn't had a relapse I'd already be in Scotland.'

'Yeah. But you're not. You're here. So why not wait and see how things go for a bit?' He watched Keir closely. 'We agreed at the start. This only works if we're both honest.' His shrewd gaze said he knew Keir wasn't telling him everything.

That phrase of Dr Rolfe's swirled in Keir's head. 'At the start...' Easy for you to say, Doc. And when was that, exactly? When did all this begin?

Of course he understood where Dr Rolfe was coming from. Keir had been the first person to write about the mental problems suffered by returning combat troops. War was his business, after all. He'd slipped through the Vietnam jungle with countless patrols, ducked when they ducked, seen what they'd seen. And seen what they did. In the name of a country that turned its back on them when they came home. No wonder some of them cracked.

'But I'm not a soldier,' he insisted. 'I'm a journalist, for fuck's sake.'

'Yes, you are. I know. And you're paying a price for years spent in a war zone. I know that too. So do you.'

He trusted this doctor. He believed in him. He believed in him because he was desperate. Despairing and desperate. He couldn't have gone on like that. If someone hadn't helped him stop the chaos inside he'd have ended it himself. Permanently.

So why couldn't he admit that he'd stopped his medication?

Why not say to this patient, listening man that he'd decided to break off contact with him?

Most of all, why couldn't he tell him about his father's letter? The deathbed confession his dying father had left behind...

The lowering sun is making a moody silhouette of the old dredger. The clunking rhythm of heavy steel buckets slows ... slows ... slows ... then ends in a piercing rusty screech. Shouts of crewmen carry across the slack water of the turning tide. He strains to hear what lurks behind the voices as he watches a tender leave the nearby harbour and head towards the waiting ship.

He begins to feel threatened and tries to pin down why, searching amongst anxious feelings as if looking for intruders, for danger. But all he can find is himself, alone, stranded on a broken-down desolate pier. His search for safe ground is leading to quicksand.

Maybe he's just feeling the effects of jet lag, insomnia, the hangover from last night's whisky? Nah, it's more than that. Something had crept under his skin in Clydebank as he'd wandered tenement streets counting the gaps blasted by Luftwaffe bombers a generation ago; visited the mass grave of unidentified Blitz victims; searched through folder after folder of yellowing papers. And pictures. Yes, especially the pictures. God knows he's no stranger to the bloody havoc wrought by high explosives on human lives but there was something about those black and white photographs – they're reaching inside him, scratching and plucking at old wounds, rattling demons' cages. He can feel his heart start to race. Tightness spreads across his shoulders, clutches at his throat.

He tries to escape the growing inner turmoil, to find safety outside, in his surroundings, in the landscape, but he has left it too late. The river has turned to rippled silver, slashed with flares of fiery red and bruised purple. From out of the sun's glare a patrol boat scythes towards him. He sees the flash of its cannons but can't hear them. His head still rings from the incoming rocket that blew him off his feet. In the village just behind him, burning thatch roars and crackles. The photographer lies crumpled ahead of him. Lenses and cans of film have spilled from his waistcoat, his Nikon lies in the dust beside his outstretched fingers, the strap still wrapped around his wrist.

He looks down at the small child on the ground beside him. One side of her head is missing. Her remaining eye has the open innocence of a doll's.

He chokes on the smoke, wipes blood from his eyes and tries to shout at the boat, to make them understand. But the harder he tries, the less sound he can make. The gunships swoop in again, low over the palm trees. The ground shakes to the whop-whop of their rotors. And he knows, somehow, he is to blame.

He curls up and whimpers.

Two

Nessa Glover had almost finished washing the steps of the main altar when Father O'Donnell came out of the confessional box, removed the stole from his shoulders, and called to her: 'Don't forget your cup of tea now, Nessa.'

'Don't worry, Father. Just let me finish up and I'll be right there.' She rinsed out her cloth, carefully wiped any trace of soapy water from the creamy marble of the bottom step, gathered together her cleaning things, and headed for the small store cupboard at the back of the church.

In the chapel house, Father O'Donnell's shadowy but snug study was a warm haven against the creeping chill of a March night. The priest rose from his seat by the coal fire. 'Hang your coat on the peg behind the door there, Nessa, so you get the good of it when you go out again.' He gestured towards the tea tray the housekeeper had left on the table. 'Would you like to be the mammy?'

Nessa was glad to oblige. She loved this little ritual, a perk of being one of the volunteers who took a pride in keeping St Brendan's Church spotless.

'And how are things at home, Nessa?' he asked as they settled to their tea and biscuits, 'How's your new wee fella? John, isn't it?'

'That's right, Father. Oh, he's a great baby, no trouble at all. Putting on weight and sleeps most of the night.'

'Thanks be to God. And the big lad, Ricky, he'll be pleased there's another boy in the house, I bet you.'

'You're right again, Father. After three wee sisters I think he had just about given up hope.' Nessa refused a second cup. 'Sorry to rush, Father, but Hugh's holding the fort at home and the baby needs fed soon.'

'Aye. Being a mother's a full-time job, Nessa. I'm sure Mary, mother of God, found that too. So God thank you for keeping his house so beautiful and clean. Let me give you a blessing before you go.'

He had just lifted his hand when air raid sirens started a low, slow moan that soon climbed to a rising and falling wail. They looked at each other. 'Do you want to go to the shelter here?' he asked.

'No. We usually don't bother. What's the point? Just about every day, Father. And it's always a false alarm. But I better be off home. Hugh'll start to worry.'

The priest held out her coat and opened the door as she put it on. She bowed her head as he blessed her.

The gloomy blacked-out streets offered no protection from the deafening beat of sirens. A full moon just managed to peer through the sooty haze that hung above murky tenement roofs. Sulphurous coal smoke caught at her nose and throat and cool air chilled her cheeks. She gripped her coat collar tightly and hurried on through the dark and wailing town. At Dumbarton Road she looked back over her shoulder towards Glasgow, hoping to see the blinkered lights of an approaching tramcar, but the road was long, straight and empty.

The sirens stopped as Nessa passed the foot of Kilbowie Road. She became aware of a cold light. Long searchlight beams swung through the sky. A new sound, a low pulsing drone from high above, grew louder and louder until it seemed to beat inside her. She looked up; endless swarms of planes filled the darkening sky. Anti-aircraft guns in the shipyard began to boom. Fiery flashes ripped the night apart, falling bombs whistled. Thunder rumbled through her. The ground beneath her shuddered and heaved. She was picked up and tumbled along the pavement like a scrap of litter.

When she managed to sit up she was facing back the way she had come. A large section of a tenement was collapsing silently in slow motion. For the first time since she left the priest, she became aware of other people. A woman was sitting near her, screaming noiselessly. A man approached, he was speaking but she couldn't hear him. She shook her head. In all directions fires were brightening the sky. Across the street a woman was kneeling over a man. Three children stood in a huddle of wrapped arms.

She picked herself up and started to run towards her own home, her own family.

As her hearing returned she could make out the repetitive sequences of whistles, flashes and deafening explosions as stick after stick of bombs rained down. Tracer shells curved up to join the swinging searchlights. She glimpsed again countless planes dark against the stars and the moonlight, sometimes flickering sharp and clear amid shell bursts and explosions.

When she reached Singer's factory, vast curtains of flame were leaping from the surrounding woodyard where tons of dried seasoned timber fuelled an inferno that lit everything around her with an intense flickering glare. The canal between her and the roaring blaze looked like a river of molten metal. She could feel the heat on her face.

She was surrounded by dense smoke that carried the sooty smell and taste of shattered buildings and burning wood. Her eyes streamed. She screamed when a yellow ball of feathers smacked into her face and landed at her feet. A canary picked itself up and flew off. Two wild-eyed dogs yelped past, their coats standing on end and their tails curled under in terror.

When she escaped the smoke, she saw that the way ahead was blocked by a building that had crumpled into the street, partly crushing a tramcar which now had a double bed balanced on its battered roof. People pulled at the rubble with their hands. Bodies were laid out on a cleared part of the pavement. She picked her way through them, all her attention on the bridge ahead that crossed the canal and led to the street where she lived. Where *they* lived, and where she could now see several gaps smashed into the roofline of the tenement row. She uttered a prayer, beseeching God to protect them.

An air raid warden stepped in front of her, stretched out his arms. 'Stop, Missus. It's not safe.' His face was black with soot and dust, apart from his eyes and lips. She tried to push past him.

'No,' she said, pointing. 'My weans, my man! We live over there! Thistle Street!'

'I know, I know,' he shouted. 'But look.' A parachute was floating slowly through the smoke and the tumult. It looked surprisingly calm and peaceful amid the glare and the noise. 'That's a mine. A ton of explosive. It'll go off any minute.'

She strained against him. They watched the parachute mine drift gently onto the damaged rooftops. There was an incandescent horizontal flash, brighter than the sun. Then the noise and the blast wave hit them with a monstrous roar that thrust them backwards and further into one another's arms. She broke free and ran.

The face of the four-storey tenement had been sliced off as if by a giant knife. Chunks of the building continued to fall. Chaotic piles of rubble reduced her run to a frantic scramble. Fires were taking hold and flames shot above the mountain of debris that now faced her. She slithered and scrabbled up its unstable surface, grabbing support wherever she could and scarcely noticing when she ripped her hand open on a broken window frame.

At the top she shielded her eyes against the blue-hearted tower of flame that roared from a fractured gas main. All that remained of number 26 – her home, her family, her neighbours – was a vast crater. Beneath the thud of her heart, the gasps of her lungs, she felt herself loosen, empty, as if life itself was flooding out of her along with the blood that

9

streamed from her wounded hand.

She became aware of voices. At the edges of the deep hole, small groups of people were pulling at the little that remained of numbers 24 and 28, calling out tentatively, wondering where to start. Then she recognised her name being called.

'Nessa! Is that you? You're here. Oh, Nessa.'

She stumbled down to Granny Chalmers, the elderly neighbour from number 37 who had been looking after the baby.

'Oh, Nessa. I was up in your place when the siren went. Your Hugh wanted to wait for you. And you know what the lassies are like. Daddy's girls every one. So they stayed with Hugh. And they kept the baby with them. Theresa said you'd like him to be there when you got home. I told them I'd take his night things across to the shelter with me. Nessa, I'm sorry. This's all I've got.' She held out a wicker basket and a baby's shawl.

'Ricky?' she asked, 'Where's Ricky?'

'He came with me, hen.' Granny Chalmers pointed at the figures dwarfed by the rubble. 'He's across there with the men. They told him to stay in the shelter, but he said: "No, it's my Da and my sisters and my wee brother. I'm coming with you."'

Nessa reached out and took the shawl from the old woman's hand. Pressed it to her face. Held it tightly.

Clydebank, March 14th 1941

'I don't think you'll get anything out of her, son. She hasn't spoken a word. Not one word. Just sits there and stares.'

Granny Chalmers watched Joe Connor struggle to take in what she was saying. He pushed his goggles higher up the forehead of his leather helmet. His grey face was haggard and heavy with black stubble. She watched his eyes flicker over the wreckage of her normally spotless kitchen to where his sister, Nessa Glover, dishevelled and dust-covered with her right hand wrapped in a bloodstained tea towel, sat on Granny Chalmers' fireside chair amidst the ash and soot-strewn mess. She held a rolled up baby's shawl to her bosom. In the bed recess behind her, thirteen-year-old Ricky had collapsed into an exhausted sleep. The room smelt of smoke and rubble.

The old woman tugged at the sleeve of the man's heavy canvas motorcycle coat. 'C'mon out to the lobby, son.' She led him into the hallway of the tiny flat. When she tried to close the kitchen door behind them, the distorted doorframe jammed it half open. She shrugged as if to say 'who cares?' and led him through the entrance door and onto the common stairway. Sunny blue sky showed through a large hole in the roof above them. She took one of his hands in both of hers and began to massage it gently. 'There's terrible news about Nessa's family, Joe.'

'Aye, some people came up to me in the street. They recognised my bike and sidecar. I couldn't believe what I was seeing. The big crater. No houses. Nothing but...' He stopped talking and she could see his bottom lip start to tremble as he struggled to control himself. 'They say Hugh, the lassies, the baby ... The whole lot of them...?'

'That blast, you've never heard anything like it. There'd been a lot of bombs before but it had gone a bit quiet. We hoped the worst was by. Then that one went off! It was as if the earth had opened and Auld Nick burst out and kicked hell out of the whole world. I swear to God, the shelter Ricky and me were in flew up into the air. We bounced about like peas in a drum before it landed again. Some of the roof caved in. People were screaming and yelling. Geordie Watson, him that's a foreman at Singer's, managed to calm everybody down then him and the rest of the men went out to see what had happened.' She shook her head.

'Did they find anything … anybody?'

'They tried for a while. But they soon knew it was hopeless. That boy sleeping through there saw things a lad his age shouldn't see. Nobody should see.'

'But maybe if they dig deeper today. There's rescue squads working in the street.'

'Aye. I spoke to some of them. Workers from Brown's and miners that's been brought in. They're digging where bits of the buildings are still standing. Tunnelling in. Listening for people that's trapped. And they've found a few. I asked them about Nessa's place, pointed it out to them. They just shook their heads at me.'

Her small wrinkled hands fluttered over the calloused skin of his palm and fingers. The muscles of his face worked as if he somehow had to chew on her words, make them easier to take in. 'Awful, son.' She squeezed his hand. 'Awful … awful. I'm sorry, Joe.'

'But here,' she said after a few moments silence, 'what about your lot? I should've asked before now. What happened in Kilbendrick?'

'Nothing like as bad as here. But they didn't miss us either. Hillcraig Terrace was hit. Two dead. Two people missing and quite a few injured. Other places hit too. There's five dead that we know about so far. But nothing like...' He waved his arms in a vague gesture. 'Nothing like this. So I'm taking Nessa and Ricky back with me. Those bastards aren't finished with us. They'll be back.'

'You're doing the right thing, son, getting them out of here. The rescue men said there's fires all over Clydebank that'll never be put out today. The sky'll be ablaze again the night. Sooner you get going the better. I'd have made you a cup of tea by now but the gas is off, the water's off, my teapot's missing and there's not a whole cup left in the house.'

She watched him go back into the kitchen and put his arm gently around his sister's shoulders. 'Nessa. Nessa. It's me. Joe. I'm taking you to Kilbendrick. Sarah and me can easy make room. It'll be safer there.' She allowed herself to be lifted from the chair. He eased her towards the door into Granny Chalmers' waiting arms and turned to the sleeping youth. A filthy hand, scarred with blood-crusted cuts, stuck out from beneath the quilt. Ricky woke at the first shake, his eyes wide in his grubby face. 'Uncle Joe...' he mumbled, 'I looked. I tried...'

'I know you did, son. You can tell me about it later. Right now I'm taking you and your ma down to stay with me and your Aunt Sarah. Your Aunt Heather's there as well.'

Granny Chalmers walked them downstairs into bright sunshine. She looked around at the ruined houses then back at the crater where the Glover's home had been. The untamed gas main continued to send its roaring flare twenty feet into air that stank of soot and sulphur. On either side of the gap left by the exploding mine, rescue squads worked at the collapsed houses. Further along the street, a fire engine fought to control a fierce blaze at Paterson's paint works, where the thick black smoke was now and again turned red by an explosion.

'My God, son,' she said, 'How did you get through that?'

'I didn't. I had to go round the back way and come in from the other end of the street. I've been making detours all the way here. It's taken me nearly an hour to come five miles. There's buildings down across Dumbarton Road and smoke everywhere. Squads of men are starting to clear a way through for traffic but there's not much moving yet. Except for people. Thousands of them, lugging bags and suitcases, pushing prams, just getting out of Clydebank. Women in their fur coats. I've never seen anything like it. Everybody that can is getting out.' He reached out and took her by the arm: 'Listen, hen. Why don't you come along with us as well? You can squeeze into the sidecar beside Nessa.'

'No, son. That's kind of you. But, och, this is where I've lived for over fifty years. I'll stay here. Thanks, that was kind of you. You've got enough on your plate.' She reached into the sidecar and embraced Nessa who didn't resist, although she continued to stare straight ahead. The old woman walked round to where Ricky sat on the pillion. The boy's arms were wrapped tightly around Joe's waist and his head nestled between his uncle's shoulders. 'You're a brave laddie,' she said. 'Look after your mammy.'

Granny Chalmers watched the motorbike weave its way through mounds of rubble towards the less damaged end of the street. She laboured upstairs to her ruined kitchen where she'd been trying to create some order since the all clear siren had sounded at half past six. Neat gatherings of sooty dirt, broken glass and shattered belongings dotted the once gleaming linoleum. She went on with her sweeping, and when the growing heaps of debris slowly forced her to a halt, she laid her brush aside and stood for some moments looking out at the broken buildings and reeking fires. Then she picked up her shovel and began to throw load after load of rubbish out the glassless window.

Kilbendrick, March 14th 1941

Dressed in his ARP overalls, Joe Connor stood with his wife Sarah at the window of their small, ground floor tenement flat. The scenes outside had silenced them both.

On a Friday afternoon Kilbendrick's main street would normally be near empty: children safe at school; womenfolk bringing in their washing and fixing the evening meal; men hard at it in the shipyard, the deafening clang of their riveting skelping around the harbour and echoing off the hills. Instead the narrow main street of the village was choked. A long line of red double-decked buses, crammed with standing passengers, trundled slowly past, then began a laboured ascent on towards Dumbarton. Flatbed lorries, loaded with a dangerous fluttering cargo of people and belongings, lurched as the drivers changed gear for the climb ahead. Motorcycles carrying up to four people weaved in and out. Laden bicycles, often with a child on the crossbar, were pedalled or pushed.

Walking people thronged the narrow pavements: family groups pushed prams and carts; parents sweated under the weight of heavy cases or weary children; solitary people, dusty, dishevelled and blank faced, moved as if following the crowd but apart from it. Here and there knots of young men and women, still in the smart clothes of last night's visit to the pictures or the dancing, shared their cigarettes and retold stories.

Further along, the road was partially blocked by the collapse of Hillcraig Terrace. A bomb had somehow blown out the walls but left intact the roof, which had settled onto the rubble creating a bizarre one-storey caricature of the original three-storey building. A squad of Joe's workmates had dismantled a sheerlegs crane in Henderson's yard and brought it down into the village where it now straddled the wrecked tenement. Their rescue operation scarcely slowed the progress of the cavalcade of refugees because traffic was in one direction only; except for an occasional fire engine or lorryload of men and equipment, everyone was heading westwards, away from Clydebank.

Aye. Nobody wants a second night of that. Joe's heart lurched at the thought. He'd seen and heard enough last night to keep him going for a lifetime, never mind the nightmares he'd uncovered this morning. Clydebank destroyed. Nessa's man and most of her weans killed. He felt a big gap open in his chest. Another night? Please. No.

'Can we not do something to help?'

Sarah's question brought Joe back to the immediate

problems. He drew her closer and kissed her hair.

'Sarah, you're only seeing a wee bit of it here. It's the same story all the way back to the middle of Clydebank. The town's in a hell of a mess. Going up through Dalmuir, big areas have nearly disappeared. Just piles of rubble. At least these folk have got out, more and more of them as the roads are getting cleared. But there are also people just sitting about in a daze. I passed a lassie and her mother. They'd pulled as much as they could out of the wreckage. It was as if they were playing houses; they'd set up their table with two chairs, and there was a chest of drawers with a radio on it, and a mattress and bedding. She was nursing a baby and the wee one was feeding a budgie in a cage and talking to it as if everything was normal. God knows what'll happen to them. Anyway, have we not got enough to do with Nessa and Ricky?'

'Maybe so. Poor souls, they've been through hell.' She gestured towards the kitchen. 'And Nessa's not said a word?'

'Not to Granny Chalmers, not to Ricky, not to me. At least she let you take her coat off and bandage her hand.'

'Aye. But she won't part with the baby's shawl. When I put my arms out to her, she just turned away and held the shawl tight to her chest, as if she was scared I was going to take it. I think she must be in some kind of shock. Of course she is. Four of the weans. And Hugh.' Her face began to crumple. 'I never thought I'd say this, Joe. But right now I think not having any children is maybe better than having them and losing them.'

Joe put his arms around her shaking shoulders, but she pulled herself together quickly. 'It's okay. I'm fine. You're needed up the road. Big Sandy was here. Said could you come right away when you got back.'

'Any word of how it's going?'

'Mrs Brownlee's youngest girl's still missing. So is the old Italian woman. They've nearly finished getting cables under the roof and they think maybe it can be lifted.' As she walked him to the door she asked: 'What about Ricky? Has he said anything?'

'He's spoken to me a wee bit. The men he was with last night stopped digging when they started finding bits of bodies. Ricky thought he'd found the sleeve of his Da's shirt and wanted to keep it, but one of the men took it away from him. Maybe that was the right thing to do. Who knows what's right anymore? While you were busy with Nessa I watched him sitting out the back with Heather. Heather's always had a soft spot for Ricky. He seemed to be telling her a lot, then I could see him starting to greet. She gave him a big cuddle. I think that'll be what he needs.'

'Aye. Heather was going to be up the road at Charlie's tonight, but I've asked her to stay with us and help. That's fine with Heather as long as Charlie can be here as well.'

'Here we go again. That lassie's never away from Charlie!'

'Joe Connor! They're due to be married in a month's time. If there's still a world left. Leave Heather be. She might stay with us but remember she's my wee sister, not your big daughter.'

'I know. But we agreed. While she's living here it's my rules.'

'What does it matter? Are any of us going to get to our beds tonight? And if we have to go to the shelter, will there be room for us all?'

'Don't worry about it.' He squeezed Sarah's shoulder. 'I'm sure it'll be okay. I'll go and speak to the neighbours. One way or another, I'll find a corner for myself somewhere.'

She whirled on him. 'No-you-will-not!' She emphasised each word, clearly, emphatically in his ear, then stood back and looked at him. 'Wherever we are, we'll be together. All of us.' And she pointed through to where her mute sister-in-law held an infant's shawl to her breast and stared into the kitchen fire, as if that said everything and no further discussion was needed. A quick hug, then Joe left.

'How about a cup of tea, Nessa?' Sarah asked as she walked back into the kitchen. There was no reply and the hunched woman curled her body away when Sarah reached past her to move the kettle across the cast iron range and closer to the fire. It began to sing almost immediately.

Three

Keir Connor braked hard and changed down. His hired car tucked itself neatly into the tight corner then surged ahead when he floored the throttle. He patted the steering wheel approvingly. 'Bet this is a change for you, mate. I think you're enjoying the drive even more than I am.' He felt at one with the car, with the stunning landscape, with the journey he was on.

A sudden steep climb took him high above the loch with a cliff at the road edge and rocky offshore islands that sprouted tall bluish pines with stout trunks and strong vigorous limbs. A quick drop and he was back into dappled flickering patterns cast by the fresh foliage of a canopy of unfamiliar trees. As he zipped along he soaked up the ever changing nuances of colour, light and tone. Sunshine here was soft and fleeting, so different from Western Australia's hard-shadowed glare and fierce heat.

He didn't try to stop his thoughts when they began to drift back to the chaos of yesterday's episode at Kilbendrick, although he knew Dr Rolfe would disapprove. He could almost hear that calm voice warning him to stay focussed on his driving, on the here and now; to leave analysis until later when he could pick a time to go through his relaxation routine then give his full attention to dissecting what had happened. But Doc was wrong this time. Working a good car along a twisting stretch of road into the Scottish Highlands was therapeutic for this patient. It loosened him up, helped him think straight.

First of all that spooky setting – the desolate shipyard, the clanging metal sheets, the wrecked pier, the rubbish strewn remains of abandoned buildings – had been a major factor in triggering the flashback. And he'd gone there after a morning steeping himself in the Clydebank Blitz while jet lagged and hungover. Then there was that old dredger with its piercing metallic squeals and screeches, its steely clunks; and the small boat's curving wake; the reddening river; the stink of decay.

And now the big one. Add into all that his own muddled feelings as he'd stood in the yard where his father – where Joe Connor – had walked, worked, spent his early life before Keir was born. Yeah. Add in the letter he'd found after his father had died, the single page of familiar spidery writing telling him that Mum and Dad weren't his real parents. Apologising for hiding the truth all of his life. Worse still, telling him that Mum had wanted Keir to know, had pled with Dad before she died, but he had resisted.

He could feel his frustration boil up again and he could feel the anger underlying it. Why hadn't his father spoken to him about it? There had been time to do that, the letter was dated two weeks before his death. But he knew there was no point in pursuing unanswerable questions. Somehow they had managed to take him from Scotland at the end of the War and raise him in Australia as their own. No wonder they'd tried to give a different spin to his childhood queries about the past, or to tell a diverting yarn whenever he asked about life in Scotland.

Ahead of him a simple elegant black sign carried the words "Laggandarroch School" in white letters. A white arrow pointed to the right. As he swung through an imposing pair of stone pillars, he had to brake suddenly to avoid a little red squirrel that bounded away from his shower of gravel, raced up one of those mighty pine trees, stood tall on the first branch, and criticised his driving with an indignant quiver of its tail. Keir tooted his horn in salute and continued along the driveway that wound up through mature woodland. When he reached open ground his foot eased off the accelerator. He let the car coast to a stop.

The grassy hill ahead of him was crowned by a castle

straight out of a Hollywood movie. Or a fairy tale.

The Laggandarroch School secretary led Keir into the headmaster's office. 'Here's Mr Connor, Dr McNeil.'

A tall upright man with pale blue eyes and a warm lopsided smile moved from behind his desk and opened his arms wide in greeting. His high intelligent forehead ended in vigorous waves of grey hair, neatly tamed by an old-fashioned side parting and a hint of hair oil. He wore a comfortable, well-made tweed suit and his corduroy shirt was open at the neck.

'Please call me Bob. We don't stand too much on formality here. First names are almost compulsory now in this kind of work.'

The man's geniality made Keir feel as if he already knew him. 'Another example of the shifting world you describe in *Children and Change* maybe,' he said as he returned the firm, friendly handshake.

'Ah. You've read my book. Kind of you to mention it. The "Doctor" by the way has nothing to do with my work here. It's courtesy of a PhD into the mating behaviour of *Somatochlora arctica*. That's a dragonfly and if you've ever heard of it you'll be about as rare as it is. I've been called "Doctor" almost as a joke ever since. I once foolishly tried to ban it here but pupils and staff just went on using it behind my back. I gave up.' He shrugged at Keir as if to say none of that mattered. 'I'm so glad to meet you at last. There's so much I want to talk to you about.'

'That cuts both ways.' Keir resisted the urge to go straight to the question that was foremost in his mind.

The headmaster picked up a copy of *Inside Cambodia: Victims and Survivors* and waved it at Keir. 'Glad to say I've returned the compliment and read your book too. Fascinating. Part of my own wartime service was spent flying bombers in Southeast Asia. Felt messy at the time but it now looks like a simple conflict compared to what the past decade

21

has inflicted on that part of the globe. Thanks for painting a coherent picture from such a complicated mess. Makes me doubly glad you're prepared to use your researching and writing skills to help unravel the history of this place. While you pursue your own researches of course.'

'Hey, it's a great bargain for me. Free board and lodgings in a beautiful spot like this and a fee at the end of it.' Now he couldn't restrain himself any longer. 'I'm really curious to know if you can help with the family questions I sent. About connections with my father, Joe Connor, and his work as a trade unionist.'

'Of course you are. My apologies. I'm going on about dragonflies and bombers and you've travelled thousands of miles on your search. So the short answer is yes, I know we can help. Here's what I suggest. Let's start with a look around. There's nothing like seeing the daily business at first hand to understand what goes on here at Laggandarroch. We can talk later over a cup of coffee, then sort out your bags and where you're staying.'

He led Keir out through the main arched entrance and onto an extensive well-clipped lawn that afforded a panoramic view of the school. 'Are you at all familiar with the architecture of Scottish castles?'

Keir shook his head.

'Ah. I'll try not to make a lecture of it. The main tower just to the right is the original Laggandarroch castle, a 16th century Scottish z-castle, so called because of its diagonal tower arrangement. The rest of the building facing us dates from the 18th century. There are late Victorian wings going up either side but you can't see them from here. This view really preserves the antiquity and beauty of the place. Not ideal for our purposes today, unfortunately. Some pupils live in the main building and others in two small modern units in the grounds. Most of the teaching takes place in a nineteen-sixties purpose-built classroom block. Why don't we start there?'

He led the way along the front of the castle. Some distance from the Victorian east wing stood a flat-roofed, two-storey building. Attempts to improve its unprepossessing aspect by painting it in blocks of bright pastel colour had emphasised rather than disguised the ugliness.

'Let's start with Science. Not because of any lingering attachment to my long ago academic enthusiasms, I assure you, but because the science classroom in this gracelessly ageing building has a very useful anachronism attached to it. An observation room. When it was built, one-way observation of families or children or patients was considered a proper and ethical practice. Not so today. To keep this room I've had to fight off opposition from Her Majesty's Inspectorate, social work directors, left wing teachers, right wing teachers and other people who've formed an instant untutored opinion at first sight of it.'

'Ah. *Children and Change* again.'

'Quite so.' Keir's comment was rewarded with a flash of the warm, asymmetrical smile. 'And there's another advantage of beginning with the education department. We can enter it from here without being seen from the classrooms. The presence of a visitor, or a headmaster for that matter, can have unpredictable effects on some of our pupils. Some of our teachers too, I dare say.'

He led the way through the entrance and up a flight of stairs to a corridor with several doors leading off it. Raising a finger to his lips, he gestured Keir through into a darkened room. A large tinted observation window made up one wall. On the other side of this a teacher welcomed a group of eight boys being led into the classroom by another man. 'Right, lads. Just get settled down while I hand out your notebooks.'

A squabble broke out between two pupils. One of them, a lanky, thin-faced boy, shouted to the teacher: 'Hoy, Greener! Greener! He's pinched my seat again!'

'No, Donny. It's not Greener. It's Mr Green – or George if you're feeling pally. And I've told you before. Nobody owns any of the seats. Just take that one behind you.'

Instead Donny charged at the other boy, wrestled the disputed seat from him and scrambled onto a table beside the classroom window. His strained face had turned adrenaline white. He held the back of the chair in his hands and was thrusting its tubular steel legs at the teacher who stood three or four paces off, not reacting although Keir could see an alertness in his face, in how he was holding himself. 'It's my fucking chair, you bastard! Don't come near me. I'm telling you. One more step and I'll fucking do it! I'll do you!'

The rest of the pupils were stamping their feet and chanting 'oof-oof-oof' in time to the stabbing movement of the chair. Between them and the stand-off at the window, the other man was speaking into a phone. He hung up quickly, then spread his arms wide and began waving the pupils towards the classroom door. Somewhat to Keir's surprise they allowed themselves to be ushered out. There were gestures of defiance and one shouted: 'Aye, go on Donny. Do him,' but there was also laughing and jostling towards the door, as if they preferred to leave the tension of the room and its unfolding drama. Keir heard steps running past the observation room door. A hefty bearded man and a tall athletic young woman pushed past the pupils and entered the classroom. Some of the children tried to turn back with them but their usher intercepted, shooed them out, and closed the door behind him.

'You're bastards, you're all fucking bastards. I'll fucking do you all!' The entry of the two new members of staff provoked the white-faced youth. He swung the chair and smashed the window. For a moment he seemed to consider leaping through the jagged hole onto the ground below. Instead, with a howl, he jumped down towards the teacher who stepped quickly away from the upraised chair, then stood still again. When the boy had turned to break the window, the bearded man had sped forward. Now he sat down slowly into a classroom chair behind the teacher, but to the right where he could keep the boy clearly in his view. The woman did the same to the teacher's left.

'You have a seat too, George,' the new man said to the teacher. 'Things seem to have got a wee bit heated. You too, Donny. Could you please sit down like the rest of us?'

'I don't want a fucking seat, Watson!' In the darkened observation room, Keir smiled at the irony of the chair clenched in Donny's fists.

'That's fine. We want you to be comfortable, though. Why don't you sit on that table and tell me what's gone wrong today?'

The boy half-leaned and half-sat on the table. The seat he was holding slowly lowered until its back legs rested on the ground but the knuckles that held it remained as white as ever.

'I'm not telling you, you big bastard. He can tell you. He was here.' He lifted a hand from the chair and gestured towards the teacher.

'Now, Donny. Language. There's a lady present.'

'Aw aye, she's some fucking lady. I don't think so. Big skinny slag, more like.'

'Well George's here. He's a teacher. An educated man. He probably doesn't even know any bad words.'

'Him? Greener? Wise up, you plonker.'

During this interchange, George Greene had eased himself to within reach of Donny. He placed his hand on the chair back and, before the boy had a chance to react, he raised his foot and planted it firmly on the seat. 'It started with a dispute about this chair, Ainsley.' Although the teacher's comment was addressed to the man behind him, he kept the boy within his field of view, but didn't look directly at him.

Donny wailed a moaning animal sound, whirled to the

windowsill and picked up a large jagged piece of glass. Ainsley Watson sprang from his seat and grabbed the boy's right wrist. Almost simultaneously the teacher took hold of the left. The two men walked Donny backwards into the room so quickly that his feet could not keep up and he began to topple. Still moving away from the window, one of the men put his free arm behind the boy's head, the other put his around the boy's shoulders. They lowered him quickly and laid him full length on his back. The woman had anticipated their movements and was already at the boy's feet. She turned at right angles to him and laid across both his legs. Keir could see her body jerk as she contained the boy's frenzied, but useless, efforts to free himself.

Meanwhile Watson had his knee on top of Donny's wrist. 'Let go of the glass, son. I don't want to hurt you.' The boy's blood-covered fingers struggled to continue their determined squeeze on the shard. Keir noticed that the inside of the left arm, which the teacher was controlling, was covered in parallel lines of old scars from the wrist to the inner elbow.

'Let it go. Now. You've done enough damage.' With that, Watson let more of his weight drop through his knee onto the boy's wrist. Donny screamed as a spasm forced his hand open. Watson carefully took the glass and laid it well out of the boy's reach.

'You bastard, you big bastard. You've broke my wrist. You big fat cunt. I'm going to get you charged!' He gathered saliva and spat in his tormentor's direction, but Watson had already turned away and was lying on the floor with his back to him, the boy's outstretched arm safely trapped beneath his bulk, a large hand pinning Donny's wrist to the floor. On the other side of Donny's head, the teacher was in a similar position. The boy ranted and struggled like a feral beast, stopping occasionally to deposit gobs of spit on the backs of the two men holding his arms. Then, slowly, he weakened. It was not a steady process and was interrupted by bouts of violent exertion and foul language which gradually became less frequent until at last he lay still like a human X, each end of which was securely held by silent adults, none of whom had spoken since the glass had been removed.

He started to cry.

When Ainsley Watson began to speak, his voice was quiet and slow. 'Don't you worry about crying, Donny. It's a good sign. It lets us know you're getting ready for us to release you.'

'Aye. Let me up. Let me go,' the boy sobbed.

'I'll know you're getting ready when you take two deep breaths, Donny. Two deep breaths. That'll help you get ready.'

'Don't start that deep breaths shite! Just let me up. Please. Watson. You big bastard, let me up. Fuck you! Let me up!' Donny's tirade was punctuated with further, hopeless attempts to free himself. Ainsley Watson merely turned his head away from a renewed barrage of spittle.

No one spoke as Donny raged, swore and struggled. When he had sweated himself to an exhausted stop, Watson let the silence develop for some time. The boy's breathing became steady and regular. Watson began again in the same soft slow tone as if nothing had intervened: 'Good, Donny. You've done really well to get yourself calm and quiet. We're making progress here. Now. Two deep breaths. Then we'll know we can start letting go. Take as long as you need. We're not going to rush you.' Donny's chest rose as he inhaled steadily. He paused, let his chest fall slowly, then inhaled again.

'Well done, Donny. I think we're ready to begin. I'm going to ask Janice to release your left leg. When she does, you can move it around a little if you want to, then keep it still. Janice, will you release Donny's left leg please?' The woman took her weight off the boy's leg then released it altogether but kept his right firmly under her control. Donny stretched the leg once then left it lying where it was.

'You're doing very well, Donny. Janice's going to release your right leg now. When you stop moving it we'll know you're ready to go on. Janice, will you please release Donny's right leg?' Janice rose and sat back on her hunkers, watching carefully as the leg moved to and fro then lay still.

'Very good, Donny. We're half-way there and making great progress. George is now going to release your left arm. You can move it if you want but remember to lie still again so we'll know you're ready for the last bit. George, will you please release Donny's left arm? Good. You've done a great job of making yourself calm, Donny. When this is finished, Janice and I are going to take you to the nurse to have your hand seen to. I'm sure she'll be able to find a cup of tea for us too. Then we'll have a chance to hear what upset you and get it sorted out. Now I'm going to release this arm.' He did. Janice joined him and together they encouraged Donny to his feet and began making their way to the classroom door.

Bob McNeil leaned towards Keir: 'Welcome to Laggandarroch Residential School,' he whispered.

Four

Joe Connor pushed back his ARP helmet, fished cigarettes and matches from the breast pocket of his blue overalls, lit up, and leaned his elbows on the wall at the top of Church Brae.

This spot, with its bird's eye view of Kilbendrick nestling in the tight turn of the Clyde, was one of his favourite places. When he was a kid, he and his pals had often dangled their legs over this high wall and argued about which of the toffs' gardens below them were ripe for raiding. The pears on the minister's tree were always September favourites. On the other hand, Henderson the shipbuilder's walled garden spread its treasures over a wide season – early rasps, strawberries, goosers, plums, apples. Then there was Dr Robertson's. Despite the threat from his spaniel, his cherry tree needed regular, critical sampling before the decision to plunder could be made. To Joe this hadn't been stealing, but an adventure that was his by right, a sort of balancing of the books. Looking back, he could see how those escapades seeded an attitude in him, a first understanding of social difference, of them and us. And they'd been stepping stones on a journey that had led him to serve his apprenticeship in Henderson's yard, to become a tradesman, to become a trade union man, too.

And he'd stood here and proposed to Sarah as they walked back from a long kiss and cuddle in the bluebell woods. When she said yes, they'd wrapped themselves around one another and gazed down on the lovely vista of river and village. He'd thought his heart would burst.

Aye, that was a world away. Now he was up here on lookout while down there Sarah cared for his grief-crazed sister and got ready for another night of ... of what? He looked eastwards towards Clydebank. Just two miles away, the damaged oil storage tanks at Old Kilpatrick continued to pour out flames and thick black smoke. In and around Clydebank itself, countless fires were still burning. He could just make out the barrage balloons above Brown's shipyard. To their left, a square mile of desolation flickered and smouldered where Singer's wood storage yard had been left to burn itself out while overstretched fire crews and rescue teams had focussed on saving human lives and dwellings. A menacing pall of smoke billowed like a warning above the devastated town.

High in the Kilpatrick Hills behind him, smoke still rose from the embers of the flimsy timber decoy towns that had been set alight last night in the vain hope of misleading the raiders. But the unmistakeable ribbon of the moonlit Clyde had beckoned the German bombers and tonight's fires would make their job easier still. Those blazing oil tanks would draw them further west and more bombs were bound to hit Kilbendrick. At this thought, his eyes sought out the wreckage of Hillcraig Terrace then, nearer at hand, the burnt-out wing of Henderson's mansion where the old woman had died. Twenty-four hours could make a hell of a difference. Boss or worker. Victim or rescuer. Life or death. For now, you could hardly slip a tram-ticket between them. Bombs didn't give a shit about the social class of the people they were blowing to bits.

Day faded into dusk. The river glittered red in the remnants of a sunset that, further to the west, silhouetted the dome of Dumbarton Rock and painted reds, pinks, blues and mauves in the western sky above the distant Cowal hills. For a moment he felt a surge of wonder that such beauty could exist in the midst of so much death and destruction. In the village below him, a light flickered in a top floor window of Erskine View. Sure enough, Maggie Thomson had forgotten

30

to close her blackout blinds again. What was it going to take before she got the message? He looked again at the flaming oil tanks and the burning town in the distance. What the fuck did it matter? Tonight wasn't going to be about blackout rules, it was going to be about survival. He dropped his cigarette end, crushed it under his boot, and set off downhill.

As he approached the foot of Church Brae he could see beneath the railway bridge the shapes of tonight's two Home Guard sentries. Although it was now almost dark, he recognised them from their shadowy outlines – Sandy Downer and Jock Wilson, respectively the shortest and the tallest in the shipyard. Sandy insistently described himself as 'over five feet', a claim that had once been put to the test in the plating shed where he had lain down and been marked out. Careful measuring put him a sixteenth of an inch over. Disbelievers subsequently claimed either that he'd kept his socks on or needed a haircut, but Big Sandy, as he was affectionately known, stuck to his guns. Despite his size, he was good for a full shift swinging his riveting hammer with the best of them. Wee Jock Wilson was a clear fifteen inches taller and about twice as broad as Sandy. Putting them on guard duty together was the one bit of evidence that old Colonel Somerville had a sense of humour buried somewhere beneath his florid and grumpy exterior.

Big Sandy's face wrinkled in concern. 'How's it looking up there, Joe?'

'Terrible. The tanks are still blazing and there's fires all over the place in Dalmuir and Clydebank.'

'Think they'll be back the night?'

'It's not what I think, Jock. I'm sure of it. The weather's perfect. They'll see the fires from miles away. Those bloody incendiaries. Makes it easier to find the target the second night. Look at last year. Birmingham, three nights. London, two nights. Liverpool and Manchester got two each as well. Aye. They'll be back all right.'

31

'After what happened last night,' said Wee Jock, 'you wonder what we're up against here. I mean. Just look at us.' He held out the makeshift weapon he was carrying, a scaffolding pole with a bayonet lashed onto one end.

'Stop complaining, you big lassie. We agreed it was night about with the musket.' Big Sandy held up an old bolt-action rifle. 'And tonight, I got not just one bullet, I got two. Bring on the Wehrmacht! Anyway,' he added as an afterthought, 'that thing you've got is too heavy for me. It's designed for big brainless people.'

'Sandy, if you kill any Wehrmacht it'll be because they die laughing. I mean, look at him, Joe. Churchill's secret weapon, done up to make the Jerries think Scotland's being defended by wee boys dressed up as soldiers. The shoulders of that battledress are somewhere round about his elbows and the arse of his trousers is at his knees.'

'Ach, the big eunuch's just jealous, Joe. He's bothered because I need a lot of room down there in my pants. Unlike him.'

'Boys, boys.' Joe pretended to placate with outstretched hands. 'Don't drag me into it. When you two are doing the sniping, my head stays below the firing line. But I'll say one thing, Sandy. You showed plenty of balls the day. Crawling in under that roof.'

'No. Don't say that. I was the obvious one to go. The rest of you buggers are all too big. No. I'll tell you who the real heroes are. Mrs Brownlee when I handed her wee Shona's body. And people like your sister Nessa who's lost her man along with most of her family. How is she?'

'Still not talking. The doctor came in and checked her. "She's one of many," he said. "Time'll take care of it." Whatever you say, Sandy, you did a great job.'

'What I can't get over is Mrs Dagerelli. I knew I was in their kitchen, at the back of the café. Most of the walls were still standing but it was a hell of a mess. And a strong stink of gas. That really bothered me. I looked everywhere I could. There was no sign of her. When I crawled back out, Ernesto wouldn't believe me. "I know she's-a-there. In-a-the kitchen. Please. Please. I know she's-a-there." So in I crawled again. Checked under the table, under the bed, in the pantry. Not a sign. The kitchen door had swung wide open. Then I noticed the door wasn't hard up to the wall. I pulled it back. There she was. Bolt upright. And stone dead. It must've been something to do with the blast. Or maybe she'd changed her mind and was at the door on her way to the shelter when the bomb exploded.'

The other two had heard Big Sandy's account before, but they listened respectfully. Joe clapped him on the shoulder. 'You did well, Sandy.' He set off to complete his rounds.

When Joe arrived home, Sarah was making sandwiches at the kitchen table. Nessa still sat huddled at the fire. 'Where is everybody?' he asked.

'Charlie's here. Heather and him are up at the shelter, just making sure everything's okay. Ricky's gone with them.' As Sarah spoke, she took Joe's arm and led him through to the front room. 'She's started muttering,' she said. 'She's done it a few times now.'

'Muttering? What d'you mean? Can you make anything out?'

'As if she's speaking under her breath. There seems to be a pattern to it. I thought I once heard her say Hugh's name. But then again, I wonder if she's praying. The rosary maybe?'

'Oh aye. I can hear the Church of Rome galloping to our aid the night, just like it did last night.'

'Joe Connor! You bite your heathen tongue. Just because you've turned your back on your faith, doesn't give you a right to mock.' Sarah despaired at Joe's attitude to the church, but never let such comments go unchallenged.

33

'Aye. Aye, I know. I'm sorry.' His apology sounded rushed and insincere. 'I'll go through and see how she is.'

Nessa didn't acknowledge her brother's greeting, but she didn't turn away or resist when he slipped an arm around her shoulders and gave her a gentle hug. The baby's shawl was now in her lap, gripped between hands that were pressed together as if in prayer. He could see her lips moving slightly. When he bent to listen he could hear a faint mumbling.

'What is it, Nessa? Are you trying to say something, hen?' He squeezed her shoulders again. 'Nessa. This is a hellish, awful thing that's happened. You and Ricky can stay here with us. We'll look after you here. Help you get through this. Help you –'

He broke off at the first low moan of the siren. He'd left his deputy, Cyril Beattie, at the post with instructions to set it off if the call came through, and Joe would get there as soon as he could. He checked the mantelpiece clock. Twenty to nine, half an hour earlier than last night. The bastards couldn't wait. There was a rush of footsteps in the close. Charlie, Heather and Ricky came in and began picking up the blankets and food that Sarah had laid out on the table.

'We'll all go up to the shelter thegether,' Joe said to Sarah. 'Then I'll have to leave. I'll try and get back before anything starts.'

At the door, Sarah faced him and gripped his arms tightly. 'No. Not "try", Joe. You promised.'

'Aye. I know, I promised. I'll be back.'

The siren had stopped by the time they reached the mound of the Anderson shelter, half buried in their vegetable plot. Joe shone his torch into its cramped interior. There was just room for a narrow bench along each side. Sarah and Heather stowed the night's supplies under one of the benches while Charlie lit two candles on the small table at the far end. Ricky led Nessa in through the doorway. Joe put his arm around his sister and helped her sit down. He could hear that Nessa's muttering had become louder, a monotonous, rhythmic undertone. Maybe Sarah was right. Maybe it was some sort of prayer. Nessa had always been one to turn to the church when things went wrong.

With Sarah, Nessa and Ricky sitting on one side and Heather and Charlie holding hands on the other, the shelter was already almost full. 'I'll see you all later,' Joe said as he closed the door.

Joe hung up the phone. 'That was Central,' he told Cyril. 'Big fleet of bombers crossed the Berwickshire coast at quarter past nine tonight. They were spotted again ten miles south of Edinburgh. Looks like our name's on them.' The two men stood outside the ARP post at the end of one of the harbour's quays. They had a clear view up and down river. The light from the full moon was strong enough for them to see detail for at least a mile in both directions. Upstream, just beyond the slipway of the Erskine Ferry, the Old Kilpatrick tanks burned out of control and threw up a spiralling, twisting red beacon. Further west, flames reddened the otherwise blacked out townscape of Clydebank.

'I think that's them now.' Cyril, his head tilted to one side, pointed upriver. Then Joe could hear it too, the faraway drone and throb of aircraft engines. Searchlights came on and started sweeping the skies. Anti-aircraft shells burst like short-lived stars.

'Okay. We've seen enough.' The two men began to run along the quay and back towards the village.

When Joe reached the shelter he could see Sarah standing outside. Bomb blasts could now be heard in the distance.

'What...? For Christ's sake get inside! Can you not hear what's happening?'

'I'm waiting for you, Joe. Listen. That muttering. It's their names. She's on her feet, saying them out loud now. I can't do anything with her.'

'Never mind! Get in!' He pushed her in through the door. He could see Heather and Charlie sitting on one side. Ricky sat white-faced between them and they had their arms around him. Nessa stood with her arms raised above her head. The child's shawl dangled from her injured hand. The other was open, palm facing out as if she was greeting someone, or perhaps warding something off. The upward flickering glow from the candles turned her face into a demonic mask. What had earlier been incomprehensible and barely audible had become loud and clear: 'Hugh-Theresa-Margaret-Sheila-John-Jesus-Mary-Joseph-Hugh-Theresa-Margaret-Sheila-John-Jesus-Mary-Joseph-Hugh-Theresa...'

There was no warning of the first bomb until it exploded somewhere near the harbour. Joe heard the whistle of the second one. The explosion was ear-splitting and from the direction of the Bendrick Inn. The whistle of the next was louder, closer, and ended in a thunderous crack and crumple that felt like a physical blow. The shelter rose and fell, its occupants thrown together in a heap as rubble thundered down onto the two feet of earth above them.

Except for Nessa. She somehow managed to keep standing and shrieking: 'HUGH–THERESA–MARGARET–SHEILA–JOHN–JESUS–MARY–JOSEPH–HUGH–THERESA–MARGARET–SHEILA–JOHN–JESUS–MARY–JOSEPH–HUGH–THERESA–MARGARET–SHEILA–JOHN–JESUS–MARY–JOSEPH–HUGH–THERESA–MARGARET–SHEILA–JOHN–JESUS–MARY–JOSEPH–'

Five

Keir Connor expected the headmaster to become involved in the aftermath of the window smashing and the restraint of Donny on the science classroom floor. Instead Bob McNeil led him briskly back down the stairs. 'Let's see if life's any quieter in the English department,' he said.

As they walked, he addressed Keir's unasked question. 'You're possibly wondering why I didn't get mixed up in the classroom stramash? That's no place for me. The trust of damaged kids like Donny is not easily won. Staff earn their authority the hard way. The last thing they need is a headmaster robbing them of it just when they've done all the tough stuff.'

The furniture in the English class had been moved back to the walls. Pupils sat on the floor in a semicircle. The teacher who sat on the floor facing them wore a one-piece brightly embroidered jumpsuit and had her legs tucked under in what looked to Keir like a meditation posture. Her steel-grey hair was pulled back into a strong single plait that almost brushed the ground. The face she turned to greet the visitors was smooth and lively.

'I've brought a guest with me today,' said the headmaster. 'This is Keir Connor. He's come all the way from Australia to see us.'

'Hello everybody.' Keir smiled and nodded around the group.

'Haw you! You spick affa funny,' blurted a pale skinny boy with carroty hair.

'Move out and make room for two more,' said the teacher when the laughter had died down. Then she added for the benefit of the newcomers 'We're having a story circle. Eric here has his hand up. When he puts it down, the next person on the left has to keep the story going.' She nodded to the headmaster who was sitting down beside the boy with the raised hand. 'And that'll be you, Dr Bob.'

Keir slipped between Bob McNeil and a plumpish girl who immediately said: 'But Gloria, it's not fair on them.' She rubbed reddened areas on either side of her nose with a gesture that looked to Keir like a nervous tic. 'They don't know what's happened so far.'

'Good point, Rosemary.' The teacher opened her arms in a questioning gesture as she directed her attention slowly around the circle. 'Well? Do you want them to know?'

'Gloria, why don't you just tell them enough to get the idea?' suggested a large youth with bad acne. 'It'll take too long to do it all again.' There were nods and murmurs of agreement.

'Okay,' said Gloria. 'I kicked us off. My cat Petra has just had seven kittens. I love that cat. She loves her kittens. But I can't keep them all. Sandra was next. She told us about when her mother came to visit her in a children's home to tell her she loved her and her brothers and sisters but wasn't going to be able to take them home just yet. Then Jo-Jo had us all laughing about the time he had a keyworker he didn't like. So at suppertime he offered to make the sandwiches. Everybody had corned beef except the keyworker who had dog food. The thing was he didn't notice.'

Keir and Dr Bob joined in the rekindled laughter.

'And when you came in Eric was telling us about his grandfather's dog which became Eric's after his Granda died. It's the only funeral Eric's been to. His feelings were mixed up. He was very sad, but he was glad to be there too. That's where you'd got to Eric.' She looked at the boy who still had his hand up. 'Do you want to go on?'

'Aye. After that we left the crem … crem…'

'Crematorium,' the teacher prompted.

'Aye. That place. Then we all went to a hotel and we had pies and sandwiches and sausage rolls, and…' he dropped his hand and turned to the headmaster with a mischievous smirk.

Dr Bob's hand shot up. 'And a man stood up and sang a song. It went like this.' In a resonant baritone he chanted:

'Your granda's dead but you are not
And life will teach you such a lot
He was old but you are young
And your life has just begun
His dog will help you to find out
What this life is all about.'

The children cheered and clapped. The headmaster silenced them with a finger to his lips and continued: 'No sooner had the singer sat down than a boy Eric's age came in, a stranger. No one knew anything about him. He came from a place...' He dropped his hand and turned to his left.

Until this point Keir had felt at home with what was happening in the classroom. As he raised his hand slowly he felt exposed and vulnerable. Then he said the first thing that entered his mind.

'He came from a faraway place where life was not peaceful. Sometimes in the middle of lessons a siren would go off and he had to hide under the desks with the rest of his classmates, crossing his fingers that a rocket wouldn't scream in through the window and kill them all, or a bomb blow them all to smithereens. Sometimes he would sit by himself in the sun and think about his life. He didn't really want much. Just the chance to grow up in peace where he and his mates and their families were safe from harm. Was that too much to ask?'

He dropped his hand. Rosemary's arm shot up. 'I know how he felt. Just a chance to grow up without problems and bad things happening. I feel like that sometimes too...'

The teacher interrupted in a quiet voice. She had caught

the slight nod from Dr Bob. 'And we want to hear more about how you feel Rosemary. But first we have to stay goodbye to our guests. They've other visits to make and we can't keep them all to ourselves,' she said amid loud groans of disappointment. As the two men made their way to the door, Eric put his hand up. 'Dr Bob, how come you always manage to sing a song?'

"Cos I am old and you are not,' the headmaster sang. Then he beamed his lopsided smile around the group, held the door open for Keir and followed him out.

'I've arranged for coffee in the boardroom.' The headmaster stopped at an arched doorway and pushed open a heavy timber door, studded with iron nails and hung on massive black hinges. 'After you.'

Keir took a few steps, stopped and looked around. The walls of the large medieval hall were oak panelled. A spectacular fireplace dominated the far end of the room. Ingle seats flanked the wrought iron hearth and the whole edifice was framed by an ornate stone mantel carved with heraldic emblems. The oak panelling that lined the walls continued up into a vaulted ceiling where the roof bosses on the supporting crossbeams were decorated with brightly coloured coats of arms.

The centrepiece of the room was an oak table capable of seating at least two dozen people. A large oil painting and a cloth banner dominated the left hand wall. The panelling between them was densely hung with smaller paintings and photographs. The line of the right hand wall was broken by two wide and deep book-lined alcoves which ended in tall windows reaching almost from floor to ceiling. Through the nearest of these, Keir could see the long sun-struck loch and the curving drive that had led him up to the school. He stood for a moment, soaking up the view and savouring smells of polish, books, a hint of smoke.

Bob McNeil made his way to the other alcove where a coffee tray sat on a low-lying table flanked by two comfortable looking armchairs. 'I think you're impressed.' He waved a glass coffee pot at Keir. 'How do you take it?'

'More than impressed. Wowee, this room is spectacular! And I take my brew black, thanks.'

'So now you know something of what we do at Laggandarroch,' the headmaster said, as the two men settled themselves into their armchairs.

Keir sipped his coffee and thought for a moment before replying. 'There's a lot to take in. What I've seen is so varied. As we moved around, I kept trying to find a way to sum up what I was witnessing.'

'And did you succeed?'

'Seemed to me that the child was always at the centre of what was happening. Is that close?'

'Pretty good. I'm very pleased you felt that.' The headmaster put his cup down and paused as if collecting his thoughts. 'You see,' he went on, 'this school was called Harmony before I took over. There was a lot of that going on at the time, calling schools and residential places by abstract nouns as if somehow the pupils would absorb those qualities.' He offered more coffee and topped them both up. 'But it doesn't work like that with children. Once upon a time, some people with more money than sense built a spanking new "child-centred" school they called "Empathy". Within weeks of opening, it was burnt to a shell by two youngsters out of their heads on vodka and Valium. So much for empathy!'

Keir smiled at the headmaster's wry chuckle. He was liking Bob McNeil and sensed something agreeably mischievous in the man. He wondered if his leg was being pulled, but nodded along while he waited for the next twist in the wandering narrative. 'So I decided it was safer to call the school Laggandarroch after the castle we're sitting in.

And there was a more serious side to it. Children, especially those we work with here, respond to real places – like this ancient building – rather than to abstract notions. But harmony remains key to what we do here. We aim to create a harmonious balance between the needs of each child and the experiences and care we provide. Not always easy, particularly since we deal with some of the most troubled and troubling young people around, kids whose behaviour can be very challenging.'

'That's what so impressed me. That lad who smashed the window had to be controlled. But it was done in a way that kept him, and the lessons he had to learn, at the centre of the whole shebang. He was being gently confronted with inescapable reality, rather than punished for what he had just done. Well, maybe not gently. But in a supportive – could I even say loving? – way.'

'I'm so pleased to hear that. You've put your finger on why we've developed the techniques that you saw being used. Donny was almost certain to harm someone. Probably himself, he has a long history of doing that, but maybe someone else too. Once he picked up the piece of glass he had to be restrained. But there's more to it. He had to be restrained quickly, safely, as painlessly as possible, and in a way that allowed responsibility to be given back to him as soon as he was ready to take it. That's key to the philosophy here at Laggandarroch. When Donny lost the place today, adults that he trusts took control until he was ready to take charge of himself again. That's why I stayed out of it. There's no place in the equation for a headmaster to appear like an old granddad, patting heads and handing out sweeties to people who've been rolling around amongst the dust and the spittle.'

'Yeah, I can see that,' said Keir. 'The setting in the English class couldn't have been more different, but again it was the children's contributions that were central. Not to forget your singing of course!'

'Ah well, I try not to disappoint. Gloria's a remarkable teacher. A couple of years ago we had a snap visit from Her Majesty's Inspectors. One of them sat in on some of her English classes. "Very interesting, Ms Honeydew," he said, "but is it English teaching or is it therapy?" "If you give me a clear definition of the difference, I'll give you a clear answer," she replied. You should have seen the look on the man's face! He'd never been spoken to like that by a teacher.' He chuckled at the memory.

Keir's eyebrows lifted. 'Gloria Honeydew?'

'Yes. Yours is a common reaction. The name has led some to speculate in all kinds of unlikely directions, others to snort at the affectation of a name change. But I assure you Honeydew is indeed her name. Gloria has a long connection with this place. She was born here when her parents were members of the original commune. And, as it happens, Ainsley Watson, the chap who took charge of the classroom incident, he was a commune child too.'

'Yeah. The commune.' Keir put down his coffee and leaned forward. 'You explained a little about that in one of your letters.'

'Indeed I did. From what you said when you first wrote, I know that part of this place's history is very pertinent to your search for information about your relatives.'

'I know for sure that my father and an uncle – they were both shipyard workers – had some connection with this place because of their trade union activities. It's very important for me to find out more, to learn what brought them here.' Keir paused. He could say much more to this likeable man, could tell him that, in the weeks that had passed since their exchange of letters, his questions had taken a whole new direction. What had started as curiosity about family history had become a fundamental inquiry into his own origins. Who his mother was, his father, who he was? But after yesterday's

43

events in the shipyard, that all felt too risky. He waited for Dr Bob to continue.

'This boardroom holds important clues to what happened here in the years before Laggandarroch became the kind of school you saw a little of this morning.' The headmaster gestured towards the picture-decked wall. 'What do you make of the two big ones over there?'

The oil painting on the left, about two metres tall, showed a middle-aged seated man, the strong planes of his angular face dramatically picked out by light streaming through a window. He wore simple clothes – loose-cut trousers and a smock-like shirt, open at the neck. Long hair cascaded to his shoulders. A large book lay on the table beside him, its title and author carefully lettered onto the spine although Keir was too far away to read them. A young girl sat at the man's feet and his hand rested lightly on her head.

The portrait contrasted with the large hanging that dominated the right hand side of the wall. It was twice as high as it was wide and reached from floor to roof. Keir was reminded of a trade union banner but with a narrative style that echoed Diego Rivera murals he'd seen. A pastoral scene at the top featured the castle that now formed the main building of Laggandarroch School. People gathered and stacked sheaves of corn; hunters with hounds chased a stag from a wood; a group of men and women danced in a circle. Further down, heavily muscled shipyard workers swung hammers; miners and ponies with blazing eyes emerged from the smoky blackness of a coal mine. Elsewhere a family sat down to a meal; a woman taught a class of children; patients were cared for in a hospital; men and women in a workshop studied drawings and constructed components of a futuristic machine. All of the scenes were linked to a dramatic central image; a giant heroic figure with a flaming torch in its outstretched right hand and a powerful head, tilted up to look towards some distant vision. This titan was being carved from a tree trunk by two men on flimsy scaffolding, one with a large axe and the other with a pneumatic drill. Banner-carrying suffragettes gathered beneath the carvers' platform. A scroll of curving letters across the top of the banner read "Harmony" and was partnered across the bottom by "Freedom, Knowledge, Cooperation".

Keir gave his judgement: 'The oil painting's old-fashioned. Romantic and a bit kitschy for my taste. It looks to the past. The wall hanging feels modern, and talks about a new future.'

'Ten out of ten. And I think that's one of the paradoxes about Fergus Abercrombie, the chap in the painting. Despite its 18th century appearance, the portrait was painted in 1920, long after he'd bought Laggandarroch Castle and founded Harmony Commune based on ideas he discovered during his travels in Europe. The book on the table beside him is *Harmony and Happiness* by the 18th century utopian socialist, Charles Fourier. The banner on the right was carried by Fergus Abercrombie and other commune members when they marched in support of a whole range of left wing causes. But you already know something about that, I think?'

Keir felt on reasonably safe ground. 'Not a lot. When I was a child in Western Australia I loved listening to stories about the castle in Scotland owned by a rich man who believed that all people were equal. Then as I grew up I began to think my leg was being pulled.'

'He was certainly rich, extremely rich at one point in his life. But then he changed.' The headmaster looked thoughtful. 'Trouble is, I really only know what I know from a book he wrote about himself. I never met the man, he was long dead by the time I came here twenty years ago. But I've lived with that portrait for years and I still can't make up my mind about why he decided on such a Victorian biblical style. Is there a hint of self-mockery there? Or is it self-deception? Or is the intention to deceive me? For sure, he's a difficult man to sum up in a few words. The childhood stories about him, did you hear them from your father and your uncle?'

'Not my uncle. No, Hugh Glover was dead before I was born. He and most of his family were killed in the Clydebank Blitz of 1941. Finding out more about that is one of the reasons I've come to Scotland. It was my father, Joe Connor, who told me about this place.'

Keir senses movement somewhere close by. Or did he hear it? He focusses. Listens. There's something wrong with his heartbeat. Steady-unsteady. Steady-unsteady. Steady-unsteady. Easy. Take it easy. That's just its rhythm. So why is it bumping in his ears? Why is he fighting the urge to gasp for breath? Oh-oh. Must stay on top of this. He can stay on top of this. He has to...

But an inner wall collapses. His attention is pulled more and more over the rubble, drawn by a beckoning whisper that lures him towards a dark corner. He chases the sound through shadows. There's a bitterness on his tongue, and the taste of unease grows as a four word chant repeats and repeats.

My father Joe Connor ... My father Joe Connor ... My father Joe Connor...

Then, from a distant light place, beyond the spell of the bewitching mantra, another voice beckons. A calmer, safer voice. He turns towards it.

'I think it's time we had a closer look at some of the smaller pictures on that wall,' said Dr Bob. 'I believe I've found Joe Connor and Hugh Glover.'

Six

'You cunts are at it!' Big Sandy Downer stretched to his full five feet, peered over the curved steel sheet that dangled in front of him. He threw a heavy rivet at the two platers who had guided the crane from the plating shed to Number One stocks where Ship 453, destined to be a three hundred ton tugboat, was currently little more than a keel, bottom plates, and a skeleton of rust-coloured ribs.

The men dodged and laughed. 'How?'

'Don't fucking how me. I'll tell you how. Because your foreman is Wee Jock's cosy drinking pal...' Big Sandy gestured over his shoulder to where Wee Jock Wilson's squad worked flat-out riveting on the port side bilge strakes. '... and because there's a bet on here, and because I was winning until you pricks brought that last plate whose alignment is straight out of my worst fucking nightmare. And because I think this plate's a dud as well. Is that enough for you?'

Big Sandy waved to the crane driver, issued directions until he was satisfied with the newly arrived plate's position, then clambered down beside the platers. 'Right. That's the bottom holes lined up now.' He slipped temporary bolts through two of the holes. His squad on the other side threaded on nuts and tightened them up. 'Now. Look at these five holes here.' He pointed to the curve where the new plate overlapped the one they had just finished riveting into place. 'The first hole and the last one are dead on. The middle one's acceptable. The other two are both out. And in opposite directions.'

'C'mon Sandy. They're not that bad. That's within agreed tolerance,' said one of the platers.

'Aye,' said the other, 'Shouldn't be a problem for the man

with the biggest podger in the yard.'

'Agreed tolerance my arse. It's not a big podger you need for that mess,' said Big Sandy, 'it's a fucking magic wand.'

'No, no. Look. If you podger the middle hole, you'll split the difference between the one above and the one below. Then those rivets'll slip in easy-peasy.'

'Is your brain on fucking holiday?' Big Sandy pushed a finger into the hole being discussed. 'Hey Cammy, son,' he called to the rivet boy on the other side of the plate, 'podger this hole for us.'

Cammy picked up Big Sandy's podger. The open-ended spanner with a tapering spike for a handle was a common tool in the shipyard, but Sandy's was four or five inches longer than anyone else's. 'Aye,' he was fond of saying, 'you show me a wee man and I'll show you a man with a big podger. Ask any of your wives.' 'Do you not mean with a big mouth?' somebody was sure to reply.

The men watched the podger extend towards them until it filled the hole. 'Hit it a wee tap with one of the hammers, son,' Big Sandy instructed. There was a clang. The offending holes remained as misaligned as ever.

'C'mon Cammy. You're a big boy. Hit it a good scud son,' shouted one of the platers.

'N-o-o-o!' By the time Big Sandy's yell registered with the rivet boy it was too late. The swing of his hammer carried all of the power and urgency of a sixteen-year-old demonstrating that he was fit to stand with the men. There was a screech of steel on steel as Cammy's well-aimed blow drove the podger almost full length through the misaligned holes. Its gleaming spike pointed towards the platers like a foot-long accusatory finger.

'Oh fuck,' groaned Big Sandy. 'That's going to take some fucking shifting. Right, you cunts.' He hefted a riveting hammer and breenged at the platers. When they scampered away laughing, he threw the hammer after them. 'Tell that fucking foreman of yours he's the biggest poxiest cunt in this whole fucking yard.'

The twelve o'clock hooter blew.

'We're going to have our pieces outside in the sun, Uncle Joe,' said Ricky Glover as he and Alan, a second year apprentice, made their way to the sunlit entrance of the engine shop.

'Now. C'mon.' Joe Connor leaned over and stared into Ricky's face. 'How many times do I have to tell you? Say that again, Ricky.'

'Sorry. Alan and me are going to have our pieces outside, Joe.'

'That's the way. There's no uncles in the shipyard, son. We're all working men here.'

Joe watched Ricky head out into the sunshine, looking every inch the new shipyard apprentice in an old pair of trousers, a collarless shirt, and a wide cloth cap on his head. Then he picked up his metal lunch box and moved to the back of the workshop where his fellow engineers were gathering. The foreman fitter, Willie Strachan, and Cyril Beattie, Joe's best pal in the shop, laid a sheet of ply across adjoining workbenches next to a charcoal forge. Other men fetched the assortment of boxes and tool chests that doubled as seats around the temporary table. An orderly queue formed at the forge where Ricky, as the newest apprentice and therefore unofficial tea boy, had earlier placed a dozen blackened tea cans to boil. Each man in turn threw into the bubbling water his preferred quantities of tea and sugar, slipped one of his tools under the wire loop that formed his tea can handle, and carried the steaming container of strong aromatic brew to his established place at the table. With the relish of the deserving hungry, they unwrapped their sandwiches and began to eat.

Auld Boab, at seventy the oldest worker in the yard, peeled one of his sandwiches apart. 'Jesus Christ! Fish paste.

That's what she thinks of me. What about you, Willie?'

'Spam,' said the foreman.

'Oh aye. Not bad. You could be in luck. Joe?'

'Cheese and onion.'

'Geordie.'

'Meat paste.'

'Christ. Nearly as bad as me.' Auld Boab carefully picked his way round the group so that he ended with Sammy Samson, just twenty years old, just one week married, and hiding his sandwiches behind cupped hands.

'Too late, son. I had a wee quick look when you were opening your box. Sliced beef. I remember what it was like when I got sliced beef on a Friday. She'd be waiting for me behind the door, half naked. It wasn't my wages she was after. No wonder you're blushing.'

'Leave the boy alone, Boab,' said Joe. 'You're just jealous.'

'Och, the lad knows I'm only kidding him. You're lucky, son. So you are.' He looked down at his large potbelly. 'The last time I was able to see mine, never mind do anything with it, was about twenty years ago.'

'Young Ricky's had a good first week, Joe,' said Willie the foreman when the laughter died down. 'But I still think you tipped him off about going to the stores.'

'Never a word.' Joe's reply was heavy with mock sincerity.

'Well, I've sent a lot of new boys to the stores for a bucket of black steam. You see some of them looking a bit suspicious, but they go along with it. I checked with Smart Alec. He never saw Ricky. The boy never got the length of the stores. But the wee bugger had the cheek to come back and make sure you all heard his answer. "They're out of black, Mr Strachan. Only the hot red stuff or the cold blue stuff left." That's the kind of lip you've got on you, Joe. You tipped him the wink.'

'Never said a word.' On the foreman's blind side, Joe's eyelid flickered.

'How's the boy's mother doing, Joe?' Cyril's question silenced the group. Heads turned in Joe's direction.

'I can see my sister coming back to herself again,' he said, 'but it's a hard road for her. It's only a few months, and it's a hell of a lot to come to grips with.'

'I think one of the worst things must be not finding the bodies, not being able to have a funeral. To say cheerio,' said Cyril. 'Mrs Brownlee told my wife that the one thing that keeps her going is being able to go and see wee Shona's grave. Take her a flower. Talk to her about how things are. But when all that's left is a big hole in the ground...'

'Aye, that's right,' said Joe. 'And there's a huge hole in her life too. She can talk a bit about it now. She's quiet a lot of the time as well. Except when it comes to young Ricky, she's got plenty to say about him. She still gets nervous whenever the boy's out of her sight, always needing to know where he is, what he's doing. I can understand why, but the lad needs to have a life too. He was bursting to get a start in the yard as soon as he turned fourteen. Never off my back about it.

'So I had to speak to her. "Nessa," I said, "it's what I did at his age, what your Hugh did as well. That's the way it is around here. It'll do him good." "Aye, maybe", she said. "But what if something happens to him? That's what worries me." "Well there's no need to worry, hen," I told her, "I'll be keeping a close eye on him, and so will the rest of the men. It's a fine friendly wee yard, Henderson's," I said, "not a huge place like Brown's where he could get lost before he had time to put his bunnet on."'

'Aye, she's coming round, slow but sure. Sarah and me, we look out for her as best we can, but there comes a time she's just got to get on with it. She's close to my wife's sister, Heather. Her man Charlie's in the Navy. Heather's working with the polishers in Brown's the now, and she's full of stories about the carry-on the women have there. Nessa enjoys hearing all that. She spends a lot of time at her church as well,' Joe added, and a disapproving tone crept into his voice.

'Each to their own,' said Geordie Scott. 'But I don't get it. How can somebody believe in mysteries and secrets about turning bread into bodies, and women getting pregnant without screwing?'

Joe turned the mockery aside with a careless shrug. 'A Protestant freemason like you, Geordie, knows about secrets and mysteries. It's all a heap of shite to me.'

Religious bigotry was a rare visitor to workforce relationships in Henderson's yard and that was fine by Joe Connor. Most of the workers were Kilbendrick men who shared the intimacies of tenement life in a wee village community. Aye, the fault line existed. The two sides went to their separate churches and life's important milestones – christenings, marriages, funerals – were carried out to the beat of different dogmas. It was a divide that affected the young, too. Catholic children went to school in one direction, Protestants in another. And sometimes when feelings were hurt, religious name-calling was practised along with the well-aimed stone or a challenge to fight that usually ended in little more than a bloodied nose or a black eye. But during the nightly football matches in the swing park, a goal scored by a Catholic foot counted just as much as one scored by the other foot, and in the pub darts team a winning throw was a winning throw, no matter the surname of the thrower or the school his kids attended. So by and large, religion was for Sundays and overlooked for the rest of the week.

There were exceptions, and Geordie Scott was one of them; Geordie who liked to boast when cradled in the boozy camaraderie of his cronies: 'I'm the proddie who'll always take a poke at a pape.' Now he put down his sandwich and his tea can. No one else moved. They all knew it wasn't the time for eye contact. Auld Boab broke a silence that now carried a seed of menace.

'Geordie, Geordie!' he admonished. 'If Joe here was a real pape –,' he nodded to Joe 'no offence Joe, but you know what I mean, you don't care about that dross any more than I do – if he was real pape, we'd be pulling you off one another by now. Isn't that right boys?' There were nods around the table. 'So, Geordie, instead of using your dazzling wit and repartee to wind people up, how no take it home and charm your lovely wife? You could be the one sitting here next week with beef on your piece, a smile on your face, and too tired to pick a fight with anybody. Especially our favourite Red Clyde revolutionary and shop steward, the man who fights the bosses on behalf of the whole lot of us, whatever shite we believe in.' Amid the nods and words of agreement, Auld Boab leaned over and patted Geordie on the shoulder. 'Right Geordie?' The only reply was a narrow-eyed, thin-lipped smile.

Willie the foreman knocked a fist on the table. 'Now, now. We agreed lads. Let's not get started on politics and union talk when I'm here.'

'It's not politics, it's theology.' Auld Boab was hard to stop once he'd started. 'Anyway, when Joe goes to that fancy castle in Perthshire it's not just trade unionists that go there. There's free-thinkers, there's university philosophers, there's men of the church. Isn't that right, Joe?'

Joe ignored him. 'Willie's right in a way. This isn't the time for workers fighting amongst themselves. Or with the bosses for that matter. Right now, the enemy's the bastards who bombed the hell out of us and blew a great big hole in my family.'

'And listen, Joe.' Auld Boab was not to be put off. 'See when you've got your shop steward's hat back on, and it's forward the revolution again, how about forgetting the capitalists? How about we just fight for a decent place to shite? They lavvies are a bloody disgrace.' And so Auld Boab brought everyone back to basics from where they moved on to the progress of the war, the weekend's forthcoming football fixtures, and the best bets at tonight's dog tracks.

The shipyard latrines were housed in a corrugated iron hut that stank of rust, shit and piss. The plumbing was simple and primitive. An inclined galvanised trough ran the entire length of the back wall and was flushed constantly by a stream of water that entered at the high point and exited into a drain at the lowest end. Above the trough, two parallel bars of four by two timber formed a continuous rough and uncomfortable perch. A dozen stalls had been formed using half-sheets of corrugated iron. They had no doors and were open at the back so that any user, with just a slight shift in position, could look along the length of the trough and count the number of bare backsides currently in production. The narrow partitions between the stalls did little to preserve the dignity of a seated worker; standing men could converse face to face and light one another's cigarettes. Despite the stench and the discomfort, it was a popular place during the second half of the lunch break.

Ricky Glover, his friend Alan and Cammy the rivet boy were in a small paint shed watching the comings and goings. Cammy was finishing his account of the jammed podger.

'... so he booted my arse good and proper. I've got to spend my dinnertime trying to get it free. And he's told me I better not bend it or take the point off it or he'll give me worse still. Shhh. Here's the wee bastard now.'

Big Sandy, a rolled up copy of the Daily Record under his arm, passed their hiding place and disappeared into the latrines.

'Right. Here's how it works,' said Cammy. He produced a large matchbox stuffed with paraffin rags and handed it to

Ricky. 'Behind the lavvies, at the top end where the water comes in, there's a hinged inspection flap. When you open it, you're looking straight down into the trough. You hold the matchbox just above it. Once Alan's put a light to it, wait until it's really blazing and ... launch! Then run like fuck.'

'Hold on,' said Alan. 'There's at least eight other men besides Big Sandy sitting in there.'

'That's why you've got to run like fuck. Listen. They'll be so busy beating out the flames on their hairy arses that you'll get a great start. Head for where I'm working. Lots of hiding places.' He shouldered a small hand winch and tackle he had borrowed and slipped away towards Number Two stocks.

As the boys crept around the back of the latrines, they could hear Big Sandy's voice, frighteningly loud on the other side of the thin metal.

'Here's two dogs for the night, lads,' he said. 'Kitty's Pet. Six thirty at Carntyne. Sitting at five to one. I lifted a few bob off her last week. She'll make a good double with Handy Boy in the seven fifteen.'

'See your tips, Sandy?' There was a pause followed by an explosive and reverberating fart. 'That's what I think of them.'

The laughter covered the creak of the inspection hatch being opened and the rattle of Alan's matches. Ricky watched fascinated as the rags erupted into flame. When he looked to Alan for a sign that it was time to release the box, his friend was already beyond the paint shed and racing towards the stocks. Ricky dropped the flaming container into the stream of water and pelted after him. Successive roars and strings of expletives erupted from the latrines as the boxful of burning rags sailed beneath the exposed rear ends of the sitting men. Ahead of him, Ricky could see Alan climb the ladder onto the floor plates of Ship 453 where Cammy stood waving, beckoning him on. 'Hurry up! Hurry up!'

Ricky was running full out as he approached the foot of the ladder. When he tried to turn and grab hold of the lower rungs, his own momentum threw him sideways. The ladder slipped from his grasp, and he slammed into the bilge strakes of the partly built ship. The point of Big Sandy's podger entered his left eye socket and didn't stop until it reached the back of his skull.

Seven

Nessa sits on a bollard at the end of a wooden pier that smells of oil and pitch. A squat round bollard, its black paint cracked and warmed by the sun.

Maybe this is my safe place, she thinks. Maybe.

But the thought nags at her. How can anywhere in the world ever feel safe again? A twist of fear in her belly. She's patient with it, gives it time to settle. It does. See, she's right. She is safe here. Now, that is, but not always. That's not how it was at the start.

The start? The word seems strange to her, strange for someone who has been tortured by lives ending. A strange scratchy foreign word. How can something begin after the end of everything?

Careful. Watch the questions. As long as she watches the questions, as long as she keeps an eye out for herself, she's okay. It's taken a long time to get here. To learn to protect. To guard.

An eternity.

Not the eternity the nuns tried to teach her about. The length of time God lived. How long she would share with Him in heaven if she was good. How long she would roast in hell if she died a sinner. Know what? God, the nuns, the devil – they haven't even started to grow up compared to the eternity she's lived through.

Sometimes she wonders if she's even the same woman it all happened to. The same Nessa.

It's not easy to piece herself back together. She wants to remember some things, but they won't leave the shadows. They sit at the edges, just out of reach, no matter how hard she tries. Then there's the stuff she hopes desperately to forget. But it's a useless hope. That stuff's going to be there forever, written in indelible pencil like the one she kept in her sewing basket so she could put nametags on their school...

No. That won't help.

Maybe the truth's simple. No matter what she'd like to claim back again, or to forget forever, her old life is over, gone, finished. Like the water flowing past her, life moves only one way and what's downstream doesn't come back again.

She watches the broad river. Bright and sunny, rippling past in a constant comforting shush. Friendly. Safe. They haven't always felt this way about one another, the river and her. There were dark nights when it howled a dismal greeting. Reached up. Beckoned her to drag her wet and weary self closer to the edge.

Join the others.

Come home.

Jump.

Then shadowy figures would hurry to her, hold her, speak words of consolation that she was beyond. She now knows they were Joe and Heather. Knows because they've told her. In her memories they are ghostly figures who will not let her bring her nightmare to an end.

She closes her eyes.

When she opens them, she's back again at the end of the pier. A scrawny patch of dandelions clings to the base of the bollard. A butterfly flutters for a moment above her sandals then lands on the nearest flower, so close that she is sure it brushes her toes. Its wings open to the sun. They capture her eyes these wings, these matching triangles of red and yellow, black and white. They draw her in until she seems to be looking through a magnifying glass, noticing the purply-blue at their edges, the fine hair on the slim brown body that separates them, the quivering antennae that end in distinct black dots. Then suddenly the wings fold together, their rainbows disappear into a thin drab line.

Her day dulls.

A sense of loss sweeps over her. If only she'd been able to catch Hugh by the arm and show him the butterfly, to point it out to Ricky, to kneel beside it with some of her wee ones.

Hugh.

Ricky.

Theresa.

Margaret.

Sheila.

John.

Her litany of sorrow.

As if to make up for its loss of brilliance, the butterfly produces a thin coiled spring that slowly unrolls then buries itself in the startling yellow forest of dandelion petals. She knows it's some sort of tongue, that the insect is feeding, although she's never before thought about such a thing.

I am getting better, she thinks. I couldn't have seen something like this; I wouldn't have noticed, have sat and watched, during…

What name to give it? My grief? Madness? Hell?

Evil was around all right, calling to her as sweetly as the river. And God? Where the hell was He? Och, to hell with Him anyway! That's where He belongs, for all the good He's been!

For a moment she has forgotten the butterfly. She is sure she didn't close her eyes, but somehow she stopped seeing. Is that what people mean when they talk about being blinded by anger? That emotions can stop you seeing the world as it really is?

She looks.

The butterfly lifts its tongue, searches through the petals, plunges in again.

Is there a noise when it sucks?

She listens hard. The breeze fills her ears. Then she hears

the soft tug of water at the timbers beneath her feet, then the calls of the seagulls, the clang of the shipyard, the shout of distant voices, wagons shunting, the squeal of dockside cranes. It's as if someone is slowly turning up the volume on a wireless set. She can hear more and more, louder and louder.

She swivels round on her bollard and looks across the busy harbour towards the nestling village. A passenger train chuffs along; ever widening clouds of smoke and steam twist and spin in its wake. Lines of washing wave at her from the drying greens of the houses that back onto the railway; brilliant flags of white, blue and yellow bunting, pennants of deep red.

Can she hear them flapping?

She feels her face relax.

She realises she is smiling.

Eight

Kilbendrick, September 1942

Nessa Glover made her way along Kilbendrick's main street. Father Paul Lamont, who'd called in unannounced at the Connor household, pushed his bicycle and walked beside her. 'I hope you don't mind me just dropping by,' he said. 'I've a feeling I interrupted something back there between you and your sister-in-law.'

Was this the moment to tell the priest that, as her own life was starting to make sense again, life at Joe and Sarah's seemed to become more complicated? But that would only be part of the story. She could understand Sarah's worry about Joe. There were times when Nessa thought her brother had suffered as much from Ricky's death as she had: that she'd still been numbed and half-mad from the Blitz, from the loss of Hugh and the children, so it was Joe who'd really taken on the burden of the terrible accident. And he'd been there, he'd seen how Ricky died.

How often had Joe said to her: 'It's the Monday that keeps coming back to me. Ricky was already out the door, proud to be with the men in the street, walking to the yard for his first day as an apprentice. You took me by the shoulders that morning and said: "Look after him, Joe. For God's sake. Look after him."' Finally, Nessa had turned on him: 'Will you bloody well stop going on about it, Joe! I know it wasn't your fault. Maybe I did say that, but I don't want to hear it ever again. What good does it do? Nothing changes.' What she really meant was that everything had changed for her, and nothing Joe could say or do could bring back her old life.

But it was something Sarah had said, not Joe, that was causing the tension Father Lamont had detected between the two women. Maybe Nessa could talk to the priest about that. But not yet. Instead she said: 'Sarah worries about me. She'll be glad to see you, Father Paul. She thinks you're a good influence on me.'

'Does she now? Maybe you're not so pleased to see me, though. I don't think you've been to mass for the last few Sundays?'

'Is this a visit from a priest or a policeman?' The words were out before Nessa could catch them. They both started to laugh.

'Sounds like you're in good form, thank God,' he said.

There was no doubt she was feeling better and had been for some weeks. The anniversary of Ricky's death last month had been not so much a hurdle as a chasm, looming deeper and deeper as it approached. But at her lowest point, amidst all the grief, the tears and the cruel imaginings, she'd felt the stirring of something new, as if she'd crossed into fresh territory, into a different life. It was a life she'd never have chosen: she'd been robbed of everything she loved; she would never again see Hugh's face, grow old with him while they watched the children flower into their own lives, their own families. Instead Ricky, Theresa, Margaret, Sheila, and John would now stay forever children: dead and gone with just memories left behind. It was an altered life alright. But a life nonetheless.

She knew too that she owed something to this tall young priest with his soft voice and his quiet manners. Her memories of the days after the Blitz were fragmentary and confused, but old Father O'Donnell was often there: holding her hand, saying prayers, offering a blessing at the service beside the common grave for the unidentified and unidentifiable victims. In the weeks that followed he was a regular support for her until the horror of Ricky's death. After that happened, she'd had enough of God, enough of belief, enough of false hope. She told Father O'Donnell as much. For a long time she stayed away from the church that had been essential to the fabric of her life since childhood. Then Father Lamont had arrived with a letter from Father O'Donnell. They've sent me this young boy as a curate, the old priest had written. Wet behind the ears and I don't know what to do with him. I'm going to try him out on some of the parish rounds. If you're not too busy, would you mind if he dropped in from time to time?

At the Bendrick Inn, they turned right onto the harbour road. Ahead of them, the level crossing gates were closed. The locomotive of a goods train sat on the line, smoking, hissing, and waiting for a signal to change. They could feel the heat from it, smell its coal smoke and its sweet oiliness. A boy of about seven and a younger girl ran up.

'Hey, mister! Hey, mister!' The boy waved as he called up to the driver and fireman who stood on the footplate watching the signal. 'Hey, mister! Throw us down a lump of coal!'

'What for, son?' The driver already knew the answer.

'For my mammy's fire!'

The driver nodded to the fireman who selected a good-sized chunk from the tender and held it up to show the children. 'Stand well out the road!' he shouted and waited as they shuffled backwards. The lump broke in two as it landed. The boy cradled the larger piece, his sister followed his example with the other, and they scampered off home to a pat on the head and a cuddle from a grateful mother. Then with a roar of smoke and whoosh of steam, the wheels began to turn and the engine slowly chuffed away, its noise receding as the wagons picked up speed and clickety-clicked past.

They walked on in silence. That was the unusual thing about him, compared to what she expected from a priest. Others tended to fill the space with predictable words: references to God's love, Jesus' sacrifice, Mary's sadness;

to the mysteries of life, to faith and to the rewards to come. The way old Father O'Donnell did. He'd heard her swear, curse, banish him and his religion to where it belonged. Hell already existed here on earth for her. You show me God's love, she'd challenged him, when families are blown to pieces, boys killed before they have a chance to grow into men. He'd come out with his dependable wisdoms spoken in his calm dependable Irish brogue, then he'd say a prayer and send her home with a blessing. There'd been comfort in that. She might not have survived without it. But this young man just left things alone. At first she thought maybe he didn't know what to say to her. Then she realised that when he did speak, it was clear that he'd been listening. He commented on things she'd said, rather than depended on well-worn words of faith and comfort.

They crossed the main line and the shunting tracks beside the harbour and were walking along the quay before she spoke. 'Those children…'

'I thought something happened. You went very quiet.'

'Yes. It was the wee boy and the wee girl. That's where the deepest pain lies for me, Father. In the loss of all my children. My sister-in-law Sarah, she's never been able to have any. I know that's a heartache for her and Joe. Especially for her. But that doesn't excuse what she said to me.' She fell silent again as they passed beneath one of the quayside cranes.

'What did she say?' asked the priest.

'We were talking about her sister, Heather. Heather got married last year but her man Charlie's in the Navy and she hardly ever sees him. To begin with, Heather was hoping to start a family as soon as she could, but now she's wondering if it would be better if nothing happened until this war's over. Then Sarah started talking to me about not being able to have babies of her own: "I've just got to accept it's God's will," she said. "It'll be for a purpose that I can't know yet. Maybe that's the way life is for us all," she went on. "Maybe what's happened to you has a purpose too."

'I exploded at her. "Don't you dare compare us. You can't understand what it's like. They grew inside me. I gave birth to them, nursed them, loved them. Then I lost them. You think we're somehow in the same place now? We're not even on the same planet!" Maybe my words were harsh, Father. But she'll never understand. She can't. Sometimes, when I see kiddies, it's as if something inside me is being pulled and twisted.'

'That's an interesting way to describe it. Somebody once said: "The twisting of the fibres makes us strong."'

'I hope this isn't some gruesome story about a martyr.'

'When did I ever tell such a thing? No, this man's name was Sinbad. That's what we used to call him anyway. Sinbad the Sailor. He didn't seem to mind.'

'Who's "we"?'

'Oh, a bunch of kids who hung around together in Dumbarton. We must have been about eleven or twelve. Sinbad lived in an old open lifeboat tied up at the quay. He'd rigged a sort of tarpaulin tent in the bow with a chimney pipe poking through for the little stove he cooked on. He had a wooden peg leg and said he'd lost the real one fighting in the Boer War.'

'You're making this up!'

'No. It's true. He used to sit in the stern carving clever little nick-knacks that he'd sell for a few farthings. And telling yarns. We loved going down there after school. Once he had us hooked he'd start talking politics. He could recite the *Communist Manifesto* by heart. Some of his stories included how he'd fought with the Bolsheviks, wooden leg and all, during the Russian Revolution, and how he was amongst the Red Clyde demonstrators in Glasgow when they were baton-charged by the police in George Square in April 1919. According to Sinbad, Scotland was just a wink away from Revolution when Churchill ordered in English tanks and soldiers.'

'But what's all this got to do with twisted fibres?'

'Ah yes. Sinbad used to say: "But remember this. The strongest rope is made from single threads. It's the twisting of the fibres that makes us strong."'

'Does the Archbishop of Glasgow know one of his curates grew up under the influence of an old communist pirate?'

'Does His Grace ever consider there might be a lefty between the pages of the New Testament? That has always puzzled me. I spent over nine years in seminaries studying Greek, Latin, moral philosophy, scripture, theology, liturgy, canon law, and all the rest of it. And never so much as a nod in the direction of what the political implications might be of Jesus' teachings.'

'I never thought I'd hear the like from a priest!' Nessa's surprise was tinged with delight. 'You'd better stop before that cloud up there splits open and a thunderbolt strikes the pair of us. I spent fifteen years married to a man who put the Trade Union before the Church, and now I hear the same sort of thing – ' She stopped in mid sentence.

They had to wait while a train of coal wagons glided across the track in front of them and was shunted slowly into place along a line that ended at a high gantry on the water's edge. A puffer, one of the flotilla of steam-driven coastal ships that supplied the Clyde estuary and the more distant west coast and islands, was moored beneath an inclined chute, which stuck out from the grey-painted tower of heavy steel beams. The leading wagon was uncoupled, pushed onto a platform at the foot of the gantry, and shackled into position.

'Let's watch,' said Father Lamont, 'I love seeing this.'

They flinched when a hooter pierced out its warning. A powerful hoist juddered the platform to the top of the tower where the coal wagon sat for a moment like a giant's discarded plaything, high above the gaping mouth of the puffer's hold. Slowly the platform began to tilt. A hinged flap on the side of the shackled truck swung open under the weight of tons of coal that rumbled and clanged onto the chute and, with a whooshing roar, spewed out in a black dusty cascade. The puffer rocked violently and, as it wrestled to accept the cargo pouring into it from the sky, sent wave after wave across the still water.

The boat settled in the water, the dust began to disperse and the hoist descended. Father Lamont held up a finger. 'How about one more?' Nessa smiled and nodded. They watched a second wagonload lift, tilt and empty, then they set off for the upper basin and the canal towpath that would take Father Lamont back to Clydebank. As they walked, Nessa picked up the conversation again: 'What I said back there... That's the first time I've mentioned Hugh like that. In the past. And my marriage. It's all in the past. It's all over.'

'I think that's what I was trying to say. Maybe, as old Sinbad believed, there's a twisting of the threads inside each of us that also makes us strong. But it takes time.'

'Do you mind if I ask you something personal, Father?'

'I won't know until you ask.'

'Back there, when you were talking about the old man who lived on the boat, I was surprised to hear you grew up in Dumbarton. I thought, with your name and your way of speaking, you'd come from somewhere … fancier, I suppose.'

'Ah. It's all my dear mother's fault. She was determined her children wouldn't talk what she called "slang". So we had to speak "proper English" at home and we were ordered, under pain of a thick ear, to do the same outside. Needless to say, I ignored the second bit. Talking la-di-da, I wouldn't have lasted five minutes in the back courts around Brewery Lane.'

'It's not fair to blame your mother. She just wanted the best.'

'The story's more complicated than that. My mother grew

up in very different surroundings. Her father was a doctor, the family home a big house in the west end of Glasgow. Her mother was an activist, fighting for the vote for women. She was one of the bodyguards who fought the police when they arrested Emmeline Pankhurst on the platform of St Andrew's Hall in 1914.

'Thanks to her father's influence she became a nurse. And thanks to her mother's influence, she volunteered in 1915 for a Scottish Women's Hospital field unit set up in France with funding from the Suffragette movement. So there she was, just twenty years old, caring for soldiers who were suffering, and sometimes dying, from the most hellish wounds. And there amongst the wounded was Bernard Lamont, a French car mechanic who'd been conscripted. By the time the war ended, he was healed, she was a Catholic, and they were married. They moved to Scotland and set up home in a tenement flat in Dumbarton where he worked in McCourt's Garage and she raised the children by a mixture of Catholic faith, basic Socialism, and "proper English". But,' he said, dropping the pitch of his voice, 'Doan't you think Ah canny speak like a local boay when Ah want tae.'

They were passing beneath the railway bridge over the narrow waterway where the two canal basins met. Their laughter echoed and bounced in the confined space and seemed to follow them as they left the tunnel and reached the parting of their ways.

'There's something I'm going to do.' Nessa hadn't realised she'd made her mind up until the words came blurting out.

'You sound surprised.'

'Not really surprised. I just don't know why I've taken so long to decide about something so obvious. Heather and Charlie moved into a nice wee flat in Clydebank after they got married. He's at sea all the time and she's at home there on her own. She's told me more than once there's room for me there if I'd like to move in. Joe and Sarah have been great to me. I don't know what I'd have done without them. Instead of me needing a break from them, maybe it's the other way about. They need the break from me! Heather's told me there's lots of jobs for women in Brown's yard. She was in the French-polishing squad, but now she's been trained as a welder. It's hard work, but there's a lot of laughing going on too. I think I'm ready for some of that.'

Father Lamont joined his hands together in a gesture of prayer and pointed them at Nessa. 'And Mass helps too. Hope to see you this Sunday.' With a quick push he mounted his bike, drew a cross in the air, and pedalled off along the canal towpath.

Nine

Keir sits at the desk in his semi-detached cottage on the grounds of Laggandarroch School. It is late afternoon but the May sunshine is still strong and the countryside shimmers. Ahead of him, the cottage garden drops out of sight down a slope, leaving him a clear view of the long, island-studded loch with its backdrop of hazy mountains whose sturdy flanks lead up to grey cliffs topped by rocky peaks. But his inner struggle keeps pulling him away from the joys of the scenery, from the caress of the cool breeze that wafts the smells and sounds of early summer through the partly open window. For the third or fourth time he squeezes the squeaking cork back into the still full bottle of malt whisky. He knows the surging heat of its peaty smokiness would bring a soothing glow to ease his chest, smooth out the quivering in his stomach. Or appear to, he can hear Dr Rolfe's voice remind him. A quick fix that he will pay for later.

The same dilemma often surfaced at the group sessions. Most of the Vietnam vets had struggled with alcohol during the years when their soldiering was over but their personal battles with the aftermath were still raging. He remembers Kenny, who'd lost his leg to a land-mine, pointing to the prosthesis that stretched out from the leg of his shorts. 'It's true what they say. In the early days, I had some serious phantom pain. But I could look down and see the bedclothes were flat as a pool table. I could pull them aside and see a bandaged stump. So I knew my body was fooling itself. When the tricks are being played up here in the old block...' he tapped his forehead, '... it's a different ball game. You know that as well as I do, mates. You're lost in a pit you've dug for yourself and daylight's a long way off. Sure, this group helps. Talking, sharing what happened to us, learning how to relax. And I'm beginning to understand what happens in my head. But when it goes wrong out there in the street, when a car backfires and I turn and there's a gook coming at me on a bicycle with a hand grenade at the ready, I can't find a way to remind myself I'm in Western Australia. That my mind's playing games with me. But I can get myself off the street and hit the booze. It'll calm me down. But only for a while. That's the rub, boys. It's only ever for a while.'

He pushes the unused whisky glass aside. Is this trip a big mistake? First, at the derelict shipyard, a bad flashback episode wrecked his visit to Kilbendrick and left him demolishing a bottle of scotch in a Glasgow hotel room. And now he's just managed to ride out a panic attack in the boardroom with the headmaster looking on. McNeil's no fool: he must have realised something was adrift while Keir struggled with a heart that was trying to thump its way out of his chest, with a lump in his throat that was trying to choke him. Somehow he managed to join the older man at the wall of black and white photographs, to listen to what he said, to follow the finger that picked out first one of his relatives, then the other. Joe Connor, he heard. Hugh Glover. He remembered stepping back, maybe covering his eyes. He remembered the headmaster's soothing voice, some words about the long journey he'd had, how there would be plenty of time to explore the photographs and the rest of the school's archive at his leisure. How the headmaster should have been more thoughtful and seen him settled in his cottage before imposing a tour of the school on him.

He makes a deal with himself. He'll go through the full relaxation technique from start to finish, he'll do all of the steps, all the breathing. If he still feels like a drink afterwards, it will be an earned treat at the end of a demanding day, not a false antidote. He sits straight up in his chair, places both feet on the floor, and lays his hands palm down on the desk. With his eyes unfocussed somewhere in the hazy middle-distance, he takes five deep and slow breaths, each time concentrating on the flow of cool air at his nostrils, the moment of balance as in-breath turns to out-breath. He places his attention on his right foot, giving a breath-cycle to each toe in turn as he relaxes it, ridding it of any tension he can find there. He moves along the foot, attending to his breathing as he relaxes the ball, the instep, the heel, the ankle. He pauses for five breaths before he moves over to his left foot, repeats the process, and begins steadily to work his way up each leg in turn.

His attention is on his stomach when his gaze snaps into focus. In the foreground, where the slope of the cottage garden drops steeply out of view, the top of a large conical straw hat has appeared, bobbing to the rhythm of footsteps, coming more and more into view as someone marches up the hill towards him. He holds his breath. The relaxed hands on the desk tense and bunch into fists. He can now see all of the hat. Then, below it, not so much a face as a diffuse shadowed area, as if the person advancing up the hill towards him is wearing some sort of mask. He leaps to his feet and can now see almost the whole figure, clad in a one-piece white overall. Wisps of smoke drift from a metal canister in its right hand. The calm inner pool he has created begins to churn. He struggles to make sense of what he is seeing but the words are all unhelpful: grenade, gas, chemicals. The figure looms in the window, a dark veil is thrown back...

Gloria Honeydew, the teacher from the English class, smiles at him from beneath her hat. 'I hope I didn't scare you. You look like you've just seen something you didn't want to. It's only me. Your next door neighbour. Checking my beehives.' She points the cylindrical copper smoker in his direction. A jet of white smoke hits the window, spreads out, and curls away into nothingness. He hears the hiss of his escaping breath and is aware of his racing heartbeat. He smiles back and hopes he's managing to cover up how foolish he feels. She beckons him out.

Ten

By the time he reached the adjoining cottage door, Gloria was already climbing out of her overalls to reveal a sleeveless white cheesecloth top and cut-off blue cotton trousers that emphasised her curves. Keir juggled conflicting thoughts: she was a very attractive woman; he hadn't fully escaped the panic that had threatened to engulf him moments earlier; and, right now, he probably looked like some sort of vacant cretin. 'That's not a conventional bee hat, I reckon?' he blurted, pointing to the large straw hat on the seat beside her.

'My coolie hat. No. But I need one that has room for this.' She pointed to her head where her steely grey hair, released from its classroom plait, was twisted into a roll and secured with a large carved comb. 'Anyway, I'm not a great fan of conventional.' She placed the rolled-up overalls beside the hat and flapped her arms as if to mime how glad she was to have them bared to the air again. When she turned to face him, he could see a faint line of perspiration on her top lip. 'I'm going to start with some chilled lemonade,' she said, 'How about you?'

'Lemonade sounds bonzer,' he said, and hoped that by the time she returned with it he'd be back in command of himself again.

Ten minutes later she returned with a large jugful; homemade, fragrant, sweet-and-sour, cloudy with fragments of lemon pulp and swimming with slices of orange. She poured some for both of them. He reached out his glass to her. 'Cheers!' he said, and they clinked glasses.

He sat on the warm bench, sipped appreciatively, and asked about beekeeping. That felt safe.

She sat opposite him on a folding chair, crossed her legs at the ankle, rested her cool glass against her tanned and folded arms, and began to talk. About how the queen bee was laying very well this early in the season so there'd be plenty of young worker bees in time for the clover flowers in June. About the drone cells that were starting to appear, maybe the colony was preparing for an early swarm? She didn't want to lose bees, so she'd have to keep a close eye on that. It would be ten-day inspections from now on. Maybe he'd like to join her one day, see for himself what happened inside the hive?

The heat of the sun, the delicious coolness of the lemonade, the murmur of her voice – Keir stifled the urge to sigh out loud. He slouched down on the bench, stretched his legs out in front, and studied Gloria as she talked. She must be around fifty, he thought, but she was very alluring. He reminded himself to keep his gaze on her face; straying eyes would not be missed by this alert, lively woman. She talked in the same engaging way she'd used in the classroom, inviting him into the conversation. When she smiled, which she did often, the turned-up corners of her mouth gave her a catlike appearance. No sooner did he have this thought than a long haired tabby-cat appeared around the corner and began to rub itself against his ankle, purring softly. He stroked its back then gently along the length of its tail. The purring became louder.

'You're okay,' said Gloria. 'Petra only does that with strangers she trusts. I'd depend on her judgement ahead of most people I know. It's harder to fool cats than humans. Are you eating down at the school?'

'I told the headmaster I'd probably stay up here tonight, get myself settled in.' Hide away, was closer to the truth. Kill that bottle of malt.

'I'll be eating in about an hour's time. Why not do what you have to and then join me for a bite? I'd be delighted. Especially now that Petra's given you the paws-up.'

'Your timing's perfect,' said Gloria as she poured Keir a large glass of red wine. 'Make yourself at home. I'm almost finished in the kitchen.'

Her cottage was a mirror image of Keir's but looked very different. His was spartan, simply but adequately furnished; hers was soft, colourful, comfortable. Varnished pine flooring glowed golden. The walls, painted white with a hint of pink, were covered with paintings. Mostly abstract, Keir noted. Always bright. A large panel of macramé, strung with black and amber beads, hung from a bamboo pole. A pot-bellied stove stood on a purple slate hearth. Beside it, a round bottle garden glowed with deep-throated miniature orchids in muted red and tiger yellow.

Keir browsed floor-to-ceiling shelves on either side of the stove. Mainly books but here and there larger alcoves contained pottery and small sculptures. The books seemed to be loosely organised. Lots of classics, then a more modern fiction section – Orwell, Sartre, Beckett, Herman Hesse – which merged into the non-fiction of Arthur Koestler, Carlos Castaneda, Allan Watts, Jung.

He was leafing through Koestler's *Roots of Coincidence* when Gloria came in carrying a laden tray. Perched at the front of it was her empty glass. 'Feel free to borrow anything that takes your fancy,' she said. 'Would you mind topping up the wine? I'm ready for another.' She began laying food out on a bare pine table.

Gloria's idea of 'a bite' was a simple, delicious meal. Half an avocado each, the seed-well brimming with vinaigrette, the soft buttery flesh topped with coarse grindings of black pepper and sea salt, then a pasta and tuna dish, drenched in thick garlicky tomato sauce and with home-baked crusty bread to wipe up the juices.

As they ate, Gloria explained how the headmaster's announcement of his visit had triggered lots of interest in both staff and pupils. 'It's been great for me in the English class. We've looked at war comics and watched *All Quiet on the Western Front*. I've read them First World War poets. And George Orwell's description of being shot by a fascist sniper during the Spanish Civil War. So much of what kids are exposed to is either sanitised or is bloodthirsty fantasy from the killer's point of view, not from the victim's. Somebody pulls a trigger. Somebody else takes the bullet. "Bang bang, you're dead." But Orwell has us living in another human being's body as the bullet enters it. The pupils won't forget that in a hurry. Or *Hearts of Darkness*, Don McCullin's Vietnam photographs.'

Keir whistled softly. 'Aren't those a bit strong for kids?'

'What's the alternative? To tell them a fairy story about good guys, bad guys? Might is right? If their generation knows the reality, maybe they'll look on war a bit differently.' Her voice had become stronger and more insistent. She raised her napkin quickly to her mouth as if to silence herself. Her eyes smiled at him. He could imagine the hidden corners of her mouth turning up into a smile too. 'Oops,' she said, 'Why am I telling you? You're the war reporter.'

She refilled both their glasses. 'How did that come about?'

'I didn't plan to be a war correspondent but looking back it seems inevitable.' He eased his chair from the table and settled back into it, wine glass in hand. 'When I left school in Kalgoorlie I didn't know what I wanted to do. I was a good enough student there: strong at sport, keen on English. I'd always enjoyed reading and writing. Lots of kids went on to the local Western Australia School of Mines, others headed for university in the state capital, Perth. None of that appealed to me. I could have followed my dad into the gold mines that paid good dollars to anybody prepared to work a shift, but that didn't feel right either. So when the local paper, *The Kalgoorlie Miner*, advertised for an office junior with a chance to do some reporting I gave it a go. And quite liked it. I did okay and within a couple of years I was a regular reporter, covering local politics, mining accidents, crime. Then, at the age of twenty, I was called up as one of the first Nashos.'

'Nashos?'

'National service conscripts. In 1964 the Australian government introduced national service for twenty-year-olds: a two-year stint, with the second twelve months chumming up the regulars in Vietnam. My date of birth came out of the hat at the very first ballot.'

Gloria looked puzzled. 'I didn't realise there was conscription, that Australia was so involved.'

'Up to our armpits. Southeast Asia's in our backyard. And our politicians went for the American analysis – if South Vietnam loses the war, other countries fall to the Commies like a set of dominoes. We were there from start to finish. Fifty thousand troops between 1962 and 1972. Half of them were Nashos, and they weren't just washing billy-cans. Half the dead and wounded were Nashos too.'

She leaned forward, her chin in her cupped hands. 'So why weren't you put off war for the rest of your life?'

'Vietnam certainly put me off soldiering. It was a world of jungle patrols, bugs, and bullets. You never quite knew what was waiting for you around the next corner. You just hoped you could spring an ambush before the other bloke sprung one on you. During training in the Queensland jungle, we were taught to out-think the Vietcong. Unlike the Yanks, we fought them the way they fought us. Guerrilla style. Face-to-face and personal. Low-down and dirty. Scary too.

'A couple of months before I was due to be discharged, we were in a forward position in the build up to the battle of Long Tan. Two journos joined us, a writer and a photographer. They stuck with us through three days of the hardest fighting, then they were off to another hot spot. I spoke to them whenever I could. They seemed to understand the big picture, not just in Vietnam but the international story, the way this conflict had the whole globe poised on the brink of something that could go either way. And they weren't killing anyone. Whenever I pulled a trigger, threw a grenade or set a booby-trap, I was fighting a war that was changing the world, but the only view I had of it was the jungle above my head and the mud beneath my feet.

'I couldn't wait to leave the Army and return to journalism. Within a year I was working on the foreign desk of the *Sydney Morning Herald* and by '68 I was back in Vietnam covering the Tet offensive for Reuters.'

He paused, slightly unsettled by the calm violet eyes, the attentive stillness on the other side of the table.

'Oh-oh. That must have sounded really self-blowing. Very macho. Hemingway lives on. Man with notebook saves the world. It's not really ... it wasn't really ... like that. It's an odd profession. And it takes its toll, I reckon.' He paused, suddenly unsure of himself. Of how much he should say. Of how much he could say. He twirled the stem of his wineglass, swished the contents around, watched the red film drain back to the bottom again.

Gloria filled the gap before it had a chance to feel awkward. 'Your contribution to the group today. When you spoke as a child who was under fire, who only wanted to be left alone, you sounded hurt.'

'Yeah ... well ... there's a whole other side to all of this.' He paused again. Be careful now. Keep an eye on yourself. Watch where this goes next. But he was enjoying the food, the relaxing wine, the empathy he sensed in this listening woman. 'Did the headmaster say much about why I was coming here?'

'Not really. Just a brief announcement that you were researching members of your family and had agreed to tie it in with some work on the history of this place.'

'Yeah, it was that simple to begin with. Then my Dad died a few weeks ago. Left me a letter telling me that he and Mum weren't my real Mum and Dad. Straight out of the blue, that was quite a blow.'

'My God! And you had no idea?'

'Not a smidge. But it's now starting to make sense of a hunch I was never really able to put into words. They were very private people, secretive almost. I grew up believing they'd lost everything in the Clydebank Blitz and emigrated to Australia just after the war when I was still a nipper. As far as I knew, they had no contact with Scotland, no letters, no birthday or Christmas cards, no phone calls. Anytime I asked, I got the same answer. The Clydebank Blitz. Sometimes I used to dig out my birth certificate. It showed Joe and Sarah Connor as my parents, him as a shipyard engineer, her a housewife, and my place of birth as Kilbendrick, close to Clydebank. So I just accepted it.'

'Did your father tell you what had happened? Who your real parents were?'

'All his life he was a man of few words, and he just left me a bare minimum in his note. That he and Mum had kept a secret from me, they weren't my parents. That when she was dying, she had wanted to tell me but he had disagreed. That he now realised I deserved the truth: I was born in Kilbendrick in 1944, but my mother was his sister, Nessa Glover, who'd lost her husband Hugh and her children three years earlier in the Blitz; Nessa died in 1944, the year I was born; he didn't know who my father was; he was sorry and hoped I could forgive them. And that was it.'

'Had you heard before about Hugh and Nessa Glover?'

'A little bit. I knew that Aunt Nessa and their oldest child Ricky survived the Blitz, although he was killed in a shipyard accident soon afterwards. I also knew that my father, at least the man I called Dad all his life, and Uncle Hugh were both active trade unionists and that involved coming to Harmony in the years running up to the war. That's why I'm here.'

Gloria switched on a light and crossed to the bookshelves.

She knelt to read the spines on a set of large books with matching covers. 'I grew up at Harmony,' she said to him, over her shoulder, 'These are mainly personal photographs, showing life in the Harmony community. But I also used to help out at events that brought in outsiders. Usually a group photograph was taken...' She picked out a volume, '1938 to 1946. Let's start with this one.' She carried the large album to the table and began to turn the pages. There were pictures of individuals, of gatherings, of people involved in various activities. She paused at a formal group posed at the front entrance to the old castle building and read the label below it. 'No. This was a visit from members of another commune in the USA, also influenced by Charles Fourier.' She continued flipping, and stopped again about halfway through. 'This looks promising. "Cooperation not Conflict" weekend. June 20th-21st 1943. Participants from all walks of life used to come to these.'

In the large black-and-white print, about twenty people were grouped informally on the sloping lawn below the castle. It was a sunny day and the men had open-necked shirts with rolled up sleeves. Some sat on the grass in loose groupings. Others stood in twos and threes, sometimes with an arm around a friend's shoulders. Towards the top of the slope, a tall white-haired man stood with his arms open in a gesture of welcome. 'That's Fergus Abercrombie, the Harmony founder, he made it all happen. He would have been in his late sixties in 1943, but he was still full of life and energy. And here's the reason it's in my album.' Gloria pointed to a gangly adolescent girl standing beside a large picnic table laden with food and refreshments. Her hair reached below her shoulders and long thin legs stretched from her light summer frock. She was holding the hand of a younger boy in short trousers and sporting a short-back-and-sides wartime haircut. 'That's me, the gawky thirteen-year-old. The boy with me is Ainsley Watson. He works at

Laggandarroch School too.'

'Yeah,' said Keir, 'I saw him in action earlier today.'

Gloria seemed not to be listening. She was studying the photograph closely, pointing at the only woman in the group. 'It was unusual to have women visitors at these meetings. And she's not from Harmony or I'd recognise her.' Below the photograph, a neatly drawn silhouette showed the numbered outlines of the people alongside a typewritten list of names. Gloria matched the woman to the index. Paused. Looked up at Keir. 'It's Nessa Glover.'

She brought the album around the table and laid it in front of him. He followed her pointing finger to where a woman sat on the grass. Her wide, pale face with deep-set eyes was framed by shoulder-length dark hair. Beside her, a boyishly handsome man grinned at the camera but Nessa's smile seemed tentative, cautious. Her hand was raised as if holding something. Or beckoning...

That's enough, he tells himself. Hold right there. Focus. Here and now. Breathing. Stay with my breathing. Stay with...

'Are you okay, Keir? All this must be tough on you.' Her arm goes around his shoulder. He feels her head rest against his for a moment, then her lips brush the back of his neck. He is on his feet and turning to meet her. Her arms draw him close into a welcoming softness. He gives in to it, lets himself be led. It feels as if he is being carried, eased through space, laid down with great tenderness. His face is stroked, his shirt unbuttoned, his clothes slid from him like an unneeded skin. Quickly? Slowly? He can't tell, doesn't care. Time belongs somewhere else, somewhere outside this cocoon. A gentle warmth covers him. Weight shifts, light dims as he is sheltered in a tent of long hair. Soft lips trace the thin scar that runs from his hairline to his eyebrow, move around his face with murmurs of comfort, explore the ridge where long ago, in a different world, a broken breastbone hadn't managed to find its way home again. The lips come up again to meet his: brushing them, nuzzling them, sucking them softly. She arches, reaches beneath, takes him in her hand, guides him home.

Her movement almost woke him, but she shushed, kissed him lightly. He seesawed between waking and sleeping, sometimes aware of distant sounds as she showered, dressed, clinked in the kitchen: sometimes adrift in a motionless, noiseless sea of deep calm. When he wakened fully, the cottage was silent. He was sure she had just closed the door behind her.

The bed was draped in white curtains and he was enveloped in soft radiant light. From the apex of the tent hung a hoop of willow containing a woven web of blue cord. Three strings of beaded feathers hung from the hoop that rotated very slowly to some slight movement of the air. As he lay and watched it, memories of the night under this canopy floated past, to be caught and savoured. How they twined and moaned. The animal howl that escaped from him. Sometime during the deep darkness they had fallen asleep, wrapped together.

Reluctantly, he turned his thoughts elsewhere. To why he was here at Laggandarroch and whether he could continue. Whether he was wise to try. He parted the curtains, got out of bed and made his way through to the sitting room. A plate and spoon were laid on the table along with a milk jug, a bowl of fruit, some fruit juice and a jar of muesli.

The glossy red apple from the fruit bowl felt firm and cool in his hand. He bit into it slowly to prolong the crunch. Sweet juice swam across his tongue.

Eleven

Clydebank, May 1943

As though striking a long grey match, Nessa Glover drew the tip of her welding rod along one of the two steel plates clamped in her workbench vice. There was a crack followed by an incandescent blue sputter as a powerful electric arc, hot enough to melt steel or burn to the bone, jumped between welding rod and metal. She leaned forward in concentration as her gauntleted hand moved the electrode slowly along the right-angled junction of the plates. Her head was encased in a heavy mask. Through its dense filter she could watch the steady progress of the line of molten metal she was laying into the angle to weld the plates together. Acrid sulphurous fumes created a now familiar metallic taste on her tongue. She liked that curious tang, the daily flavour of the welder.

She'd learned arc welding during her six-week training under the witty guidance of The Bannock. 'Yous're supposed to call me Mr Cooper,' he'd introduced himself, 'but my real name's The Bannock. So The Bannock it is. Right?' He was in charge of welding training at John Brown's shipyard for what were called dilutee workers, volunteers and conscripts drafted into industry to meet wartime demands. He'd left the eight women facing him in no doubt about the special opportunity he was putting in their path. 'Right now there's over five thousand workers in the yard alone, that's not counting another few thousand in the engine works. There's less than two hundred women, and only a dozen of them are welders. So yous could join that elite band of heroines. If yous pay attention to me, work your hardest, don't call me Mr Cooper, and only say fuck when yous get burnt.'

He started them off on oxyacetylene welding. They became familiar with the complicated looking equipment of

83

heavy steel cylinders, yards of tubing, pressure gauges and regulators. Nessa took to it. She quickly understood how to mix the gases and create the correct flame at the end of the blowpipe, how to hold the torch in one hand and feed the metal welding rod in with the other as she moved slowly along the seam she was welding.

At the beginning of their fourth week, The Bannock had an announcement. 'Yous are doing fine at the gas. I walk round the cubicles and all is peace and calm. Good flames on your torches, steady progress along your welds, rods being fed in sweetly as if yous were icing cakes. Now yous're going to have a go at electric arc. By comparison, that's welding from hell, all flash and stench and fury. But it'll weld just about anything. I'll give a demo, and then yous can all have a shot.'

Late in the morning, he called the trainees together. 'I can see yous're all trying hard,' he said. 'But just watch me for a minute. Tell me what I look like.' He picked up an electrode handset and held it out stiffly at arm's length.

'You look like you're going to shoot the first gaffer that comes through the door,' somebody quipped.

'Aye, right enough,' he said, finger at his lips to shush the laughter. 'But as well as that, I look scared stiff of this thing I'm holding in my hand. My knuckles are white, my arm's rigid, and my eyes are about a mile away from the tip of that rod. How can I see how my weld's going? But watch...' He noticeably relaxed his grip, slowly bent his arm, drew the electrode holder down to the workbench surface, and lowered his head to within a few inches of it. 'Ah. Now I can see what I'm doing.' He picked up a test piece of two lengths of steel plate that were tacked together ready to weld. 'Nessa, you seem to be getting the hang of it. Would you mind having a go at this?'

As she did, she could hear his commentary above the crackle. 'See how she's got a relaxed grip. If you're tense, you canny control it. Look at her arm. Relaxed, bent, bringing her closer in. And she's leaning over the job, staying in charge of the arc, watching the bead form, adjusting as she needs to. She's keeping it all controlled and regular. She looks as if she loves what she's doing. If it wasn't for her mask, she would kiss that weld. Only kidding, hen...' But he wasn't kidding about her newfound skill, and when her training period was over she was put straight on to electric arc welding.

Since then, Nessa had worked in the east yard smithy where she was currently making brackets for attaching torpedo tubes to warships. She pushed her helmet back onto the top of her head, picked up a small hammer and began to chip slag from the weld she had just completed. Although she had done this countless times, she still felt a surge of pleasure as the coarse dirty-coloured slag fell away to reveal the fresh glistening weld underneath: a thin shining river of steel, its ripples frozen forever. She added the bracket, her fifth so far this morning, to the pile on her workbench. Well up to target, she could afford to treat herself to an unofficial break. She knocked twice on the wall of her cubicle, received two knocks in reply, pushed aside the hessian sacking that shielded passers-by from eye-damaging flashes, and met Heather emerging from the cubicle next door.

'Five,' said Nessa.

'Six,' said Heather.

They grinned at one another and threaded their way across the smoke and din of the long narrow and fume-filled smithy, as high as a cathedral, lit by roof windows, glowing forges, and the blue lightning flashes of arc welders. A small side door behind the steel racks was the women's bolthole into daylight and fresh air. Once through it, they closed the door then leaned against it to stay in the sanctuary of its doorway, hiding not from the weather – it was a fine morning – but from the attention of any gaffer who might be on the lookout for time wasters. From where they stood they could see beyond the grubby waters of the old canal to the south bank of the Clyde where the mouth of the River Cart broke the line of the green fields of Renfrewshire. Although it was Saturday, the shipyard behind them clanged and thundered like a restless, half-mile-long monster, building new ships and repairing a never-ending stream of war-damaged ones.

It was seven months since Nessa had left Kilbendrick and moved into Heather's flat in Clydebank. The move had suited Nessa, who'd quickly been taken on at the shipyard just a few streets away. Initially she'd been assigned to the paint shop, doing preparation work for the painters. Her job took her all over the yard, onto ships which were in various stages of being built, or were already launched and being finished off in the fitting out basin, or had been brought in for repair. Although she'd been married for years to a man who worked in Brown's, she hadn't been prepared for the scale of the place. One Saturday night, in the early days of the war before the Blitz, Hugh had taken Nessa to the *La Scala* cinema to see an animation of *Gulliver's Travels*. As they walked home he'd said that watching Gulliver tied up by the Lilliputians had reminded him of the yard, except in Brown's the ships were much bigger than Gulliver, the workers building them much smaller than the little people. 'But it's difficult to explain unless you've been there.'

On her first day she realised why words had failed him. The noise was a physical assault: the duelling machine-gun clatter of riveters, the interminable whining fusillade of pneumatic caulkers, and from every corner the reverberating clangour of steel being punched and rolled by platers, hammered by blacksmiths, rammed and beaten into white-hot shapes by frame-benders. She felt the combined wall of sound explode against her eardrums, push against her skin, invade her until it felt like every part of her had been overwhelmed and was vibrating to its command.

She'd been assigned that day to help a painting squad at work on an aircraft carrier, still in the stocks at Berth 3, but soon to be launched as HMS *Indefatigable*. Her request for directions before she left the paint shop was greeted with guffaws. 'Don't worry, hen. Just look for the big wan. You canny miss it!' And she couldn't – an enormous bulk of grey painted steel, wrapped in scaffolding and rising over everything else like a huge beast that had somehow been squeezed into a world that was far too small, and had no choice but to dwarf everything else, even the four-story tenements that fringed the yard's high walls. When Nessa leaned back and craned her neck to see where the swoop of the hull flared out to become a massive flight deck as big as two football pitches, it seemed like the sky was being wiped out. Only the derricks were taller. They crowded around like a family of giant birds, swinging their long beaks to and fro, supplying everything the shipbuilders needed. And the workers themselves? Wee specks swarming like flies over acres of steel, each with a pair of hands that had somehow given life to this monster.

Now, months later, Nessa's own hands were making their contribution. Sometimes she wondered what Hugh would have thought about her being involved, even in a small way, with the actual building of the ships: what he would have said, what new things they could have talked about, if he was still here and they both worked in the yard. She enjoyed these moments. They were sad, but not so painful now. She'd done the right thing coming back to Clydebank. And Heather seemed pleased with the arrangement too. Nessa was company for her during the long months between Charlie's leaves from the Navy. And expenses were shared. Not that money mattered too much. With the constant availability of overtime and the bonuses that could be earned, both women were wealthier than they'd ever been before. They also enjoyed working together in friendly rivalry, and slipping out the side door for a break.

'I'm packing it in at the midday hooter,' said Heather. 'That's me made maximum bonus for this week. And I've been saving some coupons. I'm swapping a dirty workshop for some Glasgow clothes shops this afternoon. Fancy it?'

'No. I'm working on. There's a shop stewards' meeting later the day.'

'In the yard?'

'In Connolly's at opening time. A few people turned down today's overtime so they could go to the Bankies' game. It's a Scottish cup-tie or something like that. So the meeting's being held in the pub after the football.'

'You're really getting involved, Nessa. How did it go last night in Kilbendrick? What did Joe say when you told him you've been elected shop steward for the smithy?'

'He already knew! I don't know why we get the reputation for gossip. Men are worse. Especially trade union men.'

'So things went okay last night?' Heather wasn't going to let it slip.

'Aye. Aye, they did.'

Nessa had been surprised and pleased by the warm, teasing welcome Joe had given.

'Put the kettle on, Sarah,' he'd shouted through to the kitchen, 'we're being honoured with a visit from the new shop steward of the general smithy at John Brown's.' He put his arm round Nessa and gave her a squeeze. 'Congratulations, wee sister. I'm proud of you.'

'Joe's been telling me, Nessa,' said Sarah as she led them through to the kitchen where the table was laid with sandwiches and fresh baking, 'how did this come about? I mean, you've not been there that long.'

'Aye,' said Joe, 'shop steward before the ink's dry on her membership card. She'll be convener by the end of next week, and running the TUC next year.' He dodged his sister's playful swing. 'Seriously, how did this come about?'

88

'First things first. How do you know anything about it?'

'You've a lot to learn about Clydeside trade union communication,' advised Joe. 'Something happens in a Govan yard, and minutes later it'll be common knowledge fifteen miles down-river in Greenock.'

'Gossip,' accused Nessa.

'No, no. Industrial intelligence.' Joe winked at her.

Over tea, Nessa explained there hadn't been a shop steward in the smithy when she started there. She'd spoken up on behalf of the women welders on a couple of issues. They didn't have the full head masks men wore, instead they'd been issued with hand-held shields that increased the possibility of eye injury. And flying pieces of slag burned right through the light overalls they were given. Couldn't they have leather aprons like the blacksmiths? Old ones would do. Word got back to the shop steward convener for the yard who then approached her and explained how to hold a meeting and elect a shop steward for the smithy.

'So that's how I got involved. I'm going to a shop steward's meeting tomorrow night.'

'So I believe,' said Joe. 'Just you watch yourself with Tommy. He's a bit of a tearaway.'

'Hold on. Who are you two talking about?' asked Sarah, who was having trouble keeping up.

'Tommy Spowart. He's the shop steward convener in Brown's. He was Johnny Moore's right hand man during the apprentices' strike a couple of years ago. Young lad, bit of a firebrand. A lot to learn yet.'

'C'mon!' said Nessa. 'They won a huge victory. In no time at all, every major engineering works in the country was involved and fifteen thousand apprentices were out on strike. And no wonder! Dilutees like me were getting paid tradesmen wages after six weeks training and fifth year apprentices weren't even getting half that!'

'Oh my,' said Joe, 'somebody's been looking after your

history lessons.'

'Are you saying it's not true?'

'Of course it's true. But it's not always the right way. Young hotheads like Tommy are drawn to a fight. And sometimes they're blind to the possibilities for cooperation and compromise, of working out a way that suits both parties. Especially when there's a real fight going on. Like a war.'

Eventually Sarah had brought their sparring to a halt. She insisted that she wasn't going to spend the night refereeing a squabble she didn't understand. 'Let's speak about something else. I'm here too, you know.' She smiled, but the smile had an edge to it.

When it was time for Nessa to go, Joe had walked her to the bus stop and, just as the bus arrived, had given her a folded piece of paper. 'This might interest you, Nessa. Whatever else I might say, I'm proud of what you're doing. And trade union business – it's not a game.'

Now, in their doorway shelter, she handed the paper over to Heather. 'Joe gave me this when I was leaving,' she said. 'It's about a place called Harmony. Does that ring any bells for you?'

'Maybe. Vaguely.' Heather unfolded the sheet.

'Joe and my Hugh used to go there. Before the war. To talk about politics and ideas. I think Joe's trying to encourage me to do the same.'

'You're kidding me ... Scarper! Inside! Quick!' Heather thrust the paper back at Nessa and pointed along the building to where the bowler-hatted figure of a foreman advanced briskly in their direction.

The two women slipped back into the clamour of the smithy, its gloom broken by erratic blue flashes and then by a sudden fiery glare as the door of the main forge opened. To the orders of the master smith, a team of shadowy figures drew a large steel shaft, glowing white and orange, out of the furnace. Sparks flew and the profiles of the men took on a fierce light as they guided the heavy radiant bar onto the anvil of the steam hammer. At the smith's signal, the enormous hammerhead was released. The force of its first thumping blow sent a tremor through the ground beneath the women's feet. The clang vibrated and punched its way along the walls. The hammer lifted, struck again.

Between blows, the master smith sprinkled water on the glowing beam, as if in blessing.

Twelve

Clydebank, May 1943

Nessa Glover pushed open the door marked "Family Department" at Connolly's pub. As usual, the sign annoyed her. "Family" was a euphemism for 'the only place women get served'. At least the one at Connolly's was bigger than most, had comfy seats, tables, and a nice coal fire in the winter. She checked her appearance in the large wall mirror advertising McClay's beers. Okay. She would do. She'd clocked out of the yard at four o'clock and raced around to the public baths for a steep in one of their private tubs, a deep tiled affair where she relaxed and let an endless brimming supply of hot soapy water soak away the day's dirt and smells. Back at the flat she'd made a quick spam sandwich and eaten it as she'd laid out a dark brown tweed trouser suit and a cream blouse, tied her hair up in a headscarf, and put on some light makeup. A hint of rouge and powder. A touch of lipstick. And flat shoes. She had some walking to do later.

'Tommy in yet?' she asked Mike the barman.

'See for yourself.'

She placed her hands onto the counter, hoisted herself up, and peered over the mahogany and stained glass partition into the noisy, smoky, conversation-and-laughter-filled, men-only bar that always struck her as the true life and soul of the pub. A chorus of wolf whistles greeted her appearance. Tommy Spowart broke away from a group of men, disappeared from her view, and reappeared through the family department door.

'Hello, gorgeous. What're you having?'

'Cut the patter. I'm old enough to be your mother.'

'Aye, and good-looking enough to make me forget that.'

'So you say. That'll cost you a whisky and lemonade.

Where's the rest of them?'

'They'll be making their way down from Kilbowie Park. Full-time was about half an hour ago.' Tommy bought the whisky, a pint for himself and took the drinks to the table where Nessa had already sat down. 'Hard day?'

'Hard enough. I made a dozen torpedo tube brackets.'

'A dozen? On overtime as well? You'll be lifting some pay packet next week. I should've let you buy the drinks!' Tommy pushed two tables together and began laying out some handwritten sheets. 'There's not a lot on the agenda,' he said. 'An hour should do it. Give's a hand with the chairs. There should be another six besides you and me. Davy Kilpatrick from the plumbers won't be here. He buried his boy this afternoon.'

'The bomb explosion?' Nessa shook her head. 'Awful. Were you at the funeral?'

'I was. There was a huge turnout. Three young boys. They were all buried today. Davy's was just twelve, and he was the oldest. Playing about in a bombsite in Jellicoe Street. An unexploded bomb goes off. And they're all dead.'

'It's hellish. Just so hard on the families.'

'Y'know what's really cruel?' Tommy put down his papers as if to emphasise the point. 'Parents of lads that age aren't worrying so much now. The war should be finished before they're due for call-up. And right now it's the Jerries who're on the receiving end as far as the bombing goes. People are starting to believe we won't see their planes back here again. And then a stupid accident. A bomb that's been buried in rubble for over two years. And it kills three more kids...' He stopped suddenly. 'Sorry, Nessa.'

'Tommy, I've told you before. You've got nothing to say sorry for.' She pushed the last of the chairs into place with brisk movements that emphasised the end of that part of their conversation. 'Right. That looks as if we're ready now.'

'Aye. Good. And does our new shop steward have

anything she wants to put on the agenda?'

'I don't know if it's for the agenda. I got this last night from my brother Joe. Joe Connor, he's…'

'Oh, I know Joe. Henderson's yard, Kilbendrick. Fitting shop.' Tommy took the poster from her. 'Harmony, eh? I've heard about this. Big place in the country, isn't it? Up north. Perthshire or somewhere like that. Has there not been meetings there before?'

'They used to happen regularly, but this is the first one since the war started. My man Hugh and Joe sometimes went to meetings during the Thirties. People live there. It's a kind of community in some old castle. Everything's paid for by a rich American man who used to own factories in America before something changed his mind. Some tragedy or other. Hugh used to tell me about it when he came home. Sometimes him and Joe spent weekends there. I never paid too much attention back then. Hugh just got stuck into his books and his ideas and the socialist groups he went to in Glasgow. What he did for the union was part of something much bigger for him. Harmony was part of it too. So I want to know what it was all about. What he did there. I think I'm going to go to this.'

'Nessa, we've spoken about this before. Your man was highly thought of in the yard, as a worker and as a union man. He was one of the old school. So is Joe Connor from what I hear. Ideas men. Intellectuals, I suppose you'd call them. I can see why they wanted to go to a place like this Harmony – poncey name, by the way. But it's got nothing to do with our meeting. All the hot air spoken at some swanky castle won't put another penny piece into the pay packets of the workers in Brown's yard. And it won't send them home cleaner and safer.'

'Fair enough. But I'm going anyway. You haven't even had a proper look at it! Give's it back,' she snatched the paper from his hand and began to read. '*Harmony. Saturday*

20th and Sunday 21st June 1943. Cooperation not Conflict. New Approaches to Industrial Relations in Wartime. That's the big words, Tommy. Let me read the wee words to you as well. *An invitation is extended to all interested parties to come to Harmony for a weekend of discussion and activities concerning this important topic. Previous events have been attended by diverse groups including businessmen, trades unionists, university lecturers, Fabianists, women's activists, students, politicians, and clergymen. Anyone with a genuine interest in humanity and the roots of social conflict is welcome. Attendance is free, including food, accommodation and transport to and from Harmony by coach. Transport details and the weekend's programme are given overleaf.'*

'Free?'

'Aye. That's not free as in "Free the Workers", Tommy. That's free as in doesn't cost you a penny.'

'Ha-ha. Very funny.' Tommy paused, swigged his beer, stroked his chin. 'Tell you what. I'll come along as well. Sounds to me it's time for a young modern voice with a simple message. Like "We've been shafted long enough. Now it's the turn of the owners and bosses." Also, I know from Mike the barman that old Connolly's just acquired a very healthy increase in his stock of whisky. I'll make sure some of that makes its way to Harmony with me. Maybe it'll calm the overheated minds of some of the eggheads there. One of them anyway. You. Speaking of which, how about staying on here after the meeting. We'll be having a few drinks. And you're one of us now.'

'Thanks, but no. I've other plans.'

'Don't tell me you've got a date?'

'None of your business.'

There was running outside, feet skidding, bodies jostling, raucous shouts. A group of men in football scarves burst through the door, wrestling and pushing to hinder one another's progress. The hindmost called back over his shoulder. 'Get the wallet out, Tam. Last man buys the drinks.'

Nessa passed between the heavy iron gates at the entrance to Dalnottar Cemetery. Although she'd already walked almost three miles, she lengthened her stride, keen to reach the summit of the hill at the cemetery's centre and escape the gloomy tunnel of trees that led there.

At the top, she entered bright sunshine and paused to take in the sweep of the view. In the valley to her left, she could pick out the dominating clock tower of Singer's factory; then Brown's yard, its dense pattern of derricks dwarfed by the massive cantilever crane. Directly below the graveyard, the Erskine ferry clanked itself across the Clyde on chains, connecting the north and south banks, which soon, to Nessa's right, broadened into the estuary that reached past Dumbarton, Helensburgh, Greenock and on to the sea.

Nessa made her way to a grave with a plain headstone bearing the simple legend "Richard (Ricky) Glover 1927-1941". After a while she turned, walked a few paces, and stopped at the open area of grass that covered the mass grave for unidentified Blitz victims. In what she now thought of as her mad days, Nessa used to come here and weep helplessly, hoping that somehow Hugh would rise from the ground or step out from behind a gravestone, and the four children would follow in a line behind him. Now she accepted the grave might not even contain their remains; or there might be indeterminate pieces of flesh and bone, rotting slowly to mould. But it was all she had for their memorial. All they had too.

She sat on a nearby bench. Deep within, she felt the familiar ache: nothing sharp, nothing raging, no longer the fury that tore her to pieces then receded, leaving a blackness filled with unbearable misery. No. This was steady. Unchanging. Part of her forever. She knew it would never go away. But she knew too that it would never stop her living the rest of her life as best she could.

With Hugh, she hadn't talked a great deal about the future. Oh, he'd had his dreams, but they seemed to come mostly from his political ideas. He hoped the war would lead to a new deal for workers, to new thinking. Maybe the people working and fighting to save the country would lead it into a new socialism? She'd found this vision troubling. For her, back then, God's plan was enough, and she'd bowed her head to the authority of the church and to its teachings that the future lay in a distant, eternal, perfect heaven.

She was a long way from there now. She attended church infrequently, and when she did it was often more social than spiritual – to share the sorrow of a funeral or witness the joy of a wedding. Then there were Sundays when she wakened early and a long ingrained habit tugged her from bed, into some smart clothes and out to mass. She always felt a little confused afterwards, as if part of her resented the enjoyment she'd felt at being part of an old familiar ritual – the standing, the kneeling, the singing, the murmur of the priest's Latin, the clang of the altar-boy's bell, the smell of incense.

Father Paul Lamont always seemed to spot her amongst the crowd and draw her aside before she could leave. 'Nessa,' he'd say, 'It's always good to see you here. You know I'm always available if you'd like to talk.' Sometimes they'd walk around the chapel grounds. Or they'd arrange to meet later. He'd stopped pressing her about her declining attendance. He'd ask about her work, she'd hear something about his parish duties.

She felt indebted to him for his help during her difficult times. If he hadn't turned up, she wouldn't be where she was now. But his support and companionship had helped her move away from the church. She wondered if he realised that. If he did, he said nothing. He accepted her, seemed pleased by her achievements. That's what created the warmth between them, the bond.

'Nessa! Nessa!' She was brought back to the graveyard surroundings by her name being called. She turned and looked back down the shadowy avenue of trees. There he was! Striding up the path, his arm raised in greeting.

'Father Lamont? What are you doing here?'

'You told me you sometimes come to Dalnottar on a Saturday evening. I remembered that when I was here at the funerals this afternoon.'

'The boys killed by the bomb?'

'Yes. I buried two of them. The third was from a Protestant family. He was buried this afternoon too. Reverend Taylor took that one. But people attended all three. It seemed like half the town had come along. When the mourners eventually started to leave, I looked around and thought to myself what a beautiful place this is, surrounded by hills and overlooking the river. Yet here it was crammed today with grief and pain. And I felt a sudden urge to come back later. I just wanted to be here in peace and quiet. That's when I remembered your visits and wondered if I might find you here as well. I hope you don't mind.'

'No. No, it's good to see you. I've just walked here from a union meeting. One of the things we talked about there was the boys killed by that bomb. And how it was so cruel for this to happen long after the Blitz, just when people are starting to feel safe again.'

'I know. That makes it so difficult to comfort the bereaved. They think I can answer those questions. Oh yes, I can talk to them about God, about death, about resurrection. But sometimes I look at the faces in front of me and wonder what they're really making of that. Sometimes I wonder what I make of it myself. As a priest I know the answer to that one. It's the devil challenging my faith, waiting for it to weaken. So I kneel and I pray and I wait for God to come and strengthen me.'

'And does he come?' Nessa asked softly.

The priest hunched forward, elbows on knees, fingers interlinked, staring ahead, sharing the view with her. Time passed and dissolved her unanswered question.

'Ah well, I'd better think of making tracks.' Father Lamont broke the silence at last. The sky was reddening and shadows lengthened on the Renfrew shore. Downriver the sun dropped faster towards the cranes of Greenock.

'Me too.'

'I didn't hear anything about your union meeting,' he said.

'Nothing much you'd be interested in there. But it feels good for me. And...' she took the Harmony poster from her handbag and handed it to him, '... I've decided to go to this.'

He read the paper carefully, turned it over, studied the other side. 'I'll come too,' he said.

'You can't.' She emphasised the "can't" and laughed sceptically. 'You always tell me Sunday's your busy day.'

'Priests might not have a trade union,' he replied with a straight face. 'But we can take holidays.'

'I think you're teasing me.'

'You wait and see. I'll be there.'

They walked together down the wooded path. He stopped and squeezed her hand softly. She turned to him, uncertain. He pointed up to the edge of the trees where a pair of bats whirled to and fro, hunting insects.

Thirteen

Keir passed under the castle archway that led to Laggandarroch School's main doorway. What had the headmaster made of his flippo yesterday? Would he ask about it? So what? It happened. Explain as necessary, don't dwell on it, get on with the job.

He put his head round the secretary's door: 'G'day!'

'Good morning, Mr Connor. The headmaster asked me to let him know when you arrived.' Miss Baxter was a large lady of uncertain years whose powdered face was crowned by a neat helmet of white hair that still carried traces of the original blonde. With some difficulty, she eased herself from between the restraining arms of her swivel chair and led the way into the headmaster's study.

Dr Bob McNeil rose to meet them. 'Ah, Keir. I hope you're well rested? Travelling can be so tiring, I find.'

'Yeah, thanks, I'm good.' He wasn't sure his night with Gloria could be described as restful, but he felt more settled and clear-headed than he had for a while. 'And I've just had a fine walk down through your beautiful woodlands. I spotted a group of little deer and followed them to a clearing. Watched them from behind a tree for quite a while until the antlered fella caught a sniff of me, let out a bark, and they scarpered.'

'My goodness, you were lucky. Those roe deer are extremely shy. You must have moved very quietly.'

'Yeah, well. Jungle survival and all that, I reckon. Becomes a habit.'

'Quite so. And I'm hoping to hear a lot more about your experiences. But right now I must apologise for being in a bit of a rush. We have a staff meeting on Thursday mornings and I never seem quite ready for it. Might I tell them that you'll be able to attend the soirée tomorrow? As I mentioned yesterday, we're marking the start of the May holiday weekend with wine and cheese, and there's a lot of interest in meeting you.'

'Yeah. That'll be good.' Keir's recollection of yesterday's conversation was vague, and he was grateful for the headmaster's prompting.

'Wonderful, I'll make an announcement.' He scribbled quickly on a lined pad, which was covered in notes and bullet points. 'Miss Baxter will look after you. I've asked her to show you where the archive is stored. It's a bit cramped and airless in there so please use the boardroom table to spread your work out.' He turned to the secretary. 'I suggest you show Mr Connor the general structure and layout, then he can take it from there.' He crossed to a bookcase and reached down a heavy, leather-bound volume. 'We keep a copy of Fergus Abercrombie's book, *The Reluctant Capitalist,* as a mark of respect to the person who founded this place. Might be worth having a look in here too. Now, if you'll excuse me, I'll leave you in Miss Baxter's capable hands.'

In the boardroom, Miss Baxter opened a door set into the fireplace wall and led Keir into a windowless, cell-like room.

'I'm afraid it's not quite as well organised as Dr Bob believes,' she said as she flicked the light switch. The chamber was about twice as deep as it was wide. One long wall was taken up with glass-fronted bookcases perched on top of waist-high wooden cupboards. Behind the glass, Keir could see shelves of old books interspersed with box folders. A row of wooden filing cabinets, piled high with cardboard boxes, lined the other wall. 'Basically,' she went on, 'the filing cabinets contain any existing documents from the time Fergus Abercrombie bought the castle until his death in 1949. They're approximately date-ordered with the oldest at the back and the newest nearest the door. I wouldn't put too much trust in that, though. We believe the bookcases used to

101

be part of a much larger Harmony collection … the school assembly hall in the west wing is still called the Library. The bottom shelves contain annual log books of some kind. Those box folders are a bit of a nightmare. Some are labelled and some aren't. They seem to have a mixture of stuff in them, letters, miscellaneous paperwork, photographs.'

'So you're reasonably familiar with what's here?' Keir was beginning to wonder if he'd taken on more than he'd anticipated.

'Only what I've already told you. As far as the cupboards and the cardboard boxes go … unknown territory, I'm afraid. Best of luck with them.'

'Aaah. So the archive isn't indexed or catalogued.'

'Far from it. I suspect lots of it hasn't seen the light of day since Laggandarroch School, as it now is, came into being in 1955. It was a very different place before then.' Miss Baxter leaned forward and dropped her voice 'I think there were some funny goings on here.' She straightened up again, and Keir backed out into the boardroom to avoid the swell of her bosom. 'At least, I've heard whispers,' she said, following him. 'I'm not one for gossip myself. Oh. And Dr Bob asked me to leave you this so you can come and go as you please.' She placed a key on the large oak table, sailed across the room and closed the door behind her.

Keir searched the wall of photographs and found the one of the weekend gathering that Gloria had shown him in her album last night. His eyes settled on Nessa Glover. 'Hello Mum,' he said quietly. He waited. Yeah. That felt okay. He sat down at the table, facing the wall of pictures.

Gloria Honeydew puzzled him. He'd pushed thoughts of her to and fro this morning while he enjoyed a slow sensual shave then soaped up his body and let the elderly but brisk shower rinse him clean. Yeah, he'd lost the plot a bit when she pointed out the image of Nessa Glover. His mother. He'd better get used to the word. His mother. His dead, enigmatic mother. But his floundering hadn't been as severe as the earlier flippo in the boardroom. And what about the way Gloria had responded? Had she comforted him? Had she taken advantage of him? Did it matter? And what would happen between them now? Right now that didn't matter either – he was feeling pretty good.

Surely his change of mood wasn't simply because of a sexy night with a near stranger? Nah, he'd run round that track before, although he couldn't deny that last night's laps had been pretty special. He'd also made a strategic decision about the quest that had brought him here, and that was perking him up too. He'd begin his research by focussing on the history of Harmony – its founder, its commune, its school – and not dive head first into his own family stuff. He couldn't tear up his father's letter and pretend it had never existed. But if he made Harmony commune the centre of his attention, that might let the family ghosts come to meet him. Because trying to chase after them in his current state wasn't working. He needed to find an approach that eased the burden on himself.

Okay, the plan was impossibly black and white. No way could he avoid finding references to Nessa, to Joe, to Hugh, to others who were part of the mystery. No way when he was working in a room where their photographs hung on the walls.

A photograph of her.

His mother.

But his strategy was about a shift of emphasis, that's what felt right to him. He'd be sitting here as a researcher, as a journalist, as a writer, and maybe that hard-earned professional skin would protect him. Maybe not, but it was an approach worth trying.

For a while, he studied the dramatically lit face of Fergus Abercrombie in the large romanticised oil painting. So you're the founder, mate. You set the ball rolling. He switched his attention to the strident banner with its symbolic tale of social advancement. It sure rolled its way across a wide swathe of human activity.

How did all this come about?

There weren't many stories that could resist the six-word mantra drummed into Keir during his rookie years by Skip Rafferty, chief reporter of *The Kalgoorlie Miner*.

What? Where? When? How? Why? Who?

Six queries, simple as locksmith's picks, that could crack open the most complex of mysteries. And here he had people, he had dates, he had places. And he had a mountain of stuff that surely held the whats, hows and whys.

Time to get started.

Keir picked up the book the headmaster had given him. Inside the cover, the title was expanded to *The Reluctant Capitalist: Harmony and its Blessings*. He turned to the Introduction and started to read.

This book had a gestation of ten years during which I left the United States of America, the country of my birth, and returned to Scotland, the country of my origins. I also ventured further into Europe, to France in particular. These were years of more than just geographical adventure: I spent them exploring philosophy, and I enquired especially into the challenges of organising human relationships in the industrial world, depending as it does, in its commonest style, on two main classes of people; those who supply capital, and those who supply labour. Other styles existed before the great eighteenth century advancement of mankind called the Industrial Revolution, and others have been attempted since.

The chapters that follow will, I trust, uncover to the attentive reader where I now stand on these issues of social organisation and why I have arrived at the conclusions I have. My aim in this Introduction is to help that reader understand the inner journey that led me to write The

Reluctant Capitalist.

I, Fergus Abercrombie, was born on 1st August 1873 in Pittsburgh, Pennsylvania, the only child of Jessie and Robert Abercrombie, migrants from Dundee in Scotland to Pittsburgh in 1852. They were both from travelling stock and Robert had grown up learning traditional tinkering skills. Although he was barely twenty years old when he and Jessie arrived in the USA, he was already an accomplished tinsmith and sheet metal worker who also had a natural aptitude for the repair of clocks and other forms of mechanical gadgetry.

My father was ideally suited to the opportunities America offered to a skilled and industrious man. By day he worked as a handyman. Nighttime found him in his workshop corner of the single room he and Jessie rented in Pittsburgh, repairing clocks and watches, casting and painting lead soldiers, fashioning tinplate toys and experimenting with clockwork motors cannibalised from irreparable timepieces. His hard work and inventiveness were matched by Jessie's determination and frugality and soon the couple lived above a little rented shop where Jessie took in watch and clock repairs and sold household goods and toys. Meanwhile Robert worked in an ever-expanding backyard workshop, experimenting with larger scale production of tinplate objects, as well as ornaments and novelties made from pressed steel, brass and pewter.

Such was the success of this venture that in 1860, just eight years after he first set foot in America, my father bought a small pressed metal factory. The American Civil War started a year later. By the time it ended in 1865, and thanks to its voracious appetite for brass cartridge cases, pressed steel gun components, brass buckles, metal buttons, and other military accoutrements, Robert Abercrombie owned two large factories which, between them, employed two thousand people. He was also an innovative designer and manufacturer of tinplate clockwork toys and he and

Jessie lived in a fine mansion at Point Breeze, alongside Pittsburgh's wealthiest families.

My arrival in 1873 was a source of great joy to my parents who had begun stoically to accept their childless marriage. My father now had a son to continue not just his name but his considerable success as a man of industry. From early in childhood I was a familiar figure in his offices and factories and I was left in no doubt that he expected me to take over from him when the time came. Alas, that day arrived sooner than expected. My father succumbed to a typhoid outbreak and died in 1896. Cruel fate timed his death for 1st August, my 23rd birthday. I was at that time notionally attending college and studying metallurgy, but in truth my life was more structured around sailing, tennis, polo, and being an enthusiastic member of a set drawn from Pittsburgh's richest and best known. With unwilling heart, I assumed my father's mantle as the head of Abercrombie Industries Inc.

I spent the ensuing four years as a supposed captain of industry: but this captain was rarely on the bridge and I was more likely to be found turning somersaults from the high board at the Point Breeze Country Club; astride the saddle of a thoroughbred; or pursuing the favours of any one of several young women who wanted to sit beside me atop my recently imported Benz motorcar. By and large, the responsibilities for the running of Abercrombie Industries were left in the hands of my father's friend, and vice-president of the company, Morgan Frick.

Then, during a strike at one of the Abercrombie factories in 1900, eight picketing workers were shot dead by Pinkerton men employed, with my tacit approval, by Morgan Frick to protect the strike-breaking labour force he was using. In truth, and to my shame, I had paid scant attention to the details of how this industrial dispute was being handled, and even less to why it was happening in the first place. It is a matter of record that I was present at the meeting which agreed the strategy of using armed guards, but I have no recollection of taking part in discussion and probably, as usual, spent the meeting with my mind on other matters. Nonetheless, after the shootings, it was to me that my fellow industrialists paid compliments, praising "my" tough action, endorsing "my" determination to show misguided union organisers the error of their ways, to remind them who were the bosses and who the workers. Any protests or misgivings I expressed about such plaudits were slyly endorsed with a nudge or a wink. Yes, yes. Best not to say anything too publicly.

I became suffused with a pervasive fear, the origins and meaning of which I could not fathom. I had ingested my parent's values along with the milk of childhood: decency, hard work, resoluteness, honesty, regard for fellow man. Yet somehow my father, through his prodigious efforts, had created a ready place for me in a world of wealth and commerce where such values were counterfeit coinage. What appealed to my fellow magnates as a salutary lesson for "socialist upstarts" felt to me like foul murder, and the blood was on my hands. As I struggled with what, in hindsight, I regard as an affliction of my soul, a newspaper published a picture of the wife and family of Dawson Fenton, one of the dead strikers. It showed a poorly clad woman, carrying one child and surrounded by four others, sitting in the street amid their scant belongings after their eviction. Far from being sympathetic to the wretched woman, the newspaper highlighted her plight as a timely message to present and future troublemakers.

And that was my turning point. The fear that had paralysed me for days on end departed, and in its place came a clarity and a determination. I set up a fund to provide for the families and dependents of the dead men, sold up all my assets, made sure my mother was provided for, and came to Scotland with a considerable personal fortune. I began to research other ways of managing the links between *that troublesome trinity of capital, labour and production. I studied John Stuart Mill, Marx, Engels, Henry George, Robert Owen. But I was increasingly drawn to the ideas of the eighteenth century French philosopher and utopian socialist Charles Fourier who believed that cooperation, not conflict, was the key to a society's success and would result in happy workers and increased productivity. And this would best be achieved in self-sufficient communities, which he called phalanxes, where men and women would strive together to attain what Fourier called "Harmony", a new form of social order based upon human nature as it is, not what moralists vainly insist it must become, nor what capitalists try to shape in their own self-interest.*

The following chapters deal with those aspects of Fourier's thinking that focus most trenchantly upon the very issues that led me to sell the Abercrombie industrial empire and seek out a place where a Fourier-inspired community might be established. Such was the genius of Charles Fourier that his philosophical system extended far beyond the avoidance of industrial strife: it offered nothing less than a blueprint for harmony and happiness in all arrangements of human activity and relationships. These wider ideas, which have hitherto been unavailable in English, have implications for communal life and form the subject of a further book for the education and guidance of those adventurous souls brave enough to place themselves at the core of the new experimental community.

And now, with satisfaction at the ending of one journey and excitement at the beginning of another, I await the first arrivals at Harmony Community.

Fergus Abercrombie
Harmony
Laggandarroch Castle
February 1910

Keir sat back in his chair and searched the face in Fergus Abercrombie's portrait. What had the headmaster said? Was it self-mockery? Was it self-deception? He let his attention flick between the wall hanging with its vibrant images of human dignity and heroic progress and the romantic painting of a lone visionary. If you were chocolate you'd eat yourself mate, he thought.

Fourteen

It was early evening when Keir Connor left the boardroom. He'd made a good start. Re-connecting with his professional skills had been like stepping into a well-worn suit of clothes. His pen, his pad, his tape recorder were comforting reminders of lifetime commitment. They, and Skip Rafferty's six-word mantra, had led him through a hard-working day. Whenever stealthy memories of Gloria's bed crept in, he'd seen them off with a brisk return to the question in hand, the document of the moment, the next sheaf of photographs.

But now with the castle behind him and the road ahead leading him uphill to his cottage, Keir's thoughts turned back to his next door neighbour. How was he going to deal with Gloria? How was she going to deal with him?

He approached a rustic roadside shelter that had seen better days. Some of the half-round boards were askew and patches of thatch were missing from the roof. From inside, Keir could hear excited female voices and occasional screeches of hysterical laughter. The hut was open to the road and as he drew level he could see two girls sitting on a bench along the back wall. One of them was inhaling deeply from a plastic bag that covered the lower half of her face. The other he recognised as Rosemary, the girl he'd sat beside in the English class story circle. The reddish marks he'd noticed then around her nose were now prominent and inflamed. Both girls' eyes were bright and staring.

'I did, Kath,' he heard Rosemary say in a thick voice, 'I says to him, "Go on then, show us your big fat prick." I did.' She reached out towards the other girl. 'C'mon. Hurry up. It's my shot. You can tell one now.' She took the plastic bag, poured some liquid into it from a tin, fitted the bag around her nose and mouth, and breathed deeply. The other girl looked up and caught sight of Keir watching them. She froze momentarily, then, not taking her blazing eyes from him, reached out and shook her friend's knee.

'Rosie. Rosie. Look. We've got a real one.'

Rosemary lowered the bag, looked at Keir. 'I know him. He's from Australia. A war man or something. He came to our English class. He speaks funny. But he's gorgeous isn't he? You know what they say about Australian men, Kath?'

'No?'

'They've got really big pricks!'

The girls howled and cackled, their faces contorted as their laughter gurgled and exploded uncontrollably, their arms and upper bodies swinging to and fro in wide exaggerated movements. Keir was at a loss. He felt he should do something but he didn't know what. Then he heard the deep-throated beat of an approaching motorcycle. Ainsley Watson appeared round the bend astride a gleaming black and chrome vintage model. He swung the machine into a tight turn and brought it to a crisp halt.

'Oh fuck, it's Watson,' Keir heard one of the girls say.

'That's right, it's me.' The motorcyclist strode past Keir and planted himself confidently in front of the seated girls.

'I thought I'd find you two somewhere around here.' he said. 'Right. Let's have it.' He extended his hands towards them and made beckoning gestures. Everything about him, his voice, his stance, his movements, carried the same calm authority Keir had witnessed during the restraint of Donny in the science class.

When Rosemary spoke, her slurred voice was soft and seductive. 'Ainsley. C'mon Ainsley. Please. Can you not just leave us? Just for ten minutes? Please, Ainsley? You know me. C'mon. You know me, Ainsley. We'll come back down. Ten minutes. Honest. Pl-e-e-e-a-s-e?'

'Don't. Even. Start.' Watson emphasised each word singly, his voice firm and level. 'Now hand them over. The bag...' he beckoned with one hand, then the other, 'and the glue.'

'Oh. Fuck him. We know he's just got a wee one anyway,' said Kath. She held out her little finger and wiggled it. The girls collapsed into one another's arms, screaming and giggling. Watson waited. Slowly the plastic bag, and then the tin, were held out. He took them.

'Thank you. Now let's just stand up. You two can have a nice quiet walk back down to the school. I'll just tootle along behind to make sure you don't get lost again.' As they struggled to their feet the girls collided. Rosemary staggered backwards, hit the wall, and slumped to the ground. Keir stepped up beside the other man. 'Need a hand, mate?'

'No thanks. We'll take a minute to disentangle ourselves here, but we'll be okay.' He didn't turn as he spoke but kept his attention fully on the two girls. Keir began to wonder if his being there was unhelpful. He flitted away quietly.

Gloria's cottage door was open and she called his name as he passed. He wondered if she'd been watching for his return. She stepped out and hugged him in a way that felt natural and easy to return. She took his hand and, without asking, led him in.

'How was your day?' she asked.

'Look, about last night...' he hesitated. He felt he had to say something. Before he met the two glue-sniffing girls he'd been rehearsing what that might be, but couldn't seem to find the right words. Now he'd just stumbled into it. Gloria came to the rescue.

'I don't mind speaking about it, Keir. But there's no need. Talk might spoil a really nice time.'

'Yeah ... well ... thanks. And thanks for leaving me some breakfast.'

'You were sound asleep when I left. I didn't want to disturb you.'

'Thanks for that too. I just slipped out afterwards.' He

winced as soon as the words were out. Gloria pounced.

'You certainly didn't slip out during!' She laughed at the impact, gave him a comic nudge in the ribs. 'C'mon, Keir. Big boy and big girl time. You needed some tenderness, I was hungry, we both ended up better off. And your discrete tiptoeing away this morning was a bit wasted.' She waved towards the window and the deserted countryside beyond. 'There's not a neighbour in sight. Anyway, if you'd charged around Laggandarroch trumpeting the news from atop a circus elephant you wouldn't have shifted my reputation up nor down.' She pushed him playfully again. 'You certainly look better than you did yesterday. I suspect you're feeling better too. That's all fine by me.'

Keir shrugged and laughed with her. He needn't have worried about their first meeting. Gloria had hijacked it. He felt outflanked and sheepish. And on unfamiliar ground.

There was something different about this woman. He couldn't find anyone like her in the many brief entanglements that speckled his life, nor in the three relationships that had, in their own ways, broken a piece from his heart. Not in Annie, his wife in a marriage that now seemed like a desperate retreat from the craziness of life in war zones, a simplistic attempt to rediscover the boy from West Australia in the arms of his teenage sweetheart. Not that he hadn't loved her. He had. He still cared for her deeply, and wished her success with the mining engineer who was doing a fine job of being a new dad to the two kids Keir had left behind. And not in Pauline, the American photojournalist who'd eventually chosen life with her husband. Certainly not in Chandina, the Cambodian translator he'd promised to marry and take to Australia but who he'd last seen on the wrong side of a line of Khmer Rouge fighters. He quickly pushed Chandina away. Dangerous territory. But Gloria? Different. Oh yes. Different.

He took her hand and squeezed it between both of his.

'It's fine by me too, Gloria. Yeah, I've had a good day. But I had a weird encounter with a couple of kids on my way back here. I wonder if maybe I should have done more.'

She listened to his account of the two girls, and Ainsley Watson's intervention, with interest but no surprise.

'Two glue-sniffing girls and a bout of sexual bravado doesn't count as strange at Laggandarroch,' she said when he'd finished. 'If you'd come across two pupils studying for their exams, now that would be really weird. You did the right thing walking away. That removed their audience, their shock factor. From then on it would be business as usual for Ainsley. How was your day in the boardroom? Any progress?'

'Yeah. Some. That photograph you showed me last night? With Nessa Glover? My father, Joe Connor, is in there too. And he's in several of the pre-war pictures. So's Hugh Glover. He was Nessa's husband, killed in the Clydebank Blitz three years before I was born.

'But for the moment I've decided to focus on the wider picture. Try to understand what brought Nessa here. Try to figure out what Harmony was about in 1943, and before then. That's put Fergus Abercrombie in my sights. You knew him well I guess?'

'He was part of my childhood, part of my growing up. The community was his dream, his life. In a way, he was Harmony.'

'He's a main man in most of those photographs. Decades pass and there he is; the same welcome, the same smile. Apart from his hair going white, the years hardly seem to touch him. Difficult to believe he was almost seventy when Nessa came here. And his introduction to *The Reluctant Capitalist* is fascinating. He mentions writing a second book for community members. Did he do that?'

He was sure he spotted a fleeting change in her. Did her eyes narrow for a moment? Her lips tighten? 'You're very

interested in Fergus Abercrombie all of a sudden,' she said.
'I thought you'd came here on personal business, a family
search. Now you're beginning to sound like you're carrying
out an investigation.'

'Whoa! That's a bit strong. You can blame Dr Bob.
Thanks to his silver tongue, I also agreed to look at what's
involved in writing a history of the school. That's all.'

Her smile was back as quickly as it had vanished. 'Yes.
Yes I know you did. Maybe I have a book than can help you.
Do you know the *I Ching*?'

'That's some old Chinese tome, isn't it?'

'I don't think you're showing the respect it deserves.'
Gloria crossed to the bookshelves and returned with an old
box of dark reddish wood, decorated with raised gilded
lacquer scenes of oriental figures in gardens. She placed
the box on the table, beckoned Keir to sit beside her. In a
slow, respectful manner, she opened the box and removed
its carefully packed contents; a jade incense holder, an
embroidered silk drawstring purse, a bamboo calligraphy
brush and a cake of ink, a block of handmade paper sheets.
Underlying these, and completely filling the bottom of the
box, was the largest object, wrapped in yellow silk which
Gloria unfolded to reveal a book. Above Chinese pictograms,
its title was rendered in English: *I Ching or Book of Changes*.

Gloria lit an incense stick. Its wavering wisp of smoke
soon saturated the room with a heavy, spicy smell. She spread
the yellow silk on the table in front of her and tipped onto
it the contents of the purse: three Chinese coins perforated
with square holes. She scooped them up, closed her eyes,
and began to shake the coins together between her cupped
hands.

'I'm holding a question in my mind. "What will be the
outcome of Keir's search?" Please hold it in your mind too.'

Then she threw the coins onto the square of yellow
silk. Keir could see two had landed with an inscribed side

showing, the third had a blank face. Gloria studied the coins for a moment, moistened the ink block, and drew a broken horizontal line along the bottom of a sheet of paper. She gathered and cast the coins again, drew another horizontal line above the first. And so she continued in a slow, ritualistic manner until she had built up a stack of six lines, some of them complete, others broken.

'Now we can let the question go,' she said, 'and see what the oracle has to say.' She slowly turned the pages of the book and when she stopped, showed him the pattern of lines at the top of the page. It matched what she had drawn with the ink brush. 'This hexagram is called *Chin* in Chinese, which means "progress". So that's a good start. Because of the way the coins fell, one of the lines has special importance for your question.' She pointed to the broken line second from the bottom. 'Here's what the *I Ching* has to say about it:

Progressing, but in sorrow.
Perseverance brings good fortune.
Then one obtains great happiness from one's ancestress.'

Keir, who'd been watching with wry amusement, suddenly felt a clench in his stomach. 'Ancestress? My mother?'

'Don't rush at it,' she said. 'Give it time, mull it over. Anyway there's more. Two of your lines are classified as moving lines. Most lines are either Yang, solid, or Yin, broken. But moving lines change character from one to the other. That creates a new hexagram.'

She took a fresh piece of paper and copied the lines onto it, in the process converting two broken lines to solid. Then she consulted the table of hexagrams again. 'Aha. *Sung.* Conflict:

A cautious halt halfway brings good fortune.
Going through to the end brings misfortune.'

Gloria turned to him. 'Sounds like you should focus on your family search, get the "great happiness from one's ancestress", and leave it at that.'

'Sounds as if I'm being given some advice I didn't ask for.'

Gloria's eyes widened in mock horror. 'I'd never dream of doing such a thing to an internationally-known journalist. Oh no. I'm simply giving you access to three thousand years of Chinese wisdom, that's all. If this mere mortal was trying to influence you, it would be in the direction of a drink to celebrate your successful day.'

'I gratefully accept your advice on that.'

Gloria had just handed him a glass of wine when the phone rang. Keir could hear enough to make out a man's voice, speaking with some urgency. 'Yes. I'll come down,' Gloria said. 'Be there in a few minutes.' She put the phone down. 'Rosemary and Kath seem determined to make a night of it,' she said. 'I've some influence with both of them. I'll go and see if I can help. Enjoy your wine. And be sure to...' she wiggled quotation marks with her fingers, '"... slip out quietly afterwards."'

She gave him a quick hug and headed for the door. He heard her car start and felt an odd mixture of regret and relief.

He sat down on Gloria's chair and studied the coins, turning them over, rattling them together in his cupped hands. He picked up the book and flicked through it to find the *Chin* hexagram. *One obtains great happiness from one's ancestress*. He couldn't get over that. Some coincidence! He sought out the second hexagram. '*Sung*. Conflict,' he read. Then he stopped. Put the book down thoughtfully. Picked it up again. Gloria had quoted from a section called "The Judgement", but Keir could see that she'd omitted the first line. It read: *You are sincere and are being obstructed.* Whatever he thought of the *I Ching*, it was obvious that Gloria believed in it. So why had she edited that sentence out?

He picked up his glass and walked slowly around the

room, letting his thoughts wander as he soaked up the decor, studied the pictures, sifted through the record collection, ran his eye along the book titles. He spotted another copy of *The Reluctant Capitalist*. There was an inscription below Fergus Abercrombie's name on the title page. 'To Gloria, a bringer of joy, on her fifteenth birthday, 6th June 1945. Fergus.'

Fifteen

Dr Bob McNeil tapped a teaspoon softly but insistently on the stem of his wineglass. Conversation faded as school staff and guests turned to face the rostrum in Laggandarroch's assembly hall. From his vantage point beside the headmaster, Keir felt himself become the focus of a many curious eyes.

'Welcome, everyone. As you can see, liberties have once again been taken with our so-called Wine and Cheese party. I'm sure you'll agree with me that Matron and her ladies have produced a banquet far above and beyond the call of duty...'

He gestured towards tables laden with canapés, plates of sandwiches, rounds of quiche, bowls of salad, boards of cheese, displays of fruit, elegant flower arrangements, a brimming crystal punchbowl and rows of bottles and glasses. There was cheering and foot-stamping.

'... so I'm keeping the formalities to a minimum, then we can get on with enjoying ourselves. This is Keir Connor, all the way from Australia, who's going to be our guest for a while. Keir is researching some family connections with Harmony in the 1940s when it operated as a commune under the guidance of Fergus Abercrombie. Most of you know something about that phase of the school's history. Keir's also a journalist and war correspondent who has written books about Vietnam and Cambodia. While he carries out his personal research here, he's agreed to do some work on the history of Laggandarroch School. The board and I are delighted to have the help of such an experienced writer. I'm sure you'll all do what you can to make his stay here an enjoyable one. And please take the opportunity to introduce yourselves in the course of the evening.'

While the headmaster spoke, Keir picked out a few familiar faces. Gloria, of course. He pretended not to notice her knowing smile and nod of the head when Dr Bob asked the staff to ensure Keir enjoyed his stay. He was reassessing Gloria in the light of last night's *I Ching* session. She worked hard at being the open, liberated and unconventional spirit, but...

Next to Gloria was Janice, the woman who had played a key role in the classroom restraint of Donny. He also spotted George Greene, the science teacher, too neatly groomed for Keir's taste and wearing clobber that an Aussie man as young as Greene wouldn't be seen dead in – crisp checked shirt and tie, tweed sports jacket and nondescript grey trousers. The pretty woman beside him, his wife maybe, looked like she shopped in the same chain store. At the edge of the crowd, and within ready reach of the food and refreshments, Miss Baxter, the school secretary, paid enthusiastic attention to her glass of white. The tall bearded figure of Ainsley Watson was prominent at the front of the group. When the headmaster had called for attention, Watson had made his way through the throng pushing a pale woman in a wheelchair. She had the parchment-like skin that speaks of chronic and debilitating illness. Now, as Keir stepped from the rostrum, Watson approached, his hand extended in greeting.

'My name's Ainsley Watson, Keir,' he said. 'Sorry I couldn't introduce myself yesterday. I had my hands full with those two girls.'

'You sure had. I wondered afterwards if I could have done more to help you out.'

'You did exactly the right thing. You removed the audience. Let me introduce my wife. This is Annette.' The woman in the wheelchair held out her hand. It felt so slender and bony that Keir hesitated to squeeze. She held his gaze with glittering, washed-out eyes.

'Hello, Keir,' she said.

'How's it going there, Annette?' he asked, and meant it.

'All the better for being out at a party and meeting new

people.' Ainsley Watson, standing behind her, nodded to Keir as if approving his directness. 'I've some information that I'm sure'll help your researches, Keir,' he said. 'Maybe I could drop it past your cottage one day?'

'Yeah, please do that. If I'm not there you'll likely find me in the boardroom.'

Ainsley eyed Keir's glass. 'Let me get us a top-up,' he offered.

'Not me,' said Annette, when Keir glanced at the glass of water she was nursing. 'Doesn't go with the medication. I hear you were chatted up by two of our finest young ladies yesterday,'

'Yeah. They were pretty direct about it. I was glad when Ainsley whizzed up on that bike of his.'

'Stanley.'

'Stanley?'

'1939 Velocette KTT Mark8 350cc. Maximum speed 110 miles per hour. As ridden to victory by Stanley Woods in the 1939 Manx TT.' She spoke as if reciting a well practised quote. 'That's why he calls it Stanley. Stanley's the other love of Ainsley's life.'

'Sounds like you have competition, Annette.'

'Well I've been in this chair for going on three years. Basically, my heart's buggered and complications rule out a transplant. I just keep popping the pills and crossing my fingers. Hey-ho. It gets tiresome and it's no fun for Ainsley either, not that he complains, bless him. Passion for that bike probably saves his sanity. Takes him out and about. Gets him off to rallies. Now. Here he comes. So let's change the subject. A war journalist? How did that come about?'

Questions like that made Keir's socialising easy. He didn't overly relish the attention, but, hey, it was attractively non-fatal compared to other aspects of his profession. New people introduced themselves, chatted for a while, then made way for others. He felt welcome. As well as seeming genuinely interested, his enquirers had an agreeable concern that glasses, his and theirs, did not go empty. That, and his regular visits to the food and drink tables, ensured him a steady supply of very decent red wine. He was on a top-up excursion when the headmaster approached, leading a woman in her late twenties whose long auburn curls were beautifully set off by a dark green dress, cinched at the waist and with a tight hem just above the knees of her long, slim legs.

'Keir. I'd like you to meet Eryn Galbraith. I've just discovered that you two have something in common.' He opened his arms wide and for a moment Keir thought the headmaster was about to wrap an embrace around him and the lovely newcomer. Instead, he patted them both gently on the shoulder. 'Now I'll leave you to find out what it is,' he said.

Eryn shook Keir's hand. 'Typical Dr Bob, he knows when to be the playful one,' she said. 'I sometimes think it's one of the tools he uses.'

'Yeah. I've already seen him in action,' said Keir. 'When he took me on a tour of the school, we joined a story circle in the English classroom. In no time at all he'd entertained them with an impromptu song that led to a discussion about how we deal with the death of our loved ones. Masterly the way he did it. It reminded me of some of the things he says in *Children and Change*.'

'Ah. You do know a bit about his ideas then?'

'I read his book before I came here, and found it full of good sense. Especially when he talks about authority between adults and children. It was all new stuff to me. I'd never thought much about troubled kids who haven't had a fair crack from life. And the importance of being cared for by people who can act as good models to the youngsters. "Different, authentic and consistent adults". I think those are the words he uses.'

'And it's not just his ideas, it's the way he puts them into practice,' said Eryn. 'You can tell a lot about a school's philosophy by what happens when things go wrong. I mean, here we are in 1980 and children are still beaten with a belt in some residential schools. But not here. Instead, group counselling and other innovative techniques are used ... oops. Sorry. I don't mean to give a lecture. It's just that Laggandarroch is so far ahead of the other schools I visit. I'm a big fan, I suppose. So. Does that get us any closer to Dr Bob's tease about having something in common?'

'You're a jump ahead of me there. Everyone's been told what I'm doing at Laggandarroch. What's brought you here tonight?'

'I'm a psychologist. One of my specialties is the residential care of what are sometimes called difficult children, although in truth it's usually life that's been difficult to them. But that's not what I was talking to the headmaster about before he introduced us. I hadn't been talking to him about professional things at all.'

'So what were the pair of you talking about? There must be a clue in there somewhere.'

'About the holiday weekend. He asked if I had plans for it. I told him I was going to spend some time on my dad's boat at Kilbendrick.' She misinterpreted Keir's reaction. 'No need to be impressed, it's not as grand as it sounds. She's a converted fishing boat in the canal basin there. Well, partially converted. Dad's a bit of a perfectionist. He doesn't do things in a hurry.'

'It's not the boat. It's Kilbendrick. I was born there. During the war. That's why I'm here. You see, there was also a family connection to Laggandarroch castle. It's a bit complicated.'

'Have you visited Kilbendrick yet?'

'I have. That's a bit complicated too. It didn't work out so well.'

'My goodness. What a lot of "complicated"! And I always thought Australians were straightforward people.'

Keir thickened his accent. 'Strewth, we are, cobber. We are. Simple, that's us. It's against the law for an Australian to even say "complicated" before the age of twenty-one, and not until you can sing Waltzing Matilda backwards while drinking a pint of Fosters, mate.'

An infectious giggle shook her. Even her eyes seemed to join in. Remarkable amber eyes, shot through with verdant flecks that coalesced to form a narrow green band around the iris. You're stunning, he thought. 'I'll be visiting Kilbendrick again soon,' he heard himself say.

'When?'

'Maybe this weekend.'

'I'll be joining my dad at the boat on Sunday and we're staying over for the Monday holiday. She's called *Spaniard's Choice*. Glossy black hull, white superstructure.'

'Not a very local name?'

'She's named after a racehorse. Spaniard's Choice was the last runner in a four horse roll-up and it stormed home at twenty-to-one. That had a lot to do with Dad being able to buy the boat.'

They were interrupted by the headmaster calling to Keir. He had a portly, balding, chinless man with him. 'Looks like you're going to be claimed by the chairman of the board,' said Eryn. 'Expect to hear frequent use of the pronoun "I".' And she slipped quietly away.

True to Eryn's prediction, the chairman blew his own trumpet loudly and at length. Then his wife joined them, bringing with her the vice-chairwoman, a stick-thin retired librarian with a ghoulish interest in pressing Keir about the worst forms of death and mutilation he had witnessed. She in turn introduced him to other members of the board and so he was rotated around the room until the people he met began to merge into a blurry pattern of smiling faces, half-remembered names, and familiar questions. More and more he found his gaze drifting from his friendly enquirers to seek out the tall figure of Eryn, with her green dress and her cascading hair.

With some relief Keir spotted Dr Bob escorting the chairman and his wife towards the exit. Ah. The first move. Right. Watch for the headmaster's return. That would be a reasonable time to start taking his leave. Including saying goodbye to Eryn Galbraith.

He thought he'd been pacing himself well but he could feel a generous amount of booze begin to take charge as he listened as best he could to George Greene's account of the principles behind the restraint technique Keir had witnessed in the science class. Keir positioned himself so he could watch for the headmaster's reappearance.

'Y'see,' Greene continued. His speech had loosened and his cheeks were flushed, but he still looked to Keir like a mannequin from a high street window, 'Y'see, Ainsley and I only moved in on Donny once he picked up the broken glass. Up till then, time and patience would have done it. We'd never have touched him except maybe to pat him on the back when it was all over. And, of course, to remind him that he'd have to pay for the broken window with his own pocket money.' His wife nodded proudly, and gave Keir a look that seemed to say war reporters weren't the only heroes in the room. Fair dinkum, though a tad predictable. He felt his brain begin to numb. 'It all changed when he picked up the weapon. Not that there was much chance he'd use it on us. But we know how quickly he can cut his own wrist, so we had to deck him.' Deck? The verb didn't do justice to the skilled and sensitive way Keir had watched Greene, Ainsley and Janice control the enraged boy. Nor, Keir guessed, was it a word that Greene would use when sober. You're more pissed than I am, mate, he thought.

The hall door burst open. Rosemary the glue sniffer looked unsteady but she was fast on her feet and had reached the tables of food and wine even as heads turned in her direction. She picked up the almost empty punch bowl and crashed it to the floor.

'You. Watson. You big bastard! You and your scabby wife. I hate yous! Bastards!' She took hold of the linen tablecloth and began to tug. But, from the moment they'd spotted the girl, several staff, Ainsley Watson amongst them, had started to converge on her. There was a brief, noisy, unequal struggle. Rosemary, her legs and arms firmly held, was carried, struggling and swearing, out of the hall just as the headmaster returned.

'Ah. A gatecrasher,' Dr Bob said as the noise of Rosemary's departure echoed, and then faded, down the corridor. 'Always a sign of a good party.' But Keir saw him whisper to the school matron who was picking up pieces of broken crystal. Very soon her staff were collecting empty plates and glasses and creating the discrete bustle that signals the appropriate time to leave.

Eryn was easy to find.

'Hey, that was a kerfuffle,' he said. 'I wonder what narked that young lady?'

'Oh yes, Rosemary. A lass who's had a very difficult life. But if they can't deal with her here, they can't deal with her anywhere. She's in good hands at Laggandarroch.'

She held out her own hand. 'It's been a pleasure meeting you, Keir. If you make it to Kilbendrick, please drop by the boat. Just ask for directions to the Basin. The Kilbendrick natives are a friendly bunch, even to complicated Australians.'

He floated home in the light-headed, loose-footed company of wine. His mind flickered through the evening in a series of scenes and soundbites. Gloria's vulpine appraisal as he stood on the rostrum. Vulpine. Yeah, that'll do nicely. Do nicely too for the reddish eyes of that spooky spinster who wanted to hear all about blood and gore. And what about the robotic science teacher rambling on to the trite accompaniment of his tepid wife. And … POW! The spectacular shatter of the crystal bowl. And the fury that followed.

And Eryn Galbraith.

Oh yes. Eryn.

A debate broke out inside his head: Listen mate, she's given you a hot invite to the boat. Nah, it was fifty-fifty tops – maybe I even suggested it first. Yeah, but who made the last approach, who squeezed your hand goodbye and almost begged you aboard the Spaniard's whatsit? Okay, but I've decided to ease off that tricky Clydeside stuff and get stuck in here at Laggandarroch. No probs, you can put in a full boardroom shift tomorrow and have a Kilbendrick break on Sunday.

Who's fooling who here?

He had reached his cottage by the time the argument fizzled out. Next door, Gloria's windows were dark. No doubt she'd be up to her armpits in the aftermath of the barney that Rosemary started. He'd make sure the lights were out in his place by the time she arrived home. Anyway, he needed to get the head down so he'd be ready for a long working day.

He was scarcely through his own door before sleep reached out and led him straight to bed.

Sixteen

Keir woke early from a tender dream and lay savouring the details. Cambodia. Soft warm night. Swish and gurgle of the river currents. Shushing palms, croaking frogs. He and Chandina naked as one with the velvet star-studded sky.

A tender dream?

From Cambodia?

'Thank you,' he said, loud enough to hear.

By seven he was at his desk in the cottage window, with a full pot of coffee and the notes he had made yesterday in the boardroom. He started with a list of the names of the eighteen men identified alongside Nessa Glover in the caption of the "Cooperation not Conflict" weekend photograph. Although he'd decided his starting point would be an overview of Laggandarroch's history, he would pounce on any mention of these men along the way. Nessa spent a weekend here in their company in June of 1943. He'd been born in March of 1944. Someone in the photograph could have known who made Nessa pregnant. Could have known who was his ... his what? His "true" father? His "biological" father?

He slipped a fresh sheet into his typewriter, headed it "Joe Connor (1903-1980)" and added "Marine engineer and trade union activist. Attended several events at Harmony in this role. My father."

That would do for now. He wanted to move on to each of the others, to focus on the strangers, not the dad he grew up with. He continued to think of Joe as his father. Of course he did. Someone who had been your parent for thirty-six years couldn't simply be rubbed out on account of a deathbed letter. On account of some unexpected twist of history.

He thought back to the childhood stories. Of how his father hadn't gone to war to shoot the Germans. Instead he'd stayed in Scotland and built the ships that beat them. He'd fought another fight to make working people's lives better. How he was helped by a man who lived in a big castle. Long ago stories that became more reluctantly told as Keir grew to ask questions, to seek details. Until at last the stories were refused, the questions swept aside. Because. Because the war was old history. Because wars were bad. Because people were bombed and killed. Because it was better to forget. Because Australia was a new life. Because his father's whisky glass was filled again. Because his parents were living through one of their silences. Because his mother beckoned and hushed him with a cuddle. Long ago in childhood when he was innocent and ignorant. Innocence and ignorance. They seemed so related.

He assigned a sheet to each of the other men, leaving Fergus Abercrombie until last. This final page he divided into two columns headed "Fergus Abercrombie (1873-1947)" and "Charles Fourier (1772-1837)." Keir had figured out from his brief acquaintance yesterday with *The Reluctant Capitalist* that if he wanted to understand why Joe Connor was a regular at Harmony, and what attracted Nessa in 1943, he had to understand more about Fergus Abercrombie. That meant also understanding the ideas of the French utopian philosopher.

In the first column, he began setting out a bullet point summary of the life story told in the introduction to Abercrombie's book.

His desk telephone rang

'Hello? Keir Connor.'

'It's Bob McNeil, Keir. Sorry to bother you this early, and on a Saturday.' Keir heard tension behind the politeness. 'Are you planning to work down at the school today?'

'Yes. I'll be there quite soon.'

'Could you drop in past my office please? Something's happened, and I'm hoping you may be able to help.'

'How soon do you want me there?'

'As soon as you can.'

Keir picked up his car keys. Didn't sound like this was a day for a saunter through the trees. As he started the engine, Gloria's door began to open, but he didn't dally.

The headmaster was on the scruffy side of casual. He looked as if he had tumbled into the shapeless old sweater and tired, baggy tracksuit bottoms. His face seemed to have slumped into jowls that bristled with white stubble.

'Thanks for coming so quickly. And please excuse my appearance. It's been a long night.' He picked up a coffee pot from the tray on his desk, waved it in the air, and refilled his own cup when Keir shook his head, '... and the troubles are by no means over. I fear we're going to be the focus of some media attention. I thought you might be able to give me some advice about how to handle that. I hope that's not presumptuous of me?'

'Not at all. I'll certainly help if I can.'

'Maybe if I summarise what's happened we can take it from there?'

Keir nodded and took out a notebook.

'Rosemary, the girl who made the scene in the hall last night, is currently in hospital being treated for a broken leg and other injuries apparently as a result of being assaulted by Ainsley Watson.' Keir began making notes as the headmaster continued. 'I say apparently because police inquiries are ongoing. There are several witnesses and Ainsley's not denying that he struck the girl. I've suspended him, as I have to in the circumstances, and he's at home awaiting developments. The police are currently processing the statements they've taken and will return later today when I think there's a strong likelihood Ainsley Watson will be charged with assault.

'Before I called you I'd just had a long telephone conversation with the school chairman. You met him last

130

night. He's the local councillor, he's one of the biggest landowners around here, and he's a man of many, what shall I say, informal contacts including amongst council officials and the police. Despite it being early on Saturday morning, his phone has been busy. The head of social work. A police inspector. The editor of The Perthshire Journal.' Dr Bob counted them off on his fingers. 'I've been told to expect queries from the press.'

'Oh-oh. Okay. I've got the general picture. How do you usually deal with journalists?'

'Usually? I haven't been in this position before.'

'You mean journalists have never shown any interest in Laggandarroch?'

'Not in my time, apart from the occasional low-key mention – an item about a fund-raising sale, that sort of thing. But I've never had to deal with potentially hostile questions from people looking for a sensational story.'

'What makes you think that's what you're facing?'

Keir heard rasping as the headmaster rubbed at his chin. 'Up until a few years ago, nobody really bothered about what happened in schools like this. Bad kids were sent away from home for doing bad things and that was that. But there's been a revolution in how Scotland deals with its troublesome children. Juvenile courts have been abolished and replaced with a system that puts the welfare of the child before society's demand for punishment. The slogan "needs not deeds" captures the new philosophy quite neatly: unacceptable behaviour is a cry for help rather than a wilful or criminal act on the child's part.'

'Yeah. Sounds remarkably enlightened,' said Keir. 'What's the link to what happened last night between Rosemary and Ainsley Watson?'

'Just this. That enlightenment doesn't go down well with a lot of people who'd prefer to see the return of the birch or the fabled policeman whose one clip around the ear dependably

131

turned a hooligan into a solid member of society. So when, a couple of months ago, three boys from a residential school such as this went home on weekend leave, sniffed lots of glue, and toppled more than a hundred gravestones in an Edinburgh cemetery, the media had a feeding frenzy.'

'Ah. Okay. I'm getting there.' Keir consulted his notes. 'Glue sniffing seems to have played a part with Rosemary too. Can you tell me more about it? I know we've a problem back home with young people sniffing petrol. I think maybe that's something similar but I've never had cause to check it out in any detail.'

'You're right. Same thing. The correct term's "solvent abuse". There's a long history of intoxication using the fumes from different substances. In the nineteenth century there were public events where people were encouraged to sniff what was then called laughing gas, then entertain the audience with their silly antics. You probably won't find a doctor whose student days didn't include fun with chloroform.

'There's been a growing problem with youngsters in this country since the mid-seventies. They call it "buzzing". The most popular choice is household glue. Put it into a plastic bag, fit it around your nose and mouth, and inhale deeply. Reddening around that facial area is often what first raises suspicion. That's what put us on to Rosemary and Kath this week.'

'What started them off?'

'Rosemary had a difficult home visit last weekend. Before she came back here on Sunday, she stole money from her step-father, and went shopping for supplies. Thanks to a police campaign, shops are cautious about selling more than a single tube to youngsters. Maybe she made multiple buys, maybe she found an unscrupulous shop owner. One way or another she managed to acquire a large amount of glue, smuggle it into school, and stash it at various spots around the campus.'

'So it's a high profile problem?'

'Currently, yes. There have been a few deaths. Unfortunately, these have prompted ill-judged scare campaigns that frighten parents, teachers and social workers but have just about no deterrent effect on the sniffers.'

'And it regularly makes newspaper headlines?'

'Oh yes. Sensational ones.'

'Right. Could you give me a bit more about what actually happened last night?'

'When Rosemary went do-lally, she was dealt with swiftly and correctly. She was obviously out of control and incapable of doing anything about that. She was properly restrained, carried upstairs, and handed into the care of the staff who were on duty there. Unfortunately she managed to break free from them. She charged after Ainsley Watson who was making his way back downstairs. By all accounts she was enraged and swearing as she flew at him. You'll have to pardon my language, but I think you need to know exactly what she was shouting: "You're a lying fucker Watson. See your dying poxy cunt of a wife. She's what you deserve."'

Keir winced.

'Quite so. Not easy for any of us to listen to, never mind someone in Ainsley's position. As he warded off her attack, he hit her across the face. A hard blow – she has a black eye and other facial bruising. She tumbled on down the stairs, landed very badly and has a nasty compound fracture of her right leg.'

'Wheeow.' Keir put down his pen. The two men looked at one another in silence.

The headmaster massaged his forehead. 'Any questions?'

'Why didn't Ainsley Watson and the people who carried her from the hall see the incident through to the end? That's what worked so well when Donny was being dealt with.'

'Yes. Well spotted. Those at the party were off duty. To

133

allow maximum attendance, we'd sent as many pupils as we could home for the weekend, but there are always a few for whom that's not possible, and a small number of staff were looking after them upstairs.'

Keir wasn't getting it. 'But surely, in an emergency, it doesn't matter whether staff are technically on or off duty?'

'That's correct. The staff in the hall acted promptly in Rosemary's best interests. There is, however, an unfortunate detail. They'd all been drinking alcohol. Including Ainsley Watson. In most circumstances that would be a disciplinary matter. That's why they handed responsibility over to the duty staff as soon as they could.'

Keir could see the headlines now: 'Yeah, I get it. "Glue Sniffing Pupil Assaulted After Drunken Staff Party". You've got a bit of a dog's breakfast here. You seemed to make light of Rosemary's shenanigans at the time, but I reckon you were more troubled than you looked.'

'Yes. I was putting a public face on an embarrassing incident but I was extremely concerned about the staff and alcohol issue and wanted to get upstairs to check things out as soon as I could. The duty leader made the right decisions. She called an ambulance and sent someone down to tell me discretely there'd been a major incident but it was under control. Could I come upstairs as soon as the guests were off the premises?'

'What'll happen to Ainsley Watson? I met his wife last night. The girl's words must've kicked him where it hurts.'

'Ainsley is...' Dr Bob hesitated, '... *has been* a key member of staff at Laggandarroch. Our staff have chosen to work with some of the most disadvantaged young people this country produces. Kids who'll test for your weakness, your Achilles' heel. They'll kick, they'll swear, they'll spit in your face. They'll challenge your sexuality, foul-mouth your wife or husband, threaten your children. They'll steal your belongings. It's part of the job to live with that, absorb it, and continue to act in the best interests of the child. I'm not saying for a moment it's easy. But there is no wriggle room. Nor can there be. An assault on a pupil is both criminal and unprofessional. It can never be condoned. If Ainsley is charged he'll remain suspended until the court case. If he's found guilty he'll be dismissed.'

'I get that, but it still seems harsh to me.'

'Life's been very harsh for our pupils. Most are at the end of a destructive downward spiral. Out of control at home, out of control at school. Parents can't cope, schools throw them out, their foster placements collapse, children's homes pass them on like damaged parcels. They come here. They test us and test us. Gradually the message sinks in. We can handle them until they learn to do it for themselves. They're safe from harm here. They're the ones who deserve a second chance. That's why, if Ainsley assaulted Rosemary, he won't get one.'

'Yeah. I can see that now. So let's talk about the media. You might find it helpful at this stage to make a distinction between the detailed information we've been discussing, and the facts that a journalist is likely to uncover at this stage. Adopt a simple strategy – don't give out any information that a journalist doesn't already have.'

'I'm not sure I follow you.'

'You know from the school chairman that questions are already being asked. Journalists will learn that a pupil from this school's in hospital with injuries. They might also find out the police are involved, but that's by no means certain. I think you should prepare a press release – I'll come to that in a moment – that simply confirms someone has been hurt.'

'A press release? Really? Please don't think I'm challenging your judgement, you're the expert here and I'm most grateful for your help – but my instinct is to say as little as possible.'

'Yeah, I can understand that. Try looking at it this way.

It's a dead cert that journalists will come creeping around asking questions. The worst thing you can do is try to say nothing when something's already known. Saying "no comment" makes it sound like you're trying to cover up. But you can stay in charge of what you do say, and only add to it *if* and *when* you have to.' Keir scribbled on his pad then read to the headmaster the few lines he had written. '*Laggandarroch School. Seventeenth of May nineteen-eighty. One of our pupils is receiving hospital treatment following an incident at the school yesterday. The child, whose family has been informed, is comfortable and is expected to make a full recovery.* As you can see, lots of information's omitted: the name and gender of the pupil, the injuries, which hospital, the details of what happened, the involvement of the police. You're simply confirming the basic information that journalists will have, but not giving them anything else to feed on.'

'Yes. That's making sense to me. Most helpful. How do the journalists then get the press release?'

Keir thought for a moment. 'It's very early days and it's a developing situation. Your best bet's a holding statement until the police decide about charging Watson. This is a holiday weekend, and that'll probably work to your advantage. At a guess, the most that's likely to happen today are a couple of telephone calls from any Sunday papers who've picked up on Rosemary being injured, probably through contacts they have at the hospital or in the police. My advice would be to read the press statement out to them on the telephone and say absolutely nothing else, whatever questions they might ask. If anyone turns up unexpectedly, give them a copy and say no further information's available at this time. And stick to that, because they'll be persistent.'

'Should I speak to them myself?'

'No. Or if you have to, don't identify yourself as headmaster or the quote'll be attributed to you and you'll also be pressured for more information. It's probably a good idea to have someone act as the school spokesperson.'

'Right. Anything else I should do?'

'Yeah. Plan ahead. Depending on what happens, you could be in for a lot of media scrutiny. Believe me, they'll focus on the sensational; staff violence, a boozy party, glue-sniffing pupils, and all the rest. You can try to balance that with press releases. It would be a good idea too if you have information available about Laggandarroch School: your staff, your pupils, your way of working. You've told me about the positive feedback you've received from school inspectors. Get positive quotes from those reports and have them typed up. That brochure you sent me? Make sure you have plenty of them available.'

'Fine. I see where you're coming from. I'll give Miss Baxter a call and we'll get to work. She never flinches at being here when circumstances require it. You know what?' The lopsided grin flashed briefly. 'I think she'd love to be our press spokesperson.'

He stood up and held out his hand. Keir shook it. 'Thank you,' the headmaster said. 'I'm in new territory here, and I can see it could get worse before it gets better. But, to quote myself, "Fear of the new is the enemy of change."'

'I'll be working upstairs in the boardroom if you need me,' Keir told him.

Seventeen

The grandfather clock in the corner had just struck noon when Dr Bob joined Keir in the boardroom. He looked much more his usual self, freshly shaved and comfortably clad in generous navy cords and a loose-fitting grey linen shirt, but his face was sombre.

'Are you stopping for lunch?' he asked.

'I'm not planning to.' Keir gestured towards a plastic box. 'I've brought a snack to keep me going. I want to put in a full day here, then I'm heading off to Kilbendrick for tomorrow and Monday.'

'Really?' A cheeky smile parted the clouds. 'Why don't you go round by the harbour? I believe Eryn Galbraith will be on a boat somewhere there. You remember Eryn? You met her last night?'

'Yeah, sure I remember her.' Keir ignored the headmaster's fishing.

'Ah. Good. Good luck.'

'Any developments?'

'Yes. The police are coming at four o'clock this afternoon. They want Ainsley to be present. I've phoned him with the news.'

'How is he?

'He seems stoical. Prepared for the worst. Not too keen to talk about it at this stage. Understandable, I suppose. Apart from the call from the police, all's quiet downstairs. Miss Baxter is perched like a predator beside the telephone, ready to pounce on the first journalist who tries to winkle information from her. In the meantime she's working on extracts from Inspectorate reports.'

He laid his hand lightly on Keir's shoulder. 'Thank you again for your advice. Much appreciated. By habit I'm a keen consumer of news and current affairs. But my school and I possibly making the headlines? Ah. I'm finding that a most uncomfortable prospect.' He breathed deeply and let out a sigh, as if both to accept the situation and dismiss it from their conversation. 'Now. How about you? So glad to see you making an enthusiastic start on the project. Very early days, of course, but how's it looking?'

'I've decided on a two-pronged approach. I'll delve into the archive here, which'll help with Laggandarroch's history and also give me an understanding of what brought my rellies here in the 1940s. I'll combine that with some work in the Clydeside area. That's where Kilbendrick comes in.' He turned an innocent face to the headmaster. 'Honest.'

'Yes. I'm convinced.' Dr Bob pointed to a large tattered oilcloth map rolled out on the boardroom table. 'That looks very interesting. "Harmony Community, Laggandarroch Castle, Perthshire". I don't remember seeing it before.'

'I think it's the original version of the map that appears in Fergus Abercrombie's book. It gives the overall layout as well as these detailed floor plans. I found it behind a wooden filing cabinet during one of my trawls through the cupboard. I suspect that dark hole has lots of other treasure to yield.' Keir picked up *The Reluctant Capitalist*. 'Maybe this has too. Have you read it?'

'Not cover-to-cover. I've picked at it now and again out of a sense of historical duty. It seems very dated now. I don't mean any disrespect to Fergus here,' he nodded towards the portrait on the wall, 'if it hadn't been for him and his generosity we wouldn't be talking in this fine room today. By all accounts he was a charismatic man who inspired others to great levels of loyalty and commitment but, alas, I find his prose rather leaden.'

'Believe me, he's a literary wizard compared to Charles Fourier,' said Keir. He picked up another book. 'This is a nineteenth century translation of some of Fourier's ideas and, oh boy, it sure is dense in places. I don't think the

139

translators deserve the blame. They were dealing with some weird ideas and strange vocabulary. Sometimes it seems like he's making up words as he goes along. But I can see what attracted Fergus Abercrombie. Fourier rejected the Industrial Revolution because, to his mind, its production methods inevitably cause economic and social conflict. That conflict in turn alienates us from what Fourier called "Universal Harmony and the satisfaction of our Passions."' He used his voice and his hands to stress Universal Harmony and Passions. 'Our mate Fourier is a big fan of Emphatic Capitals.'

'Fergus Abercrombie picks up on Fourier's themes in his own book,' Keir continued. 'There were several Phalanxes – that's what Fourier called his idealised communities – in the USA in the mid-nineteenth century. In France too. Compared to Harmony, they were all short-lived, and Abercrombie was sure that was because they had cherry-picked the parts of Fourier's thinking that suited them and dismissed the rest. Abercrombie believed he would succeed where these other communes failed, because he would lead the community towards a more pure expression of Fourian philosophy. He also hints that some of Fourier's more unusual ideas would become the basis for some sort of inner circle. He seems to be saying that there would be a two-tier aspect to the commune. Does that tie in with what you know of Harmony's history?'

'In truth, I don't know a great deal about it.' Dr Bob gestured around the boardroom. 'This was all here when I took over more than twenty years ago. Fergus Abercrombie had been dead for a decade by then, and I don't think the Harmony commune survived him for long. Apart from the school, that is. It lived an odd hybrid life before a charitable trust took it over in the mid-nineteen-fifties. There were still a few commune members around, Gloria Honeydew and Ainsley Watson amongst them, who either worked in the school or had jobs locally. They didn't speak much about

Harmony. What they did say painted a picture of an idealistic community which aimed for self-sufficiency and where traditional artisan skills – weaving, carpentry, blacksmithing and so on – were valued.' He pointed to the map. 'I believe there were some well-equipped workshops here in the west wing. Also, you'll notice that the original commune school wasn't in the castle. It was in this large wooden building which was pulled down in the nineteen-sixties to make way for the classroom block.

'But to get to your question about a two-tier Harmony. When I arrived there was tittle-tattle floating around about the breakup of the community after Fergus Abercrombie's death. Something about a split into two groups. And there were murmurings about unconventional family and sexual arrangements. I never paid much heed. Just think about it. An experimental commune? In douce Perthshire? You bet there were rumours, and the spicier, the better.'

Keir was studying the floor plans of the main castle building. 'The boardroom here, and the rooms above, are labelled Upper Seristery. Whereas the hall we were in last night and the surrounding rooms are called Main Seristery. Does that mean anything to you?'

'No.' Dr Bob checked *The Reluctant Capitalist*. 'Those terms don't appear in the index.' He unfolded the map that formed the book's endpapers. 'This map's labelled differently from the one you've discovered. Here the boardroom is called Meeting Hall. Downstairs is the Library.'

'I wonder why the difference? There must be some significance to it.'

'You could always ask your neighbour Gloria about life in the commune.' Dr Bob pointed to the girl in the "Cooperation not Conflict" weekend group photograph: 'You know this is Gloria? The girl here?'

'Yeah. With Ainsley beside her.'

'Just so. The lost days of innocence. Who'd have thought

it?' Dr Bob studied the photograph silently for a few moments. 'Thanks for taking my mind off the other business, but I'd better get back downstairs. I'll let you know what happens with the police.'

When the door closed behind the headmaster, Keir studied the two youngsters standing side by side at the picnic table. Ainsley, with his short trousers and his cropped hair, looked like a young boy. The long-legged girl beside him teetered on the edge of womanhood. Ask Gloria? Nah. Doesn't feel right. Not for now.

A motorcycle engine broke his concentration. He checked the grandfather clock. Three-fifty. From the window, he watched Ainsley Watson shut off the engine and pull the gleaming machine back onto its stand. He strapped his crash helmet around the front forks, smoothed his hair and beard with the palms of his hands, and headed for the castle's main entrance. Barely ten minutes later, an unmarked car crunched the gravel and parked beside the motorcycle. Two men about Keir's age, dressed in dark suits and ties, walked purposefully towards the school. One had a brown folder under his arm.

It was almost five o'clock when Keir heard voices outside and watched as Ainsley was led to the police car and driven away. The boardroom phone rang, and he was soon on his way to the headmaster's office.

'Terrible news. But not unexpected. Ainsley has been arrested on a charge of assault and has been taken to the police station for processing. He'll be released on police bail later today pending a court appearance.'

Keir thought through the implications. 'Those facts will almost certainly become known. But your strategy remains the same. Stick with the press release for now. If anyone asks about a member of staff being charged, Miss Baxter should tell them to contact the police directly about that. Have there been any enquiries so far?'

'Just one. From the *Sunday Standard*. It's a broadsheet, a quality paper. The reporter tried to push Miss Baxter on a couple of points. Mainly looking for more details of the incident itself and whether or not the police were involved.' The headmaster gestured towards the window. 'He might as well have tried to push over one of those mountains. He also asked if he could interview me. She told him to phone again about that on Monday.'

'Fine. That's all been well handled. Is there a date for the court appearance?'

'Not yet.'

'Let's hope they take their time. The rules here are the same as back in Australia, in fact we borrowed them from you. In the early days of an incident journalists can publish pretty much any detail they dig up. Once someone's charged the case becomes *sub judice* and the media can be charged with contempt if they report anything that could affect court proceedings. It's taken especially seriously when minors are involved. That should work in your favour for now.'

'What about the reporter who wants to talk to me?'

'Speak to him. But if he knows by then that a member of staff has been charged, tell him right away that you're unable to discuss such details and refer him to the police.'

Dr Bob rapped sharply on his desktop. 'Better than that – I should have thought of this earlier – I can't discuss or identify individual children. There's an issue of pupil confidentiality.'

'That's spot on. Client confidentiality debars you from speaking about any specific incident but you're happy to talk to him in general terms about what happens here at Laggandarroch. Send him the information Miss Baxter's working on. Or, if you feel okay about it, invite him to collect it in person, maybe look around. My guess is you won't see him. He's after a juicy story, not an account of the valuable work you do here. "Good news is no news" as the hacks say.'

Keir handed the headmaster a piece of paper. 'I'll be spending a couple of nights at Barton Hotel near Kilbendrick. Contact me there if you need me.'

Eighteen

Keir looked around the smaller of the two circular docks that formed the figure-of-eight mooring area known as the Kilbendrick Basin. Water from a canal cascaded noisily over a lock gate and flowed past a motley collection of boats in various states of repair or, in a few cases, of decay. None of them matched the description Eryn had given, so he followed a short section of canal that passed beneath a disused rusty-red railway viaduct and flowed into the larger lower basin. Beyond it, he could see the broad tidal expanse of the River Clyde sparkling in the hot afternoon sunshine.

Just one vessel had the classic profile of a wooden fishing boat – graceful lines sweeping down from a high prow, superstructure set well back to accommodate a large hold, masts fore and aft. Her glossy black hull, broken only by white lines picking out the waterline and the scuppers, reflected the ripples in shimmering highlights. Her name adorned the bow in proud gold script: *Spaniard's Choice*. She was moored on the far side of the basin within a stone's throw of the river. There was no sign of anyone aboard, but Keir could see the hatch covers were off and could hear the sounds of work in progress – hammering punctuated now and then with the whizz of a power saw.

To reach the boat, he had to cross lock gates where water tumbled twenty feet into a chamber connecting the mooring basin to Kilbendrick harbour. The walkway was a bare wooden board. When Keir stepped up, he could feel it shudder to the roar of the cascading water that fell in a continuous glassy sheet until it crashed into frothy turmoil below, spitting up flecks of yellowish spume that climbed towards him in the turbulent air. There was no handrail; instead a slack rope was threaded through eyes in intermittent iron rods. Keir pulled his gaze away from the hypnotic uproar beneath and began to edge across. Beyond the harbour he could see the desolation that once had been Henderson's yard. The swirling updraft from the waterfall at his feet bombarded him with the same contradictory smells that had contributed to his troubles during his visit to Henderson's just a few days ago: sweetness, grass, ozone; and beneath these, dark echoes of oil, sulphur, rot.

His knuckles whitened around the hand rope as he felt the maelstrom pull him towards it. He struggled to keep himself upright. Safety was not far away but his feet seemed glued to the walk board. With a great effort of will, he forced his left foot forward an inch or two, then his right, then his left again, until at last he was able to step down onto solid cobbles. He took a deep breath then headed towards *Spaniard's Choice*.

'Keir! Keir! Great! You made it!' Eryn waved a welcome from the deck. She was wearing pale green overalls. Lengths of auburn curls escaped from beneath a floppy cotton hat. A man's head appeared at the top of a ladder into the hold.

'Dad, it's Keir. I told you about him.'

The man climbed onto the deck and waved Keir up the short gangplank. 'Welcome aboard.' He held out his hand. 'I'm Vincent, Eryn's father.' The warmth of their greetings chased away the dark shadow that had ambushed him on the lock gates. He hoped his smile was up to the job.

'Why don't you take Keir up to the galley and fix a cup of tea?' said Vincent, 'Just give me a shout when it's ready. I can manage down below now that the framing's up.'

'You mean, "do something useful and stay out of my way."'

'Nonsense. It would have taken me twice as long if you hadn't been on the other end of those four-by-twos.'

'Hear that, Keir? All I'm good for is to hold the end of a plank. I never get to do the skilled stuff.'

'You will. Every good boat builder has to spend an apprenticeship just holding on to the far end.' He disappeared into the hold.

The galley aft of the wheelhouse was long and cramped, but the windows that formed one side created a bright airiness and gave a wide view of Kilbendrick nestling beneath steeply climbing hills. A narrow table was fitted along the window wall; a cooker, a sink, work-surfaces and storage space took up the other side. Keir sat at the table out of Eryn's way. As she sorted out the tea, she chatted about how her father planned to keep *Spaniard's Choice* as a sea-going vessel. He was converting the large fish hold into more living space – a lounge and kitchen as well as two good-sized cabins. But for the moment they had to use the original galley and the cramped crew quarters below it.

Keir felt he had to interrupt. 'It's a shame to mention professional stuff on such a fine day but I'd best tell you before your father joins us. That carry-on at the end of Friday night's party ended very badly.'

She listened while he summarised Rosemary's injuries, Watson's arrest, and his own discussions with the headmaster. 'Has anything appeared in the Sunday papers? We never buy them when we're here.'

'Nah. I've had a quick scan. Nothing. It's a non-story until they discover a staff member's been charged with assault. If the other elements – staff drinking, pupil glue-sniffing – leak out, they could make juicy headlines. There might be rocky days ahead.'

Eryn was quiet while she thought over what he'd said. 'Thanks, you were right to tell me. I'd have hated to find out from sensational media stories. I'll talk to the headmaster and I'll arrange to see Rosemary. But for now, it's the May holiday, the sun's shining, and the tea's brewed. I'll give Dad a shout.' She turned at the galley door: 'And I've still got your complicated Kilbendrick history to hear about.'

'Yeah, but only if you're interested.'

'I am.'

'Okay. Why not come with me to the village? I'll clue you in on the way there.'

At her father's suggestion they had tea in the wheelhouse. Upriver, the Clyde passed beneath the high, gentle arc of the Erskine Bridge, then disappeared around a bend in the direction of Clydebank. Immediately downstream lay Kilbendrick harbour, then the river, with craggy hills on one side, and lush woods and fields on the other, continued to widen towards the estuary and the far hills.

'That's a brilliant view!' said Keir. 'And you get a different look at the boat from up here. She's a stunner.'

'Thank you,' said Eryn's father. 'She was built as a herring drifter in 1937. Forty-seven foot, heavy larch over oak timbering. Properly looked after, the hull will last forever. One-hundred-and-ninety-eight horse power, five cylinder Gardner diesel. Nine knots cruising, twelve knots max. Gaff ketch rigged...'

'Dad. Dad.' Eryn held up her hands as if begging for mercy. 'Way too much information.'

'Are you a shipbuilder to trade?' Keir asked.

'No. I'm an industrial designer. Although I mostly teach now, at a technical college in Glasgow.'

'Industrial design. Hmm. That's a vague area for me.'

'It's quite straightforward. Think about an object's function. And about its form. Then understand these two qualities are inextricably linked. Take this boat; she was designed to sail in wild seas, to catch fish, store them, and bring them and her crew safely to shore. The requirements of that function also give her a beautiful form. If she had been built ugly, she wouldn't do her job so well.'

Keir pointed upriver to the pencil-thin line of the Erskine Bridge and the twin needles of its cable-supporting towers. 'If I'm following you,' he said, 'that bridge is elegant because it's well-designed to span the river and carry traffic safely across it. Would you take it that far? A causal connection between beauty and function?'

'Yes, I would. An intellectually elegant solution to a design brief will also be aesthetically pleasing. The beauty of that bridge is fundamentally linked to the way it's designed and constructed. Technically, it's a box girder suspension bridge. One of the first in Britain. They begin by erecting the two cable towers, then build the slim box girder sections out from each side. It was a great day when they met in the middle.'

From behind her father's back, Eryn was trying to catch Keir's attention. 'Okay, Dad,' she said. 'Keir's got some business to see to while he's in Kilbendrick.'

'That'll take me to the Bendrick Inn,' said Keir. 'I could buy you both a drink, maybe a meal?'

'Not me. I've big plans for what I want to get done this weekend. I'm sure Eryn'll want to go. She's fed up holding planks for me, as she calls her essential work aboard this craft. But don't expect culinary treats in the Bendrick. A hot pie if you're lucky. Which reminds me, Eryn said you're interested in the Clydebank Blitz.'

'Yes. That's one of the reasons I'm here.'

'I lived through it. I'm from a Bankie family. I was just eighteen. In fact I received my call-up papers a week after the Blitz. I'll never forget the awful scenes of those two terrible nights. But what I remember most was the camaraderie, the determination of people to stick together, not to be broken by the destruction raining down on them. We didn't seem to dwell on the loss of homes, the maiming of people, the deaths. You were more likely to hear a funny story than a horror story when people got together and talked about it.'

Eryn was watching her father with tolerant bemusement. 'Dad. I can usually follow your roundabout storytelling. But what's this got to do with eating at the Bendrick?'

'Ah yes. Thanks dear. The Bendrick pie. You see, when the bombers struck, people had been ignoring air raid warnings for over a year. Always false alarms. So they didn't run for the shelters until the bombs were exploding around them. In those days, dentures were poorly made and lots of people removed them after they'd finished their evening meal. So this family were racing for their lives when the grandfather turned and started to run back to the tenement. His son raced after him. "Where the hell are you going Da?" "Ah've forgot my false teeth." "False teeth?" the son roared. "D'ye think that's pies they're dropping?"'

Keir's appreciative chuckle triggered a hiccupy two-tone laugh in the other man. It started softly then gradually became more raucous as he luxuriated in his own joke. Keir felt Eryn tug his shirt sleeve. She led him gently out of the wheelhouse door and down onto the deck.

When Eryn stepped off the gangplank and headed for the lock he had crossed earlier, Keir felt uneasy. 'Do we have to go that way to Kilbendrick?' he asked.

'It's quickest,' she said.

'It's just – I didn't feel very safe coming over. Could do with a better railing, maybe?' He'd have preferred to say nothing, but what if he then made a fool of himself?

'It's fine. I've used it hundreds of times.' They were approaching the long wooden beam, made of heavy square timber, that was an extension of the lock gate and was used to swing it open and shut. Eryn ran the remaining few paces, sprang and landed neatly on the beam's flat top. 'C'mon,' she shouted, holding out her hand. 'I'll take the high road and you take the low road. Come on!' she urged more forcefully when he hesitated, 'I've done this loads of times.'

When he took her hand she immediately set off at a brisk walking pace along the top of the beam. He didn't know how to protest and when he reached the walk board and she shouted 'Hup' he had no choice but to step up onto it. She continued along the top of the lock gates, slightly ahead of him, pulling his hand steadily. He was scarcely aware of making the crossing, then he heard her shout 'Down,' and he was off and back on solid ground again. She jumped down beside him and landed with a gymnast's bounce. 'There,' she said.

He stifled his laughter, afraid it would come out as hysterical. He felt pleased with himself and even more delighted with her. 'How on earth...?' he began.

'I was around here a lot as a kid. I was a bit of a tomboy and played with some local daredevils.' She nodded at the lock gate. 'That's nothing compared to some of the antics we got up to.'

'Well, you've certainly impressed me, lady. So you grew up here?'

'No, I'm a city girl from the centre of Glasgow. But Dad's always had a boat of some kind here. And he always made sure they had at least a couple of bunks so we could stay over for weekends and holidays. We'd go cruising down the Clyde too, sometimes as far as the open sea.'

'And is your mum a sailor too?'

There was a pause. Had he asked the wrong question?

'Mum died when I was quite small, I was just three years old.'

'Oh my, I'm so sorry. What happened?'

'She suffered from what people back then called a bad chest, in her case bronchitis that could become chronic for periods. Then in 1952 Glasgow was plagued by winter smog, a serious form of pollution caused by a combination of fog and coal smoke, basically. And it can be lethal for people with existing breathing problems. The old and infirm tend to be the victims. Mum was just twenty-seven when she developed pneumonia that proved fatal.'

She gave a helpless shrug. 'And that was that. Dad became a single parent. And I learned to be a fearless lock gate walker. What about you? I'm very curious.'

Keir gave a brief summary during the five minute walk to

Kilbendrick. That suited his mood. He felt good in himself, had a beautiful lively companion, and didn't want to take any risk of blighting their day. By the time they approached the Bendrick Inn, Eryn knew only that he had already planned the trip to research his Scottish background, then his father died and left Keir a letter explaining that he and his wife Sarah were not in fact Keir's biological parents.

Keir led Eryn past the pub door and further down the village street. 'I'd like to show you something else first.' He stopped outside Sadie's Kut and Kurl, a shop on the ground floor of a tenement building. 'That's where I was born.'

'In a hairdresser's shop?'

'No. At number one Erskine View, Kilbendrick on 25th March 1944. The home of Joe and Sarah Connor. That's what it says on my birth certificate.' He pointed to the lintel above the common close that gave access to the various tenement apartments. Carved into the sandstone was "Erskine View 1860". He then led Eryn up the close to the first door on the right. It bore the number one. 'That's the original door into what's now the hairdressers. I called in there last week. The owner confirmed that it was converted to a shop in the nineteen-sixties.'

'But how does Nessa – your real mum – fit in?'

'I'm hoping I might find an answer or two back there in the Bendrick Inn. Something I learned in my cub reporter days. You can do worse than start in the local pub.'

'I can see how that might work in your home territory. But here you're going to stand out like a beacon with that Australian accent.'

'Yeah. I've thought about that. Also, I don't know why my parents were so determined to hide the truth from me. So I don't plan to give too much away, probably just say I knew them in Australia. If pushed, I'm the son they adopted over there, but I won't go any further than that.'

The Bendrick Inn was a smoke-stained Formica-and-

152

linoleum pub. The large lounge area was busy. Eryn waved to some other boat enthusiasts. The bar itself was L-shaped, and the short leg of the "L" created a neuk where a group of regulars was comfortably at home. A barman, with the worldly ennui of a man who's seen it all and can't find much to get excited about, and with his shirt buttons threatened by a generous belly, moved between the locals and the two waitresses who scurried to and fro keeping the lounge customers happy.

'Australian, eh?' he said as he poured Keir's order. A shout of 'G'day mate!' came from the end the bar, followed by snickering laughter.

'G'day fellas.' Keir nodded and smiled towards the group. 'I'm hoping I can find out something about people who lived in the village during the war. Connor was the name.'

'Connor,' the barman said. 'There's a few Connors about here. Have you got an address? First names?'

'Yeah. They lived across the road. Bottom flat in Erskine View. Joe was his name. His wife was Sarah.'

'Was? So they're dead?'

'Sadly, yeah.'

'What were they to you?'

'I knew them in Australia. They emigrated at the end of the war, I think.'

'I was just a boy,' the barman said. 'But it does ring a bell for me. C'mon Erchie. You're the local encyclopaedia.'

The florid battered-looking character with a peaked engineer's cap had already turned towards Keir, his index finger raised to emphasise a point he'd yet to make. 'You're asking an interesting question there, son,' he said. He slipped off his stool and moved closer, preceded by the reek of stale beer. You smell like you've been in here for days, mate, thought Keir as the man studied him closely with boozy eyes: 'There was a bit of a mystery about what happened to them. There was a lot of talk at the time. But it was long ago,

I'm sketchy on the details.'

'Did you know them?' Keir asked.

'Aye. Joe Connor worked in Henderson's shipyard, in the fitting shop. And he was the shop steward for the yard. A well-respected man. They were a well-respected couple. Then there was some kind of family trouble. Caused quite a bit of bother. Joe was in a fight here one night. That wasn't like him. Then him and his wife disappeared. They just vanished. But then, it was the wartime. Funny things happened. Australia, eh?' Erchie scratched at his heavy stubble, as if deciding what more he should say. 'Listen, young yin, you should talk to Cyril Beattie. He worked in the fitting shop alongside Joe. They were pals. Mind you, I'm not saying Cyril'll talk to you. People always said he knew more about what happened, but he never wanted to speak about it. Maybe he thought some things were best left alone. Maybe they are, son.'

'Where can I find him?'

'Ask your girlfriend. You're off a boat in the basin, hen, aren't you?'

'Yes?' Eryn looked puzzled.

'If you've needed any engineering done, you'll know Cyril. Cyril,' he insisted, as if repeating the name emphatically would prompt recognition. And it did.

'Oh, Cyril,' she repeated, smiling. 'The engineering shop. The arches.'

'Aye. Cyril.' He showed her a set of tombstone teeth.

Keir looked from one to the other. 'C'mon, clue me in. Who's Cyril?'

'We passed him on our way here,' Eryn told him. 'His workshop's under one of the railway arches. He was outside in the sun stripping down an engine.' Keir took her by the hand and headed for the door. 'Thanks, fellas,' he shouted over his shoulder.

'What was that all about?' he heard the barman ask, as

the buzz grew at the bar.

Cyril Beattie was finished for the day.

'Joe and Sarah Connor, eh?' He put down a hefty padlock and turned to face Keir. His eyes narrowed and he tugged his oil-stained cap firmly onto his head. 'Who's asking?'

'I'm a friend. I knew them very well in Australia…'

'Who's asking?' He leaned slightly forward onto the balls of his feet.

'They made me really interested in Kilbendrick, and the Blitz. So I thought…'

He raised his hand to silence Keir. 'Could you maybe try a wee bit harder, my friend. Who's asking?'

'My name's Keir Connor. I'm Nessa Glover's son.' The words seemed to release themselves.

'Aye. I can see her in you.' He pulled open one of the doors he had just closed. 'Fancy a cup of tea? I'll shove on the kettle.'

Nineteen

So they're both dead? Aye. I wondered. Seventy-seven you say? That'd be right enough. Joe was just about ten years older than me. We were good pals, but I looked up to him too. He was kind of a big brother to me, Joe was.

The last time I saw him was 25th March 1944. Aye, that's right. The day you were born. I might as well warn you straight away. There are lots of things I don't know, that I can't help you with. But I can give you a truer story than the likes of Erchie McKerrel. Erchie was just a boy at the time. He looks older than me? Aye well, he's spent a lot more of his life in the Bendrick. He probably can't remember what day of the week it is, never mind what happened in 1944. A few well-pickled shreds of gossip, that'll be his lot. I'll tell you what I know. Hear me out first and then I'll answer your questions. If I can.

I wasn't the only one that looked up to Joe. I'll tell you this, you earn your respect in a shipyard, it's not handed out like sweeties. Joe Connor had two things in his favour. He was a first-class marine engineer. One of the best. I served my apprenticeship under him. No small thanks to Joe that I'm not a bad fitter myself. The other thing people admired, Joe was a man of principle. He set up the first union in Henderson's, he was the yard's first shop steward. He led the first ever strike in 1932. It was a dispute about the lack of washing facilities in the yard and Joe won the right for people involved in unusually dirty work – repairing inside a ship's boiler, say – to get time off with pay and go to the public baths in Clydebank. Even got the employers to pay their bus fares and admission. He'd a brass neck, Joe. The Henderson brothers weren't fit for him.

Then he started going to a place in Perthshire with his brother-in-law, Hugh Glover. Aye. Nessa's man. It was some kind of a big castle, run by a rich American guy who was full of fancy ideas. Oh, you're staying there? Right. Harmony. Aye, that was the name of it. Well, Joe and Hugh came across notions there that had a big influence on them. Why fight about things if you could find ways of working them out? Co-operate, don't knock lumps off one another. That's why, when the war started, Joe wasn't keen on walkouts or strikes, and sometimes that made him unpopular with other people in the union.

But Joe changed. It was something that happened during the war, but I'm not sure the war caused it. Oh aye, it was hellish, Hugh and the four kids being killed in the Blitz. For a long time, Nessa was in a terrible state. Hardly ever speaking, just rocking by the fire nursing her wean's blanket, or walking about like a zombie in all weathers. But a lot of people had to face up to the same kind of things. And there was somebody else to blame for it. The Nazis. The bad guys. They sent over the bombers that flattened Clydebank. No, I don't think that's what started it with Joe.

More likely it was the death of Nessa's eldest, Ricky. He was the only one besides her to survive the Blitz. Nessa and him came to stay with Joe and Sarah in Kilbendrick after the rest of the family were wiped out. Then Joe got the lad a start as an apprentice in Henderson's. He was proud of that, y'know? I remember him telling me, I've got young Ricky a start next week in beside us in the fitting shop. So that'll be him and me walking up and down the road together. Aye, he was proud of it all right. I think he saw Ricky as a chance to have the son him'n Sarah never had.

Then the boy was killed during his first week at the yard. Freak accident. One minute Ricky was a young lad having a laugh with his new pals, next minute he was dead. There's a tradition in shipyards. If two from the same family work there, and one of them's injured or killed, the other helps with the rescue, the recovery, whatever's needed. In Ricky's case, that was a hell of a job. Y'see, what happened to the boy … no. I'll spare you the details. But it was tough on Joe. Aye. Real tough on him.

Nessa was starting to come back to herself, but when Ricky was killed she turned around and headed right back into the dark place in her head where she'd been living since the Blitz. She'd sit alone at the end of the pier, just staring out over the water. When that started, Joe and Sarah were really worried. Finally they just had to accept it. She'll not move, Cyril, Joe told me. What are we supposed to do? Drag her home? Carry her? She'll not move. She'll not talk. We just have to leave her. But he was worried sick. Blamed himself for it. Took it really hard.

Two things helped Nessa, and Joe had mixed feelings about both of them. One was her religion. The Connors and the Glovers both came from Irish-Catholic people. Maybe it doesn't happen in Australia, but in the west of Scotland, we can tell your religion from your name. Connor, so your people were Catholics. Beattie, so my folk were Protestants. Joe didn't give a toss about that stuff; he was too busy making everybody in the world equal. I don't give a toss about it either.

Some do, though. Joe's wife Sarah was never away from the chapel. Nessa was the same, but after the loss of her family she took a scunner at it. Then this young priest appeared and started visiting her. He came down from Clydebank, from the chapel that Nessa belonged to before the Blitz blew her life apart. There was a bit of tongue-wagging about it. Ach. Mostly it was a bit of fun, but there was one exception. Geordie Scott. Geordie worked in the fitting shop as well, alongsides Joe and me. He wasn't from the village, he travelled back and forth to Clydebank. There was a nasty side to Geordie. Not to put too fine a point on it, he was a big bluenose bastard. Sorry. Pardon my French, hen. Geordie didn't like Catholics, or papes as he called them.

Now, there wasn't much of that kind of bigotry went on in this wee village. Ach, maybe a bit of name-calling between the kids, but nothing really bitter. We just got on with one another, by and large. But Geordie Scott, he liked to have a go at anybody he considered a pape. Sometimes he'd try it on with Joe, but not often. Joe was too smart for him, he'd just leave Geordie looking stupid. That wasn't too hard because, to be honest, Geordie wasn't the shiniest rivet on the boat. But somehow, over Nessa, Geordie got to him.

I said there were two things that helped Nessa get back on track. The other one was her becoming a shipyard worker. About a year after young Ricky's death, Nessa moved out of Joe and Sarah's, moved in with Sarah's sister Heather in Clydebank, and got herself a job in John Brown's. Aye. She did, son. She started as a labourer, then she got herself trained as a welder. And by all accounts, she was a bloody good one. That wasn't the end of it. She joined the union and became a shop steward!

It was as if Nessa got a chance at a second life. And she took it. To begin with, Joe was pleased. For a start, him and Sarah didn't have the same worry about Nessa. But then she became more of a militant than he was, and started hanging about with some real firebrands. That bothered Joe, but there wasn't much he could do about it.

Right. Let's get to 1944. There was a really cold spell in January, snow and weeks of freezing temperatures. Me and Joe, we were stripping down the engine on a wee coaster that was in for repairs. Christ, it was like a fridge on that boat, the spanners gey near freezing onto our fingers. Joe'd been awful quiet for a couple of days. He looked worried and he looked tired, but if I tried to ask about it, he just shrugged off the questions.

The day we started up the rebuilt engine, the engine room began to get warm until it was fine and snug down there. We put our feet up, lit fags, and sat watching the dials and listening. Then out the blue he told me what'd happened. Three nights earlier, in the middle of a snowstorm, Nessa turned up carrying a suitcase. She was pregnant, well on too. Could she come and stay with them until she had the baby? Well, that knocked the feet from Joe and Sarah. They hadn't seen her for a while, but that often happened. Like I said, she'd made a new life for herself, and she'd been staying with Heather for maybe a year. So they had no idea. After a lot of argy-bargying, they agreed to take her in because Heather's man, Charlie, was coming home wounded from the Navy and she couldn't stay on there.

I mean, what else could they do? I said that to Joe. He'd made me swear to keep my mouth shut before he told me, because him and Sarah had put conditions on Nessa. Aye, she could live there, but stay in the house, out of sight, until you were born. Then leave, taking you with her. Joe, I'll tell nobody, I said to him. But it'll be a miracle if you can manage to do that in Kilbendrick.

It's difficult to explain about a wee village like this unless you've lived here. Sure, people have their secrets. But they're hard to keep. What is it they say, walls have ears? Believe me, in a Kilbendrick tenement the walls have lugs like soup-plates. So secrets kind of seep out. Usually as a bit of a rumour to begin with. Then people start asking questions.

I said nothing to my wife. Not a word. But one day she asked me outright: Is Joe's sister Nessa staying with them?

Where'd you hear something like that? I asked her.

A bit of gossip in the post office, she said.

I didn't tell Joe. In fact, I never spoke to him about Nessa unless he raised the subject first.

The day you were born was a Friday and it was also the day when it all blew up in Joe's face. It was dinnertime, and we were sitting round the fitting shop eating our pieces and drinking our tea as usual.

160

How's that sister of yours these days, Joe? asked Geordie Scott. Her that's at the welding in Brown's?

Everything went quiet. You could've heard a mouse farting.

Nessa? Aye, she's fine thanks, Geordie.

Is she? I heard she was seen walking along the shore this week. And she's up the duff. Size of a house. About to pop any day.

Joe turned the colour of whitewash. He put down his piece and his tea-can. I put mine down too.

Geordie wasn't finished. I wonder if that young priest she used to hang about with got the leg over? Now. Will this count as a virgin birth, Joe? If the priest podgered her?

Joe's speed nearly beat me. I knew what he was going to do and I was probably out of my seat ahead of him. I flung my arm around him, but he was determined to get to Geordie and he carried me along with him. Geordie was trying to get to his feet when Joe reached him, and the three of us ended up on the floor in a tangle, Joe and Geordie trying to hit one another and me the meat in the sandwich. The rest of the lads pulled us apart and Geordie was bundled out the door.

You're right out of order, Geordie Scott, I could hear Willie the foreman telling him as I tried to calm Joe down. But Joe wasn't having it. He kept trying to breenge past me and two other men who were blocking his way. Out my road! he was roaring. I'll kill that bastard. Aye, the man I had to hold back that day was a different Joe Connor.

At finishing time, Joe and me walked home from the yard thegither. Well, not just us. At least half the yard walked down that hill every night. And, on a Friday, a lot of the men that didn't live in the village came down for a pint or two in the Bendrick with their mates. So we were in the midst of a fair crowd. And you can bet your boots there was a lot of whispering going on about what had happened between Joe and Geordie.

By this time, I'd got a bit more out of Joe. He'd been up at five that morning. That's when Nessa's waters broke. He'd ridden up to Clydebank and brought Heather back in the sidecar. It'd been arranged that she'd come and help when it was Nessa's time.

So I don't know what I'm going to face when I get home, he told me. It's been in my mind all day. The last thing I needed was that bigoted bastard winding me up.

Aye. I can understand that, I told him. And he's an ignorant bigoted bastard right enough. But you can usually dance rings round him.

Aye, usually, he said. But not today. Today's not very usual.

Maybe so. But you let yourself down earlier, Joe. You're going to have to screw the head about this.

I was glad to hear that Joe was going straight home. Usually on a Friday we went into the Bendrick first for a couple of pints. As I says, a lot of the lads did. Including Geordie Scott and his cronies.

Well, best of luck in there, I said to him when we reached his close. I hope everything goes well.

I'll tell you in ten minutes, he said. Unless you don't feel like a pint the night?

Joe, you know that's not a good idea,'I told him. What's got into you?

Nothing's got into me, he said. So I'll soon be across there drinking a pint with you as usual.

He was as good as his word. When he walked in the door of the Bendrick there was a pause in the conversations. Not a silence, just a kind of hiccup. Joe acted normal as he came across to our usual place at the bar, but I could see he was worried. I shouted up a pint for him.

They chased me out, he said to me quietly. Told me they've sent for the doctor and I'll just be in the road.

It'll just be a precaution, I said.

I hope so. Doesn't seem right, though. Nessa's already had five. You'd think it'd be straightforward enough.

He picked up his pint, put it to his lips, and slowly tilted it. His Adam's apple bobbed as he downed that pint slowly, steadily and in a oner. Give's two more, Rab, he shouted to the barman. And two nips.

No. I'll skip the whisky, I said.

Make it a double for me then. Joe gave me a hostile kind of look.

I laid my hand on his shoulder. Joe. Take it easy. You're not yourself. I know there's a lot going on. But take it easy. Please.

He shrugged me off. Keep your advice to yourself, Cyril. The last thing I need is you girning at me.

That's when I realised the pub had gone quiet. And this time it really was a silence.

Is it not a bit early for wetting the baby's head? asked Geordie Scott from behind us. Or are congratulations in order?

When Joe turned he took his pint with him and poured it over Geordie's head. It was the last thing he expected, and when he raised his hands to clear his eyes, Joe sunk a fist into his belly. Geordie double up and went down on one knee. Rab the barman had vaulted across the bar and stood between the two of them, nose to nose with Joe.

Right Joe, he said. You know the score. Take it outside.

The pub emptied and formed a ring around the two men. Joe took off his boiler suit and rolled up his shirtsleeves. Geordie was still holding his belly. One of his mates came over. Right, you sneaky bastard. He'll need a minute before he's ready.

He can take as long as he likes, said Joe. Then he's going to get the hiding that he's needed for a while.

I couldn't recognise my pal Joe. I'd listened to him arguing against conflict. This was the guy who encouraged cooperation in return for fair pay and practices, who preached that education and ideas were the key to the advancement of the working man. And now here he was, strutting like a game-cock and talking like a gangster in a B-movie. I knew one thing. The point of no return was far astern: there was no way of stopping what was going to happen.

When the two men squared up to one another, you could see that Geordie was a fair bit bigger than Joe. Taller, heavier. But he was fleshy, quite a belly on him. And he looked wary. I don't think I was the only one who realised I was looking at a different Joe Connor. But only one of us was facing him. And I don't think anybody fancied changing places with Geordie.

The two men started circling, watchful, fists ready. Have you ever noticed there's times when a crowd seems like it's just one big animal? Aye, well this was one of them. A big restless animal that held its breath, stood on tiptoe, watched and waited.

That's why Heather's voice sounded so loud. Where's Joe? Joe! Joe! What's going on? she shouted as she tried to push her way through.

When Joe turned to look, Geordie took his chance. He stepped in and hit Joe a hell of a scud, sent him flying into the wall of men. He didn't go down, but that was maybe because the crowd held him, shoved him back in. But I don't think so. Because he came straight at Geordie at some rate of knots.

Geordie was helpless after the first punch. He wobbled in a sickening kind of way. He'd probably have gone down if Joe'd left it at that. But he didn't. He kept going. Planting his feet, picking his punches, and hitting Geordie as hard as only a brutal man can. Three. Four. Maybe five times more. He wasn't just driving Geordie ahead of him, he was driving the whole crowd. Finally it parted and Geordie collapsed. Joe wasn't finished. He got on top of him and kept punching until he was dragged off.

Know what bothered me the most? And it still stays with me? Joe's grunts as he put in those last punches. I can hear them now, oomph ... oomph ... oomph ... as he gave it his best shot every time. Okay, Geordie was seriously out of order with his comments and was asking for a good belt on that big mouth of his. Maybe even a couple. But nobody deserved the destruction that Joe was handing out that night.

Joe was covered in blood. That first punch of Geordie's had split his eyebrow like a burst orange. But his eyes were blazing, and it was taking four men to hold him as he tried to get back at Geordie. Let me go. I'll kill him, I'll kill him, he was shouting.

I remember thinking, you're no killing him, you're killing yourself. Yourself and everything you stand for. This isn't murder. It's suicide.

Then Heather was shaking him, pulling him, screaming at him. Joe looked around the crowd as if he saw it for the first time. He shook his head, turned, and followed her.

That was the last time I saw Joe Connor.

Twenty

Shadows had lengthened. The dropping sun sent a long angled shaft of light through the open door of Cyril Beattie's workshop – a theatrical spotlight that picked out Cyril, perched on a workbench and swathed in a halo of smoke from a freshly lit cigarette. Opposite him, in the shadow, Keir Connor and Eryn Galbraith sat low on two old car seats, a rapt audience to the story they had just been told. Questions raced and tumbled through Keir's head, too many to pin down at once. Where to start? He picked up where Cyril had ended.

'You didn't see him again? Didn't follow him across to the street?'

'No. After Joe left with Heather, all the men went back into the pub and I went with them. At first all the attention was on Geordie. His pals carried him in. He was in a mess and well out of it. They got water and towels from behind the bar and cleaned him up as best they could. Once they'd sluiced off the worst of the blood you could see the damage: burst nose, eyes swollen shut and circled with cuts, lips bulging with splits. Slowly they got him back on his feet and, arms draped around the shoulders of two mates, he was led off catch a bus to Clydebank. People drifted back to their drinks. I knocked back Joe's untouched double whisky and ordered myself another, and a pint to go with it. A couple of people tried to speak to me about what'd happened but I waved them away. I wasn't for talking.

'I thought about going across to Joe and Sarah's. But what use was I going to be there? I thought about going home but then I'd have to try and explain to my wife things I could hardly explain to myself. So I just stayed and got drunk. Maybe that didn't help anything, but it didn't make anything worse either.'

'What about next day?'

'I tried, but he wasn't there to see. Sometime in the night Joe slipped away on his motorbike with you and Sarah in the sidecar. I never heard from him again.'

'What about my mother? Nessa?'

'Your mother died that night. I'm sorry, son.' Cyril hitched himself down off the workbench and out of the sun, as if he'd had enough of the limelight. 'Look, I've told you all I know first hand. Anything I added would be guesswork. Or worse still, gossip. Tittle-tattle. If I was in your shoes, I'd have a hundred-and-one questions. So before you start, why don't you go and ask the person with the best answers. Heather. She was with your mother that night. She was with Joe. Heather Ross.'

The blood rushing in Keir's ears made his voice sound faraway: 'Heather Ross?'

'Aye. I wondered. Sarah Connor's sister Heather. Joe's sister-in-law. One way or another I suppose that makes her your aunty. She's still in Clydebank. You'll easy find her. Her man Charlie runs a wee business from the house. Fishing tackle and stuff like that. "The Fly Caster" he calls it. Now. See's your cups.'

Keir watched Cyril collect the empty tea cups and rinse them at the sink. Eryn stood and reached a hand down to him.

'C'mon, Keir,' she said. 'Time to go.'

Cyril, his elderly body still lean and compact within the oily shell of its boiler-suit, his face wrinkled against the smoke rising from the cigarette between his lips, closed the workshop's sliding doors and snapped home the heavy padlock. Keir felt like embracing him. Instead he held out his hand. 'Thanks, Cyril. Thanks a lot,' he said as they shook hands. It seemed so inadequate. But in the absence of anything else, he said it again.

'You're welcome, son,' Cyril told him. 'It's been good to

167

meet you. Just a wee word of advice. I kind of take things in my stride but not everybody's like me. Maybe you should give Heather a bit of a warning, not just turn up the way you did here. The poor woman could die of shock, know what I mean? Thirty-six years later and you just turn up? You'll find a phone number for The Fly Caster in the Yellow Pages.'

Cyril's leathery hand gave Keir's a final squeeze. 'Good luck, son,' he said. 'You too, hen.'

Keir and Eryn stood on the wooden hump-backed bridge that crossed the small stretch of canal connecting the two mooring basins. Eryn suggested they go back to *Spaniard's Choice*. It was almost nine o'clock and they'd had nothing to eat. She could fix them an omelette. There was a spare bunk if he didn't want to drive. She was sure her father wouldn't mind.

If Eryn had been on her own Keir wouldn't have hesitated. But her father's company, the small talk, the teasing jocularity? Nah. That's not what he needed. So he made a lame excuse about Laggandarroch and wondering if there were messages back at the hotel.

Eryn didn't push him any further. 'I understand,' she said, and laid her hand on top of his. 'You've had quite a day today. A lot to take in.'

He studied the sluggish flow of the water, cautious about what to say. Yeah, there was a lot of new information. But there was something else too, a swirl beneath the surface.

'How do you feel? Try to get in touch with the feelings.' When he'd first heard Dr Rolfe talk like that he'd resisted, dismissed it as so much psycho-babble. Early on, in the privacy of his consulting room, the man had been gentle but insistent. Later in the veterans' group, Keir began to understand the importance of underlying emotions for him and people like him. The flashbacks, the panic attacks, the flying flippos — in their different ways they were surface storms caused by deep undercurrents that were denied, washed aside with booze, banished beyond memory. Because they were too hard to look at, to face up to. They were too hard to feel.

Today's events had stirred the depths, created whorls and eddies he needed time to explore. But he didn't want Eryn to think he was shutting her out.

'How'd you like to come with me to see Heather?' he asked. 'Once I've made contact with her. As long as she's up for it.'

'Yes. Definitely. I feel involved after today. How're you feeling?' Eryn waited. Quietly.

'I don't know how much sense this is going to make,' he said, after a while. 'In 1944 Joe Connor battles outside his local pub. Twenty years later, a young Australian nasho goes to war for Queen and country, then becomes a newsman dodging bombs and bullets to bring the truth to the world. They seem miles and years apart, but they belong in the same landscape. It's a landscape to do with men and honesty: what we say compared to what we do; what we believe in our heads, then what we act out with our bodies. For me it's here-be-dragons territory, full of dark corners and hidden demons. Strewth. I'm spouting riddles. What an idiot! First time I meet you I go all complicated, and now I'm Mr Confused.'

'After listening to Cyril's tale, I'd say you've good reason to be.'

They walked to his car holding hands. 'Go carefully, Keir,' she said when he was leaving. She kissed him lightly on the cheek. 'You're a good man.'

Keir stood in the Bendrick Inn car park. The steady buzz of conversation from the bar was punctuated by occasional laughter, raised voices, the chink of glass. Street lamps flooded Kilbendrick with an ugly orange glow. Across the railway track behind the pub, two lines of light pricked their way along the harbour wall and pointed towards the basin where he'd said goodnight to Eryn.

Thirty-six years ago, a horde of men left their drinks behind and swarmed out to form a ring around Joe Connor who was about to beat a man to the ground. Then continue to beat him senseless, maybe trying to kill him. Joe Connor. My father. My dead father.

He remembered the disbelief when he'd first read the letter. Dad wasn't my father? Mum wasn't my mother? He might as well be told Australia was Africa, up was down, the sun was the moon. This man and this woman had been his certainties; his life-givers, his carers, his moral touchstones. Then suddenly some spidery lines of an old man's writing told him they weren't.

The mum and dad he loved were being shouldered aside by a pair of silhouettes. One had a name. Nessa. Dad's sister. She was one of those shadowy rellies who'd disappeared in that long ago war, except now she was also a face in an old photo. The other silhouette was empty – nothing more than a large question mark there.

Mum was someone else.

Dad was someone else.

Maybe he was someone else too.

That's what had begun to push at him as he stood on the bridge beside Eryn and tried to make sense of the swirl inside. He was now on a search for his 'real' mother, his 'real' father. Maybe somewhere in the centre of the mystery he'd find the real him, the real Keir beneath the war-dirtied, battle-zone-fatigued, armoured shell.

He could've talked to Eryn back there. He thought that's what she'd wanted too. But the truths that began to tiptoe along his tongue were closely stalked by warnings. Tread easy here. Tread easy.

Men and truth, a minefield for the unwary. A minefield

where the presence of violence changed the rules, changed the values, changed truth itself. So that only those who'd been there, who'd walked in the same shoes, could ever really understand.

Only those who'd been where he'd been could ever understand how bits of a dead human could be turned into a grim joke...

When the new bloke triggered the booby trap, he disappeared in an eardrum-splitting explosion that had a red centre and a pinkish haze to it. The section corporal ordered the squad to spread out, find as much of the body as possible, and wrap it in his hoochie before the casevac chopper arrived. Keir found his intestines, a long glistening greyish-purple tangle, dangling from a low branch onto the muddy trail. The coils were still warm as he gathered them. 'Here comes a grunt with the guts for the job,' quipped Banjo McAulay, 'but I've got the brains.' He was carrying the head.

And everyone laughed, as if there was a good joke to be found in the parcelling up of the leftovers of a fellow man. Everyone laughed?

It made sense at the time. That's the hard bit. Keir and his mates knew the score. They were going home in three weeks. They'd scraped through the battle at Long Tan. They'd made it this far, learned a lot together, trusted one another. When the reo arrived to replace a casualty, they'd clued him up as best they could, but they walked well away from him. He'd too much to get the hang of, and they didn't want to share his mistakes.

People who've been there, who crawled the same jungle trails, who saw what he'd seen; people like that can understand. Ordinary humans who weren't there, unspoiled people like Eryn, never will. It's that simple. That complicated.

Banjo McAulay and the other diggers went home when their time was up. But Keir went back. He went fucking back. He convinced himself there was testimony to be given, a witness account to be told. History was in the making and the world could – the world should – learn its lessons. That's what he told himself, when the truth was more bodies, more lives blown apart, more bits of people. And the never-ending smells – chopper exhaust, explosives, thatch smoke, burning flesh, decaying corpses. Screams. Pain. Death. Always death. Always loss.

You crazy, truth-seeking, self-deluding…

He felt a bubble of humour begin to surface, a black, wry bubble. Maybe they run in the family, men who stand outside the Bendrick Inn staring at the bloody evidence of what they do and trying to square it with the fine words they say. Or write.

Did Joe face up to what he did that night? Or did he bury it? Or did it torture him forever?

He followed Joe's footsteps across the street and stood outside Sadie's Kut and Kurl. His imagination airbrushed away the hairdresser's plate-glass window and door, replaced them with sandstone blocks and an original window to match the apartments upstairs. He dimmed the orange streetlights to wartime blackout, took himself back to the evening of 25th March 1944.

On the other side of that window, he had just been born. Nessa, his mother, was dying.

When Keir picked up his room key, the hotel receptionist handed him a message. *Events moving quickly. Phone when you can. Bob McNeil.*

But that wasn't what he did first. Instead he borrowed the Yellow Pages and quickly found what he was looking for in the Fishing Tackle section.

The Fly Caster
Superior hand-tied flies,

rods, reels, and tackle.
Est: 1950. Prop: Charlie Ross.
17 Merilees Avenue, Clydebank.

He copied the address and telephone number into his notebook, under the heading "Aunt Heather".

Twenty-one

'I hope you haven't put yourself out because of this,' said Dr Bob. 'I thought you were away for a few days.'

'No, my plans were open ended,' Keir replied. 'After we spoke last night, my gut reaction was to come back. There's too much happening too quickly for my liking.'

'Far too much. I couldn't believe it at first, but now that Ainsley's disappeared...' The headmaster shook his head, leaned forward onto his elbows, eased his temples with slowly circling fingertips and began to expand on the brief summary he'd given Keir on the telephone.

'Rosemary now claims Ainsley was having sex with her. She confided in one of the nurses and the hospital called the police. At previous interviews Rosemary said she'd made a scene at the wine and cheese do, then tried to attack Watson, because he was on the trail of her glue-sniffing and was gradually finding all her hidden supplies. This time she told a different story. She said a physical relationship began between them around Christmas. Kisses and cuddles to start with, then a bit more and a bit more until they were having intercourse.'

'My God ... how likely's that?'

'How likely is it that a member of staff in a residential school is sexually involved with a pupil? I suspect it's more common than many people want to believe. These are changing times for the world of residential child care and mostly for the better. There's more openness about issues that might previously have been swept under the carpet. In the past, order was often maintained through fear and violence. Now staff who hit children run the risk of being charged with assault. But, for reasons that escape me, there is much less clarity as far as staff/pupil sexual behaviour is concerned.

'In pursuing our aim of harmonising the needs of each individual child with the experiences we give them, physical contact between pupils and staff has an important role. Lots of pupils have missed out on cuddles and comforting. As you saw, physical restraint is sometimes needed. Games and horseplay have their place. But sexual contact by staff is an abuse of trust, a criminal offence, and will not be tolerated here.'

'How d'you reckon the possibility of false accusation? That Rosemary's being vindictive, making this up? Why tell a nurse she'd just met? Why didn't she confide in someone else here at Laggandarroch?'

'You raise an interesting point. Turns out she told a similar story to Gloria Honeydew. Gloria's been spending a lot of time visiting her because whatever else has happened, one of our pupils is in hospital with a serious leg injury. She deserves the sort of support other kids would get from their parents. Gloria only heard the sexual claims the day before Rosemary told the nurse. When I asked why she hadn't passed that information on to me immediately, she said she was treating it as confidential until she had a chance to learn more from the girl.'

'Is that acceptable?'

'Trust between pupils and staff is a very important aspect of our work. You saw first hand just how well Gloria could get children to open up. Pupils will only do that if there's a strong bond of trust. So yes. I think that's acceptable, for a short time at least, if it will help the pupil bring important information into the open. Anyway, it's out of my hands now. The police will decide whether Rosemary's telling the truth. And whether Ainsley will face further serious charges.'

'Is there any word of him?'

'None, last I heard. The police are hopping mad that he's given them the slip. They called at his house unannounced to take him in for more questioning. He and his motorbike were missing.'

'How's his wife?'

'She's in hospital for observation following what appears to be another heart attack.'

'Heck ... the poor woman. Can she handle much more of this?' The enormity of Annette Watson's plight silenced him. He remembered the squeeze of her slender hand, the glittering washed out eyes that held his gaze.

He shook his head. 'So what about the journalists? Any more contact?'

'The chap from the *Sunday Standard* phoned back. He was clearly frustrated by my insistence that, for reasons of confidentiality, I couldn't speak about any individual pupil. I invited him to come and see the school at work but he was less than enthusiastic. Muttered something about being a newsman and that was a job for features. Nobody else has been in touch so far.'

'Good. Let's hope it stays that way. Things might change when Ainsley's caught, but we can deal with that when the time comes. The combination of Miss Baxter and a press release should hold the fort for now.'

A large brown envelope awaited Keir when he opened his cottage door. He laid it on the desk, consulted his notebook, and dialled the number for The Fly Caster, angling supplier, Clydebank. When a man answered he asked for Heather.

'Hello? Heather here,' said a friendly, ageing voice.

He'd thought hard about what he would say. 'Hello, Heather. My name's Keir Connor. I'm here from Australia, and I'm trying to trace some relatives while I'm in Scotland.'

'Keir? Connor? From Australia?'

'Yeah. My parents came from near Clydebank. I was born in Kilbendrick. During the war. 1944 in fact. 25th of March...' He left it there.

She broke the silence with a moaning whisper, 'Oh ...

my … God.'

He waited.

'Keir? So that's what they called you.'

'That's right. So I'm thinking that maybe you knew my mother?'

'If you're who I think you are, you're right about that. Sarah, my sister … and Joe? How are they?'

'I'm really sorry, Heather. Both of them have passed away. Dad – Joe – a few weeks back at the end of March. Mum three years ago. In Kalgoorlie.'

'Just a minute.' He could hear the phone go down, a door opening, some distant murmuring. Long moments passed before he heard returning footsteps. When she said hello, her voice was different, thicker. A lump grew in his throat.

'Look, I know this is very sudden,' he said. 'A bolt from the blue, really. Maybe you need some time to think about it?'

'Where are you?'

'I'm in Perthshire. Just a couple of hours away.'

'Could you come and see me?'

'Yes. Please. I can be there whenever you want.'

'The sooner the better,' she said. 'Just let me talk to Charlie.' There was another pause, more distant murmuring. The man's voice sounded comforting and reassuring but too indistinct for Keir to hear what was being said. Then Heather was back: 'How about tomorrow night? Seven-thirty?'

'That'd be terrific! Is it okay if I bring a friend?'

'Yes of course, son … and Keir?'

'Yeah?'

'Welcome home.' He heard her breath catch and now he was sure she was weeping.

'See you tomorrow,' he said softly.

'Tomorrow,' she said, and put down the phone.

He felt something give, then his own tears started to flow, unexpectedly and without any commotion, a gentle filling up of the eyes and a spilling over. They trickled down the sides of his nose, gathered along the seam of his lips, plipped softly onto the page of his notebook beside the entry for Aunt Heather. He cradled his head in his arms and surrendered to what was happening.

Time passed.

He didn't hear the door open, the footfalls approach. Soft hands stroked the back of his neck.

'Shhh, Keir. Shhh, shhh,' said Gloria.

He stood and turned to face her, wiping at his wet cheeks like a child. She wrapped her arms around him and moulded herself to him, her lips fluttering around his face, seeking his mouth. Keir shrugged himself free, then pinned her arms to her sides. 'What are you doing here?'

'Keir. Keir.' Her tone was placatory. 'When I came home, I saw your car outside. I just came in to say hello. I'll leave you alone. We can talk later.'

He was already pushing his irritation aside. Maybe this was an opportunity? A penny had begun to drop for him a few nights earlier, when she'd left him alone with the *I Ching*. A second penny had started its fall earlier today when the headmaster was updating him on Ainsley Watson. Now the pennies were landing together and adding up to more than tuppence. You know what, he thought, there's one or two things I'd like to ask you, lady. So let's keep cool here.

'You just came in at the wrong time,' he said. 'I'm fine. Maybe it didn't look that way, but I'm fine. Good in fact. But I could do with a cuppa. Could you put the kettle on? I'll go and give my face a splash.'

While they drank their tea, Gloria was keen to make sure he was fully in the picture about recent developments. 'Poor Rosemary,' she said. 'You may not know that it's common for girls to develop a crush on staff?'

'Really? So you think there's nothing behind what she's saying?'

178

'Nothing's established so far. I'm worried that Ainsley's being found guilty before we know what's true and what's not. That's what I wanted to talk to you about. You know how much I admire Dr Bob and his approach to the work here. But sometimes his commitment can blinker him. He seems to have a lot of respect for your judgment. Maybe you could encourage him to look at it a bit more from Ainsley's point of view. To see the whole picture.'

'The whole picture? You're concerned about the whole picture? Good on you, Gloria, that makes a nice change.' He watched her look of puzzlement turn into wariness. Oh yeah, Gloria. Good riddance to the false face. Now where are you going?

'I don't get you. What do you mean?' He could hear aggression in her voice now.

'Maybe a quote will help. Like, "You are sincere and being obstructed."'

'Who's sincere? Who's obstructed? I haven't the faintest idea what you're going on about.' But her face belied her denial. Keir knew he was on track.

'Tut-tut,' he said. 'Poor memory. That *I Ching* reading you gave me? When you advised me I should stick to my own family business and keep my nose out of what had happened at Harmony? You forgot to warn me that I was a sincere bloke who was being obstructed by somebody. Because you knew who was doing the obstructing. You. Thing is, I still don't know what scent you're trying to put me off. Maybe we could talk about that? And while we're on the whole picture, why don't you tell me how you managed to tip off Ainsley Watson about Rosemary spilling the beans? And why you're trying to protect him?'

He could have said more, but Gloria was already wrenching open the door and storming out. Yep, Keir thought, actions speak louder than words – especially when Gloria's doing the door slamming.

Twenty-two

Any sense of triumph Keir felt at confronting Gloria Honeydew faded as quickly as the sounds that followed, angry footsteps across the gravelled area outside their cottages then the slam of Gloria's front door. He could have done without her surprise visit. Not because she'd found him weeping and upset – he'd long ago been forced to give up any nonsense of big boys not crying – but because their verbal duelling seemed shallow compared to how he'd been feeling before she'd popped up and wrapped herself around him like a wet towel.

There'd been nothing bogus about his telephone conversation with Heather Ross. A connection had been made not just with her, but internally too. As if a barrier had collapsed that had been separating different bits of himself from one another. He could almost convince himself he'd felt a rumble as the blockade came down. He remembered Dr Rolfe's explanation of a flying flippo: extreme stress and anxiety caused 'depersonalisation' when the self seemed to split in two and one part became a detached observer, watching the distress of the other self. What he'd experienced after talking to Heather felt like the opposite, like a joining together.

Oh-oh. He was going all psycho-babbly on himself. Look, keep it simple. He'd discovered Heather Ross. She was his aunt, for Christsake! She'd lived with Nessa during the war, she'd been there when he was born and when Nessa had died! She was a linchpin between his old, safe, Australian life and his new, puzzling origins. He was going to meet her. She'd have lots to tell him. No wonder he felt as if a gap had been bridged.

Maybe his battling with Gloria was about connections too. Had he taken the wrong track in trying to keep

180

Laggandarroch's history separate from his own family search? After all, Nessa Glover, Joe Connor, Gloria Honeydew, and the missing Ainsley Watson all appeared in the same 1943 photograph.

The envelope he had picked up from the cottage doormat lay untouched on the desk, his name scrawled across it in a hasty, irregular hand. He opened it and took out a slim hard-bound book, its title picked out on the front cover in gold letters. *Harmonious Love.* The author was Fergus Abercrombie. The contents page listed just four chapters.

1. Introduction
2. The Theory of Passionate Attraction
3. The Nature and Uses of Love in Harmony
4. The New Amorous Institutions.

He opened at the introduction and began to read:

The three chapters that follow are the first translation into English of a little known volume Le Nouveau Monde Amoureux *or* The New Amorous World *written by the eighteenth century French philosopher and utopian socialist Charles Fourier whose ideas influenced me to set up the Harmony Community. I discovered* Le Nouveau Monde Amoureux *when I was studying Fourier's work in Paris some years ago. I arranged for its translation and for a small number of copies to be printed. I did so with the intention that, once the Community had been established, the ideas explained in this book would be made available to those members whose attitude and commitment were such that they could be placed at the very centre of the Harmony experiment as members of the Upper Seristery. The presence of this book in your hands signifies you as one of that number. Welcome.*

You are already familiar with Fourier's concept of the "social minimum" as a key principle of life and work at

Harmony – the guarantee of a minimum of food, clothing and subsistence as a right to every member in the community. This right eliminates poverty and inequality and makes work a fulfilling experience carried out in a spirit of cooperation and enthusiasm, rather than an unwilling drudgery necessary for mere survival. Much more is said about these matters in my other book, The Reluctant Capitalist, *which I know you will have studied closely.*

This book, Harmonious Love, *introduces you to a Fourian idea just as fundamental to communal life as the "social minimum". Fourier called it the "sexual minimum". He saw a very close parallel between the two concepts. Just as the social minimum guaranteed material security and comfort, so the sexual minimum ensured a guaranteed level of sensual pleasure in the world of amorous relationships.*

I will recognise at once that, within our Western culture, industry, capitalism, labour, poverty, social lifestyle, and so forth are common subjects of discourse and debate. However the organisation and pursuit of our amorous, sensual lives does not attract the same discussion or scrutiny. These aspects of our lives occupy more clandestine and hidden territory: indeed it is that very secrecy, and what Fourier describes as the hypocrisy and enslavement of marriage, that fuel his thinking and his Utopian ideas about sexuality. Therefore, unlike The Reluctant Capitalist, *where I weave my own life and thoughts into the matrix of Fourier's notions to achieve a synthesis that offers a blueprint of how Harmony might function socially, in the chapters that follow I present you with Fourier's words only. I do this in the hope that, through open-ended discussion and sympathetic experiment, we of the Upper Seristery can explore this hitherto neglected but fundamental aspect of Fourier's vision.*

Because of the sensitive nature of the ideas which unfold in the following pages, it will be necessary to carry out these explorations within the confidential confines of the Upper

Seristery.
Fergus Abercrombie.

Keir examined the book's fly-leaves for evidence of ownership. They were blank. He began turning the pages, his eye catching now and then on quaintly stylised language or arcane vocabulary: *The Three Goals of Passionate Attraction; The Eight-Hundred-and-Ten Harmony Personality Types; The Pentatones; The Omnitones; Amorous Anarchy.* On page thirty-one, early in the chapter called "The Nature and Uses of Love in Harmony," a small section of text was lightly underlined in pencil:

'Love can neither be expressed nor satisfied in civilisation, since the only form in which it is tolerated – marriage – is a coercive bond which extends only to the purpose of reproduction. There are no legal sanctions for any form of love which is consistent with the desire of nature to establish human bonds and to harmonise society.'

He found another underlining a few pages later:

'The law condemns to death a pauper who is driven by hunger to steal a loaf of dark bread, and it protects and honours the hoarder who inflicts famine on thirty million men. And what of today's law-makers? Oblivious to their obligation to provide a minimum of subsistence, they are even less willing to grant a minimum of sexual gratification. They suppose that the sexual needs are less urgent than the need for food. This is an error. Even though a person can do without sexual intercourse and not without food, it is certain that the need for tactile or sensual pleasures causes as many social disorders as does the need for subsistence.'

More unusual and fantastic terms began to appear in the section called "The New Amorous Institutions": *Vestalate; Damselate; The Striplings.* And there were more frequent underlinings.

'The adolescents of both sexes form a group called the Damsels. The Damsels will only have limited contact with the court of love. They will not be invited into the Seristeries where the high degrees of love are practised. There are limits to the amorous liberty which they enjoy, and they are not allowed to participate in the more exceptional varieties until they have finished their education.

'So many friendly relations are established in Harmony between people of widely divergent ages that it will become commonplace for a young lad to begin his amorous career with an elderly woman and for a young girl to begin with a mature man.

'Only half an infidelity is counted if a Damsel has an affair with one of the priests or priestesses who, in view of their age, are given special advantages. Any Damsel may redeem an infidelity by spending two nights with an elderly priest or priestess.'

Keir placed the book carefully on the desk. What the heck? He slid his hand into the envelope. Nothing. He looked again at the scrawled handwriting. Blue ball-point, rushed, the two words of his name forming an untidy line that rose from left to right. And that was all.

No. That wasn't all. He knew now that Fergus Abercrombie had written his second book. And somebody had sent him a copy of it.

He dialled the number of the clinic where Eryn worked. A secretary checked her availability and put him through.

'Keir,' she said. 'Nice to hear from you. I've just a couple of minutes before my next client.'

'How'd you like to meet my Aunt Heather tomorrow night?'

'Tomorrow night? I'd love to. Call me later – after four's good – and we can sort out the details. Anything else?'

'No. Not much happening here. The police are looking

for Ainsley Watson. He disappeared on his motorbike after Rosemary claimed it was sexual between them. Gloria Honeydew isn't swinging with a straight bat. Oh, and somebody's sent me a book that goes back to the original Harmony commune. It's got sex, sex and sex on every page. Apart from that, it's quiet as a nunnery here.'

Silence. Then Eryn asked: 'Keir. Is this all true?'

'Scout's honour!'

'We're going to have a lot to talk about tomorrow night after we've seen Heather. How about going back to the boat? We'll have the place to ourselves.'

'Sounds pretty darn good to me.'

He went through to the kitchen and poured a large malt whisky. He studied it until he was sure he wasn't deceiving himself. Nope, not to help him hide, not as an aid to amnesia. This drink was rightly his because he'd earned it.

He topped his glass up with water. Cheers mate, he said.

Twenty-three

He placed a butt of red wool just where the slim frond of golden pheasant crest was tied in to make the tail of the fly. Then he formed the body by winding silver tinsel along the shank from the butt to the hook's eye and back again. For the hackle, he selected a Chinese hen feather, dyed light blue, gave it three turns around the shank just below the eye, tied it in place, then added beneath a small throat made from mallard flank. He removed the half-tied fly from the vice and held it up to the clear evening light streaming through the window. Fine. Everything was lying just so, the way he wanted it to be. Time for the wings.

The shallow crescents of feather that would form the wings were about as long as his index fingernail and narrower than the cuticle. They were laid out in two identical groups, one for each wing. From the left group he took two slivers of dyed goose shoulder, one yellow, the other red, and melded them together with a confident stroking motion that caused their tiny fibres to interleave. Using the same technique, he married on a piece of blue goose shoulder, then completed the wing with a narrow barred strip of feather from a mallard's flank.

He was tying in the pair of wings when he heard the doorbell. He checked his watch. Right on time. He hoped Heather wouldn't get too upset. It had taken her a long time to settle down after that phone call. And she'd hardly slept all night for excitement. But they'd done plenty of talking, and she'd thought a lot about it. In between hoovering, polishing, washing the windows, and the house a palace before she even started on it. And baking. There were enough scones and cakes to open a shop. Aye. She'd be okay.

Merilees Avenue was in one of many developments of

neat roughcast houses that had grown up around the edges of Clydebank in the nineteen fifties and sixties to compensate for the Blitz damage to the town's centre. The tidy lawn and colourful flower beds in front of number 17 were enclosed by a close-clipped privet hedge. A wheelchair ramp led up to the front door. Keir felt Eryn squeeze his arm as the distant bing-bong faded and was replaced by the sound of approaching feet.

The woman who opened the door had well-groomed steely curls, rimless spectacles and a broad smile. What had once been a young woman's curvaceous figure had eased out into a comfortable roundness. Her arms opened in welcome. 'Keir! This is great, son! I can hardly believe it!' She embraced him enthusiastically then stepped back, holding his hands as she studied him.

'Hello there, Heather. This is my friend, Eryn Galbraith.'

'And welcome to you too, dearie,' said Heather, shaking Eryn's hand. 'Now come away in, the both of you.'

She led them up a carpeted corridor with doors on both sides. Attached to the first of these was a large painted sign of a man thigh deep in a river pool, fishing rod curved high, the long loop of his line curling fantastically to spell out The Fly Caster in cursive script.

'I told Charlie we'd look in on our way past,' Heather said, as she knocked on the door and pushed it open. A rack of fishing rods stood along one wall. Rows of shelving on the facing wall were stacked with an orderly arrangement of bags, reels, lines and assorted tackle. In the middle of the room, a man in a wheelchair was hunched over a worktable, his head bent very close to a fly-tier's vice. 'Here they are, Charlie. Keir and his friend Eryn.'

'Just give me a minute. If I don't tie off this head, I'll be in trouble.' He stayed focussed, his face in profile, the lens of his spectacles almost touching the fly he was working on. He gave a few precise twists with the chrome tool he was holding then, with a small pair of scissors, snipped the fine thread that attached the tool to the completed fly. He sat up and spun the wheelchair to face them.

'Hello, folks,' he said. 'I'm Charlie.'

Keir stepped forward. He grasped the outstretched hand and tried not to register any reaction to the dreadful asymmetry of Charlie's face. The right profile, which had been visible as he worked, was more or less normal although the lens of his heavily framed spectacles was exceptionally strong so that his magnified pupil almost filled the frame. The left lens was blanked off with opaque black glass. That side of his face looked as if it had melted, flowed, then re-solidified.

The brow was smooth pink scar tissue that extended back onto his scalp where occasional bristly patches of hair struggled to survive, like cactus in a desert. Most of the ear was gone, and the stubby flap that remained bore little relation to the outline of the original. Ripples of burn-damaged skin cascaded down his left cheek, halfway across his lips and gave an unnatural pink glaze to his neck before disappearing beneath his shirt collar. The left corner of his mouth was pulled down into an immovable cusp.

When Keir glanced down at Charlie's left hand he could see a thumb, index and middle finger protruding from a pink amorphous blob. He stepped aside to allow Charlie to greet Eryn and stood beside the worktable, enthralled by the precise elegance of the multicoloured fishing lure.

'Have a right look at it. Here...' Charlie took the fly from the vice and dropped it into Keir's outstretched palm. 'That's a Silver Doctor. A fully dressed salmon fly. I've based it on an old pattern that was first tied in 1850. Good fly to use when the water's a bit low. Sea-trout will snap at it too.'

'I guess making something like that takes a fair bit of practice,' Keir said.

'Aye, a wee bit right enough. Not bad for a man with half

a hand and one eye, eh?' A smile lifted the good side of his face and suddenly comedy and tragedy co-existed, as if their masks had been bisected and two disparate halves united.

'Way better than not bad, Charlie. She's a stunner,' said Keir, handing back the fly.

'We'll leave you to it, Charlie,' said Heather.

'Fine, pet. I've plenty to do. You'll be okay now?' Heather gave him a nod as she ushered out Keir and Eryn.

The bright airy sitting room looked out onto the neat garden Keir and Eryn had seen from the street. They'd persuaded Heather to delay her offer of tea on the basis they'd recently eaten and needed time before they could do justice to the splendid display of home baking. Now they sat together on a sofa facing a fireplace where the broad mantelpiece was covered with a proud array of framed photographs: Heather, young, lovely, and in a white wedding dress, stood beside a smiling, undamaged Charlie, tall and proud in his navy uniform; then two girls marched through time from left to right – as infants, as toddlers, in school uniforms, the graduation photograph of one, the wedding photograph of the other.

Heather perched on the edge of an armchair she'd drawn so close to the sofa that her knees almost touched Keir's. 'Charlie was in the Navy during the war. A gunner. He was trapped in his turret when the ship was bombed then went on fire. He nearly died. He's blind in one eye and needs a lot of help in the other one but it doesn't stop him. Charlie just gets on with life, that's his great gift. He loves tying his flies and running his wee business, he does most of the gardening, he plays darts and dominoes down the pub. You could search for a long time before you found someone as contented as Charlie and I'm happy for him. But even after all this time I sometimes still wonder how it would have turned out if he hadn't been wounded, because then Nessa could have stayed on with me to have the baby…'

She stopped. Her eyes glistened. She reached out and took Keir's hands in hers, '... to have you.' She shook his hands vigorously. 'Keir. Keir, this is great. And I'm not going to spoil it by bubbling. But I can't help thinking, if Nessa had been able to stay with me ... the thing is, as well as losing Nessa and losing you, I lost my sister and my brother-in-law that night. Sarah was the only family I had. But she and Joe took you, and I never heard from them again. Not one word. Ever.' She shook her head and closed her eyes. Her grip on Keir's hands tightened. Then she released them and sat back, as if to look at him afresh.

'Now, I know there's a lot you need to find out,' she said. 'And I'll do my best to help you with that. But can you tell me a bit about them first? Please. That would make it easier.'

'Yeah, let's give that a go, Heather. Where would you like to start?'

'How did they end up in Australia?'

Keir did his best. He was two years old in 1946 but he had vague memories of the noise and smell of the ship, of being in a crowded cabin and another woman trying to comfort him while his mother was being sick and his father wasn't there. Later on he learned they'd sailed from Portsmouth. Joe had worked in a shipyard there and somehow that'd helped them get places on the first immigrant ship to sail after the war. On board, men and women had been separated at night, so his dad couldn't be with them all the time.

As far as Keir was concerned, he grew up with Mum and Dad in Kalgoorlie where Joe worked in the gold mine. They loved him, cared for him, always made him feel wanted and special. His birth certificate said they were his parents, so he'd had no reason to doubt that until the letter his father had left for him just a few weeks ago.

Heather listened intently. Then, as if she couldn't contain herself any longer, she leaned forward and took his hands again. 'But why didn't they let me know? Just a note. To say they were okay, you were okay.'

'I don't know the answer to that one, Heather. I've done a lot of thinking about it. I look back and wonder, to try to understand them.' He felt Eryn's arm slip around his back, squeeze gently.

'You see, they were always vague about Scotland. I was told about Aunt Nessa's family being killed in the Blitz, and that she'd died during the war too. But the way I was told discouraged questions. They'd left Scotland to get away from the awful things that happened. They had a new life now. Some things were best forgotten. Some things were best not asked about. That's the message they gave me.

'When I was a young lad, Dad used to tell me stories about going to this big castle where there lived a good man who helped people make their lives better. I just dressed them up in my head like people in a fairy story. As I grew up I started to ask different sorts of questions. Once, I was maybe eleven, twelve at the time, I heard Dad complain to Mum about some fellas who were threatening to strike at the mine. "But aren't they doing that to make it fairer, Dad?" I asked him. "Like you and the man in the castle used to do in Scotland?" "That was long ago," he said. "The war changed all that." Meanwhile, behind his back, Mum shook her head at me as if to say: "Shhh! That bad old war. Don't ask any more. Leave it alone." Now, I'm beginning to figure out why.'

'When did my sister die? How? Please, I need to know what happened to Sarah.'

'She died three years ago, from breast cancer. She had a peaceful painless death in a hospice. Dad and I were there at the end.' As Keir gave details he began to understand more clearly the tragic link that tied him to the quietly weeping woman. Heather had lost her family when he was born, and his arrival triggered their disappearance. The big sister who'd stepped in and looked after Heather when their parents had died, who'd kept a roof over her head until she got married and moved on – that dear sister and her husband just vanished into the night, taking the newborn baby with them. Heather had spent thirty-six years not hearing, not knowing, just living with the pain of an unhealed wound, thirty-six years when he'd had Sarah and Joe all to himself. And when in turn they'd died, he'd been able to say goodbye to them, to grieve. What did it matter whether they were his real mum and dad? Who had the most to cry about here?

'C'mere, Heather.' He rose, drew her to her feet and hugged her to him.

'Sarah was thirteen years older than me, and Joe twenty years older, so they were almost like a second mum and dad. They were very good to me, and I'm sure they'd have taken me in even if they'd been able to have family of their own,' Heather positioned the cake plate so it was almost touching their hands.

'You know what it's like when you start growing up. The people who look after you seem a bit fuddy-duddy, old fashioned. I liked Joe Connor, but he could be stiff and he put his foot down when he wanted to be boss. Sometimes I used to think he'd swapped one religion for another. Catholicism for Socialism. And Sarah – it would have needed an operation to separate her from the Catholic Church.

'I used to love it when Nessa, Hugh and the Glover tribe came to visit. Suddenly the house was full of noise and fun. I was the kids' aunty and they created a big fuss about that, made me feel really special. Joe and Hugh would find an excuse to go across to the Bendrick Inn, I'd take all the young ones to the swing-park, Sarah and Nessa would cook a meal. Then we crammed around the kitchen table – four adults, a gaggle of kids and me somewhere in the middle.

'By the time the war broke out, I was starting to go my own way. I'd met Charlie and I was crazy about him. He was tall, handsome, a great dancer, and full of fun. Joe was suspicious but Sarah used to take my side. She might have been prudish and strait-laced, but she was still my big sister and she stuck up for me.

'Maybe you think Joe and Sarah used the war to cover-up where you came from, who your real mother was. And right enough it sounds like they did. But there's no denying the terrible effects those years had on our lives. Clydebank was devastated in the Blitz. Hugh, the girls and the baby were killed just about quarter of a mile from here. Blown to pieces. The next night in Kilbendrick, Charlie and I were sure the rest of us were finished as we clung on to one another in a wee shelter while the buildings crashed down all around us. Above all that dreadful noise, Nessa screamed out the names of the dead ones like a mad woman.

'But she survived it. That and the death of her boy, Ricky, a few months later. In fact she didn't just survive it, she turned her life around. That's when she came to stay with me in the wee flat where Charlie and I lived down near the shipyard. He was away at sea all the time, and Nessa and I were both working as welders in Browns, so it made sense to share the expenses and give one another company. We made good money too. I was quite happy just to enjoy myself, buy clothes, go to the pictures, the dancing. Charlie didn't mind. He trusted me, and he was right to trust me, but I still had a lot of fun.

'Nessa, now she went a different way. She got herself involved with the trade union and shipyard politics. That kind of drew her into Joe's territory in a way that didn't really please him. Oh aye, and there was a young priest involved as well, a Father Lamont. Then something happened during a weekend when they all went to that castle in Perthshire.

'I never quite got the whole story at the time but from what Nessa told me, and other things I've figured out for myself, I've managed to piece most of the jigsaw together.'

Twenty-four

Nessa Glover moved to and fro, unable to decide which window to sit by. Was it going to be the view of the fairytale castle? Or did she prefer the countryside of woodlands, loch, fields with sheep and cows, far mountains – and nearer to hand, the neat rows of the vegetable gardens, the lines of fruit trees, the henhouses? Every so often she turned and looked around her room with the same sense of wonder she'd felt when she'd first entered it last night. A peaceful place with walls of white-painted wooden boards, a neatly made single bed, a plain table and chair, a wall cupboard that now held the belongings she'd brought to Harmony for the "Cooperation not Conflict" weekend.

She'd felt slightly anxious when she'd realised she was the only woman attending, but it meant she had this lovely room all to herself.

Finally she placed the chair by the window that looked towards the countryside panorama. And there she sat, soaking up the scene in front of her and letting the events of the previous twenty-four hours drift past as they chose.

She'd worried in case she missed the coach yesterday. She'd been amongst the first to clock out and had pushed her way to the front of the crush at the shipyard gate, waiting for the howl of the Friday night hooter. After a thorough scrub at the public baths, she cut short the long soak she so much enjoyed and raced home to Heather's where she put on her makeup, dressed in the clothes she'd ironed and laid out the night before, and packed the rest of her things into a small case.

She'd arrived early at the pick-up point outside Clydebank

Town Hall. The Friday night pavements were crowded, mainly men in working clothes. Some had decided a couple of drinks were enough and it was time to head home and hand over the wages, some criss-crossed between the pubs that filled every street corner outside the shipyard walls. Others who'd skipped the pub altogether were now smartly dressed and escorted their wives or girlfriends to the cinema. Reminders of the war were everywhere too – uniformed soldiers on leave, sailors with girls on their arms, the rubble-filled gaps in the tenement rows.

She stood facing the direction that Father Paul Lamont should arrive from. If he arrived at all. She'd twice been to mass since their meeting in the cemetery. Both times he'd made a point of greeting her but had moved on quickly to other parishioners. 'We'll have plenty of time talk soon,' he'd said. Did he mean it? Was he really coming to the Harmony weekend?

She'd expected him to be easily spotted in the throng. Instead the handsome man in open-necked shirt, sports jacket and trousers was almost beside her before she recognised the priest. He put his suitcase on the pavement and held out his hand. 'Hello, Nessa,' he said.

'Father Paul,' she said as they shook hands formally, 'I don't know what to say. I didn't recognise you.'

'Why should I wear my working clothes on holiday?' he asked. 'No one else does. Nope, the black suit's banished to the wardrobe for the weekend. So is "Father". My name's Paul. Plain Paul. I've left the Father bit back there in the chapel house. It'll be waiting for me when I return, but I'm not taking it to Harmony with me.'

Before Nessa could think of an answer, her name was shouted from across the street. Tommy Spowart had emerged from Ross's pub and now weaved his way towards them, narrowly missed by a tramcar that clanged an angry bell at him. 'Hello, gorgeous,' he said. 'See they tramcars, think they own the road.'

'You've been drinking, Tommy.'

'Just a couple of wee swallies,' he said. 'The boys I usually drink with on a Friday decided to give me an early start.'

More like an early finish, thought Nessa. She was introducing Tommy to Paul Lamont – minus the Father – when a single deck coach turned off Glasgow Road and pulled up beside them. They climbed aboard to join the dozen or so passengers already there. All men, Nessa noted, and no familiar faces, but lots of smiles and friendly greetings. She made her way to an empty seat towards the back of the bus. Paul Lamont sat beside her. Despite Tommy's loud boisterous greetings – 'Hello there, boys ... How are yous all ... Nice to see yous all' – he followed Nessa and Paul all the way up the aisle and slipped into the seat behind them.

The next stop was at Kilbendrick to pick up Joe Connor. This time the calls of welcome were much more personal, with Joe greeting people by name and shaking hands with several of them. When Nessa stood up and called to him, he smiled and waved back, but when he reached her and recognised her companion, his smile faded. 'Father Lamont? You're just about the last person I expected to see on this bus. And out of uniform too! I nearly didn't recognise you.'

'Believe it or not, I'm entitled to holidays the same as everyone else, Joe. When Nessa showed me the poster about this weekend, I decided to come along, and to leave the priest back in the chapel for once.'

'Is that right? I thought you lads signed on for life. Or is it eternity?' Joe's tone had an edge to it.

The men held one another's gaze, and only broke off when Tommy stood up from behind Nessa, his breath as beery as his smile. 'Howdy, Joe.'

'Tommy Spowart! Well, well. Nothing but surprises back here.' Joe left it at that and went forward again to sit beside a bearded man who appeared to have kept a seat for him.

'That brother of yours can be right snotty,' Tommy said to Nessa. 'Maybe we're not good enough, compared to who he's sitting with.'

'Who?'

'The beardie boy beside him. That's Danny Freedman.' Tommy shook his head at the puzzled Nessa. 'C'mon, hen. You've a long way to go here.'

Paul Lamont helped Nessa out. 'Danny Freedman. The Independent Labour Party. He's a famous Red Clydesider. Part of the same lot as Jimmy Maxton and Manny Shinwell.'

'Aye, Davie Kirkwood as well, before he became a turncoat and joined the Labour party.' Tommy gave Paul Lamont a boozy, approving look. 'At least your pal here knows his stuff,' he said to Nessa.

Another passenger was picked up in Dumbarton. 'That's it now, folks,' the driver announced. 'We've near enough a three hour run to Harmony, so you can all sit back and take it easy.' Nessa heard the squeak of a cork from the seat behind. There was a pause, then Tommy stood up behind them and reached forward an open half-bottle of whisky. 'Anybody fancy a wee relaxer?' he said. When they refused, he began to sway his way along the aisle, repeating his invitation. Some men took a polite sip, most waved the offer away. When Tommy returned to his seat, Nessa could hear him helping himself again before the cork squeaked back into the bottle.

Soon afterwards, Joe came back to where the three were sitting. 'Could we have a word, Nessa?' he asked and, without waiting for her answer, led the way forward to a vacant seat right behind the driver. There was no trace of humour in his husky whisper. 'What's going on here, Nessa? First you turn up with that priest who's trying not to look like a priest, and then up pops Tommy Spowart and proceeds to make an arse of himself in front of everybody else on the bus.'

'Just you back off for a minute, Joe,' she said. 'I've come

here as me, myself, on my own. I'm not here as Tommy's buddy and it's none of my business how anybody on this bus is dressed. For that matter, I'm not here as Joe Connor's wee sister, holding out my wrist for a slap. Why I'm here, and what I do here, has nothing to do with anybody else. If you've got a problem with what "that priest" is wearing or not wearing, that's between you and him. Same goes for Tommy.'

She could see Paul Lamont's concern when he rose to let her back into her seat. She sensed him looking sideways at her tense face and she experienced again the same feeling of being split about what she wanted from him. Half of her wanted him to take her hand the way he had when they walked in the cemetery. The other half feared that he would. He didn't.

Tommy snored behind them; conversations here and there were lost to the thrum of the engine and the creaking of the coachwork; occasional heads nodded gently to the curl of the road and the sway of the suspension. Then Paul Lamont reached out and held her hand.

It was after eleven o'clock when the coach pulled up in front of a long wooden building.

'Right, gents,' said the driver, 'this is your stop, but the lady stays on to the next one.' A chorus of teasing "ooohs" and "aaahs" greeted this announcement. Someone's shout of 'Hey, what happened to equality?' brought cackles of laughter.

Tommy Spowart had been sleeping it off for the last couple of hours, but he'd woken when the bus stopped. He still looked the worse for wear. 'You going to give us your new address, gorgeous?' he asked, slurring some of the words.

'You going to give us peace, Tommy?' she answered.

Once the driver had organised men and baggage and shown them into their dormitory, he drove her further uphill to a larger wooden building.

'This's the school for community children,' he explained as he carried her bag up the steep wooden steps that led to the entrance porch, 'but there's no classes at the weekend. Nobody'll bother you.' He led the way along a corridor and opened a door at the end. 'Hope this'll be okay, it's a nice wee corner room.'

She'd looked around, stunned.

Today had been one of the most unforgettable days of her life. After breakfast this morning she'd met Fergus Abercrombie who stood at the doorway of the meeting hall and greeted each person as they arrived. He was an imposing presence, powerfully built for an elderly man and with a mane of vigorous white hair that curled almost to his shoulders. When Nessa shook hands with him, she had a strange feeling that the clear slate-grey eyes studying her were somehow able to see beneath her surface, to look into her. She felt captured by his gaze until he gave her a brisk nod and turned his attention to the next arrival.

Once everyone was assembled, Fergus Abercrombie mounted a rostrum at the front of the hall and spoke to them in a strong voice that still carried an American accent.

'Welcome to this "Cooperation not Conflict" conference at Harmony. It's good to see some old friends and some new faces. This is the first time it's been possible to meet since the war started. We're a smaller group than usual, but thanks to careful management of the community's petrol ration, we've been able to send one coach to the west and one coach to the east. Luckily, we're a self-sufficient bunch here at Harmony, so feeding you isn't a problem, and you won't be asked to produce your ration books.'

Nessa joined in the cheering. For breakfast they'd had porridge with lashings of fresh milk, large jugfuls straight from the Harmony commune cows, thick, creamy stuff of a richness Nessa didn't think she'd ever tasted before. Then bacon and scrambled eggs with as much homemade bread and butter as she could eat.

Fergus Abercrombie outlined the weekend's programme. Talks on a variety of topics would be followed by discussions where each member of the group would be expected to contribute. 'You represent different viewpoints and different experiences. Some of you have spent almost a lifetime considering the ideas we'll be discussing. Others are newer to the issues and perhaps bring a fresh viewpoint. I know from the experience of previous weekends that we've much to teach one another. The greater the effort each one of us makes, the more we will all learn.'

Then he led off with a talk called "The Birth of Hope" that explained the background to the "Cooperation not Conflict" weekends. It was a summary of his own life and how he'd come to set up the Harmony community. Nessa listened with a growing sense that she was hearing something new and important. Before the war she hadn't paid a great deal of attention to Hugh and his ideas. He was the father of her children. He worked hard in the shipyard to pay the rent and put the food on the table. She was the homemaker, the mother at the centre of the family. She'd respected the principled stance he had to his trade union work, but in truth she'd seen it as a luxury compared to her own never-ending hard work of running the house. In her new life as childless widow and shipyard welder, she'd drifted into being a shop steward and up until now had operated in a localised, practical way. She listened to the complaints and issues of her fellow workers and took them to local foremen or to the shipyard shop stewards' meetings that Tommy ran. Talk of capitalists and owners, workers and exploitation, initially sounded to her like a foreign tongue, understood by members of a closed society she had not yet fully joined. She was beginning to understand the words, but the relevance of the ideas to the world she lived in wasn't always clear to her.

Now Fergus Abercrombie brought the dry language alive with his own story of the rich industrialist whose eyes were opened by the fatal impact on others of his own wealth and power. He spoke with clarity and with an energy that seemed to reach out and draw Nessa in. By the time he finished, she felt as if she'd known him for years.

Apart from one or two polite questions, there was no discussion when Fergus Abercrombie finished talking. The purpose of his speech had been to set the scene and he ended by saying he had established the Harmony commune so that like-minded people could pursue an ideal. He recognised life was different for others present who worked in the real world of capital and labour where the problems were complicated, the challenges tougher.

'And so it gives me great pleasure to introduce the next speaker, a man known to most if not all of you as an important figure in the history of Clydeside – Danny Freedman. Danny's talk is entitled: "Is Cooperation the Slippery Slope to Concession?"'

The man who'd been Joe's travelling companion on the bus was about the same age as Fergus Abercrombie, but there the similarities ended. Freedman was a small restless man of wiry build with a full dark beard, light grey on the chin. Above his heavy eyebrows, his careworn forehead contrasted sharply with his large, perfectly smooth, bald head. He used no notes and avoided the lectern where Abercrombie had stood to deliver his precise, authoritative, fatherly talk. Instead Danny Freedman roamed the podium, gesticulating, pointing, and challenging his audience often in colourful language that seemed to paint pictures in Nessa's head.

'Before we can talk about cooperation we have to talk about conditions,' he argued at one point. 'Conditions draw forth men and movements. There would be no Labour

201

movement without the conditions that brought it into being. And as a result the collar on the neck has been eased where it hurt most. But the collar remains in place. So the question is: What does it mean to cooperate with the hand that straps the leash onto the collar?'

By the time Freedman finished, he hadn't closed the door on cooperation, but Nessa felt he'd plastered it with warnings and words of caution for anyone curious about what might lie on the other side. Lively debate followed. Tommy Spowart, apparently none the worse for last night's antics, was in firebrand mode.

'I hadn't expected a man of Brother Freedman's reputation to hide the truth behind some fancy words. The fact is, and he knows it, the rise of the Labour movement is nothing less than a revolution in action. To be successful, a proletarian revolution must be continuous. And revolution *is* conflict. Cooperation has no place in it. Although you wouldn't think that if you listen to the watered-down rubbish which is spouted by the traitorous Labour party, rubbish that's now infiltrating the trade union movement itself.'

That brought Joe to his feet. 'Tommy Spowart's not being straight with us. The words he's just spouted aren't his words. They're from the mouth of Leon Trotsky – a ruthless man, with ruthless ideas. Right now, this country's fighting for its very existence against another ruthless man with ruthless ideas, a man whose sole ambition is to plunge the whole world into war. That's the real lesson we can take from what Tommy tells us; ruthless people cause endless human misery and conflict.' Joe paused for a moment. 'And while I've got the floor, there's something concerning me that I must bring to this conference's attention. Someone else here isn't what he appears to be.' He pointed at Paul Lamont. 'That man there's a Catholic priest and for some reason he seems determined not to be honest about it.'

Everything seemed to slow down for Nessa. She watched

Paul uncross his legs, get ready to stand up.

She beat him to it.

Fergus Abercrombie's earlier announcement that everyone was expected to contribute to discussion had filled her with dread. She had no trouble speaking to her fellow workers or within the jokey friendliness of the shop stewards' meetings. That was very different from finding the right words to say in front of a crowd of strangers, and she'd decided to keep her head down and just listen. But now she heard her words come out as if someone else was speaking.

'Honest?' Nessa spoke directly at Joe. 'Surely a person's honesty isn't in the clothes they wear but in the ideas in their head, in the words they speak. You've attacked this man, without waiting to hear any of these things.' Now she looked around the others. 'I thought this weekend was about "Cooperation not Conflict". So far, I've listened to one man support non-stop conflict, and watch another attack somebody who hasn't even spoken yet. Does anybody want to start speaking about cooperation? Is that not why we're here?'

When she sat down she was shaking, but she felt different. In a good way.

Twenty-five

Harmony, June 20th 1943

From her seat in the window, Nessa watched the shadows lengthen in the gardens and orchards, the sun slip down towards the Perthshire mountains. Not much longer now until nine o'clock. And then they'd be together, just the two of them.

In the course of the day, they'd been careful not to seek one another out. The conference group was small and they were never too far from one another. When chance placed them face to face across the lunchtime table, they exchanged a fleeting, private smile. The only time they turned their backs on caution was when the photograph was being taken on the lawn at the front of the castle. Then they had sat together on the grass.

There was a soft knock. Nessa checked the tinplate alarm clock on her bedside table. Just gone half-past eight. She opened her door to find Fergus Abercrombie standing there with a book in his hands. 'I wonder if I could have a word with you, Nessa?'

'Sure … sure, that's fine.' Her head was racing. He mustn't feel unwelcome but she couldn't be late. 'Please come in. I'm afraid I don't have too much time. I'm meeting … I've said I'll join the others quite soon. I hope that doesn't sound cheeky?'

'Not at all. I won't take long.'

She offered him the chair and she sat on the edge of the bed.

'I hope this room's comfortable enough,' he said, looking around.

'Comfortable? It's wonderful. This room, these views, all for myself. I can hardly believe it!'

During the day's events, Nessa's eyes had often sought out Fergus Abercrombie. Whether he was addressing them from the podium, sitting quietly amongst the others, or sharing a meal, there was something about him that drew her attention. Now, as he perched on a plain wooden seat in the window of her small room, it seemed to her as if he was too big for such a simple place, as if he belonged somewhere more dramatic, a temple maybe with hills behind, shafts of light.

'I'll come straight to the point,' he said. 'You're making an important contribution to this conference. Your first words this morning steered the discussion in a most eloquent and helpful way. And later, when you spoke about the terrible losses you suffered in the Blitz, then how your life has changed since, it was … I would go as far as to say it was inspirational. Your story moved people.'

Nessa felt herself begin to blush. Nessa Glover? Inspirational? She studied her hands.

'Oh dear, I fear I've embarrassed you. That's not what I intended. Let me say what I came to say. Thanks to Charles Fourier, and to my own experiences, I've worked out much better ways for society to organise the whole troublesome business of wealth creation and industrial production. I'm certain that our lives no longer have to be enslaved by the greed and exploitation that have blighted our social and economic history.'

He turned slightly in his seat and gestured out of the window. 'That's why Harmony exists, and it delights me that you and the others come here to explore my ideas, to add your own, and then go back into your everyday worlds and try to use what you've learned to make conditions better for other people. I encourage you to do that. But I know that the changes you can bring about will be limited. Oh there are those, young Tommy Spowart amongst them, who believe the proletariat will rise up in a tidal wave of revolution that will wash the world clean of capitalism. Time'll teach them where reality lies. And for the rest, they'll learn to find satisfaction in small victories and marginal gains, and to persuade themselves that these represent the green shoots of evolution towards a distant paradise.

'For some of us, that's not the best way. I set up the community at Harmony so that like-minded people can experience, here and now, the utopia that's possible on a small scale. I explained a little about that in my opening address this morning. It would take too long to explore my ideas in full, but I'd like to leave you this copy of my book, *The Reluctant Capitalist*. It explains in detail why I left the larger world of commerce behind, and gives an account of the principles behind our lifestyle here at Harmony.

'I've also come to make you an invitation, to return to Harmony and experience life here for yourself. We often make arrangements for people – people who I think might make suitable residents – to stay for a few days, a weekend perhaps, and sample the lifestyle. Please think about it, and in the meantime enjoy the rest of the weekend.'

When he'd gone, the only clear thought she could muster was that she'd never before met anyone like him. It was as if he could see into her, could see something that she couldn't see herself.

In the June dusk, Nessa and Paul Lamont walked hand-in-hand along a farm track at the foot of the hill.

Their plan to find time together had been made during an extended afternoon break for a group photograph on the castle lawn, then a generous picnic of sandwiches and cake washed down by unlimited amounts of tea, milk and lemonade. As they relaxed in the sun, the participants had enjoyed the comings and goings on the road below. Two horse drawn carts, each pulled by a tall, muscular Clydesdale, plied back and forth carrying hay from one of Harmony's fields. When an empty cart arrived, workers threw up large forkfuls which were stacked higher and higher until the hay reached the top of the cart's holding frame. Then the driver clambered onto the shaggy load, shook his reins, and the cart lurched into motion along the track and out of sight. Paul had leaned closer to her as he pointed to one of the disappearing wagons. 'Let's meet down there this evening,' he'd whispered.

Now as they walked, Nessa told Paul about her unexpected visitor. 'I can't get what he said out of my head. He's inviting me to try out life as part of the Harmony commune.' She waited, keen to hear from him, but nothing was forthcoming and they walked on in silence until she couldn't wait any longer. 'C'mon Paul, you're being very quiet…'

'Yes I am. Something strange is going on. You see, I was planning to tell you about the conversation Fergus Abercrombie had with me.'

'With you? When?'

'After dinner was over, and you'd left, I decided to go too. The men were lighting up fags, conversations were breaking out. Didn't appeal to me, and I decided to go for a walk. He came after me, and asked if I minded if he joined me.'

'Both of us? That seems quite a coincidence.'

'That's what I think too. He took a different tack with me, though. With you he came at it from the political angle. With me it was belief.'

'Belief?'

'He said he'd pricked up his ears when Joe attacked me for being a priest in disguise. I tried to tell him the story about being on holiday – and I must admit it sounded like a feeble excuse – but he waved my explanations aside. "What matters to me is that you're a man who can believe. You couldn't have become a priest unless you were able to put belief first. The Harmony community is an act of faith on my part. I admire believers. And I need believers here, people who can make a commitment on the basis of their faith in an ideal." Then he made the same kind of invite that he made to you. I'd be welcome to come back again and try it out for myself. Borrow and read his book if I wanted to find out more about Harmony and its background. He left me very thoughtful and with a strange sensation that he can see something ahead for me that I'm only beginning to glimpse myself.'

'That's spooky. I feel something like that with him too, as if he can see what's going on with me, can read me somehow. Why's he spoken to both of us though?'

'There's no possible way he could have guessed there's something going on between us.'

'What is going on between us, Paul?'

Ahead of them lay the destination of the loaded hay wagons they'd watched earlier in the day. A cobbled yard in front of an old wooden barn was almost filled with an army of newly built haystacks, their conical tops carefully raked into neat watertight thatch. Paul led her deep into their midst where the air was thick with a smell that reminded Nessa of warm toffee. He turned to face her and took both her hands.

His kiss was clumsy and vigorous. She was forced backwards and could feel cut ends of the hay stems catch at her blouse and prod her shoulders. When she tried to move he pressed himself harder to her until she was trapped between him and the haystack.

'Paul,' she said. 'Paul. Stop. Wait.' The pressure eased. When she disentangled herself, his arms dropped to his sides and he stood awkwardly, facing her. She cupped his face in her hands and kissed him very softly. 'Paul. Wait.' She put her finger to his lips to silence anything he might try to say. 'Shhhh.' She led him through the door of the barn. The floor was deep with fresh hay. 'Wait,' she said when he tried to reach for her again. She knelt and patted the straw beside her. 'Come here. Lie down. Just wait. There's no rush.'

Twenty-six

Are you sure you've both had enough? Och, you'll manage another wee slice. That chocolate sponge is Charlie's favourite. Or a bit of shortie to finish with? It's my own recipe. No? Well, if you're sure. Just help yourselves if you change your mind. Now … Aye…

Maybe I'll start with the time Nessa went to that Harmony place. She came back from that weekend a changed woman. Joe came back an angry man. Paul Lamont came back and left the church.

Funny how two days can affect lives so much, isn't it?

Who's responsible when things change? Or maybe I mean who's to blame? See, Clydebank was nearly destroyed in two days. Lots of lives were lost. But other people did that. Climbed into their planes, flew over our heads and dropped those hellish bombs on innocent folk. Aye, that was somebody else. But the things that happened to Nessa, Paul Lamont, Joe Connor, my sister Sarah – their lives changed because of what they did, decisions they made. I've had a long time to think about it, and that's the best I can come up with.

Sometimes when I watch my Charlie tying his flies or wheeling his chair around the garden and flicking weeds out from between the roses, he seems like a lucky man to me. Oh dear, that doesn't sound right. What I mean is, he just had to cope with what somebody else did to him. Blowing him up, burning him half to death. Mind you, all those shells he fired at other people, maybe somehow it all balances out. Och. I'm havering and probably not making much sense. You must want to hear about your mother, so why don't I just get on with that.

I knew that something important had happened to Nessa during her time at Harmony. Not that she told me, not to begin with anyway. In fact she was very quiet. Too quiet, not like her usual self. It was late on Sunday when she got home. She made an effort to tell me what it had been like, about the room she stayed in, about the endless food they'd eaten as if there was no such thing as rationing. Of course she had to tell me something, she couldn't just say nothing at all.

Just one last thing, I asked her, when she said she was tired and going to bed. Did Father Lamont turn up? Yes he did, she said. She gave me a funny look that left me wondering.

We'd talked about him off and on. Mainly it was about how grateful she was for the help he'd given her. Then just a few weeks before she went on that weekend, he'd turned up unexpectedly when she was visiting the graveyard one Saturday night. When she told him about Harmony, he surprised her and said he wanted to go too.

I think he's just kidding me on, she told me when she got home. But I could see she was excited.

D'you fancy that priest? I asked her. He's a bit of a dish right enough.

Don't you be daft, she told me. He's just a boy compared to me. He's barely started to live, compared to what I've been through.

At the time I remember thinking: I didn't ask his age, Nessa. I asked you if you fancied him. That left me wondering too.

Anyway, as I said, she came back from that weekend very quiet. Thoughtful too, as if she had something on her mind. Then, a few nights later, I came home from working overtime and she'd a nice meal waiting for me. She was considerate that way; in fact we were good to one another, when I look back.

How about a wee drink? she said when I'd finished eating. Now it was very rare for us to drink at home in those days. We might stop in for a couple on the way to the dancing, or when Charlie came home on leave, and we always made sure there was some in the house just in case, because it could get scarce at times. But this was quite unusual. She poured us a whisky each, downed hers quickly and topped us up again.

And that's when it all came pouring out. Something had happened between her and Paul Lamont. But that wasn't all. Fergus Abercrombie, the man who ran Harmony, had invited them both to come back there. Maybe they'd even be able to stay. I couldn't believe what I was listening to. I couldn't make sense of it. Nessa! To me, the one dependable thing about your mother was the way her two feet were firmly planted on the ground. Yet here she was talking as if she'd walked into a fairy tale.

There was a loud knock at the door. I just about jumped out of my seat. Maybe it was the whisky, but I had this daft idea that we shouldn't even be talking like this, and somebody had found out. But no, it was worse than that. It was a telegram boy with news of what had happened to Charlie.

That telegram turned my life on its head and I had no time to think about Nessa. Charlie was in the Royal Naval Hospital and not expected to live. I was given compassionate leave from the shipyard and a travel warrant to take me to Plymouth where I spent the next two weeks holding his hand and talking to him whenever they'd let me into the ward. Soon I was in there every day. I think they realised it helped him when I was with him. And it did. Eventually he was out of danger, but after that came weeks of treatment. Plastic surgery was still very new and experimental but, believe me, they did a great job when I think about what he was like to begin with. But it took a long time, and I was away a lot, until he was finally allowed home six months later. So I don't know all the details of what was going on in Nessa's life during that time.

She had become much more open, though, and during

211

my spells at home she would update me on what was happening. The big news was that Paul Lamont had given up the priesthood. Big news from Nessa, that is, because as far as the church was concerned, it was all hushed up. She told me that when he told the parish priest, Father O'Donnell, that he was planning to leave, the old man must have made a phone call. Within an hour, a car arrived from Glasgow with two priests who tried to persuade and bully him into going with them to some sort of monastery where he could pray for guidance and get help to sort his ideas out. But he stuck to his guns, and at the end of the day there was nothing they could do to stop him.

A few weeks later he was staying at Harmony. I don't know where he was before then, although once, on a trip home, I got a strong feeling that someone had been staying in the flat with Nessa. She'd been back to Harmony for weekend visits, and from the way she was speaking, she was starting to think about making her future there with him. In fact I could hardly get her to talk about anything else. Harmony this, Harmony that. I stopped giving my own opinions. It was her life, and I had enough on my own plate to think about. Nessa, I said to her, I know you'll do whatever you want to do. My main concern is to get my Charlie home. That's my priority.

And then something went wrong. Well, two things, really. First of all, there was some kind of falling out between Nessa and Paul Lamont. I don't know what caused it, but the romance between them hit the buffers in a big way. By this time, Charlie'd been transferred to convalesce at the Royal Naval Hospital near Edinburgh, so I was working in Clydebank through the week and spending my weekends across there. Then, early in December, Nessa came back from a weekend at Harmony. She was upset and tearful, and when she wasn't crying she was really angry. I've made a big mistake, she said to me. Paul Lamont isn't what I thought he was. That's not all. I'm pregnant, six months on.

I'd noticed her putting on a bit of weight, but I hadn't said anything. I had plenty to think about in my own life. Charlie was making great progress and the plan was to have him home at the start of the New Year. Nessa, I said. I'm sorry to hear all this. You deserve better. But I nearly lost my man and now I'm going to have him home again. In January. That's what comes first for me, so there's not going to be room for you here. I'm sorry to tell you that at such a bad time. Do you want me to talk to Sarah?

No, she said. I understand your position, Heather. Leave it to me. It's between me and Joe. I'll deal with it my way.

You see, Joe and Nessa hadn't spoken since that weekend at Harmony in June. "Cooperation not Conflict" it was called. What a laugh! They had that name the wrong way round, because the result was a hell of a lot of conflict. For my family. For your family.

I'd heard from Sarah about how Joe had come home livid. I've already said that Joe Connor could be a bit steely, a bit severe. I think that sometimes comes with pride. Joe did a lot of good as a trade union man. He got a good name for that, and his reputation went wider than just the yard. People would come to his door in Kilbendrick, ask his help if they'd housing trouble, or with the Ministry of Employment, stuff like that. He also enjoyed the fact he was pals with some of the well-known people in left-wing politics. He thought Nessa had given him a showing up, turning up on the Harmony bus with Tommy Spowart and a priest in disguise, as he saw it. But what really got to him was how Nessa had stood up to him in front of a whole meeting. Put him in his place.

Worse than that, he thought there might be something going on between Father Lamont and Nessa. That was too much for Sarah. It's a blasphemous accusation, she said to me, and I've told Joe to his face. As if that would have bothered Joe.

You could see it coming a mile away. There was going to be an explosion and it was Nessa's business when and what she told Joe and Sarah. It wasn't up to me to light the fuse. I just held my tongue.

In the end, she told them nothing until she turned up on their doorstep on a snowy January night. You know, that was probably as good a plan as any. I've said that Joe could be proud and prickly, but deep down he was a good man and he couldn't abandon his own flesh and blood. They didn't accept her with good grace, though. She was to hide away in the house, nobody was to know, and after the birth, she and the baby were to leave.

A few days after I got Charlie home, just as I was putting Nessa and her troubles to the back of my head and beginning to put my own life together again, Paul Lamont turned up at the door looking for Nessa. I barely gave him the time of day. I told him he should be ashamed of himself and the trouble he'd caused. Her whereabouts were none of his business. I didn't dare tell him the truth because if he'd turned up at Kilbendrick there'd have been mayhem, maybe even murder.

Of course Joe and Sarah had to speak to me eventually and that wasn't easy for them. When they did, during one of their visits to see how Charlie was getting on, it was a very tight-lipped conversation. Joe was furious with Nessa and Sarah still didn't want to accept what had happened. I left them in no doubt it was none of my business but I said I'd come and help when it was Nessa's time.

And sure enough, Joe arrived for me early on that March morning. By then, Charlie was a dab hand on his wheelchair. He could move around the flat and get himself in and out of bed. He kept telling me he'd be okay if I didn't get back home that night.

Don't worry, I told him. Everything'll go fine and I'll be

here in time to make your cocoa. Little did I know.

Nessa's labour had barely got going. She was glad to see me, gave me a big hug and I thought, you know what, you're looking great, Nessa. And the other two? There was a big difference in the way they were coping. Joe looked awful, white-faced, chewing at his lips, not knowing what to do, until finally Sarah put his piece bag over his shoulder and ushered him out the door. Go and get an early start, Joe, she said. It'll do you good to keep busy.

As soon as he left, it was as if a burden lifted from Sarah and she almost looked happy as she bustled around getting things ready, keeping an eye on Nessa's progress, making tea for us all. See, the thing was, although Sarah had none of her own, she often helped at births, in fact she was often asked for. You have to remember, in those days women had their babies at home and somebody with a good reputation for helping was in big demand.

A kind of a bond grew between us as the day went on. It was as if the approach of your birth drew us three women closer and closer. Nessa'd had five before, so giving birth held no surprises for her. By four o'clock in the afternoon, her contractions were coming thick and fast and there wasn't much for Sarah and me to do, other than to encourage her to push when they were at their height and to mop her brow in the wee breaks she was getting in between. Half an hour later Sarah clapped her hands and gave a wee cheer of delight. Well done Nessa, she said, your baby knows the right way out. I can see the top of its head.

Then out you came. You started crying right away and Sarah wrapped you up and handed you to Nessa. He's a fine wee boy, Sarah said. Now let's have the afterbirth and we'll be as right as rain.

But nothing happened for what seemed like ages. Sarah fussed over Nessa and checked for any developments. Then she gave me a nod towards the door and followed me out. I don't like it, she said. That's over half an hour. Everything should be out by now. She's starting to get hot and there's too much bleeding. Nip to the phone box and call Dr Robertson. Tell him what's happening and ask him to come as soon as he can.

Dr Robertson was there in about half an hour. He scrubbed up with carbolic and hot water and set to work. He tried everything he knew but he couldn't stop the bleeding. Sarah sent me to the lobby cupboard to fetch some sheets. When I took them through I could tell things were bad from the look on her face. Dr Robertson spoke to us without looking up from what he was doing. One of you go across to the pub for Joe, he said. Tell him he'd better come and see his sister.

You were sleeping in Sarah's arms, so I went. I ran. I could see a mob of men on the flat ground beside the Bendrick Inn. I was shouting for Joe, but I couldn't get through. Then a gap opened up. There was a man on the ground and Joe was sitting on his chest, punching him and punching him. They were both covered in blood. I grabbed Joe, screamed at him, it was as if he was under a spell or something. Then he came out of it, got up, and I led him away.

Sarah got a real shock at the state Joe was in but the doctor brushed it aside. He had more important things to deal with. There's major bleeding and I can't stop it, Joe, he said. There's nothing more I can do. We're losing her.

Joe let out a wail and knelt on the floor beside the bed. No, Nessa, he groaned, his lips almost touching her. No. No. No. No, Nessa. C'mon. Please.

She just faded away. She was far gone by the time Joe arrived, and she just kept slipping into her last deep sleep. Sarah and I were holding onto one another and crying. Joe continued to kneel beside the bed like a man lost in a nightmare, looking at Nessa's pale face, now deathly calm and relaxed. It seems to me now that we all stayed like that for a long time.

Then Dr Robertson put his arm around Joe's shoulders. With his other hand he gently tested the swelling around the gaping split along his eyebrow. One thing I can do is stitch that up for you, he said.

He covered Nessa's face with the sheet, eased Joe's hands from his dead sister's, and led him through to the kitchen. They were gone for a fair time, talking in low voices. Then Dr Robertson called for Sarah and she went through, hugging the baby – hugging you – tightly to her.

When the three of them came back through, the doctor said he had to leave. He'd be stopping in past Massie, the Clydebank undertakers. On the way, he could give me a lift home. It's getting late, he said, and I know you'll be getting worried about Charlie.

I didn't feel right leaving things the way they were, but Dr Robertson assured me that Joe and Sarah knew what to do and the undertaker would treat this as a priority. So I let him drive me home.

When the hearse turned up at six the next morning, Nessa's body was washed, dressed and laid out on a fresh clean bed. Joe, Sarah and the baby had gone. There was an envelope on the table and a note from Joe for the undertakers. He hoped the money he'd left would be enough and he thanked them for their help. There was also an envelope addressed to me. Inside was a note from Sarah. She was always very slow and fussy with her writing but this had been done in a real hurry. I've still got it, but I can tell you from memory what it said: "I don't have time to try and explain what we're doing. I don't even know if I can explain it to myself, but it feels like the right thing. I'm sorry, Heather. You and Charlie look after yourselves. God Bless. Sarah."

Charlie and I did look after one another. We've had a good time together, and raised our own family along the way. I can't imagine my life without the joy of my daughters. It was different for them: Sarah, childless and hurting at being denied motherhood; and Joe, who'd been so hopeful for young Ricky and then blamed himself for the boy's death.

And there you were, a motherless infant. I can just about understand why they did it. But, dear oh dear, they caused an awful lot of hurt too.

Do I know what happened to Paul Lamont? No. My guess is he stayed on at Harmony, for a while anyway. After all, he'd given up his whole life to live there. Where else did he have to go? But I don't know for sure. I used to see Tommy Spowart now and then. He came round to my house not long after Nessa's death and, you know what? He was heartbroken. Tommy became quite big in trade union circles, had his finger on quite a few pulses. A few years after the war, 1949, 1950 maybe, I met him on a tramcar. He told me that the Harmony man, Fergus Abercrombie, had died a year or two earlier and, as far as Tommy had heard, the people living there hadn't been able to keep it together without him.

Twenty-seven

Keir and Eryn didn't leave Heather's house until after eleven o'clock. On the doorstep she squeezed from them yet another promise that they would return soon. Only then was she willing to give them both a last embrace, first Eryn then a lingering cuddle for Keir.

'Don't worry about me getting upset,' she told him. 'I feel better than I've felt for a long time, now I know what happened to the three of you. Not knowing, that's what's painful. It eats away at you. Don't get me wrong, I've had lots of happiness and good things in my life. But I don't think there's been a day when my heart didn't ache.

'And listen, what about a visit to the grave? All of us together? Have a think about that.' Then, still unwilling to part company, she walked them to the car while Charlie waved his farewells from a window. 'I hope you don't have to drive all the way to Perthshire?' she asked Keir.

'No. Eryn's dad has a boat at Kilbendrick. We're staying there.'

Keir said very little during the drive. Heather's story swirled around his head and painted rich pictures of Nessa Glover: her despair and descent into near madness after the Blitz's brutal theft of her family; remaking herself as a skilled shipyard worker and union activist; her love for Paul Lamont, followed by her sense of betrayal for reasons only to be guessed at; throwing herself on the mercy of a brother she had offended at the Harmony conference; the tragedy that unfolded in Kilbendrick when Keir was born and Nessa died; then Joe and Sarah's slipping off into the night with the infant, never to be seen or heard from again.

As the people and their lives played and replayed in his mind, one face kept pushing itself to the front – Heather, tonight, in her own living room, pleading with him to tell her what had happened to the family who had disappeared without trace all those years ago.

Another disappearance joined the cavalcade of thoughts and memories. Jacko was the one true friend he'd made in the army. They shared the same birthday, but their lives were at very different places when they were called up. Keir was a trainee journalist. Jacko had just been voted Australian young magician of the year. He used to joke that if the national service ballot had been held in a theatre he could've switched the ball with their birthdate written on it. Jacko had brightened many miserable jungle days with his card tricks, slight of hand, a spot of grenade juggling. He would never crack a light about how conjuring worked. Ask him how a trick was done and he'd beckon everyone closer, put a conspiratorial finger to his lips and whisper 'Shhh. It's magic'. Until the night he said 'Okay, fellas. Just this once. Here's an important trade secret. Never end with a vanish. Because if you do, you'll send the audience away with a hole they can't fill.' Then the day before their final pull-out he forgot to follow his own advice. He was tail-end Charlie on the very last patrol. When the platoon stopped for a brew he wasn't there any more. Gone.

They'd trained together. Fought a war together. Laughed and cried together.

Vanished never to be seen again. Not the faintest trace.

Just like Joe and Sarah. Gone. Pulled up stumps, took the baby with them and left a bloody great hole in Heather's life. You can't rub out a hole. You can't bandage a void. Heather's torment wasn't caused by memories, or events that haunted her, or recollections to fret over, to rework this way and that. No, she suffered precisely because she had no history to feed on. Her total ignorance of what had happened to Joe, to Sarah and to Keir had kept the wound open. Yeah. Her suffering tonight was real all right. Here. Now. There was nothing phantom about the anguish still chewing at her thirty-six years later.

The sign for Kilbendrick shook him alert. He realised he'd been nodding his head slowly as his thoughts worked themselves out. A sideways glance showed Eryn's light-reflected face staring straight ahead as if she too had plenty to mull over.

He parked the car. They held hands as they made their cautious way around the poorly lit mooring basin to the dark shape of *Spaniard's Choice*.

'Got a torch?' Keir asked at the top of the gangplank.

'No need,' Eryn unlocked a door, reached into the darkness and flicked a switch. There was a pause for a couple of seconds then a generator coughed into life somewhere below the deck. Almost immediately a light came on above them. Eryn led the way into the boat, switching on lights as she went. A bottle of wine and two glasses sat on the table in the deep alcove at the far end of the main cabin.

'Goodo,' said Keir. 'Somebody knew we were coming.'

'And now if somebody else wouldn't mind opening the wine, I'll sort out the heating.' Eryn scampered up the companionway into the wheelhouse and returned in a minute or two, closing the hatch behind her. 'We'll soon be cosy,' she said as she took a glass from Keir and joined him on the alcove's soft bench seating. The generator sent a comforting vibration through the wooden hull and Keir could feel warmer air begin to replace the evening chill that had greeted them. 'Cheers!' he said.

'Cheers!' She sipped her wine and smiled at him. He watched her face become more serious. 'That must've been quite a night for you, Keir.'

He swirled his wine, watched it leave a purply-red translucent curtain around the glass. 'Yeah. Bit of a humdinger, alright,' he said at last, 'I just can't dodge the feeling that the most innocent person paid the highest price.'

'Who?'

'Heather. She didn't deserve to lose her sister, her brother-in-law, and the newborn me. During all the years Joe and Sarah were raising me, we had one another. I just took it all at face value. They were my mother and father and that was that. But now I know they cleared off with a baby who wasn't theirs and gained a new life for themselves. They won a son and a fresh start. Heather, who'd done nothing wrong, lost everything.'

Eryn settled deeper into the seat beside him, crossed her ankles. He felt her leg rest against his. 'Not everything. Charlie came back to her.'

'Yeah, you're right. They went on to make their own family life, but she lost the last of her kin, a sister who'd been a second mother to her. Then had to wait all this time, not knowing, only to find out Sarah and Joe are dead, and they died without ever contacting her again. That hit me like a ton of bricks tonight, especially when she spoke about it gnawing away at her for years. Day after day.'

'Me too. You could feel her pain. Disappearance. Then total silence. It must be harder to bear than someone's death.'

He refilled their glasses and thought about that. 'She's given me a lot to chew over.'

'Yes. You were very quiet on the way here.'

'Yeah, I learned a lot tonight. Feels like I learned something about myself too, but that's proving slippery to pin down. If I try to explain it'll just sound obvious. We all say there's nothing we can do about the past. Let bygones be bygones. Live in the present. The future takes care of itself. All that stuff. But yabbering on doesn't make it easy, doesn't make it happen. Instead we let the past nick the present and when we do that, our future's hijacked too.'

By flying flippos, he thought, flashbacks, nightmares, old ghosts. All just re-creations of history. All imagined inside my own bloody head. Yeah. All buggering up my life…

'Or that's what some of us do,' he said. 'Me for instance.'

'You looked as if you were working something out in the car.'

'Oh-oh. So you spotted the nodding donkey in the driver's seat. Holy heck. I hardly know where to start, Eryn.' She said nothing. Sipped her wine. Waited. The chug of the generator made a comforting backdrop to the calm, easy silence that enveloped them. He jumped in. 'Okay, you're in the psychology business. Have you heard of Post-Vietnam Syndrome?'

'I have, yes. Earlier this year it was included in a new diagnostic category called PTSD, or Post Traumatic Stress Disorder to give it the full name. A very disabling pattern of symptoms brought on by traumatic experiences.'

'Yeah, well it's been screwing up my life for a long time. Though I didn't understand that until I met a shrink – oops, a psychiatrist, and a good bloke to boot – called Dr Rolfe a couple of years back. He had a special interest in the problems of soldiers returning from Vietnam and I was interviewing him for an article on what he'd started to call Post-Vietnam Syndrome. As I listened to him listing the symptoms I had the spooky feeling that he was looking inside me and describing what my life was like. Worse still, I'd been a greedy bugger and grabbed most of the heavy stuff – depression, too much booze, broken marriage, failed relationships, flashbacks, panic attacks, flying flippos…'

'Flying flippos? That's a new one to me.'

'That'll be depersonalisation to you. One day at the Vets' group, Dr Rolfe talked about a state caused by extreme stress. He described it as a feeling of being estranged from yourself; you're an external observer, detached and looking down at this separate "you" who's going through the most intense personal anguish and turmoil. "I'm with you there, Doc," said one of the guys. "You're talking about a flying flippo." So that's what we called them from then on.'

'How long did you spend in Vietnam?'

'First I was a soldier there, courtesy of the Aussie government. Two years National Service with the second one spent in combat. Then I went back as a war correspondent, in and out of most of the Southeast Asia hotspots – Nam itself, Cambodia, Laos, back and forth for the best part of ten years.'

'I'm no expert, but I know that's a very long time to be in the thick of a war zone.'

'Too true. Then I began to work out with Dr Rolfe's help that being there in two different roles – first a soldier then a journalist – probably made the consequences worse for me. See, when you're in the army, you don't have choices. You do what you're told to do. Sometimes you're ordered to do some bloody awful stuff, you and your bunch of mates. That's a key part of it, you're a team of young guys all in it together, sharing extreme actions in an extreme environment, sharing secrets you'll probably never tell anyone else.

'But as a journalist you choose the assignments, you put yourself on the firing line and describe the carnage and horror you find there. If there's a price to pay for that, there's no-one to blame but yourself, and that's one I have to cop.'

'Dr Rolfe sounds good. Are you still involved with him?'

'To be honest, I'm in a bit of a muddle about that. I was planning to jack it in with him before I came to Scotland but then my Dad died, left me that letter, and all that's put me up in the air again.'

'I'm not surprised after hearing Cyril's account, then Heather's story tonight. Are you okay to talk about it? Had you any suspicion your mum and dad were hiding a big secret from you?'

'Not when I was a youngster. Parents are magic people to small kids, I think. No questions asked. From as far back as I can remember they spoke about leaving Scotland after the terrible tragedies of the war. Why should I have doubted any of it? I had memories of the ship to Australia, and I had

224

my father's early stories – about his fight to improve life for his fellow shipyard workers; how I was called Keir after a great man who fought for the ordinary people; how those terrible Nazis had rained bombs out of the sky and killed all the important people in Mum and Dad's life so they left Scotland forever – stories that were indelibly etched in my mind along with the whisky fumes from the glass that always seemed to be at his side.

'As the years passed I began to ask more questions just like growing kids do. Looking back now I think Dad became quieter and quieter while Mum did her best to shush me up. Eventually I accepted the way it was. I had a birth certificate that proved what they told me, so what was there to fret about?'

'Your father's letter said your mother had wanted to tell you the truth. Did she give you any hint of that?'

'Sometimes, with a drink in him, my father would start to talk about their old life in Scotland. My mother always seemed nervous when he did – I can understand why now. I used to hear them arguing later in their bedroom.

'At irregular intervals, maybe a month or two apart, she would announce on Sunday that she was going for one of her private walks. My father tried to hide his annoyance but I could see it in his face. Once, when I was about twelve years old, I followed her. She went straight to St Mary's Catholic church. It's famous for several reasons including its position at the edge of Kalgoorlie's red light district. As all the boys at school knew, some of the working girls could be found there at mass on Sunday, sitting together on the right hand side. That's where Mum went. She sat behind a group of prostitutes and listened to mass on her own. I left her to it. She didn't know I'd been there and I never talked to either of them about it.'

'Keir, that's a very touching story. All of this is. Touching and potentially very stressful. Any troubling episodes since you came to Scotland?'

'Yeah. A major flashback during my first visit to Kilbendrick and a bit of a flying flippo when Dr Bob was showing me some photographs in the boardroom.'

'Did he realise something was amiss?'

'I can't be sure. Maybe. I just covered up as best I could and scarpered.'

'He might have been a good person to talk to about it…'

'No. I had another chance in the boardroom yesterday. I didn't tell him then either.'

'I wonder why.'

'Vietnam. Most of my strife goes back to Nam. To war. When Dr Bob flew bombers against the Germans and the Japanese that was seen as a good war. Decent people against the fascists. The white hats against the black hats. Your dad's joke about the Clydebank pies touches on the same thing. Ordinary people whose honest decency will destroy evil, whose humour will beat the Blitz. Their homes might be blown to smithereens, their friends and family dead or maimed, but they'll be unbroken, because they know they're in the right.

'Vietnam was so different. Hundreds of Australians killed, thousands wounded. Yet returning soldiers were booed and spat on, because of a war that no one seemed to want or to understand. "A war without honour" it was called at the time. Meanwhile I shot at the Vietcong as a conscript, then couldn't wait to get back as a reporter. Oh, at the time I had lots of noble ways of explaining that to myself, but now it feels like I was addicted to some foul drug, hooked on the black side of what humans do. Brutality. Cruelty. Violent death. Evil deeds. How can I talk to people like Dr Bob and your father about that?'

There was lots more he could say.

About how he'd persuaded himself he was an important bringer of "truth" from Vietnam. The one to alert the world, to confront political movers and shakers with the results of their complicity. Instead all he did was witness ugly, murderous symptoms, caused by mighty powers who stamped their gory boots all over the wishes of the Vietnamese people. When that had begun to hit him over the head, he'd curled up into a boozing basket case, enslaved by the past while his present slowly leaked away like blood into a paddy field.

About how Joe Connor had blabbed on about tolerance, cooperation, the unity of man, an end to class war and exploitation. In reality, he wouldn't give a fair shake to people like Tommy Spowart or Paul Lamont. The day before he left Scotland for good, he beat a fellow worker to a bloody pulp then skulked off into the night never to be seen again.

Instead he shut his mouth and gave in to an irresistible urge to stretch. He closed his eyes, arched his back, straightened out his arms and felt flutters of tension begin to ease as his vertebrae separated, his shoulder blades opened. He held himself at maximum extension for a moment, then relaxed with a deep sigh. Eryn stroked the soft skin on the inside of his arm. He opened his eyes. She was gazing at him with a look that was unmistakeable.

He watched the green-flecked eyes widen a little, as if saying hello. He felt foolish. This beautiful woman had been looking at him like that while he'd been rabbiting on like a misery guts! What an idiot! He met her gaze, stroked her cheek, studied the symmetry of her mouth. Kissed it lightly. Then a little harder. When he felt her lips seek more he eased back, lowered his head, nuzzled gently at the softness beneath her chin, followed the line of her pale cream neck. His nose parted a curtain of auburn curls and ravished the trapped scents of coconut, musk, skin. He kissed her earlobe gently, breathed his heat into the little dip behind it.

She wriggled. 'Kiss. Kiss,' she breathed. Tongue tips touched, played together.

Eryn broke off the embrace, stood up, reached out to him.

Twenty-eight

Keir wakened to the sound of seagulls. Eryn was spooned up to him, her knees tucked in behind his, her groin tickling his buttocks, her breasts soft against his back. Her arm curled across him and her relaxed hand cupped him loosely. Her. Beside him, against him, over him, touching him.

She stirred. He turned to face her, kissed her softly. They reached for one another.

Later he woke from a light doze to find her propped on her elbow, watching him. 'Hello, gorgeous,' he said. 'D'you know that the standard Australian breakfast for post-coital lovers is coffee and Vegemite toast?'

'I can do everything except the Vegemite. Marmite any good?'

'Yeah! But let me do it. I want you to look at something.' He rummaged about the clothing-strewn floor for his bag and handed her the copy of *Harmonious Love* by Fergus Abercrombie. 'I told you about this on the phone, posted through my letterbox in a plain brown envelope. Quite appropriate, given the steamy contents.'

'Who sent it?'

'I can't be sure. Hand delivered. No letter. Just my name scrawled on the front.'

'It seems to be in very old-fashioned language.' Eryn was flicking pages.

'From the 18th century French of Charles Fourier. Apart from a Fergus Abercrombie intro. As well as writing the utopian socialist stuff that inspired Abercrombie, the old frog philosopher had some pretty spicy notions about sexual antics in the commune.'

'Really? Doesn't that seem odd, turning up in the midst of the Ainsley Watson business?'

'For my money there are far too many coincidences

and I'll give you very short odds on some of them being connected.' He started ticking them off on his fingers. 'For instance. This book turning up out of nowhere. Watson being charged with sexual hanky-panky then disappearing. Rumours of unconventional goings-on at the Harmony commune ... and let's not forget last night...'

'Unlikely on this side of the bed.'

'Yeah. Same here.' He grinned back at her. 'But also. Let's not forget we heard about Nessa and Paul Lamont making more visits to Harmony before it all went sour between them. Know what? A few of them appear in that same photograph on the boardroom wall at Laggandarroch. Fergus Abercrombie's there. So are Joe Connor and Nessa Glover. I'll bet you the young fella sitting on the grass with Nessa is Father Paul Lamont. Hey, the young Ainsley Watson's there too, along with Gloria Honeydew.'

'Gloria. I'd forgotten about her. Didn't you think she was up to something? How does she fit in?'

Keir heard warning bells. Careful. Let's not give away too many details on Gloria yet.

'Hmmm, that's still not clear, other than Harmony being the common factor. Why don't you have a flick through the book while I fix the toast and coffee? Fergus Abercrombie's intro's worth a read and look out for the underlinings by whoever owned it.'

'You might need a hand through there.'

'I'm pretty sure I can figure it out.'

As he suspected, *Spaniard's Choice* did the figuring out for him. He filled the kettle at the galley sink and plugged it into the nearest socket. After a short pause, he heard the generator kick in. La-la-la-ing to its rhythm, he held out his arm to receive an imaginary partner, waltzed his way along the narrow passage between sink and table and switched on the small portable television perched on an overhead shelf. A black and white news bulletin appeared. As Keir danced and bobbed around, finding the bread, the Marmite, the cafetière, the ground coffee, he bounced his high spirits back at the newscaster's solemn recital of world events.

'Emergency workers trying to approach Mt St Helen, scene of Sunday's major volcanic eruption, have encountered utter devastation. It's now clear that a large part of the mountain disappeared in the massive explosion...'

Nothing compared to the explosions and earthquakes aboard *Spaniard's Choice* in Kilbendrick, mate. The resulting tsunami swamped boats on the other side of the basin.

'In the recent Quebec referendum, sixty percent of voters rejected a proposal to move towards independence from Canada...'

Who cares, mes amis? You speak French, the language of love. What more do you want? L'amour toujour. Toujours l'amour.

'And now it's time to join your local news team...'

Well, if the Scottish headline isn't Eryn Galbraith and Keir Connor, you're not up to speed, boys and girls.

'A man was killed early last night when the motorcycle he was driving collided head-on with an articulated lorry near Stirling. The victim has been identified as Ainsley Watson, a forty-seven-year old man who worked at Laggandarroch Residential School...'

Keir pushed his face as close as possible to the small screen, scrutinising the picture of the damaged lorry with debris scattered around. The camera zoomed in on the rigid front forks of an old-fashioned motor bike, onto the glossy black petrol tank with its single gold-painted word: Velocette.

'... in Perthshire. The road was closed for five hours. The lorry-driver was unhurt but badly shocked. He said the accident came out of the blue and he had no time to react. It was a sunny evening and conditions were good. He watched the motorcycle's approach because it was an unusual vintage model and travelling very fast. Suddenly it veered across the white line and smashed into the front of his lorry.

'Police have confirmed that the victim was being sought in connection with the assault of a pupil at Laggandarroch School. Their investigation is ongoing.'

Keir braked quickly and switched off the ignition. A television news crew had set up in the middle of Laggandarroch School's driveway and a sound technician with a finger to his lips had turned to face Keir's car. He left his car door open and crept up the grass verge until he could hear what was being said by the broad-shouldered news presenter, dressed in a suit and sporting a crew-cut, who addressed the camera in a Scots accent with a tough edge to it.

'... who was killed outright last night when his motorbike collided with an articulated lorry on the A811, four miles west of Stirling.

'Ainsley Watson worked here at Laggandarroch School in Perthshire. You can see the school buildings on the hill behind us. It's a residential school specialising in the care and education of forty disadvantaged young people, both boys and girls.

'When I spoke earlier today to the school's headmaster, Dr Robert McNeil, he confirmed that Mr Watson had worked at the school for thirty years. However Dr McNeil said that, for reasons of professional confidentiality, he was unable to give details of events involving individual pupils. Perthshire police have confirmed there is an ongoing investigation into a pupil assault here, and said their enquiries have not ended with Mr Watson's death. They will release another statement in due course. So there are likely to be further revelations about what has been happening at this peaceful-looking school nestling in the Perthshire countryside.

'Harold Anderson, STV News, Laggandarroch School,

Perthshire.'

The crew held their positions for some seconds, until the presenter, listening into his earpiece, said 'Right, boys, that's it.' He approached Keir. 'Thanks for sussing that. We were going out live there.'

'Yeah, I thought so. I'm in the business. This as close as you can get to the school?'

'You'll get in the front door up there, but you'll have a job getting past the old bird in the office. She'll hand you a press release with bugger all in it and a folder of bumf about the place. Then you won't get another word out of her. I eventually managed to get the headmaster on the phone. Courteous old codger. Just went on about his hands being tied for professional reasons and referred us to the police. In more ways than one. We hadn't long started filming around the school when a couple of plods arrived in a car. Told us we were on private property. As a special favour we could film from down here but not a foot closer.' With that off his chest, he gave Keir a more critical inspection. 'And who are you with anyway?'

'*Sydney Morning Herald*. There might be an Australian connection.'

'Australian connection?' But Keir was already heading back to his car.

When he entered the office, Miss Baxter's fierce glare melted into a smile of welcome.

'Keir! Dr Bob'll be glad you're here. I'll take a note through. He's on the phone, talking to the chairman. Could be a while. You've heard the terrible news?'

'I heard the TV bulletin this morning.' Keir shook his head. 'It's shocking, scarcely believable. I'll be upstairs when he needs me.'

In the boardroom he made straight for the "Cooperation not Conflict" weekend photograph. The caption confirmed the name of the man sitting on the grass with Nessa. Paul

Lamont. Keir studied him – early twenties, strong masculine build, face still boyish. He leant towards Nessa and she towards him. Their arms were touching. Keir now knew that Nessa was in her late thirties when the picture was taken but she looked younger. They both smiled for the camera. Joe Connor smiled too from his place in an informal grouping of five men standing behind the seated pair. Keir took his time, moving between the three innocent-looking smiling faces that now carried the history he'd learned from Cyril Beattie and Heather Ross. A priest, a woman welder and a shipyard engineer. Two of them became lovers and gave life to him. The third stole him away and became his dad. Destiny can sure take some funny twists and turns.

Then there's Ainsley Watson, the boy with the short trousers and the wartime haircut who stood beside a gangly Gloria Honeydew at the refreshments table. The man who found his fate in a twist of the handlebars and the front end of a lorry. Had he planned it? Had he watched the oncoming traffic for a suitable target? Did he think about it at all or just act on a desperate whim?

The headmaster arrived, joined Keir at the photograph and pointed an accusing finger at the young Ainsley Watson. 'What a bastard! Ah. I think I shocked you there. Can you think of a better word for a man who uses a position of trust to abuse others? To abuse everything he's supposed to stand for? Then when he's found out, slams himself into a lorry? No thought for anyone else but himself. Selfish bastard to the end.'

'Yes. Bastard's in the mix alright. How's Mrs Watson taking it?'

'Poor woman's currently on a life support machine. Mercifully, the heart attack that put her there happened before he killed himself. I'm told that recovery's not a possibility. There's no hope for her. Now they have to decide when to switch the damn thing off.'

He threw his arms wide as if to declare the whole world crazy. 'Have I told you that I trained as a natural scientist? Yes. Yes I thought I had. When war broke out I was in my final year of an honours course in Zoology and Biology. After I was demobbed from the RAF I completed a PhD about rare Scottish dragonflies. Fascinating insects. Always been a passion of mine. Then I changed my plans when I realised that war had left me with an eagerness to learn more about the behaviour of a different creature. The human being. Much more complicated, unfathomable at times, but very skilled at finding justification for his more errant shenanigans.

'Normally I'm too optimistic to be drawn to cynicism. But people like him – that bastard – they help me understand why Jonathan Swift had us as a pernicious race of little odious vermin.' With that he punched Keir lightly on the shoulder. 'And there endeth today's rant. Thanks for listening. It's not the easiest of times.'

'You've certainly coped well with the press,' said Keir. 'I met a pretty frazzled TV news team when I arrived. The knuckle-dragging frontman was doing a bad job of trying to make a big story out of nothing.'

'I had good advice.' The lop-sided smile flashed briefly. 'And Miss Baxter's turned out to be a natural bulldog for seeing off news-hounds.'

'Are you getting anything from the police?' asked Keir. 'Why are they still digging now that Watson's dead? Have they got their eye on someone else?'

'They're being tight-lipped with me. But I've just been talking to the chairman whose ear, as always, is very close to the ground. I understand a police search of Ainsley Watson's house uncovered material that's kept their interest alive but I don't know what it is. Also, Gloria Honeydew's been questioned. Usually she's very open with me but not on this occasion. Gloria's Gloria. I can't push. It's her business. She knows I'm here if she needs me.'

Keir gestured back at the photograph. 'Ah yes, Gloria. She and Watson, they more or less grew up together. I wonder what the police are after?'

'Maybe she'll talk to you about it. She's certainly very keen to know your whereabouts. She's been at me several times. Did I know when you'd be back at the school? Did I know where you were staying? She was so insistent that I gave her the Barton Hotel number in case you were there. You seem very important to her at the moment. In fact,' he checked his watch, 'she'll be in her classroom now. She's timetabled for lesson preparation but I'd be most surprised if that was amongst her priorities today.'

Through the classroom window, Keir could see Gloria sitting on the floor with her back to him. She had on the same brightly coloured jump-suit she wore when he'd visited the English class with Dr Bob. Her steely grey hair was once again gathered into a thick plait. She was hugging herself and rocking gently back and fore, as if to soothe a pain. He felt like a voyeur spying on something he shouldn't see.

His knock on the classroom door was followed by silence. Then a shuffling of feet. The Gloria who opened the door to him looked old and haggard. Gone was the physical presence and self-confidence, the sensuality that keeps the years at bay. Now she looked as if age had taken her hostage. Her eyes looked leaden and washed out, the laughter lines crumpled to crow's feet.

'Dr Bob said you were looking for me.'

She didn't reply but invited him into the room with a curt nod. She sat back down on the floor and gestured for him to join her.

'Awful business with Ainsley,' he heard himself blurting out. 'I know the two of you go back a long way…'

She held up a hand. 'Don't bother. Don't even go there.

You haven't the faintest clue what you're speaking about. Just listen for once. There are things I have to tell you'

Keir took *Harmonious Love* from his bag. 'While you're at it, could you give this book a mention?' he asked.

'Don't worry. I'll come to it.'

She paused for a moment, as if looking inward to collect her thoughts. 'The last time we met you accused me of deliberately misleading you, and of trying to protect Ainsley. You were right on both counts.'

She seemed to have decided to be truthful. Why could he still hear underlying hostility? What was bugging her?

'On our first night together, as soon as you mentioned Nessa Glover was your mother, I realised you brought danger with you. When I "found" her in my photo album, that was a charade. I already knew she was in that picture. And Paul Lamont. I wanted to see if you knew about him too. You didn't seem to. But still, I sensed the threat you brought. Then after your first day in the boardroom, when you came back with snooping questions about Fergus Abercrombie, that's when my alarm bells really began to ring. Nessa was your starting point. I realised how important it was to keep you focussed on her as much as possible, and discourage you from digging into other people.'

Keir could have told her that he knew a whole lot more now, but he decided to play dumb and keep her talking. 'For the life of me I can't work out how I brought danger,' he said. 'Or how I did anything threatening.'

'Oh really? Must be nice to be such an innocent.' For a moment, Gloria's tone was sharp and combative. Then the weariness was back. She continued in the laboured manner of someone who doesn't expect to be understood. 'What causes what? Here in the "civilised" West we think time's a vertical arrow. Present events have past causes. And they'll have future consequences. The old Chinese knew better. Synchronicity. The web of events happening now. In the present. That's where the important connections exist that make things "happen". But you don't get that, do you? You just barged in with your bloody questions about the past and with no inkling of the trouble you could cause. You know what I really thought about you? I thought, Why don't you just take your precious mummy and run away home to Australia, Mr Big Brave Pathetic War Correspondent. And leave everybody else alone. But I couldn't fool the *I Ching*. That's why I had to edit what I told you about its findings.'

Keir could follow what Gloria was saying, but he wasn't sure where she was trying to take him.

'Hold on,' he said. 'I came to Laggandarroch to try and solve the mystery of my parents. Not to create problems for anybody.'

'Parents? What's so special about parents? You're so bourgeois, Keir. What are mummy and daddy, this highly honoured pair who're responsible for so much sentimental slush? D'you know what they are? They're just people who fuck. Just like you and I fucked. Just like Paul Lamont fucked Nessa Glover. What's the big deal about that? Does it really matter whose fuck you come from?'

He knew he was being goaded, but Gloria's punches weren't landing. Heather had given him so much more to think about. Loss and pain. What makes people important to one another. Makes people care. Love. About Joe and Sarah who'd taken him away and raised him as their own precious son. About living. Here. Now. Thanks, Heather.

Compared to all that, Nessa Glover and Paul Lamont were names from ancient history, patterns of black and white emulsion in an old photograph. Yet for Gloria they were targets to attack every time he opened his mouth. Fine. Say nothing. Why push at a door that was opening anyway? He waited.

She sat upright and unmoving. He could hear her breath settle; become quieter, more regular. He guessed she was doing something to make that happen, to calm herself. Then she reached out to him. 'Can I have the book please?'

She sandwiched *Harmonious Love* between the palms of her hands and closed her eyes. When at last she began to speak, Keir wondered if she was talking to him or to herself.

'The tickle of his beard. Smells of pipe tobacco and fresh soap. That beautiful, rich, persuasive, voice. The rumble of his laugh.' She lowered her head. Her chest rose and fell to the beat of her breathing.

Silence.

Outside a wood pigeon coo-roo-coo-ed, paused, coo-roo-coo-ed again. Distant voices flared, mostly laughing at a plaintive, indistinct protest.

Silence.

At last Gloria straightened up and looked at him.

'Someday, when the world's ready, Fergus Abercrombie will be recognised for what he was. A genius. A brave, adorable, genius.' Her voice was soft. Keir could hear reverence. 'Nothing to do with intellect or creativity. No. A true genius. A guardian spirit who made people flower. In Harmony. In Love.'

She stroked the book gently, held it to her cheek.

Keir gambled: 'That book obviously means a lot to you Gloria,' he said. 'Why did you post it through my door?'

She jerked as if from a dream. 'Me? It's a long time since I've had the comfort of holding one of these. I'd never have parted with it.'

'Then whose is it?'

The softness left her. Her mouth tightened again. Her eyes flashed with an intensity he could almost feel. Then she shook her head gently to and fro and gave him a tired smile.

'Keir, Keir. You're going to find out. But I'll get there my way. All you have to do is listen. Believe me, if you want to understand, that's the best way. Just listen.'

Twenty-nine

I was born in the Upper Seristery at Harmony in 1930. Liza Honeydew, the woman who gave birth to me, had joined the community some years earlier along with her husband, Norman. By the time I arrived their relationship was very different. Ask me who my father is and I can only point to the possibilities. Maybe it was Norman Honeydew, but it's just as likely to be any other man from the Upper Seristery. Or Fergus Abercrombie himself. Or it could've been one of the youths who Liza initiated into the joys of harmonious love. That's why questions about parents don't make sense to me. Don't really matter.

You didn't react when I mentioned the Upper Seristery, so I guess you've already had a look in Fergus's book. Of course you have. So you know there's a lot of unusual language in there. We've Charles Fourier to thank for that. Fergus liked to use Fourier's original terms when he could. It was a way of thanking the man, I suppose. But he went much further than Fourier.

That's what made Fergus such a brave inspiring genius.

Fourier thought. Fergus acted.

I'm not trying to put down Charles Fourier's ideas. Far from it. They were genuinely revolutionary and fit to change the world. He not only solved the problem of how to share a community's wealth fairly, he put people's sensual satisfaction at the heart of his ideal society. But they were also ideas that finally destroyed the Harmony dream.

Before Fergus set up Harmony in 1910, other people had tried to put Fourier into practice. But these were partial attempts. Yes, they organised the life of the communities around economic sharing with everyone receiving a fair social minimum, but they ignored the sexual freedom that was fundamental to Fourier's vision. Maybe it was prudery, maybe it was ignorance, maybe it was fear. *Harmonious Love* was just a handwritten French manuscript until Fergus came across it in Paris almost eighty years ago and had a small number of English copies printed. I doubt there are many still in existence. This might even be the last one.

Fergus was determined that the community he founded would become true to both sides of Fourier's ideal, the erotic as well as the economic. And so, without meaning to, he created a fault-line that eventually split his dream apart. I find that hard to say even now, and I certainly couldn't have said it back then. But it's true. There were two separate Harmonies.

It worked like this: people who wanted to join usually came for a trial period of a few weeks. If they couldn't manage that but were promising candidates, they came for weekends. That's what happened with Nessa Glover and Paul Lamont. I haven't forgotten about them. I'll get to them soon enough.

Trialists and newcomers joined the Main Seristery and had their communal meeting rooms in the castle although they lived in other buildings around the grounds. Life for them was organised according to the principles explained in Fergus's first book *The Reluctant Capitalist* – gardening, looking after crops and livestock, producing goods in the workshops, making decisions together, sharing work and its proceeds in a fair and equal way. For many people, that was enough to satisfy their need to turn their back on the crazy confrontational system that had disillusioned Fergus and forced him to turn his back on industry. During the forty years of the commune's existence, many Harmonians lived, and some died, happy with the simple and satisfying cooperative lifestyle they'd created together in the Main Seristery.

Members of the Upper Seristery lived and socialised in the castle's upper floors. We were committed to fulfilling both sides of the Fourian vision, and *Harmonious Love* was our guidebook to a new sensual life with sexual freedom and passionate fulfilment.

Fergus shared his time between the seristeries. He was a skilled reader of people with a sharp instinct for identifying those who might be suitable to join the Upper Seristery. He would gradually introduce them to the second main theme of Fourier's dream, the abandonment of conventional sexual arrangements for a much more open system based on an erotic minimum for everyone. At any hint of resistance, he would deftly turn the conversation elsewhere and leave that person alone, for the time being at least. Any sign of interest and he would cultivate them until he was sure they were well suited. When they joined the Upper Seristery they were given a copy of *Harmonious Love* and, with full ceremony, they were initiated into the Temple of the Senses.

And he was always on the lookout for recruits. He could recognise potential in people before they saw it for themselves. People like Nessa Glover and Paul Lamont. I remember him telling the Council he'd spotted two possible members at that weekend conference – a disillusioned priest and a woman who was ripe for a new life. He was sure they were attracted to one another and he'd invited them to come back and experience life at Harmony. Fergus usually had unerring judgement in selecting people, but he made a mistake with Paul Lamont. Only one person spotted it. Nessa Glover.

I was just a girl in 1943 when Nessa and Paul Lamont began to make weekend visits. He was the one I mostly noticed. To my adolescent eyes he was devilishly handsome. Oh, no one could touch Fergus as far as my adoration was concerned, but he was a patriarch, the very soul of Harmony. Paul on the other hand was like a young hero to me. I became his secret shadow, surreptitiously following him around and feeling empty when I wasn't near him, so I was thrilled when he soon left the priesthood to become a full time Harmony member.

The other side of the coin was my bitter jealousy of Nessa when she made her weekend visits. I made it my business to keep tabs on them. I knew they used an old hay shed to spend intimate time together, and there I lurked in a shadowy corner, watching and listening.

From that hiding place I witnessed their final separation. They lay together in the straw, sated and relaxed, and started once again to talk about their future. It was a regular topic and I was becoming encouraged by what I saw as increasing disagreement: the more committed he became to Harmony, the less enthusiastic Nessa seemed about joining as a full-time member. But my growing fear was that he was beginning to win the day. As well as being good-looking he was a very persuasive talker, not in the calm, authoritative way Fergus was, no, Lamont's style depended much more on switching between determined argument and a hypnotic honeyed tongue, and the more he talked, the less Nessa seemed able to counter him.

Everything changed when he told her how Fergus had introduced him to the higher level of Harmony, to the Upper Seristery, and the scales had fallen from his eyes. Social equality was only a half-truth unless in was accompanied by sexual equality. He was a changed man and Nessa must join him in this transformation. Then he began to describe what had happened to him in the Temple of the Senses. She was on her feet in a flash. He grabbed her by the shoulders to stop the words that came tumbling out of her. She smacked him hard across the face and raced away.

I never saw Nessa again. In a few months time I left the Damselate and Paul Lamont, aided by Fergus, initiated me into the Temple of the Senses. He was my mentor when I initiated Ainsley Watson just a year later.

You look like you're not taking this in. Or maybe it's

disgust. One way or another I couldn't care less. My heart remembers how wonderful that time was for me. How true. How right. It's impossible for outsiders to understand the bonds that grew between us. Fergus and me. Ainsley and me. Paul Lamont.

And then, suddenly, Fergus died. Quietly. In his sleep. He'd shown no signs of slowing down although he was seventy-three. On his last day he was full of his usual drive and energy – a morning in the gardens, an afternoon in the carpentry workshop. Work stopped early that day for the Exchange, a weekly meeting that involved the whole community and was followed by a communal meal. Later, back in the Upper Seristery, he attended the Temple of the Senses before going to bed. Then next morning he was gone.

Our leadership and inspiration went with him. Cracks soon began to appear. At the following week's Exchange, a plan was brought forward by the Main Seristery to reorganise the community into a single group so that everyone could live within the castle itself. There was strong resistance from the Upper Seristery, especially from Paul Lamont and others who were beginning to rally around him. But the Main Seristerians outnumbered us in the Upper by about three to one. There were two other strong points in their favour. They lived mainly in wooden buildings that were starting to deteriorate. And the system of upkeep and maintenance of Harmony's resources meant they effectively controlled our access to machinery and equipment.

Life limped along, disharmonious and unresolved, for months. Paul Lamont and his group negotiated a deal that allowed them to buy another place where they planned to pursue what Lamont had started calling the pure mission of Charles Fourier and Fergus Abercrombie. I decided not to join them. By that time I'd begun to see something in Lamont, and pure wasn't the word that came to mind.

C'mon, Keir. I see the raise of the eyebrow. I guess the

word 'pure' in this context stretches your petty notions of acceptable sexual behaviour to the limit. Let me stretch them a little further. Under Fergus's guidance, what happened in the Temple of the Senses was pure. Spiritual. The complete expression of erotic passion. Lots of people were helped, their lives changed. Mine included. No one was harmed.

But a different smell came from Paul Lamont, a smell that Fergus had missed and that my adolescent infatuation couldn't recognise. Now I recognised the whiff of brimstone that would taint any group he led, so I followed my instincts and stayed behind at Harmony. Ainsley Watson went with Lamont's group to an out-of-the-way farm. Their dream ended in ruins after a woman defied Paul Lamont's orders and took a seriously ill and pregnant twelve-year-old girl to the nearest hospital. Lamont disappeared into thin air just one step ahead of the police. It was years before I discovered where he'd gone.

Life at Harmony changed too. There was a puritanical upwelling. It didn't last long, but during that time, copies of *Harmonious Love* were gathered up and burnt. I cried as I watched my copy go up in flames, but there was nothing I could do to resist what was happening. I was barely seventeen when Fergus died and had grown up entirely in an atmosphere of benign cooperation where conflict scarcely existed. And with him gone the Upper Seristerians were now a very weakened group.

This copy of the book? It belongs to your dear Daddy, Paul Lamont. That's right. Belongs. I eventually learned where he was from Ainsley Watson who'd known all along. After the incident with the pregnant girl, Lamont used his silver tongue to scurry back to the Catholic Church. I doubt he shared the whole story of what he'd been up to, but he played the part of the penitent priest convincingly enough to find a home for himself in a remote community that exists to help priests who have crises of faith. Yes. A bit ironic, eh?

Lamont wants to see you. Ainsley told him you'd turned up here, asking questions about Joe Connor and Nessa Glover...

This is the painful bit for me. What happened in the Upper Seristery took place in an atmosphere of openness and love, but it looks as if Ainsley Watson and Paul Lamont have been living lives filled with deception and the abuse of power. Ainsley took me into his confidence about Lamont's whereabouts and convinced me the man had undergone a genuine change of heart. But who am I to believe now? The Ainsley who was having sex with Rosemary? The Ainsley who liked to make favourites of vulnerable girls? The Ainsley who used to give me a wave and a toot as he passed on his way to give the girl on the pillion "a spin in the country"? Now I wonder if he was really taking them to Paul Lamont. And I feel soiled.

For most of my life I've sneered at words like evil, seen them as just more evidence of a toxic society's need to divide unrestrained human spirit into what it likes and what it doesn't. Now I'm having to think again...

Lamont gave Ainsley the book to deliver to you, along with a note asking to meet you. That was before Rosemary, before everything changed. I don't know why Ainsley delivered only the book. Events overtook him probably. You know that I've been questioned by the police? I think they found Lamont's letter along with whatever else they discovered in Ainsley's house, and I think I'm mentioned in it. But I can only guess. And I can't figure out why he wants you to have *Harmonious Love*. To prepare you for what he wants to say to you? I don't know. I've ended up the messenger.

And here's the message. He'll phone you at Barton Hotel on Friday morning. If you don't answer, he'll do the same the next morning then he'll stop and you won't hear from him again.

There's no point in asking me questions. I'm unlikely to know the answers and I don't really want to know them either. By doing what he did to Rosemary – and whoever else – then being caught, Ainsley Watson opened a door on history. That history is now hot on Paul Lamont's heels. He deserves what's coming to him. And I want nothing more to do with it.

There was a time when they were both very special to me. Deeper than brothers, deeper than family. That's why I'm delivering this message. That's why I tried to take some of the heat off Ainsley. But this. What they've been up to. It's despicable. Filthy. Abusive.

Everything about Fergus was good. What we did at Harmony with him was true, wholesome, full of hope for the future. Now they've spat on it, turned heaven into hell. And as for Ainsley's final, selfish, destructive act…

That's enough.

Please leave.

Thirty

'It's hotter than yesterday and its not finished yet.' The ticket clerk at Dumbarton East rail station volunteered this information like someone whose opinion is not to be doubted.

'Goodo.' Keir took his ticket and marvelled once again at the Scots' relationship with weather whose fickleness seemed to dominate their lives. 'Looks like another scorcher,' he'd been told in the petrol station this morning. Then the hotel receptionist welcomed him with 'Hello, Mr Connor. Another cracker of a day!' Why such a fuss over two days of temperatures that were often beaten during a Kalgoorlie winter?

He boarded the next Clydebank-bound train and within a few minutes was speeding along the estuarine flats of the Clyde, past the handsome white-painted Barton Hotel. He'd stopped there just long enough to check in and take his weekend bag to the room. Well, to the honeymoon suite to be exact, the only vacancy available at short notice. He'd hesitated at the price then talked them into rolling Thursday, Friday and Saturday into a weekend package for two. When Eryn had been able to take his call in a brief gap between client appointments he told her there'd been important developments and he would be at the hotel for the next three days. Would she like to join him? Would she ever! She'd be there Thursday night. She could talk her way out of a Friday morning staff meeting but had a full diary of appointments in the afternoon. 'And then, I'm all yours.'

'I'm all yours too.'

There were few passengers on the train and a pleasant breeze rippled through the carriage. The Clyde dominated the view from Keir's window seat. The tide was full and under a clear blue sky the river was a shimmering unbroken sheet maybe half a mile from bank to bank. How steady and constant it seemed to him, in contrast to the ongoing drama and turbulence of the past few days. Yet, despite its placid look, it too was on the move, flowing steadily down to the sea.

Unlike him. He was heading upstream, against the current, towards the past, hoping to fill gaps in a picture that was coming more and more into focus.

Nessa now had a beginning, a middle and an end. That basic underlying structure, the skeleton from which her life-story hung, was unlikely to change much now. But if he could clarify details, sketch in locations, then maybe he would know her better. Because he was growing to like Nessa, to like and admire her. She seemed to stand in bright counterpoint to the fragmentary, disturbing picture of Paul Lamont that Gloria had painted yesterday.

What did he make of Lamont, the rogue priest who'd made Nessa pregnant? His father? Now that was a trickier question. He'd heard Lamont's name for the first time from Heather just two days ago, along with hints that he'd somehow done the dirty on Nessa. Now Gloria had told him the man was alive and wanted to see him.

And what about the contrived way Paul Lamont had chosen to get in touch? Gloria had told him enough to put together a likely scenario. Either Lamont knew he was on the police's radar or he was making a pretty good guess about it. His response was to hide or at least control how he could be contacted. That spoke of probable guilt. Keir could have asked Gloria what the police knew of the links between Ainsley Watson and Lamont but he deliberately hadn't. In her state, she might just have clammed up on him. More importantly, as long as he didn't know Lamont was on the run he didn't have to tell anyone else about meeting him.

Thinking about Nessa made him feel good – warm and calm inside. Thinking about Lamont made him uneasy. But they could both wait for the moment. He leaned back and closed his eyes. Ah, Eryn.

The train stopped at Kilbendrick. Beyond the platform lay the rusty, weed-strewn wilderness of Henderson's shipyard where he'd shuddered in the grip of flashback hallucinations, ducking the shells and staring guiltily at the corpses. His arrival in Scotland and his early visits to Clydebank and Kilbendrick now had a far-off, nightmarish quality – bleak, distant pictures viewed through the wrong end of a telescope. He'd been jet-lagged, he'd been drinking too much, and his beat-up mind was a plaything for memories and delusions. That seemed a long way off now, not so much in time as in how he was starting to feel...

A high embankment carried the railway across the centre of Clydebank. Keir easily identified the shipyard from his vantage point on the station platform — beyond the roofs of the tenements, tower cranes crowded the sky in a forest of steel, their elegant counterweighted jibs balanced like the heads of great wading birds.

When he reached the main gate, the sign above it read "Marathon Manufacturing". A man in uniform was talking on the telephone inside a glass-fronted gatehouse. Just outside the door, an elderly security guard sat in the sunshine. He was in his shirtsleeves. The Marathon logo was emblazoned on the peak of his cap and on the breast pocket of the jacket hanging from his chair back. The open clipboard folder propped on his lap didn't quite hide the racing newspaper he was studying.

'Any good tips, mate?' Keir asked.

The clipboard snapped shut, the man's eyes narrowed in appraisal. 'Try Steve's The Boy. Kempton. Four o'clock,' he said in a neutral tone.

'I was hoping this was John Brown's yard.'

'You're at the end of a long queue there, son. Clydebank's full of people who hoped it would be John Brown's yard forever. No. This used to be Brown's. It's owned by Yanks now. Building oil rigs. Not that we gave up without a fight. You know? The work-in?'

'The work-in?' Keir shook his head.

'Where've you been living for the last ten years son?'

'Australia. Vietnam. Cambodia.'

'Thought as much. You'd have to be living places like that not to know about the work-in. National news it was. The shop stewards locked out the management and the workers took over the yard. We ran it ourselves, built ships, met all the delivery targets, drummed up new orders. It was in the papers, on the telly. For months!'

'You used to work here?'

'I did. Man and boy. Forty years at the welding. And look at me now. Monkey on a fucking stick.' His self-mocking smile was uneven and gap-toothed. 'So, can I help you, son?'

Keir gave a simplified version. He'd come from Australia to fill in gaps about his family. His mother had worked as a welder in Brown's during the war. The security man remembered the dilutees as they'd been called at the time. Some of those women had been great welders, he said. He didn't know them personally. He'd worked in the West Yard at that time and the women were based in the old smithy in the East Yard. Would Keir like to see it? They couldn't go into it for safety reasons but on a day like this the doors would be wide open and they'd get a good look inside. He knocked on the glass and gestured to his mate that he and Keir were heading into the yard.

Soon they were beneath the towering presence of some of the cranes Keir had seen from the railway station. The guard led the way towards some long high-roofed structures that formed the upstream boundary of the shipyard.

'The first one of these is the old smithy,' he said. 'It's changed a bit but not that much. Shipyard owners liked making money but they weren't always so keen to spend it.'

When they rounded the end of the building, Keir was looking through high wide doors that reminded him of an aeroplane hanger. In a long tunnel-like building, amid a clanging din lit by the crackling blue flashes of a small army of welders, fabrication was taking place on a scale that made midgets of the men doing the work. Curved steel plates were being brought in at the far end and welded into longer tubular pieces as they progressed through a sequence of workstations towards the doors where Keir and his escort were standing. Whining overhead, electric hoists moved the growing segments along the assembly line.

'It was a lot simpler when your mother was here,' the security man shouted in his ear. 'A lot noisier too. Forget all the bright lights, and the fancy cranes. Forget all those roof windows as well. It was a lot darker. A lot smokier. The far end was right out of hell – the red roar of the main furnace and the batter of the big steam hammer. You didn't half feel it through your tackety boots when that thing let loose. Your mother would have worked in the welders' cubicles, just about in the middle of the building, surrounded by shelves of steel that made a cave all the way up to the roof.'

Keir could imagine an immense gloomy, church-like building, reeking, clanging and shaking while Heather, Nessa and their workmates wielded their welding torches like fireflies as they did their best to win a war, to defeat the people who'd delivered death and destruction from the sky.

The old man tugged on Keir's shirtsleeve. 'We'll have to get moving, pal. C'mon and I'll show you something else before you go.'

They trooped back beneath the cranes until they reached the upper end of an immense concrete ramp that sloped gently downwards until it reached the river's edge and slipped beneath the surface.

'This is it, son. Building Berth 5. Over a thousand feet from end to end. *The Lusitania, Mauretania, Queen Mary,*

Queen Elizabeth, *QE2* – they all started life here as a line of keel plates. The best ocean-going liners ever built. That'll ever be seen. And we built them. Created not just boats, but beauty. If you weren't part of it, it's hard to know how that feels. So here's a wee story.

'One night during the work-in I came off shift and went across the road to Connolly's where a lot of the older hands used to drink. I walked into a deathly silence. People sitting stunned. A couple of men in tears. They'd just seen the news on the telly. The *Queen Elizabeth* had sunk in Hong Kong after she'd gone on fire. These guys weren't pansies. They were some of the toughest you'll ever come across. But there they were, greeting like weans.'

Keir could see that the old man's eyes had filled. Now he drew Keir's attention to another building berth and the outlines of an almost completed drilling rig. 'Would you look at that?' he said. 'Three big tin cans with a biscuit box stuck on top of them. And as ugly as sin. Where's the pleasure? Where's the pride? When I look at that, I'm glad I'm too old for the welding.'

Back at the gatehouse, Keir shook hands with his guide and asked directions to Thistle Street where Hugh and Nessa Glover had lived with their children. He decided to walk the couple of miles and set out at a brisk pace. The sun continued to blaze, and it was warm work; but it was now late afternoon, and he wanted to be sure he was back at the hotel before Eryn arrived.

Thistle Street was in Dalmuir, a western suburb of the town, and his route there took him through the centre of Clydebank. After he passed the town hall and the library, he began to notice occasional gaps in the tenements lining Dumbarton Road, the main thoroughfare to the west. Sometimes the three- or four-storey buildings ended in a neat vertical wall where the only evidence of the homes that had once been there were the lintels marking the positions of long disappeared chimneys and wall cupboards. Some distance along the road, the building began again as abruptly as it ended, in another vertical wall containing similar ghostly reminders of human presence in what was now thin air. Occasionally the gaps were filled with replacement homes, built to blend sympathetically with the original architecture on either side. It occurred to Keir there must be some measurable relationship between the lengths of the gaps and the quantity of German high explosive that had caused them.

As soon as he crossed the bridge where the Forth and Clyde canal marked the Dalmuir boundary, he turned into Thistle Street and made his way along the right hand tenement row heading for a large gap in the middle of it. He noted the numbers of the communal entrances as he passed. The last one was Number 22. When he reached the gap he began counting his paces.

The space was grassed over and contained a children's play park – some swings, a group of yellow-beaked ducklings mounted on springs, a mound with a slide bedded into it and a climbing frame on top. Two young mothers sat chatting on a bench. Keir took fifty paces to reach the other side. The first communal entrance there was Number 30.

The facing tenement across the road was complete although he could see it too was missing a section further along. He crossed to get a better view of the gap he had just paced out. Like those he'd seen earlier, the walls on either side carried mute relics of the missing houses. One land mine, three sections of communal living obliterated. He knew the Glovers had died at number 28, the middle one. So those silent outer walls were once the homes of their neighbours. He looked towards Clydebank and imagined Nessa witnessing the moment of impact. He saw her climb the pile of rubble and look into the hell that had consumed her family. Saw the old woman approach her with the infant's shawl.

The two young mothers on the bench were watching him intently. One of them crossed the grass, called out to him

'Can I help you?' Keir could hear her suspicion.

'No. It's okay. Someone I … a relative, lived here. Lost her family in the Blitz.'

'Oh dear. I'm sorry,' Her look changed to one of concern.

As Keir walked to Dalmuir railway station, he turned over and over in his head what he'd almost said in answer to the wary young mum.

Someone I know lived here.

Someone I know.

Someone I know.

Thirty-one

Keir made a deep, solemn bow at the honeymoon suite door then gestured Eryn forward with an extravagant wave of his hand. He watched her face as she took in the large four-poster bed, the window view of the wide estuary, the smoked salmon and ice-bucket on the table, the roses.

'Whe-e-e-e!' She kicked off her shoes, spun across the carpet and threw herself backwards onto the bed's quilted softness.

Keir waved a menu at her. 'What d'you reckon we take a quick squiz at this and order a room service dinner for around eight? Means we can relax for an hour or so.' He reached for the champagne.

'Before you open that, can we talk about you? How was Clydebank? Everything go smoothly?'

'Yeah. All good. Lots to think about but no sign of the old demons. It's beginning to feel as if that flashback stuff has decided to stop giving me a beating and has taken off to trouble someone else.'

'Interesting. That sounds like good news.'

Keir stripped the foil from the champagne cork and unwound the sealing wire. 'Yeah. A few mornings back, just after I'd arrived at Laggandarroch, I found myself standing in the woods watching a family of deer. I'm sure I'd been standing there for a while, totally absorbed. What really struck me was my calmness inside, the absence of any threat, any anxiety, any lurking ghosts for me to guard against. It's a long time since I felt like that. I'm hoping it'll stick around for a while.' He gripped the cork tightly in the circle made by his left thumb and forefinger. 'And you're helping too.'

'That counts both ways. But I guess the real test will be when you're next under stress, not in peaceful countryside ... or bobbing about a honeymoon suite with a bottle of bubbles in your hand.'

Keir placed the base of the bottle in the palm of his right hand, gripped it tightly, and began a slow steady rotation. When he felt the cork give, he let it ease out with a deep satisfying pop. 'That's it, Doc, consultation's over.'

The girl who brought their meal had an air of youthful innocence. Keir watched her eyes widen at the sight of a bare-legged man in a dressing-gown at eight o'clock on a Thursday evening. When she was unable to restrain her urge to look into the room beyond, he took hold of the tray to catch her attention then gave her a bold, wicked wink. She blushed and sped away.

'What have you been up to?' Eryn sat up and watched him carry the laden tray to the table.

'Scaring a local and enhancing my reputation all at the same time.'

As they ate, he updated her on developments at Laggandarroch – his encounter with the television crew, the headmaster's reflections, and how, despite Ainsley Watson's suicide, police investigations were continuing and Gloria Honeydew had been questioned.

Most of all, he spoke about his meeting with Gloria; how she'd finally come clean about her detailed knowledge of Nessa Glover and Paul Lamont; her mind-boggling story of Fergus Abercrombie, *Harmonious Love*, and the sexual elite of the Upper Seristery; the painful ripping apart of the Harmony community after Abercrombie's death; and the final revelation that Lamont was alive and wanted to meet Keir.

He made no mention of his own entanglement with Gloria. He'd felt uneasy when Eryn had questioned him about her after they woke up together aboard *Spaniard's Choice*. But not now. One way or another it was in the past and there it would stay.

Eryn listened intently and still managed to give full attention to her food. He watched her gnaw at a chicken leg, pull it apart and nibble off every tendril of flesh then wipe her chin with her napkin and reach for another piece. When she'd had enough she sucked her fingers clean one by one then used a piece of bread to scoop up every last gravy-soaked morsel. She spoke just once during his account. After he told her how Gloria had passed on a message that Paul Lamont wanted to see him and would phone the hotel in the morning, she stopped eating, shook her head and said 'What?' in a tone that sounded somewhere between disgust and disbelief.

When he was finished, her first question was about Gloria. 'Can you believe her? Why are you trusting her now when you know she deliberately misled you before about Nessa and Lamont?'

'She was a different Gloria this time. She'd dropped her mask and I think she had truth rather than deception in her mind. She was hurting to a point where she didn't care any more what I thought. Grieving, maybe that's a closer word.'

'For Ainsley Watson?'

'Maybe in the way a sister might grieve for a brother who'd let the family down, hadn't lived up to expectations. It wasn't just for Ainsley though. Her memories and feelings for Fergus Abercrombie were very strong, and for the old Harmony life where the usual sexual rules for mothers, fathers, sisters, brothers, lovers, had been kicked right out of the park and replaced with a free-for-all. Maybe more than anything she's grieving for the past, for a lost golden age that's now come to a shabby end.'

'But it doesn't sound like those feelings applied to Paul Lamont.'

'Just the opposite. More like she saw him as the evil wrecker who destroyed the dream, who soiled Fergus Abercrombie's pure vision, who was somehow involved in

257

the downfall of Ainsley Watson.'

'So why is she acting as Lamont's messenger?' Eryn shook an emphatic finger.

'That's a good question. I can't be sure but I think part of the answer is she wants to finish a job that Ainsley took on.'

'You didn't ask her?'

'No way. A question like that would have had me looking at the outside of her classroom door. Maybe she wants me to learn something about Lamont, something that'll damage him.'

'Right. This is where I really start to get worried. What are you getting into, Keir? The police have interviewed Gloria. What's her connection? When you read between the lines of what she told you, could it be that Ainsley Watson was supplying girls to Paul Lamont? Shouldn't you be talking to the police instead of making arrangements to meet this man?'

'I've been mulling over most of that. Those only become real questions if he phones tomorrow, or maybe the next day. Or maybe never. This is tonight. You and me. Tonight.'

Later, he took her face between his hands. 'You've hijacked me. Bewitched my mind and I can't get you out of it. I just want more and more of you.'

Later still, he tried not to disturb her as he slipped from beneath her sleep-heavy weight. 'Good night, my lover,' she muttered as she turned onto her side.

'Good night, my lover.' He stroked her hair, planted a soft kiss on the back of her neck.

They were having a morning soak in the sunken jacuzzi when the telephone rang.

'Hello? Keir Connor here.'

'Ah. Good. Fancy meeting up later today?' Paul Lamont's voice was an ageing husky whisper that also managed to sound confident. Keir could hear Clydeside origins beneath the educated accent.

'Yeah. Let's do that. Would you like to come to the hotel?'

'Ah, no. Somewhere more open. I need to get all the fresh air I can these days. D'you know the Erskine Bridge?'

'Yeah.'

'There's a cemetery nearby on your side of the river.'

'Yes. Dalnottar. I know where it is.'

'Good. You can park there. Let's meet at noon. About the middle of the bridge? There's a wonderful view from up there.'

Keir replaced the phone. 'He wants to meet on the Erskine Bridge at noon today.'

'That's ridiculous. This whole situation's crazy and getting crazier. Keir, are you sure about meeting this man? He worries me. I think he's a controller. He manipulates people and probably abuses them. Look at how he's setting you up.'

'He's like that if we believe Gloria Honeydew. You said as much last night, but that's not enough for me. I need to make up my own mind about him. It's got nothing to do with whether or not he's my father. I've pretty much sorted that out in my mind. Whatever the rights and wrongs of Joe and Sarah Connor stealing me off to Australia, they were the parents who raised me. There's no way Paul Lamont can hurt or trouble me now.' He drew her to him, kissed her, held her close.

'I want to tell you something,' she said. 'The other night? Aboard the boat? I'd decided I wasn't going to let anything happen between us. A glass of wine as we talked about our visit to Heather's. Maybe a goodnight kiss or two. Then off to separate bunks. Not that I didn't fancy you. I did. Right from the start at the wine and cheese do. Although I didn't know as much then as I do now, I realised you had a lot to sort out so I decided to take it easy. Maybe help you if I could and save romance for later. But after I watched you deal with Heather then listened to you talk in the cabin…'

'… you fell for the knuckle-head who was blabbing on about a lot of self-absorbed rubbish while the most beautiful woman in the world sat looking into his eyes.'

She silenced him with fingertips on his lips. 'Keir. Please. Stay serious for a minute. I'm worried for you.' He had the good sense to shut up while she gathered her thoughts. 'You told me that Gloria described Lamont as having a whiff of brimstone about him. She might be on to something. Let me tell you a story now.

'As part of my training I elected to do a forensic psychology placement at Carstairs. That's Scotland's secure psychiatric hospital for the criminally insane, some of the country's most dangerous people are locked up there. I was supervised by Dr Silvas, a much-respected forensic expert. He invited me to carry out a blind assessment of a patient without first consulting the available case files. I found myself forming a sympathetic picture of a young man about my age who had a strange hypnotic presence. It was partly physical: he had pale, almost ivory-looking skin, large eyes so black the pupils were scarcely visible, long dark curls; but it was also because of the calm steady way he told me about the dreadful life he had experienced. When I presented my findings to Dr Silvas he revealed that my subject was a notorious young man called Eamon McLuff who had raped, mutilated, and murdered three children, and his true background bore little relationship to the persuasive story I'd been fooled by. "A very small number of people force us into an uncomfortable corner, Miss Galbraith," Dr Silvas told me. "In thirty years of this work I have met only three. Eamon McLuff is one of them. The simplest word to use for them is evil." I was shocked and I challenged him. Surely a psychologist couldn't believe evil people existed? "Yes I can," he told me, "but not as a professional diagnosis."

'You can walk away from this now, Keir. Haven't you

found out enough?'

'No, it's a goer for me, Eryn. I've turned it over and over in my head all day while I followed Nessa's footsteps through Clydebank. If history had played out a different way and Nessa was the one who was alive and had asked to see me, I would be there like a shot. You're right though, everything I've learned about Lamont says he's turned out to be a pretty shifty bloke. But without him I wouldn't be here talking to you about it. He's asked to meet me and I believe he's due that. So I have to meet Paul Lamont just this once. It'll be okay, don't you worry.'

They had time for a walk along the estuary shore before Eryn had to leave for her afternoon clinic appointments. She was steeped in the lore of the Clyde, thanks to a childhood spent aboard the various craft her father had owned, and knew this area well. That long grassy island just being surrounded by the rising tide? The site of a crannog – a two-thousand-year-old stilted dwelling and dock complex where a forty-foot dugout canoe had been excavated, so Clyde shipbuilding went back a long way. And those buoys in the middle of the river? They marked the half-mile of Golborne's Lang Dyke. He was an eighteenth century engineer who'd designed a stone structure to harness the river's current and deepen the shipping channel.

While Keir listened, an idea began to form. The Clyde wasn't just a stream of water. It was an entity, a being that threaded through the lives of the people who lived here, sometimes giving, sometimes taking away. He remembered Cambodia, and Chandina talking to him about her reverence for the river spirits she called Nata. Each year she travelled back to the Siem Reap river to join with her family and honour the Nata at the Water Festival. Maybe that's what connected the stone age man and his log boat to the people who built the great ships – the spirit of the river itself, a spirit that drew tears from the eyes of tough workmen and inspired the lament of the old man who had showed him around the rump of a world-beating shipyard. Keir too felt its influence – the river wove together the stories of the people who'd brought him back to Scotland and played a part in the life of the woman who might keep him here. In a couple of hours time he would stand high above it and wait for Paul Lamont. Am I being woven in too? he wondered.

He pointed upriver to where the two towers and slim curve of the Erskine bridge gleamed white in the strong sunshine. 'What a great day for a stroll across that beauty!' he said. 'Whoever I meet up there.'

'Don't depend on it. I don't think this'll last.'

'What's with Scots people and the weather?' he said. 'Can't they just enjoy three summer days in a row?'

'Look behind you.' She pointed down the estuary where cotton wool clouds were building above the distant mountains. 'That line of cumulus probably marks the edge of a cold front. It could turn nasty. Trust me. I'm a Clyde boatman's daughter.'

'Just because I come from a hot climate doesn't mean I melt in the rain. I'll be okay.'

Eryn gestured more emphatically downriver. 'I'm not talking a light shower. If squalls develop ahead of that lot, they can be very unpredictable, very violent. The rain could be hitting you at fifty knots – that's close to sixty miles an hour, the way you count – so keep an eye on the sky."

Keir widened his face into a mock horror mask. 'Oh gawd! Help! C'mon!' He took the giggling Eryn by the hand and set off in an exaggerated slow motion run back the way they had come.

They kissed goodbye in the hotel car park. Eryn lowered her car window. 'Take care on the bridge. The river can be a trigger for you, and up there you're wrapped in its sights, its sounds, its smell. And be very careful with Lamont.'

Thirty-two

Keir parked beside Dalnottar Cemetery gates and followed a footpath that dipped into a cool, pleasant wooded glen. He leaned into his stride as the track began to climb steeply towards the approach road to Erskine bridge. A final flight of concrete steps took him up onto a pedestrian pathway that ran along the very edge of the bridge. When he peered over the chest-high safety rail on his left he was surprised by the height he'd already reached. The glen he'd walked through was now well below him, its tall treetops a mottled carpet of green sweeping down to meet the blue-slated roofs of Old Kilpatrick village. On his right, a double set of safety barriers separated a cycleway from the southbound dual carriageway traffic. Beyond the central crash barrier a second dual carriageway took traffic northwards. Ahead of him the bridge swept around a left-hand bend and on towards the curved central section, suspended a hundred feet above the river from its two elegant, pencil-slim towers. Somewhere up there he was going to meet Paul Lamont.

As Keir climbed, his first warning of approaching traffic was a gritty whizz that increased in volume and pitch, zipped past in a swirl of slipstream then decreased and slowly faded as the drivers sped on towards the summit of the bridge. When he reached the suspended section, he felt the bridge become alive beneath his feet – cars caused a small jerking shake, an articulated lorry earned a precise bounce for each axle and left a rippling aftershock.

He was almost at the first suspension tower before he had a clear view of the road rising towards him from the other end of the bridge. There was no-one in sight. In both directions, the empty dark tarred pathway trembled in the sunshine. He checked his watch – ten minutes to midday – then rested his arms on the railing and looked upstream. The river disappeared around a bend but its position further on was signposted by the tangle of shipyard cranes at Clydebank. He used what landmarks he could to recreate the route he'd walked to Dalmuir yesterday. From up here Thistle Street seemed a mere step away in space yet its bomb-gapped roofline travelled back forty years in time. Back to the world of Nessa Glover and her family. Of his newly discovered Aunt Heather. Of Father Paul Lamont.

He put his back to the safety rail and looked downriver. Now he was looking across the width of the bridge and into the world of Joe and Sarah Connor. Henderson's shipyard. The newer concrete buildings marking the bombsites either side of the tenement where Joe and Sarah had lived, where he was born, where Nessa died. The Bendrick Inn. The harbour slumbering in the noonday sun.

He was struck again by how the river beneath his feet seemed to tie worlds together, to connect lives, unite past and present. Back home, Aboriginal people believed the earth was crossed by songlines that guarded the culture and spirituality of all living beings. Maybe the Clyde did a similar job.

Below him, he could pick out the black hull of *Spaniard's Choice* in the mooring basin but his gaze didn't linger there. Further down the estuary, Eryn's weather warning was starting to shape up. The large puffy clouds she'd pointed out when they walked beside the Clyde had grown into dazzling snow-white and dove-grey pillars that jostled one another higher and higher into the sky. Beneath these soaring columns, darker clouds coalesced into a dense purple-black curtain that obliterated river, shores and hills. Ahead of this ominous backdrop, the distant sunlit town of Dumbarton glowed like a stage set.

He reached a ceremonial plaque that marked the midpoint of the bridge. Ahead and behind, the pedestrian path was deserted. He checked his watch. It was just past noon.

Beyond the second suspension tower, a dark figure began to emerge from the shimmering curvature of the bridge – first the head and shoulders, then the upper body, finally the legs. The man's head was down as if he was struggling with the climb but his slow, stooped walk was purposeful. As he came closer, Keir could see he was wearing an ageing black suit with baggy knees and wrinkled sleeves. He must be sweltering inside that outfit, Keir thought.

The newcomer stopped and lifted his head. Damp strands of lank grey hair framed a face whose yellowish pallor showed through a haze of white stubble. His breathing rasped and his lips tightened with each in-breath. The eyes that studied Keir shone from deep bluish sockets; the brow above them was glazed with sweat.

'Hello, Keir,' said the same husky voice he'd heard on the telephone.

'Hello, Paul.' Without being sure why, Keir took a step backwards. Since seeing the 1943 photograph of Nessa at Harmony, he had carried in his mind not just an image of her but also of the boyishly handsome priest who sat on the grass beside her, the man Heather described as 'a bit of a dish'. But he found little to recognise in the gaunt apparition in front of him. Keir had an urge to swallow but his mouth was dry. There was something weird about Lamont, and he sensed danger. But it was more complicated than that. He felt pity too. The man looked weary, sick, almost done. A sudden cool breeze scurried up the river, shivered at Keir then passed as quickly as it had arrived.

Lamont put down the lightly filled holdall he was carrying, took out a half-full wine bottle, unscrewed the top, and reached it into the space between the two men. A stale sour smell wafted across to Keir. 'At last the son joins the father. Let us commune together.'

'Thanks, Paul, but no. Just a tad early for me.'

'You misunderstand. I'm not offering a social drink.

Wine has already been taken today at many masses across the land.' He spoke like a schoolmaster who, after so many years in front of the class, has forgotten how to have a conversation.

Is this the booze talking? Keir wondered. Or is a screw loose? 'Ah. I guess I follow what your saying, but that's still no to the drink. I don't do the god-bothering stuff either.'

'What a pity. In that case, I'll share our libation with the river.' Lamont's Adam's apple worked as he slugged from the bottle. He paused, poured a little wine over the safety barrier then helped himself to a few more swallows before fixing his glinting eyes on Keir again. 'This is holy wine...' he gestured the bottle's gaudy yellow label at Keir 'made for centuries by my Benedictine brethren, God bless them.'

'Right oh, but now the ceremony's over, maybe we can start talking. You have first go, Paul, you sent out the invitation.' Keir aimed for a neutral tone. The old man clearly wasn't very stable and the situation was hard to predict.

Lamont took his time. He returned his attention to the bottle, checked its level, decided against another swig but left the cap off. 'Keir ... Keir. So you were a boy. And now a man. I've thought about you a lot. Wondered. Keir ... I loved her. Nessa. Your mother. I knew she was pregnant. Maybe that's why she lost faith. Maybe I didn't do a good job of explaining about the life we could share at Harmony, although I doubt that. I've always been good at convincing people, making them believe, helping them see where the truth lies, what I could do for them and they for me.

'I told her it would be our dream come true. Equality, spirituality, sexuality, all rolled into one. She became very angry. "Maybe your dream," she said. "Not mine. Not my child's." And she stormed out. We never met again...' He stopped abruptly and grabbed at the railing as a police car sped up the bridge towards them, siren shrieking, then raced past. He took another pull at the wine bottle. 'Did you tell anyone about our meeting?'

'No one who drives a police car, that's for sure.'

'My life's become rather … tangled … recently. I suspect my dear old friend Gloria's told you something of that.'

'No, she didn't say much.'

'Really? Maybe she tired herself out talking to the police.' Lamont's eyes searched Keir's as he waited for his answer.

'Police? What would Gloria talk to them about?

'Time's short,' Lamont said. 'Shame if we wasted it on cat and mouse games. I hear you've been asking questions at Laggandarroch. I'm sure she told you about the breakup of the commune, and probably painted a black picture of me in the process.'

He waved a hand at Keir as if to forestall a response. 'Yes, my commune came to an unfortunate end. An unnecessary end. Luckily I found a refuge but recent events have forced me back on the road again.'

'Travelling pretty light, Paul.' Keir gestured at the near-empty holdall.

'I don't have a long journey planned.' He paused for a few moments, as if collecting his thoughts. 'We had the skills to look after that pregnant child, you know. We had done so before. And it was a fundamental tenet of my teaching that those outside would not understand our life. Fourier himself taught us that.' He straightened up and with the intensity of an evangelical preacher he began to declare words that sounded to Keir like one of the passages underlined in *Harmonious Love*. 'The law condemns to death a pauper who is driven by hunger to steal a loaf of dark bread, and it protects and honours the hoarder who inflicts famine on thirty million men. And today's law-makers suppose that the sexual needs are less urgent than the need for food. This is an error.'

Lamont stood tall as he shouted the last word and for a moment Keir glimpsed the charismatic man he might once have been. Then his shoulders slumped and he gasped for three or four breaths before continuing. 'But we were betrayed by one of our number and, as prophesied, the police were determined to stick to their misguided opinions. Outsiders can't grasp a truth that is based on higher values. You won't understand. How can you?'

'Funny you should say that, Paul. I served my stint in a closed society too, in a combat platoon in Vietnam. A war zone's a long way from normal life. I've done my share of stuff that "they" wouldn't understand.'

'Ah. So you have your secrets too. Good. Like father like son. I hope you've learned the most important lessons. Secrets bring power to some. Enslavement to others. Be one of the powerful ones, my son.'

Eryn's words about evil came back to Keir, Gloria's whiff of brimstone. He again sensed something black, something dangerous in this man, in the coaxing tone of his husky voice. He broke eye contact and looked around, at the tall suspension tower ahead, down to the Clyde beneath them, at the purple wall of cloud creeping its way upriver. He focussed himself. Waited. Then spoke.

'No, we're not the same, Paul. We're different. I can recognise that what happened to me screwed up my life and damaged me in the process. Slowly I'm conquering my demons. I think you're damaged goods too, but you won't understand that. Instead you hide away, pretending to be a priest while Ainsley Watson's been bringing you young girls to abuse.'

'Pretending to be a priest! I never stopped being a priest! I've always been a priest. I knew that in childhood, knew it before I was ordained. I was a priest at Harmony, the one who understood Fergus Abercrombie's vision, the right one to lead after he died. I am one of the consecrated – nothing on earth can alter that. Nothing. No-one.' The almost empty bottle quivered in his hand.

'Oh yeah, Fergus Abercrombie's vision. I understand it

much better now thanks to the book you sent me. Thanks too for underlining the bits about the priest's duties. Breaking in young girls for sex. I didn't realise that was a fringe benefit of the job.'

'Damn your blaspheming tongue!' His mouth twitched and grimaced. White spittle gathered at the corners. 'My priesthood isn't there to be criticised, it's there to be recognised! Honoured! I took the privileges that were my due. It is spelled out in *Harmonious Love*. "Any Damsel may redeem a transgression by spending two nights with a priest." Ainsley never faltered. No. Ainsley never faltered. All the girls he brought were transgressors.' He lifted an orator's arm and his voice rose to a hoarse crescendo. 'And the church lost its faith in me then found it again! Welcomed me back with open arms!'

Kilbendrick had disappeared under a towering wall of cloud. A powerful gust of wind tore at them and howled around the cables. The bridge lurched beneath Keir's feet. He saw Lamont stagger sideways then Keir had to close his eyes against a flurry of rain that stung like hail and plastered his shirt to his back. The shower passed quickly and the wind dropped to a stiff, chilling breeze.

A quizzical look had softened Lamont's face. He was looking at Keir as if seeing him for the first time. 'Your mother had faith in me, but she lost it.' He rubbed his brow in a gesture of weariness. Shook his head. 'A priest needs people who believe in him.' He moved closer with his arms held wide. His chin had sagged, his mouth was open and he looked old and vulnerable.

The squall that hit Keir slammed him hard against the safety barrier and for a moment he thought he was going to be lifted and blown over it. He threaded his arms through the bars and held on. The bridge began to buck beneath him. The howl in the cables rose to a banshee shriek he could feel in his stomach. He forced open his eyes against the relentless needles of rain and could make out the blurred black figure of Lamont pinned against the barrier. Yet there was movement. The black shape was lifting itself up … up … up … to the top of the barrier. Legs scrabbled at the safety rail, scrabbled again, found purchase. Lamont raised both arms into the storm and was whirled away.

A loud bang on the road behind Keir was followed by crashing, splintering, then a piercing high screech that got louder and louder as it raced towards him. A voice shouted 'Incoming! Incoming!' but he was sure it came from inside his head. Even as he curled himself into a tighter ball, as he felt the fear churn in his guts and waited for the explosion, he knew this was unlike any weapon he had ever experienced, knew that he was on a bridge in a storm, knew … then he was battered across the back, thumped on the head, pinned down by an unstoppable force.

The howling in the suspension cables eased to a moan. The bridge stopped bucking and the pressure on Keir slackened. He pushed back against a piece of white panelling that was pinning him down, then crept out from under it. He wiped at the wetness streaming down his face and found it was blood.

'Are you okay?' A man was pulling debris aside to reach him. 'I just saw you at the last minute. We were all over the place. I could hardly see a foot in front of me. Then she flipped.' He gestured over his shoulder at the mangled remains of a white caravan, on its side but still hitched to a car slewed across the road.

'Did you see the other man go over? There was another man here. He went over. Did you see him?'

'What? Oh my God! Who? Was he with you?'

Keir shook his head in bewilderment, unable to fit the question to what had just happened.

A woman joined the man and between them they helped Keir to his feet. She mopped blood from his face. 'It doesn't look too bad,' she said. 'Let's get out of the rain. I can fix that up in the car.'

Keir allowed himself to be led.

'I'll find an emergency phone,' the man called after them.

The woman was gentle as she cleaned Keir's cut. 'Was he someone you knew? The other man?' she asked.

'His name's Paul Lamont,' Keir said. Then stopped. What more could he say? He was my father? He was a phoney priest? He was a child abuser?

The woman didn't press him, but he felt trapped within her silence. He'd overcome a potential flashback, pushed it away before it could unleash its fiends. Before that, he'd met the man who gave life to him, and their brief time together had been marked by confrontation then ended in what looked like suicide. Now, more than anything else, he needed to be alone. When the woman's husband returned and began, with the help of a lorry driver, to right the wrecked caravan and clear debris from the road, Keir escaped the car on the pretence of going to help them. Instead, he walked past a line of halted vehicles, back to the centre of the bridge, leaned on the barrier, looked down at the slate-grey water far below.

A sudden flash of rage surprised him. Its target was not Paul Lamont but Joe Connor – Joe, the steady quiet dad who'd raised him in Kalgoorlie. Did he have to write that letter? Conjure all of this up from beyond the grave? Kick off the train of events that led to this bridge, to the awfulness he had just witnessed, had just taken part in? The answers arrived slowly, steadily. Of course Joe had to write the letter. If his mother had had her way Keir would have learned the truth long before. It was a truth he was entitled to. A truth he deserved.

He was shivering and soaked to the skin. The rain was easing and the wind had dropped to a stiff breeze. The dark mass of the squall marched relentlessly on upriver where nothing could be seen but its black wall towering high above him. He turned his back on it. Downriver the sky was already starting to brighten.

There's no blame.

No one to be angry with.

Not even himself.

He heard distant sirens, saw flashing lights approach.

Thirty-three

Keir pushed Charlie Wilson's wheelchair up the steepest stretch of road leading to the top of the small hill that formed Dalnottar Cemetery. They joined Eryn and Heather who stood beside a simple headstone that bore two names: "Richard (Ricky) Glover 1927-1941" and "Nessa Glover 1906-1944". A third line read: "As close as we can be".

'Hello Nessa Glover, hello Ricky,' Keir said to himself. That felt fine. 'Hello Mum,' he added. That felt fine too. Eryn squeezed his hand.

After a minute or two of silence, Heather turned and led the group to a large granite memorial that stood on an open patch of grass barely two coffin lengths from Nessa's resting place. 'If the bodies of Hugh and the kids are anywhere, they're in this mass grave,' she said. Three massive grey slabs perched side-by-side on a long scalloped plinth. The inscription on the tallest, central slab read "Dedicated to the memory of the citizens of Clydebank who lost their lives through enemy action in March 1941".

'Whatever else Nessa went on to do after the Blitz, her family had meant everything to her. That's why she wanted Ricky to be buried up here, as near as possible to the others.' Heather paused, as if remembering Nessa say those very words to her. 'Aye, Joe and Sarah left a lot of questions in their wake after they disappeared, but one was easy to answer – where to bury Nessa.'

Below the graveyard, beyond the trees of Dalmuir public park, Keir once again picked out the gap in Thistle Street where the parachute mine had wiped out Hugh Glover and four of his children. He knew there had been worse family losses during the two terrible nights when tons of German high explosive blew great holes in the firestorm created by thousands of incendiary bombs. Just across Dumbarton

Road from the Glovers, fourteen members of the Rocks family perished in Jellicoe Street. Three streets away, ten of the Diver family died at 76 Second Avenue. Six Dohertys at Napier Street. Six Skinners at Crown Avenue. His eyes roamed between the memorial and the sunlit rooftops.

Charlie, rakishly piratical in a black eye-patch and with a colourful handkerchief protecting his scarred scalp from the sun, wanted to pay his respects at other graves. Eryn offered to go with him. Heather led Keir to an isolated seat.

'Nessa used to come here,' she told him. 'Sometimes, when she and I lived together, I came along with her. Once, she told me she never felt more at peace than when she sat here, feeling the family close at hand. "See for yourself, Heather," she said to me, "I can sit here and look at the street where we lived in Dalmuir. I can see the school the kids went to, the steeple of the church where Hugh and I got married and the youngsters made their first communions. I can see the cranes at Brown's where Hugh worked. I can look down to Kilbendrick and Henderson's yard where Ricky died. And when I sit here looking at all that, they seem to be standing behind me, looking over my shoulder. I'm not saying it's a happy feeling, because it's not. There's a deep ache to it. Maybe that comes from them. They're cut off from me, and I'll never get them back. But I can still feel them. No, it's not happy, but it's calm." Strange that, isn't it?'

Heather frowned. 'Paul Lamont met her up here too. She said it was a coincidence the first time he turned up, but I wonder about that now after what you've told me about Harmony and all that sexual carry-on he got up to. I understand now why she dropped him like a hot potato, but do you think he was fooling her right from the start?'

'I can't be sure, but I don't think so, Heather. I think they fell for one another. Nessa had found her way out of a black hole and started a new life for herself. Lamont was a handsome red-blooded young bloke who had started to question his commitment as a priest. They took a good hard look at one another and liked what they saw.'

He gestured towards the pillars and curved deck of the bridge filling the sky ahead of them. 'He told me up there that he'd loved her. Then, near the end, there was a moment when all his phoniness and play-acting deserted him. "She lost faith in me," he said. He looked shattered, worn out, hopeless. I almost felt sorry for him then.'

'You're sure he meant to do it, to kill himself?'

'Pretty sure. The rain made it hard to see, and I was on the ground with my arms through the bars, trying to stop the wind picking me up and blowing me away. From what I could make out he didn't try to stop himself going over.'

Keir studied the midpoint of the bridge. 'No, it was more than that, Heather. He scrabbled around like he was trying to lift himself on to the top of the safety rail. The moment he got there, he lifted his arms up high and gave himself up to the storm. He was a dead man once he did that, so if he didn't want to kill himself he had a funny way of showing it. What's more, he'd already told me he didn't plan on travelling very far. He was in bad shape, and he knew he was a wanted man. Yes, he meant it all right.'

'Aye. Well, Hell mend him.'

'I think he already lived in some weird personal hell, with not much of a future once the police got their hands on him. He was soaking himself in booze, and had spent years hiding away in some refuge while fiddling with the youngsters Ainsley Watson fetched for him. Now they're both dead, and can't do any more harm, I don't think people like Paul Lamont and Ainsley Watson deserve too much of our time. I think they deserve to be forgotten, not remembered. And yet if Paul Lamont hadn't met Nessa, I wouldn't be sitting here talking to you like this. There's the tricky bit.'

She clapped her hands. 'You're so right,' she said. 'That's so right, son.'

Eryn and Charlie approached. He was in full flow, waving his arms about. Eryn was laughing. Heather shook her head. 'That poor lassie must be ready for a break. Charlie's got a lot of pals from his Navy days buried here. He must have at least five stories for every one of them, and they're not all clean.' She nudged him gently. 'She seems a very nice girl, Keir.'

'She's terrific.'

'Good … good.' Heather nodded her approval. 'I hope we'll be seeing a lot of you both. My two daughters are bursting to meet you.'

Charlie brought his wheelchair to a crisp stop. 'Why does everybody sit and watch that river when there's a much better view behind you?' he asked.

'Maybe something to do with the way the seat's facing, Charles,' said Heather.

'Och, you're all living limited lives.' Charlie spun his wheelchair into a complete turn. 'Away and get yourselves seats that can point whatever way you want.' He waved Keir to him. 'C'mere Keir, till I tell you about the hills up there.'

The long ridges of the Kilpatrick Hills filled the skyline above them for as far as they could see in both directions, bright agricultural green on the lower reaches, brown and craggy grey above. Charlie spoke of the volcanoes that had poured out sheet after sheet of lava, of the ditch in the lower slopes where the Romans had built a wall to try and contain the Scots, ' – but they couldn't hold us back. They just had to pack it in and go home.' He pointed out the wooded gorge that cut through the hills above Kilbendrick. 'That's Glenarbuck, it's like a doorway to the hills. I know it like the back of my hand up there. When I was a kid, there were two lairds who claimed they owned all of that between them. Rubbish. Hills like that don't belong to anybody. I used to creep up Glenarbuck, dodge the gamekeepers on the moors and teach myself to fly fish on the high lochs. The Black Lynn. The

Humphrey. Those memories kept me going during a lot of hard times at sea. And many a painful night when they were patching me together again.

'Thanks to those hills I became an expert fisherman, learned to tie my own flies, to make my own equipment. Dead handy the way it's turned out. Takes a lot of money to keep Heather in the lifestyle she wants.' He raised his good arm as if to ward off a slap that never came.

'That's enough from you, I think it's time we got going,' said Heather.

When they rejoined the road that ran down towards the cemetery gates, Charlie held out his hand to her. 'I'm going to go for one, hen.' She passed him a pair of heavy industrial gloves from her bag. 'Now you watch what you're doing, Charlie,' she said resignedly.

'Don't worry. The road's dead straight. Luckily this eye I've got is great for straight lines. The one I lost…'

'I know, Charlie. The one you lost was for looking round corners. I've heard it a million times. He'll tell you in a minute the gloves are his GT brakes.'

'Look folks, here are my GT brakes.' He fitted one of the gloves onto his fire-damaged hand, wriggled his good hand into the other, manoeuvred his wheelchair to the top of the slope, and pushed off, his hands pistoning back and forth as he worked to build up speed.

'God! Will he be alright, Heather?' Eryn asked.

'Don't worry about him, hen. He thinks he's indestructible and I think he's probably right. Devil looks after his own.'

As if she could sense that Keir needed to be on his own, Eryn put her arm around Heather and pointed after Charlie. 'We better get down there in case there's pieces to pick up.' The two women hurried off.

Keir watched Charlie's downhill progress. He couldn't deny a tug of envy – not at the man's madcap behaviour, although he admired his ballsiness in the face of the handicaps he had to live with – but at his satisfaction with his lot, his uncomplicated enjoyment of life. They had both been damaged by war but the causes and the consequences seemed very different to Keir. Charlie had spent four years as a conscripted naval gunner in a largely set-piece war that continued to be viewed as a victory for good over evil, civilisation against the dark forces of fascism. Keir had spent two years as a conscripted infantryman in a muddled, dirty guerrilla-style never-properly-declared war where battle lines were ill-defined and there were no clear aims or noble ideals. When Charlie's war ended, he put it behind him and got on with his life. When Keir's conscription ended he couldn't wait to return as a war reporter. Charlie's wounds were physical, obvious, and brought medals and admiration. His own were hidden inside his head and came with guilt, shame, self-blame.

But he was healing.

He was sure of that.

And he was falling in love.

He was sure of that too.

He retraced his steps and sat again on Nessa's favourite bench. Somehow the two dead women he now thought of as his two mothers made sense to him. Nessa was blameless. Admirable. She'd rebuilt her life after the Blitz robbed her of all she cared about, and she'd flowered in ways she wouldn't have done – couldn't have done – if the war hadn't happened. Sarah's star hadn't shone so brightly but she'd been a decent woman who'd wanted to be honest with him, instead she had quietly managed her burden of guilt.

His dead fathers were another matter. He turned them over in his head, comparing what he knew. How had Joe squared what he did – beating a fellow man into an unconscious bloody mess, skulking off into the night with his dead sister's baby, fleeing to a foreign land and a life based on a lie – how did he square all of that with his noble principles;

his belief in fairness, justice, equality, in a commonweal based on cooperation not exploitation? What about Paul Lamont? He too had started with ideals that had led him into a religious life but there was nothing spiritual left in the deluded, abusive alcoholic who had leapt to his death.

But he could see an important difference between the two men. Joe had turned his back on what he believed because he thought something good – a new life for himself, for his wife, for Keir – could be won from the tragedy of Nessa's death. Lamont's ideals had led him to the utopian community at Harmony where he distorted them into an odious parody so that he could abuse his position to exploit and damage other people. To do evil things.

Maybe a fair summing up was this – Joe Connor was a flawed man, Paul Lamont was a bad one.

Keir had seen enough in his life to know that evil happened. He had no truck with fancy arguments about whether actions were evil or people were evil. Evil was evil, and he recognised it when he met it. He also felt that in his life to date, with all his frailties, his failings, his infidelities, his wrongdoings, he hadn't committed an evil act.

Except – except – what did his two years of soldiering add to the equation? He'd been around that territory a few times with Dr Rolfe. He knew the psychiatrist felt he was shutting something away, but he hadn't denied his war deeds. It was more that he saw himself as an eighteen-year-old lad who'd been put in a uniform, given a gun and sent off to somebody else's war. He'd never pretended that he hadn't pulled the trigger, that he hadn't thrown the grenades. But was he doing evil, or was evil being done to him? He knew that sounded like an excuse, a slick piece of sophistry, but it was the best he'd ever been able to come up with. So far, anyway.

Balancing it all out, did he end up on the good side? Maybe he was in the same box as Joe. Good, but flawed.

Doesn't sound too bad, mate.

Maybe, just maybe, the man he'd been, the man he was now, the man he would become, would add up to that. Flawed but good.

Maybe. He hoped so. But how could you know the truth of a life while it was still being lived?

Ah ... the truth. Funny how the truth kept sticking its nose in. "The first casualty of war is the truth." When he'd heard that old journalistic chestnut for the first time, he swore it would never apply to him. He'd tell the truth, whatever the price. And maybe he had. Until horror, destruction and human misery wore him down. Pointless death upon pointless death in a world where "the truth" was constantly hijacked by politicians, tortured and executed by despots, shot and blown to pieces by the arms' pedlars.

Pointless death? Not really. Inevitable. That's all death was. All death is. People like Paul Lamont and Ainsley Watson try to control it by choosing its moment. But they end up as dead as the man who's shaving when an aneurism pops in his brain, as the child who forgets to look both ways, as the ninety-year-old who lets a breath out and just can't manage to take the next one in.

As dead as the woman in wartime Kilbendrick who succumbs to a post-natal haemorrhage.

As dead as the little girl whose fingers he gently uncurls from her mother's mutilated corpse, who wraps her arms around his neck and stares into his face with wide startled eyes, who, after the patrol boat mistakes them for Vietcong, lies on the ground beside him, missing one half of her head...

Stop. Stop there. It's all history. All in the past. Nothing to be done. Nothing.

He feels like he is emerging from a long battle, one he is not sure if he has lost or won, only that it is over.

He lets his eyes roam.

The roofs of Clydebank and the clutter of cranes where the shipyard that once built the world's finest ships is now an

280

assembly line for ugly oil rigs.

Kilbendrick with its harbour, its mooring basin, the rusting wasteland of Henderson's yard.

The twin towers and connecting sweep of the bridge ahead of him and beyond its arch a glimpse of the distant estuary, the distinctive humps of Dumbuck hill and Dumbarton rock.

The surrounding ridges of the Kilpatrick hills at his back.

And the river connecting them all, the timeless spirit of the Clyde just flowing on and on...

Acknowledgements

I am indebted to my skilled and honest first readers; my wife Julie Wyness and my writing buddy Ruary Mackenzie Dodds. Thank you both: without you, this book would not have fulfilled its potential.

Some friends and family read and commented at various stages during the long process of turning a few notes into a finished novel; others shared knowledge and experience of fields as diverse as shipyard practice and salmon flies. I am forever grateful for the help and support you all gave, with a special thanks to Megan Woods who not only advised me on Australian matters, but close-read her way through two versions of the complete work.

Thanks to all at Ringwood Publishing who contributed to the production and marketing, and in particular to my editor Ida Birch Kofoed, with whom it was a pleasure to work.

For information on the French Utopian philosopher Charles Fourier (1772-1837), I drew on *The Utopian Vision of Charles Fourier*, ed. Jonathan Beecher and trans. Richard Bienvenu (Jonathan Cape Paperback, 1975), from which the Fourier quotes on pages 183 and 184 are sourced.

About the Author

Frank Woods was born in the shipyard village of Bowling where he grew up within sight, sound and smell of the River Clyde. Amongst his earliest memories is the clang of riveters' hammers from the local shipyard where his father worked as a fitter.

At the start of the Clydebank Blitz, his mother was in bed nursing her firstborn when a string of bombs hit the village and flattened the tenements on either side. Luckily, they both escaped unhurt.

After completing a geology degree at Glasgow University, Frank worked as an exploration geologist, journalist and primary school teacher before embarking on a twenty-five-year career as a psychologist with a specialist interest in disadvantaged children and their families.

Before moving to their current home in Fife, he and his wife lived for thirty years in rural Aberdeenshire where he balanced out professional life by gardening, keeping bees, woodcarving, playing blues harmonica, learning t'ai chi and writing.

Writing has been part of his life since his teenage years. Published work includes journalism, poetry, short stories and a biography - *Dancer in the Light: the life of Gerda 'Pytt' Geddes* (Psi Books, 2008).

Where the Bridge Lies is his first novel.

Other Titles from Ringwood

All titles are available from the Ringwood website and from usual outlets. Also availble on Kindle, Kobo and Nook.

Ringwood Publishing
www.ringwoodpublishing.com
mail@ringwoodpublishing.com

Memoirs of Franz Schreiber
Charles P. Sharkey

The Memoirs of Franz Schreiber gives a unique perspective on the trials and turmoil of life in Germany during the First World War, its aftermath and the lead up to the Second World War. When Franz Schreiber and his mother get the news that his beloved father would not be returning to their home in Berlin from the battle fields of the First World War, their lives changed in unimaginable ways. Following Franz as he grows into a man, the effects of war are endless, and the story of his life is littered with love, tragedy and danger.

ISBN: 9781901514643   £9.99

Checking Out of the Hotel Euthanasia
Gerard Graham

Graham's satirical comedy follows Rab Lennon and his Glasgow cronies on their adventure to blow up Hotel Euthanasia in revenge for the assisted killing of his parents. Along the way we find ourselves tripping over deep-rooted views, bumping into uneasy feelings and finding ourselves lost along the winding path of reality. You may just find yourself turning down an unexpected route.

ISBN: 9781901514407   £9.99

The Activist
Alec Connon

"The Activist is an entertaining and heartfelt antidote to sea tales penned by hunters and fishermen. In it Tom Durant joins a colourful crew of activists to turn the tables and hunt the hunters, chasing the whalers who ply their trade in defiance of an international ban. In telling Tom's story, Connon contrasts the best and worst of people as they face off across the mountainous seas of the Southern Ocean." Callum Roberts, Professor of Marine Conservation at the University of York.

ISBN: 9781901514254   £9.99

Millennial Munros - A Postman's Round
Charlie Campbell

Millennial Munros is the inspirational story of an ordinary bloke doing something extra-ordinary. Campbell completed an unprecedented endurance event, breaking the world record for a continuous self-propelled round of all Scotland's Munros, 284 mountains over 3000 feet in height. He averaged nearly six Munros every day, and cycled or swam between them. Charlie's entertaining account of his adventures is complete with maps, routes and other details to help inspire others to tackle these mountains.

ISBN 9781901514339   £9.99

Two Closes and a Referendum
Mary McCabe

An engaging tale of ordinary people in an extraordinary time. This novel brilliantly captures the growing excitement and fervour of the 2014 Independence Referendum that changed Scotland for ever, as ordinary citizens explored their identity and wrestled with the hopes and fears that surrounded the choice they were asked to make.

ISBN 9781901514483   £9.99

The Gori's Daughter
Shazia Hobbs

The Gori's Daughter is the fictional story of Aisha, a young mixed race girl, daughter of a Kashmiri father and a Glaswegian mother moved into the household as mistress alongside the Muslim wife and the children from both relationships.

Her whole life is a constant struggle against the rejection and hostility her background generates in both Glasgow's white and Asian communities. The book graphically documents her fight to offer her own daughter a culture and traditions she can accept with pride. The book sheds a relentless light on an aspect of Scottish – Asian relationships that is seldom acknowledged.

ISBN: 9781901514124   £9.99